THE
WOMEN
OF CATAWBA

HILDA STAHL

THOMAS NELSON PUBLISHERS
Nashville • Atlanta • London • Vancouver

Published in Nashville, Tennessee, by Thomas Nelson, Inc., Publishers, and distributed in Canada by Word Communications, Ltd., Richmond, British Columbia, and in the United Kingdom by Word (UK), Ltd., Milton Keynes, England.

Library of Congress Cataloging-in-Publication Data
Stahl, Hilda.
    The women of Catawba / Hilda Stahl.
        p.   cm.
    ISBN 0-8407-5080-3 (pb)
    1. Man–woman relationships—South Carolina—Charleston—Fiction.   2. Women—South Carolina—Charleston—Fiction.   3. Charleston (S.C.)—history—Fiction.
    I. Title.
PS3569.T312W6   1993
813′.54—dc20   93-32557
                                                                                          CIP

Printed in the United States of America
4   5   6   7   -   98   97   96   95   94

FOREWORD

HILDA STAHL was an exceptional woman. She had a dream that she shared with anyone who would listen: to see her books published all over the world, touching the hearts of her readers.

The *White Pine Chronicles,* her first historical adult series, was the frosting on her cake. She had dreamed of writing this type of series for years and it finally came true. *The Covenant, The Inheritance,* and *The Dream* were not just stories to her; they were a way to reach you, her readers, to let you know that any dream you have is possible because of the covenant Jesus has made with you.

This book, *The Women of Catawba,* was the very last manuscript that my mother finished. We hope this book will help you realize that you can be led by the Lord in every area of your life. With the leading of the Lord you can walk in victory.

Anyone who knew my mother would tell you she was a woman who decided what she wanted and went after it. She passed that strength and determination on to the children she spoke to in classrooms, young ministers just starting out, and beginning authors needing a guiding hand. My mother always had a word of encouragement for anyone who asked her advice.

Hilda Stahl may be gone from this earth, but she will never be forgotten. She has touched so many lives that she will live on through their memories. My mother never gave up, no matter what the odds were. When she first started writing, people actually told her not to bother, that she didn't have what it took to be a successful author. Even with seven children to take care of, she proved them wrong.

Her favorite time of day was when the mailman came and brought all the wonderful fan mail. She would sit and read each letter, feeling encouraged to keep writing. We would like to dedicate this book to all of you, her readers, as a way to say thank you for your love and devotion.

In loving memory,
LAURIE ANN STAHL MURRAY

*T*rembling with fear, Taylor Craven glanced toward the gangplank of the *Carleena* where James Rawlings had gone to speak to the captain. A cold May wind flapped Taylor's long, gray cape about her slender body. Lifting her hand up to her bonnet, she secured a stray wisp of light brown hair back into place. Ships with their enormous masts and spars stabbing the overcast sky lined the Liverpool dock. The smell of the sea overpowered the reeking odors of rowdy, muscled workers and sailors, barrels of fish, and stacks of goods.

Taylor bit her lower lip and clasped her gloved hands together. Her crystal blue eyes darted around the dock. What was James thinking? Why wouldn't he want her to take a nanny for Brooke for the voyage to America when they'd already agreed it was for the best? Leaving England would be hard because it had always been her home, but it was also a relief since she wouldn't be constantly reminded of the loss of her dear husband, Floyd. However, to sail to the ends of the earth with a year-old baby without help was frightening. Why had James said they'd take Bernice if he'd had no intention to do so? Taylor frowned. She'd never trusted James as Floyd had. But then Floyd had grown up with his cousin—played with him and been educated with him. Perhaps Bernice hadn't heard James's instructions correctly.

Hiding her fear behind a smile, Taylor turned back to Bernice who stood with her gloved hands on the wooden carriage handle, looking agog at everything around her even as she shivered in the cold. Gooing, little Brooke sat inside the carriage with blankets tucked around her. She had Taylor's light brown hair and blue eyes and Floyd's happy smile. Pulling her cape closer to her, Taylor lifted her eyes from Brooke to look at Bernice. She was seventeen years old and slight of build, with a nose too long for her narrow face and wide blue eyes. Today she wore a gray bonnet with a matching short gray stole over a dark blue wool dress with long sleeves and a high collar. "I thought you were going with us," Taylor said as calmly as she could.

Bernice's eyes widened and she pressed a hand to her throat. Her rosy red nose was like a lighthouse beacon on her pale face as she squeaked, "To America? So far away! Wild people live there! I could never go. Pirates on the high seas, I've heard. 'Tis not safe, mum."

Taylor trembled. She'd heard the same things. She watched two ragged boys dodge around her and race after a yowling orange cat. Her heavy skirts swaying about her feet, she turned back to Bernice. "I'm sure there are laws in America. After all, it's 1800, not the Dark Ages. We will be quite safe."

But then, she reasoned, why discuss America with Bernice? It was more important that she confront James about a nanny!

Bernice shivered and touched her gray stole. "Me wrap is too lightweight for such weather, mum."

"I can see that." Taylor fingered the clasp on her gray cape. "I'm sorry you're cold. If I had another cape, I'd give it to you."

"You're a nice one, mum."

Taylor didn't feel very nice. She wanted to scream at Bernice for not telling her she was tending Brooke only until they reached the merchant ship. Taylor was trying to control her anger with the girl, but it wasn't easy.

Brooke whimpered and Bernice immediately bent down and talked to her until she gurgled happily again.

Thoughtfully Taylor watched Bernice with the baby. Maybe she could convince Bernice to go with them after all.

Her voice took on a pleading quality. "Brooke needs you, Bernice," she said. "So do I. Mr. Rawlings would pay you well. Would you please go with us?"

Giggling nervously, Bernice waved her gloved hand. "Oh, but I can't go, mum. Mr. Rawlings hired me to see you on the ship. Then I'll be going back to the Parkers' babies to tend them. They're expecting me back today."

A shiver ran down Taylor's spine. So James had planned it all along! But why?

Gone was the pleading tone. "Bernice, please wait here with Brooke," Taylor commanded. "I must speak to Mr. Rawlings at once."

"Yes, mum." Bernice shivered even as she wheeled the carriage forward. "I'll tuck meself and the babe out of the wind near these crates."

"Yes, you do that. I won't be long." Taylor bent over the carriage and smiled. "Mama's baby is so precious!" Taylor said, as she kissed Brooke's cold cheeks and retied her little pink and white bonnet. "I'll be back soon."

Brooke laughed and cooed and reached out for Taylor.

Taylor hurried away, her blue eyes flashing with determination and her chin high. She dodged around a pile of barrels, stepped over a thick coil of rope, lost sight of James, then spotted him with his back to her talking with the captain of the *Carleena* at the edge of the gangplank.

Her nerves tight, Taylor hesitated, the noise around her making her ears ring and the smells making her stomach lurch. In her twenty-five years living in a neighboring village first with her parents, then her husband, she'd never set foot in Liverpool until now. It certainly was full of noisy people without manners! Maybe she should've waited near the baggage with Bernice like James had said. He did hate to be interrupted during a conversation. Still this was different. Straightening her shoulders and lifting her chin high, she muttered, "This can't wait."

She'd go to James and speak immediately to him about Bernice no matter how angry he became. Just the thought of his temper made her tremble. It was frightening to face James's anger! His tongue was rapier-sharp and he was prone to break anything in sight. One of the reasons she'd refused his offer of marriage when she'd had to decide between the cousins, Floyd and James, was his temper. She'd cared for both of them, but Floyd had been kind and considerate of others and had not a sign of a temper. On the other hand, James had charm and good looks, but could fly into an uncontrollable rage. And in the past two months that he'd been with them while doing business, she'd noticed his temper was even worse, especially toward Floyd.

Abruptly she pushed thoughts of Floyd away. His death was still too new and the pain too raw. She couldn't burst into anguished wails on the Liverpool docks! Later she'd deal with her loss, later on the voyage to Virginia and to James's plantation.

With the wind whipping her cape around her, Taylor walked purposefully toward James and the captain. Just before she reached them a short dark man with a mouth-covering mustache parked a small cart piled high directly in her path. She started to edge around it to James's side, but stopped at the sound of James's voice. She'd wait until he finished speaking with the captain; then she'd go to him. Sparks flying from her eyes, she locked her gloved hands together. Oh, but it was hard to wait!

James was saying, "I want the marriage performed before night falls tonight, Captain."

"I'll see to it."

Taylor tensed. *Marriage? Before nightfall?*

"And you'll see to a cabin for us," James said more as a command than a question.

"Of course. I want you and the future Mrs. Rawlings to have every comfort on the voyage."

Taylor pressed her trembling hand to her throat. *The future Mrs. Rawlings?*

James laughed. "I've waited years to make Taylor my wife. I won't wait another day."

Taylor gasped and reached weakly out to the cart for support. James was going to force her to marry him! And because of the debt, she'd have to do as he said. Her stomach knotted painfully. She couldn't marry him and live with him as his wife! She had to do something! But how could she escape him? Who could she turn to for help?

Desperately she looked around at the throng of rough-hewn workers, raucous sailors, and fast-talking merchants. Would anyone help her? Sighing raggedly, she shook her head. She was only a woman—a woman with a debt to pay. She'd have to get Brooke and run. But where could she go?

Silently she prayed for help. "God is with me," she whispered to herself. "He has helped me in the past, and He won't stop now."

James's voice rose and she heard him say, "Captain, if your men see my slave Cammie, hold her for me."

"I hope you never find her," Taylor whispered fiercely. Cammie was only a few years beyond being a child, too young to work the way James worked her. He cuffed her hard if she didn't obey immediately or if she didn't do a job correctly. Just this morning he'd slapped her when she couldn't get the high collar of his shirt to lay right.

Taylor heard James say, "I should be back shortly. Send someone to pick up my baggage."

Her heart roaring in her ears, Taylor rushed back to where Bernice was waiting with Brooke. Bernice looked warmer as she stood in the shelter of the crates and bent over the carriage, telling Brooke to look at the monkey on the man's shoulder who was walking by.

Taylor glanced back the way she'd come. Had James spotted her running along the dock after he'd told her to stay with the baggage? She turned to Bernice. "Mr. Rawlings will be here shortly."

Bernice looked up and smiled. "Then I can go."

Taylor shot a look behind her to make sure James wasn't within sight, then turned back to Bernice. "He'd be very angry if he knew you told me you weren't going to America with us."

Bernice paled. "I forgot it 'twas a secret, mum."

"No matter." Taylor patted Bernice's hand on the handle of the carriage. "Don't mention it to him and I won't either."

Bernice let out her breath in relief. "Thank you, mum. You've a kind, gentle heart."

"Thank you." Taylor forced a smile while her brain whirled with ideas on how to get away from James. She dared not arouse his suspicions, or he wouldn't let her out of his sight.

Just then James stepped around the baggage. His eyes were full of anger. "Have you seen Cammie?"

Hiding her fear from him, Taylor shook her head. She had to be very careful of what she did and said. "If you want to look for her, I'll see to the luggage."

He smiled and took her arm. "No need. You come with me. We'll look for that blasted girl together."

The touch of his hand on her arm sent a shiver of fear down her spine. She wanted to pull away, but she dare not. Her heart was an icy stone in her breast, but with her head high and her spine mainmast straight, Taylor walked beside James along the noisy, smelly dock. Over the sounds of shouting and cursing her ear was tuned to hear Brooke, but soon they were out of earshot. Silently she prayed for protection for Brooke and Bernice.

Her heavy skirts swaying around her feet, Taylor walked beside James around bales of silk and chests of tea. How could she get away from him? She had no one to turn to. Her parents had died in the plague two years after she'd married Floyd. And now her sweet Floyd was dead. A shiver ran down Taylor's spine as she realized she had no one to protect her. She couldn't tell James she'd changed her mind or he'd send her to debtor's prison. Then what of Brooke? There was no one to tend her. It all seemed so hopeless, but she knew God would provide an answer for her. She wouldn't lose her trust in Him!

James stopped and turned to Taylor, flipped back his cape, and poised before her like a dandy. He cut a handsome figure in his buff-colored coat, his long lean legs covered with matching tight buff-colored breeches tucked into high black leather boots. The high collar of his white shirt forced his chin up to give the impression he was looking down on her. His black top hat sat squarely on his dark head.

His blue eyes crinkled as he smiled. "You'll like Rawlings Plantation, my dear Taylor. It has been my dream these past four years for you to live there."

Taylor forced a smile. Four years ago she'd married Floyd Craven, choosing him over James Rawlings. She'd thought James had gotten over his hurt and anger as well as his desire to wed her. How wrong she'd been!

James laughed lightly. "I planned for both you and Cousin Floyd to live with me on the plantation. Of course, now it's too late for Cousin Floyd. He'd be pleased to know you and the baby will be there with me."

Taylor shivered, but not from the blustery wind. His words were meant to waylay her fears, but they made her realize even more how devious he was. She clutched her gray cape to her, covering her dark green traveling dress. The chill reached deep inside her where a cape couldn't help. Her heart constricted painfully as the realization struck her again. Floyd was dead! Last month he'd been struck down in the street by a carriage and had died two days later.

Thankfully James had been on the scene to take him to the hospital. James had paid the bills for the hospital and the funeral. Her hands trembling, she nervously fingered the bow at the side of her neck that kept her small bonnet in place. Because Floyd had died in debt to James, she, as Floyd's widow, was forced to do what James wanted—which was to sail with him to the Rawlings Plantation in Virginia. James had said he'd call the debt canceled if she did that. She had wanted to refuse to go with him, but she'd known she couldn't—she had to do what James said. But no longer! Debt or no, she was going to escape!

His face softened and he took her gloved hand gently in his. "What wide, sad blue eyes you have, my dear. I'll put a sparkle in them—on my word as a Southern gentleman." He touched her cheek with the tip of one finger. "And I'll put roses back in your cheeks." He released her hand. "You'll like Virginia. You'll put aside these unhappy times in England, and you'll forget Cousin

Floyd who wasn't right for you anyway. Soon you'll be proud to call Rawlings Plantation your home."

She wanted to correct him, but she'd learned it didn't do to speak against anything James said. "You've been good to me, James." And he had this past month! What a charlatan he'd been!

He tipped his hat and bowed. His dark hair hung well over his collar and was held back in a tail with a wide black ribbon. "I shall do everything to make you happy."

She wanted to cry, "Then set me free!" But she only lowered her eyes.

Just then a wheelbarrow of goods pushed by a thin, ragged boy loomed up before them, almost knocking into Taylor. James swept her out of the way, scowling at the boy.

"Watch where you're going, bumpkin!" he snarled.

Taylor cringed at the anger in James's voice. She faced him squarely. "James, don't! The boy doesn't deserve your anger."

"Come along, Taylor." James Rawlings gripped her arm and scowled at her. His cape fluttered in the wind. "It's not for you to chide me."

She pressed her lips tightly together and walked around a cage that held a chattering monkey.

A baby cried. Her eyes wide in alarm, Taylor whirled around to see if it had been Brooke. The crowd parted and Taylor could see Bernice in the distance beside the carriage, still waiting at the pile of baggage. Taylor frowned. She'd wanted to hire her own nanny, but James had insisted on the woman of his choice. Now she knew why.

"I think Brooke is crying for me," she spoke insistently.

"You can't hear her over the hubbub." James scowled and pulled Taylor back around. "I told you not to be concerned with the baby. Bernice is quite capable."

"I want to go back to them."

James urged her forward. "I must see if Cammie is at the *Alicia*. She could've gone there to see the crate of parrots she'd seen earlier. She was dazzled with their bright colors."

Taylor's head spun. Should she run away now? She bit the inside of her lower lip. Why think such a daft thing?

A few minutes later James stopped by the *Alicia*, but there was no sign of Cammie. James asked around, but no one had noticed her.

He turned to Taylor with his sneering comment. "She might be at the baggage again. Can't trust a Negra out of your sight. She'll pay for running off like this."

Taylor bit back a scathing retort. She'd told James how she felt about owning slaves. Still he'd brought Cammie with him to tend him on the voyage to England. James had had her sleep in the pantry on the floor. Now because of the debt, the house belonged to James and he could keep all the slaves he wanted. While James and Floyd were talking in the front room Taylor had sneaked two blankets and a pillow to Cammie.

"The house is too cold at night to sleep on the floor without a cover," Taylor had said with a smile as she gave the blankets and pillow to Cammie.

"Thank you, ma'am," Cammie had said lowering her eyes shyly, hugging the blankets to her thin body. "I chilled clear to the bone. I won't never forget what you done for me."

Now, without speaking, Taylor lifted her skirts and hurried after James back to the baggage and to Brooke. Bernice had given Brooke a biscuit and she was gumming it contentedly.

James looked around with a frown. "Where'd that blasted Cammie get to? I told her to ride here with Delmer and stay with the baggage even after it was loaded on the *Carleena*," James said, punching his fist into his palm.

"Maybe Delmer knows where she is." Taylor kept her voice light. Delmer did odd jobs in their village until he made enough to go to the local pub. James had paid him handsomely to cart the baggage and Cammie to the docks. Probably he'd left Cammie and the baggage as quickly as he could and had gone for a drink. James turned to Taylor. "I'll ask around for Delmer. Stay here." He impatiently waved his hand to indicate that she should stay with the stack of luggage and Bernice. "Someone will be coming to load the baggage. If you see Cammie, keep her with you." His face dark with anger, James looked around. "I'll skin that girl alive when I find her!"

Taylor shivered. She knew one of the punishments to runaway slaves was being skinned alive. Surely James couldn't be serious!

❦

"Please don't be angry with her," she pleaded. "She could've gotten lost."

"You know nothing about darkies, madam!" James snapped looking down his nose at her. "She's run away before."

"Then let her go, James! She's a human being and shouldn't belong to anyone."

James gripped Taylor's arms and pushed his face close to hers.

"Cammie is my property, madam! You shut your mouth and don't speak again until I give you leave!"

Taylor flushed. Angry words boiled up inside her, but she bridled her tongue. She had to keep her wits about her or by nightfall she'd be wed for the rest of her life to James Rawlings. Finally she lowered her eyes and tried to look as humble as she could.

James abruptly released her, then patted her cheek. "That's better. I suppose you could come with me to look for Delmer."

Taylor moistened her lips with the tip of her tongue. She had to convince him to let her stay behind! "I'd be of more help if I saw to the baggage while you look for Cammie. You don't want to be late boarding the *Carleena*."

His brow knit as he contemplated her suggestion, then he nodded. "The captain said he'd send someone right over." James smiled and lifted her fingertips to his lips, then kissed them. "Thank you, my pet."

"You're welcome," she whispered. Oh, how she wanted to wrench her hand free!

He swung away, his cape billowing out behind him. "Bernice, help Mrs. Taylor."

"I will, sir." Bernice huddled closer to the crates to keep warm.

Taylor waited until James was lost behind a dray before turning to Bernice. "It's not right for you to stand here freezing when I can see to myself. You run along now."

"But Mr. James will be angry, mum!"

Taylor managed a smile. "I'll explain to him. Did he pay you?"

Bernice nodded.

"Then run along."

"If you're sure, mum." At Taylor's nod of assurance, Bernice kissed Brooke and bobbed a curtsy to Taylor. "Thank you kindly."

Watching Bernice hurrying away, Taylor took a deep, steadying breath. Relief coursed through her slender body. Now she could make some plans. Where should she go? She had to act quickly before James returned. He probably wouldn't look further than the pub at the end of the docks.

Just then a man with two young ladies and a boy about twelve years stopped nearby. The man looked harried and grim. He hailed a short, broad sailor carrying a heavy rope over his shoulder and asked, "Where can I find the merchantman, the *Falcon*?"

The sailor motioned with his head. "Three ships yonder, gov'ner."

"It is the ship heading for Charleston, South Carolina, at first tide, isn't it?" asked the oldest girl. She had long blonde hair and wide sad blue eyes.

The sailor nodded, tugged his cap, and strode away.

Taylor's heart leaped. Charleston, South Carolina! From the maps she'd studied with Floyd she knew it was in America and a good distance from Virginia. She could go there! She wheeled the carriage closer to the man.

"Excuse me, sir," she attempted with a weak voice.

He cocked his dark brow and pulled off his black top hat.

Taylor flushed. She wasn't used to begging for help. "I'm also going on the *Falcon,* but I can't manage on my own, it seems."

The man looked at her as if he hadn't heard her.

"My baby and I will be traveling on the *Falcon.*" Taylor motioned to Brooke who was leaning forward to coo at the brown-haired girl.

The girl smiled. "You have a darling baby."

"Thank you." Taylor looked helplessly at her luggage. "I don't know how I'll get my things to the ship."

"Call a porter," the man said impatiently.

"I don't know how."

A tall gentleman, standing on the far side of the family, stepped forward and doffed his top hat, revealing blond hair with a trace of gray at the temples and eyes as green as the sea. He'd almost given up hope of making extra money on the voyage. He'd thought Yates Marston and his children might be the answer, but they weren't. Now a pretty woman in need of his assistance practically fell in his lap.

"Allow me, madam," he said, with a bow. "Mr. Marston is occupied with his children, but I am alone and will be sailing on the *Falcon* also. My name is Andrew Simons. Permit me to be of service to you."

Taylor hesitated, then nodded. What else could she do? She had to have help. "Thank you." She turned to the baggage beside her and pointed out her four trunks and a portmanteau.

As Mr. Marston and his children walked away, Andrew Simons hailed a rough-looking porter. "Make haste and load the luggage on the *Falcon.* Tell Captain Crawley that Andrew Simons gave you leave to load them."

The porter wheeled away her luggage just as another porter approached Taylor.

"I'm to load baggage for James Rawlings, madam."

She nodded and motioned to James's trunks. "Yes. These things. Please hurry!"

The porter ducked his head in acknowledgement and quickly loaded the trunks and supplies, shouted for a man to get out of the way, then wheeled the load toward the *Carleena*.

Andrew Simons watched in thought. Something was going on and it would probably be worth his while to find out what. He forced back a chuckle. This was definitely his lucky day.

Just then Taylor saw Cammie motion to her, then duck out of sight behind bales of silk. What could Cammie want of her?

Her pulse racing, Taylor turned to Mr. Simons. "I must tend to some business, then I'll join you on the *Falcon*. Again I thank you for your help."

"You're most welcome." Smiling, he tipped his hat. "I forgot to ask your name."

Taylor's head spun. She knew she shouldn't give her correct name, but she couldn't think of a new one fast enough. "Taylor Craven, sir."

"Mrs. Craven. See you on board." Andrew Simons tipped his hat again, smiled, and strolled away. He stopped behind a hogshead of tobacco and peered around it at Taylor Craven. He'd seen the black girl motion, and he'd felt Taylor Craven's tension. This appeared to be a situation worth checking into.

Her stomach an icy knot, Taylor wheeled the carriage around crates to bales of silk and peeked around them. Cammie was just slipping between the bales in a perfect hiding place for such a slightly built girl. She wore a gray cotton dress with a black shawl over it and a black bonnet.

"Cammie," Taylor whispered urgently. "I'm here." So intent was she on speaking with Cammie that she was not aware of Andrew Simons creeping close enough to hear without being seen.

Her black eyes wide in terror, Cammie peeked out at Taylor. "I been waiting to talk to you. I couldn't run away till I did."

"But why?"

"I got to warn you, Missy Taylor!" Cammie plucked at her shawl, nervously wondering if she should tell Missy Taylor everything she knew.

Glancing around uncertainly, Taylor wondered what Cammie was going to warn her about. Had she known all along about James forcing her to marry him?

"What is it, Cammie?"

"You can't go with Master James," Cammie burst out saying. She quickly slapped her hand over her mouth with her eyes wide in fear. Had she made a mistake telling Missy Taylor not to go? No, she knew the Lord had told her to warn Missy Taylor. She was doing what He had directed her to do.

Taylor frowned. What a strange thing for Cammie to say. "I'm not going to, but I don't have time to explain," she said hurriedly.

"I running away from Master James, but I had to warn you before I left," Cammie said hoarsely.

From his hiding place Andrew Simons chuckled softly. A runaway! He could hear the jingle of gold coins.

"Good!" Taylor said. "Come with me to South Carolina and help me with Brooke. Would you like that?"

Cammie's black eyes brimmed with tears. She'd stayed hidden until she could get Missy Taylor alone. Was this the answer Jesus had for her? In her heart she knew it was.

She nodded hard. "Yes, yes! I go with you, Missy Taylor!"

"We must hurry!" Taylor looked around, but didn't see James yet. She dare not relax. He could be back any time. "Come!"

Cammie crept away from the bales of silk, darted fearful looks around, then walked with Taylor. "I be the one to wheel the baby, Missy Taylor."

Reluctantly Taylor gave up her hold on the carriage. She didn't want to take time to argue the point. She'd have to get used to Cammie serving and caring for her. Personally she hated the idea of owning another human being, but she had learned to keep her opinion to herself around James. He had not appreciated Taylor's voicing her objections to owning slaves when he had first arrived in England.

Blood pounding in her ears, Taylor hurried toward the *Falcon* with Cammie wheeling the carriage. Taylor could feel the tension in Cammie. At every sound behind her she jumped, expecting to feel James's hand on her shoulder.

Andrew Simons silently followed Taylor Craven and the runaway. He'd make sure they boarded the *Falcon*; then he'd find this James Rawlings.

At the gangplank of the *Falcon* Captain Crawley stepped forward with his cap under his arm. "You must be the passengers Mr. Simons said would be coming."

"Yes." Taylor nodded, barely able to speak around her dry throat. "I hope there's no inconvenience this close to departure."

"None at all. Your nigger can stay below deck."

Taylor's eyes flashed. "I need her with me to help with the baby, Captain." Her chin set in a stubborn tilt was just daring him to tell her this wouldn't be possible. She was determined to have her way in this situation.

Captain Crawley scowled. Just then he caught sight of Andrew Simons who gave him the go-ahead.

So he agreed. "We can make an exception if we must. Welcome aboard. Your trunks are in the top cargo where you can get to them with ease. The portmanteau is in your cabin. Pay my clerk over there."

Taylor wanted to look behind her to see if James was coming for her, but she kept her eyes on Captain Crawley. She couldn't stay in sight of the dock a moment longer.

With her most determined voice, she insisted, "I must get my baby inside out of the wind. May I pay later?"

Captain Crawley shrugged. "Mr. Simons spoke for you, so I'll allow it." He turned to shout for a porter—a short, broad man with heavy dark pants and a black pullover shirt. When he arrived, the captain said gruffly, "See them to their cabin."

Cammie darted a look behind her as she lifted Brooke out of the carriage. Was she finally free of Master James?

The porter picked up the carriage and walked easily up the gangplank onto the *Falcon*.

The smell of wet canvas heavy in the air, Taylor followed him with Cammie carrying Brooke. Taylor stepped on deck and heard the lap of the water against the hull and the shouts of the sailors. Was James watching them, ready to force them off the *Falcon* and over to the *Carleena*? She shuddered. She had to get out of sight immediately!

The porter led them down the companionway to the cabin. Lanterns dimly lit the way. Smells of wool, tar, and oak beams along with unidentifiable odors permeated the air. He opened the wooden door, lit the lantern inside, wheeled the carriage inside, left the door ajar, and hurried away.

Taylor stepped into the small cabin that smelled of the burning lantern. Two narrow shelves partly framed by boarding hung one above the other on the wall. Staring at them in shock, Taylor realized they were beds! The portmanteau and the carriage took up much of the remaining space.

Brooke squirmed and cried.

Taylor took her from Cammie, sank to the edge of the bed, and shushed her. "I have a biscuit for her in her bag."

Cammie handed Taylor the bag.

She found the biscuit with one hand and held it out to Brooke. Cammie shivered. "I glad you brought me with you."

"So am I." Trying to sound cheerful Taylor forced a small grin. "I wouldn't want to be around when James finds us gone. He will be very angry."

Cammie leaned weakly against the wall. She had to tell Missy Taylor the truth no matter what!

"I got something to tell you, Missy Taylor, and you're not going to like it." Cammie hesitated for just a moment, getting Taylor's full attention. "Master James plans to kill me dead for what I seen him do."

Taylor's breath caught in her throat. "What did you see him do?"

Cammie closed the door and whispered, "I saw what he done. He run right over Master Floyd with the horse and buggy."

"What?" Taylor cried in consternation, startling Brooke so badly she let out a loud wail. Taylor quieted her the best she could in her anguished state.

"He done say it be an accident. But 'tweren't no accident, Missy Taylor."

"No, no, no!" Taylor helplessly shook her head. A bitter taste filled her mouth, and she thought she was going to vomit.

"He done it deliberate-like. I knows. And he knows I knows." Cammie clasped her hands together. "That's why I runned away. He thought I be too scared to run again. Cammie not too scared this time. I know Jesus be with me and take care of me."

Taylor's mouth felt bone dry. Would Cammie make up such an appalling tale?

"You gonna faint dead away, Missy Taylor?"

"I'll be fine in a moment." Taylor took a deep, steadying breath. She felt almost too weak to hold Brooke.

"You already knows what a bad man Master James be. Else you would of married up with him when he wanted. He told me all about you before we came on the big boat. He told me this time he was gonna marry up with you and take you back home with him."

Taylor trembled and almost lost her hold on Brooke. James had planned to marry her, yet she was already married to Floyd! So James had planned to kill Floyd even before his visit!

Taylor pressed her face against Brooke, and this time she was the one who whimpered.

t the *Carleena* Andrew Simons asked the captain to point out James Rawlings. Andrew chuckled when he saw him. He was dressed like an English dandy even though the captain had informed him that James considered himself a wealthy American.

Andrew stepped forward and doffed his hat. "Mr. Rawlings, a word with you, sir," he said politely.

James frowned impatiently. The man before him was impeccably dressed—every inch the English gentleman. James had always wanted to be an English gentleman, but he hadn't been born to the right family. Living in America had given him the chance to become what he was all along in his heart—a blueblood.

"I'm in a great hurry, sir." James gave barely a glance to the other gentleman.

"Andrew Simons, at your service. I have reason to believe you're looking for a young slave named Cammie."

James stiffened. There was something about Andrew Simons he didn't trust. "What is it to you?" he asked.

"I've seen her. And I am willing to tell you where—for the right price."

James forced himself to smile. The price a common worker would charge was one thing. What Andrew Simons would call a right price was something else.

But after all, the man had to be bluffing. "My slave and my traveling companion are already on board. Step aside and let me board," James demanded.

Andrew chuckled. "Sir, I know where both are. And they are not on board."

James's pride reared and he wouldn't allow himself to back down for anyone—especially not an English gentleman! Taylor had to be on board since the baggage was already loaded.

"You are mistaken, sir," he snorted.

Andrew narrowed his eyes in thought. He had seen James Rawlings' type before. His response was even. "I suppose if they aren't on board, you'll sail to Virginia without them."

"I plan to return home to attend an important ball at my plantation in June in honor of the governor of Virginia. He, of course, will be attending." That should put Simons in his place!

"Would you stay behind to find your slave and your traveling companion if they aren't on board?"

"They are on board! And nothing will make me miss my return voyage!"

Hiding a mocking smile, Andrew bowed low to James Rawlings. "Have a safe voyage then. And when you have your first dance with your charming lady, think of me."

James's eyes flashed with anger as he walked up the gangplank to board the *Carleena*.

With a jaunty air about him, Andrew Simons strolled back to the *Falcon*. He learned where Taylor Craven and the slave were staying and hurried down the companionway to see them. He knocked on the door and chuckled. This was going to be quite an adventure.

Inside the cabin Taylor jumped, striking her head on the top bunk.

Her eyes wide in fear, Cammie started praying silently. Had Master James found them out?

Taylor swallowed hard. Was it James? Had he somehow found them? She peeked in the carriage to make sure Brooke was still asleep and then her voice wavered, "Who is it?"

"Andrew Simons, Mrs. Craven. May I speak with you?"

Sighing in relief, Taylor eased the door open a crack. Mr. Simons stood there with his hat in his hand, a smile on his face.

"Yes?"

"We'll be underway soon. The clerk wants your fare. I said I'd escort you to him."

"I'm sorry, but I really can't leave my cabin now."

"He won't wait, Mrs. Craven. I'm sorry."

Taylor took a deep, steadying breath. She couldn't have them put her off the ship. "How much is it?"

He told her. "If you want, I'll take it to him and save you the inconvenience."

Taylor's stomach knotted. She didn't want to trust a total stranger with her money, but she couldn't take the chance of James seeing her if she left her cabin. He could easily board the *Falcon* looking for her or Cammie.

So she acquiesced gracefully. "Thank you. I'd be very grateful. Just a moment and I'll get my money." She closed the door and pulled out the folded notes tucked carefully in the pockets tied around her waist and under her skirt. Before sailing she'd sold a brooch Floyd's mother had given her years ago, as well as two rings her mother had inherited from her grandmother. After paying for their voyage she'd have only a few shillings left. She opened the door a crack and handed the money to Andrew Simons.

"I'll get the receipt later," she reminded him.

"I'll save a place for you at my table for dinner. I'll give it to you then," said Andrew with a smart bow.

"Thank you." Taylor forced a smile and closed the door. Then she turned to Cammie. "There. That's taken care of."

Cammie smiled. Then as Brooke woke up and cried, Cammie reached in the carriage for her. Her grimace spoke only too well of a wet diaper.

Taylor watched Cammie unpin Brooke's diaper. The acrid odor filled the cabin, but Cammie's voice was gentle as she said, "I take care of you, Missy Brooke, and I take care of your mama." Cammie touched her stomach. "And when this baby be born, I take care of him, too."

Taylor gasped. "You're going to have a baby?"

Cammie nodded.

"But . . . how can you? I mean, who's the father of the baby?"

Cammie looked uncomfortable. "Master James has me warm his bed most every night since I got of age. This baby from him."

Her head spinning, Taylor sank back weakly. How could Cammie make such a statement in such a matter-of-fact way? "I . . . I didn't know."

"It be true." Cammie sighed heavily. "I won't never tell my baby his daddy be a killer."

Taylor trembled. And James had planned to marry her! How despicable of him! She brushed weakly at her burning eyes as she breathed the words, "Thank You, God, for saving me from that wretched man!"

"Yes, thank You, Jesus," Cammie said with a nod. "I been praying to get away from that man. Now, I is happy!"

Taylor took Brooke from Cammie and held her fiercely. They were free and going to a strange new place called Charleston, South Carolina, in America.

Just then the door opened and the porter set a case inside, then stepped out to make room for a woman to enter. As short and slight as Cammie, but older by a few years, she was well dressed and had black hair under her small blue bonnet, which was a shade darker than her wide eyes.

Taylor stared at her in shock. "This room is taken."

"I'm to share it with you, or so that captain said. I'm Maida O'Dell and I'm going to Charleston with my aunt and uncle." She couldn't say she was the poor relation brought with them to wait on them hand and foot and had no choice where she stayed. She just kept the smile on her face even though it was almost impossible.

Taylor touched Cammie, then Brooke. "Cammie is sharing it with me and my baby. Where will you sleep?"

Maida looked around helplessly. Where would she sleep? "I paid for a bed. My uncle did, at any rate," she admitted.

"I will sleep on the floor," Cammie said quickly. After all, she wasn't used to a bed except when she slept with Master James.

Taylor sighed heavily. There was barely enough room to stand on the floor. "I suppose you'll have to."

Cammie smiled. "I be happy, Missy Taylor!" The floor was much better than sleeping with Master James. She didn't say it aloud because she knew white ladies blushed at such talk.

"I'll get the porter to bring a mat and a blanket." Maida eased around her case and out the door. Biting her lip, she stood in the passageway. She'd counted on privacy, but even that was denied her. Tears welled up in her eyes, but she quickly blinked them away.

Inside the cabin Taylor carefully laid Brooke in the carriage and covered her up. Taylor smiled at Cammie. "It'll be a tight squeeze the next few weeks, but we can make it. We're free!"

Cammie sank weakly to the floor and pulled her legs tight against her body. "No more Master James! Thank You, Jesus!"

What exactly was waiting for Taylor at the end of the voyage? Not one image popped into her head. She shivered and wrapped her arms tightly around herself also.

❧

Biting her lip to hold back tears of frustration and loneliness, Maida O'Dell carried the rolled straw ticking and wool blanket down the companionway toward the cabin she was forced to share with strangers. Was there any way life could change for her? Must she stay forever in servitude to her aunt and uncle? Birthday last she'd turned thirty. Just thinking about it made her want to wail at the top of her lungs. She was a spinster, caught in a deadly trap. Freedom was beyond her grasp.

Just then she bumped into someone and lost a grip on the bedding roll. It fell from her arms and unrolled just as if it was a flag unfurling at the man's feet. She stared up at him with a gasp of humiliated horror. He was shorter than her uncle, but taller than the sailors, and he dressed like a gentleman. His dark brown eyes were full of sorrow. "I'm terribly sorry, sir," she muttered. Her face burned with shame, and tears filled her eyes.

He bent to retrieve the bedding, rolled it, and flopped it over his shoulder. "A porter should be carrying this for you!"

She nodded, feeling even a deeper shame. Her uncle wouldn't allow her ever to have money, and a porter wouldn't help her without a fee, but she couldn't very well tell this man.

He stood with the rolled bedding flung over one shoulder and a slight frown on his face. But his voice was gentle as he said, "Allow me to introduce myself. Yates Marston, bound for the Catawba Plantation near Darien, South Carolina."

"Maida O'Dell. Bound for Charleston with my aunt and uncle to visit their friends." Maida reached for the bedding. "Thank you for your help."

He stepped back a pace. "I'll carry it for you," he offered. "Show me the way to your cabin."

Her heart lurched and suddenly she knew a way to be free—marry Yates Marston! The bold thought made her feel light-headed. Then another thought came quickly behind the first—what if Yates Marston was already married? He was well into his thirties by the look of him.

She had to know! So taking every ounce of courage in her she said, "Sir, what would your wife say about your helping me?"

Yates flinched, pain flashing in his eyes for an instant. "My wife is dead, God rest her soul."

Maida saw the pain cross his face and felt bad for her selfish question. "I'm sorry." And indeed she was sorry for his sake, but relieved for her own sake. She reached for the Irish charm she'd inherited from her father and gently touched Yates Marston's arm and looked compassionately into his eyes. "That's the sorrow I see in your eyes. It's that sorry I am, sir."

Yates peered closely at Maida. "You're very perceptive in one so young."

She flushed. Because of her slight build she was always taken for someone younger than she was. "I'm not as young as I look, sir. And I'm much stronger than I appear." She reached for the bedding. "Please don't trouble yourself on my account. I can manage on my own."

He shook his head. It wasn't right that she had to fend for herself. He wanted to help this woman. He'd been so wrapped up in the grief of losing his wife while giving birth to his son and in getting his three children and himself off to America that he'd not taken time to see anyone's needs but his own.

"Allow me. It would give me pleasure," he insisted.

Maida smiled and her eyes sparkled as blue as sapphire. "Thank you."

She fell into step beside him toward her cabin. The lanterns cast shadows on the wall as they passed them. "I am used to waiting on myself. I've been rather like a servant in my uncle's home since I was fifteen."

Maida couldn't believe she had just said that. What would he think of her now? She was a poor servant and he, an English gentleman. She was so ashamed of her position that her words sounded stilted. "Here it is. Thank you for your help."

Yates felt the sudden tension in her words and wondered about them. His right hand reached out to briefly clasp hers as he remarked, "It was pleasant meeting you. I'll see you again. I'd like to introduce you to my children."

"I'd like that, sir. Thank you." Trembling, Maida opened the door and stepped inside with the bedding. The smell of a wet diaper stung her nose.

Yates caught sight of a Negro girl and a white baby and his heart sank. Did the baby belong to Maida O'Dell? Was she married? Why should it trouble him? Then he caught sight of the woman who'd spoken to him earlier on the dock and he breathed a sigh of relief. Surely the baby belonged to her. Smiling, Yates walked to his cabin. Maybe the trip wasn't going to be as taxing as he'd supposed.

Inside her cabin Maida tucked the bedding between the wall and the carriage. "I'm sorry it took so long."

"Thank you kindly, ma'am." Cammie smiled. She'd never been waited on that she could remember—except by Missy Taylor.

"Maida." She frowned and shook her head. "Call me Maida."

"She won't," Taylor said with a chuckle. "I've been trying to get her to call me Taylor for two months now. I finally gave up. Cammie, please see to Brooke's dinner. She'll be hungry soon."

Cammie looked around helplessly. "Where do I go?"

"I know where the galley is," Maida said. "That's the kitchen. You'll have to fix food for yourself and the baby."

Taylor looked puzzled.

"I heard someone say it was expected of servants." Maida turned back to Cammie. "I could show you." Maybe she'd catch sight of Yates Marston again.

Cammie looked to Taylor for permission.

"Yes, go with Miss . . ." Taylor frowned. "I'm sorry, but I forgot your name."

"Maida O'Dell. Please, call me Maida. We're going to be sharing the room and I would like us to become friends."

Taylor couldn't see any harm in that, so she agreed. "And call me Taylor." She turned to Cammie. "The food I brought for Brooke is in the trunk with the blue tag. Fix the food there in the galley, then bring it here. I'll wait here with Brooke. She'll be waking again soon and will be very hungry, so please hurry."

Much later when Taylor learned the gangplank had been lifted, she left Cammie in the cabin with Brooke and walked with Maida to the galley for dinner. She'd heard it was served at six so the cook could put out the fire and the porter could extinguish all the lamps each evening just after seven. Fire was a hazard on the ships and the crew took great care to keep one from starting.

Taylor trembled at the thought of the ship catching on fire. She'd heard dreadful stories of all passengers dying when a ship caught fire. She pushed the awful thought away. God was with her, and no fire was going to burn their ship!

As they neared the galley Maida caught a whiff of pork. "My aunt said noon meals would be scarce, but the dinner more filling. I must admit I am feeling rather hungry."

Taylor was still too nervous to be hungry, but she didn't tell Maida.

"Have you met anyone besides me, Taylor?"

"Andrew Simons," she admitted.

"I met a nice gentleman, Yates Marston." Maida kept her voice light so as not to give her audacious plan away.

Taylor nodded. "Yates Marston. Yes. Mr. Simons knows him. I saw him with three children but no wife. I wonder if he's a widower?"

Maida nervously fingered the brooch at her high collar. She tried to keep her voice level as she asked, "You don't have your eye on him, do you?"

Taylor frowned, then gasped as she caught Maida's meaning. She slowed her pace and stared in shock at Maida. "Yates Marston? As a husband, you mean?"

Maida barely nodded.

"No! Of course not!"

Maida relaxed and managed to smile. "He seems a fine man."

"Andrew Simons seems to be a fine man, too."

"Yes, I suppose he is." But for some reason Maida didn't like Andrew. She hadn't formally been introduced to him yet, but she'd observed him on deck with her aunt and uncle just after they'd boarded. He seemed too smooth-talking, like the kind of person who did something for what he could get out of it.

Just then Andrew Simons walked into sight, bowed slightly to both of them, and smiled into Taylor's eyes. "I was coming to escort you to the dining room."

"Thank you. How very thoughtful of you." Taylor introduced him to Maida. They smiled and exchanged greetings. Maida excused herself and started walking into the dining area.

Andrew held out a paper to Taylor. "Here is the receipt for your passage."

She breathed a sigh of relief as, without looking at it, she tucked it through the slit in her skirt and into her pocket. "Thank you." She could trust Andrew Simon after all. She smiled at him and he smiled back, then they walked together behind Maida to the dining room. It was quite a large room with four tables—each with six chairs to a table and lit by lanterns. Laughing and talking guests sat at the tables.

Maida spotted Yates Marston with his children. She wanted to sit with them, but she knew it wouldn't be ladylike to invite herself. She saw her aunt and uncle at the captain's table and knew she didn't want to sit there.

Andrew seated Taylor and Maida at the table between the captain's and the one where the Marstons sat. Two other passengers were already there. Andrew introduced them as Ardith and Paul Collingwood, bound for Charleston where they lived.

While they ate pork, rice, beans, and bread, Taylor and Maida talked with Ardith about Charleston. The men spoke in hushed tones about the killings done with the guillotine in France, the hardships of war, and the large profits made from slave ships going to America.

Maida finished the last bite of gingerbread and drank the last of her water. She was still hungry, but she knew she couldn't ask for more food. It was rationed to last the entire trip.

"Maida, come here!"

Flushing at her aunt's harsh tone, Maida turned to find Aunt Erica frantically motioning to her. She stood awkwardly, found her legs to walk with the roll of the ship, and excused herself.

"I'll see you at the cabin later, Taylor." Maida smiled at the others. "It was nice meeting all of you." And she hurried away before her aunt could call her again.

Under the woman's good looks was a heart of stone, Maida thought. Erica demanded service and loyalty at any cost. Her uncle was almost as bad, although at times he was kind to her, perhaps because her mother had been his sister. When Aunt Erica wasn't around he sometimes told stories of when they were children.

Maida lurched forward and grabbed the back of her uncle's chair for support. Flushing with embarrassment, she forced a smile. "What can I do for you, Aunt?"

"Help me to my room." Erica carefully stood to her feet and gently shook her emerald green dress to fall in graceful folds to her small black slippers. A diamond necklace flashed at her breast. She swayed, and then gripped Maida's arm with strong, white fingers. "Don't just stand there! Help me! You know I can't walk on this rolling ship without help."

Across the room Yates Marston saw the embarrassment on Maida's face. He wanted to get her away from her aunt, but he didn't move. It really was no concern of his.

His daughter brushed back her blonde hair before plucking at her father's arm. "Papa, please help me. I'm sick again."

Yates sighed heavily. "Laurel, resign yourself to going to Catawba and you'll feel better."

Laurel scowled and jerked her hand away. "Papa, my home is England and always shall be! When I am of age, I'll return, and I'll marry Jason Portland!"

Her sister rolled her eyes.

Her brother groaned, then leaned close to Kendra and whispered, "Kendra, let's go on deck."

"Good idea, Reid," Kendra nodded. She slipped from her chair and hurried away with him.

Laurel saw them go, but she was too upset to complain. She ran from the galley, lurching from side to side with the roll of the ship.

Yates groaned. The children needed a mother. He wasn't good at dealing with their tantrums or needs or surreptitious manner. Finally he stood and walked slowly out of the galley. Maida and her aunt and uncle were several feet ahead of him. The aunt's shrill voice carried back to him and he cringed.

In the galley Andrew took Taylor's arm and walked her to her cabin. He wondered suddenly what James Rawlings was doing aboard the *Carleena* now that he knew Taylor Craven and Cammie weren't on board?

Making his tone as casual as he could, he observed, "By the time you wake in the morning we'll be long gone from Liverpool. Will you be sad to leave it behind?"

She tensed. Was he suspicious of her? She'd try to be noncommittal. "It's always hard to leave something familiar. Don't you think?"

"I suppose."

"Where are you from, sir?"

He held his hands up. "Andrew. Please. We'll be together for at least four weeks and I'd like us to be friends."

"Where are you from, Andrew?"

"Originally from London, but I've lived in America since after the war."

"Do you have a family?"

He hesitated. It wouldn't do to tell her he had already had three wives and seven children between them. Well, the ready lie then. "I was married just out of university, but my beloved wife died more than ten years ago."

"I'm sorry. My husband died only a few weeks ago." Her voice broke and she couldn't go on.

He lifted her hand and gently patted the back of it. Was it possible she was a rich widow? Could it be his good deed would pay off more than he'd anticipated?

"I feel your pain, my dear. If I can be of any further help, let me know," he murmured.

"Thank you," she whispered.

He squeezed her hand and let it go. "Good night. I'll see you tomorrow."

"Yes." Taylor smiled through her tears. "I appreciate your kindness." She opened the cabin door and slipped inside.

Andrew chuckled under his breath and walked jauntily to the captain's quarters. This was a story worth telling over a glass of brandy.

Inside the cabin Taylor stepped over Cammie who was sound asleep and peeked in the carriage. Brooke slept on her tummy with her bottom high in the air. Taylor kissed her fingertips and touched Brooke's soft, warm head.

"Good night, sweet baby girl," she whispered. How thankful she was to have Brooke—a part of Floyd. They'd hoped to have five children, but now he was gone. Not just gone, she reminded herself angrily, but killed by his own cousin!

Tears burning her eyes, Taylor undressed and slipped on her nightgown. She crawled in the bottom bunk and lay with her eyes open and her heart racing. She was on her way alone to a strange land.

"Floyd, I need you," she whispered brokenly. He'd provided a good home for her these four years. When she'd learned she was going to have a child, she'd been overjoyed and so had Floyd. Secretly she'd been afraid they'd never have a child, so when Brooke came along, she'd been happier than she'd ever been before. Now Floyd was gone and Brooke would never get to know him.

Taylor brushed at her eyes. She couldn't spend the rest of her days in tears, so she prayed, "Heavenly Father, comfort my heart and help me to raise Brooke to be a strong woman of faith."

❦

The passage continued uneventfully. A few days later in her aunt and uncle's cabin Maida helped her aunt undress and slip on her nightdress. "Do you want your hair braided tonight, Aunt Erica?"

"Of course! Don't I always?"

Maida bit back her anger. Often her aunt wore her hair tucked into her nightcap because she thought a braid would hurt her head. Quickly and carefully Maida braided the woman's hair, then helped her into the wide bed. "I'll tell Uncle he can come in now," she whispered. Erica never undressed in front of her husband. She said it was too uncivilized.

Erica flipped on her side and closed her eyes. Her voice was demanding. "Come at seven to help me dress in the morning."

"Yes, Aunt." Maida's head felt ready to explode. How many years would she have to tend Aunt Erica?

In the passageway Maida found Uncle Samuel patiently waiting to be allowed in the cabin. "She's in bed," Maida said tiredly. "Good night, Uncle."

"Good night, Niece." He reached for the door, then turned back.

"Maida, I promised your aunt I'd speak to you about your conduct."

Maida froze. How she hated these lectures! After all, she was thirty, not thirteen!

Her uncle nervously fingered his high collar. He began with a lecturing tone. "You are forced to share a cabin with a black servant and a woman beneath your station. You must be polite, of course, but don't be friendly. You are, after all, our niece and you must conduct yourself in a proper manner." Maida knotted her fists. "I am your servant, Uncle," she said bitterly. "I am no different from the black servant Taylor Craven has."

Swiftly her uncle lashed out with his hand and slapped her cheek with a sound that echoed in the passageway. "Don't be impertinent!" he cried. He jerked open the door, walked in, and slammed it shut.

Maida burst into tears and ran blindly down the passageway.

Yates saw her running toward him, and he knew she was crying. He caught her arm and brought her up short.

"Don't!" She struggled, then stopped when she realized who it was. She had known Yates for only a few days and with each day her resolve to marry him had grown stronger.

"I want to help," he said in a low, firm voice.

All the strength drained from her body and she stood before him as limp as a used neckcloth. "There's nothing you can do," she whispered dejectedly.

"I can tell you I'm sorry."

She lifted her head and fire shot from her eyes. "Will that set me free of them? No! And I do not need or want your pity, sir."

"I am sorry."

"Then marry me! Only a husband will release me from them!" She gasped. Had she really said that? Her face burning with shame, she ran to her cabin and slipped inside, gasping for breath. Now she would never be able to face Yates Marston again!

Marry her! That was impossible. He had just lost his wife and newborn son. Her suggestion was too ridiculous—wasn't it? His head tilted in thought, Yates stood in the middle of the passageway. He was lonely and his children needed guidance. Maybe he should marry Maida. With his brow knit in thought Yates started toward his cabin. He'd have to give this idea some thought.

❦

Several days later, without her bonnet or her wrap, Taylor carefully walked on deck as the *Falcon* pitched and rolled. After a week of damp wet weather it felt good to feel the wind in her hair and the sun on her face. She breathed deeply of the tangy salt air. It cleared her head of the smells of Brooke's dirty diapers, tar and coal oil, and rancid bilge water below deck.

Immense canvas sails billowed out in the vast blue sky. She peered over the side at the green sea, its waves topped with white foam, rushing by with unrelenting speed. The water stretched on and on until it touched the unending blue sky. She trembled. She was free of James Rawlings, but what would she do in Charleston? Could she find a way to support herself and her child?

Just then Kendra Marston stopped beside Taylor. Kendra was sixteen years old, the same as Cammie, but younger in the ways of the world. She had good manners, but she had never been outside her schoolroom.

Taylor smiled and squeezed Kendra's hand. "Is your papa over his anger at you?"

Kendra chuckled and leaned close to Taylor. "I can talk Papa out of anything. He's forgotten all about Reid and me going below to see if there are slaves on board." Kendra sighed heavily and looked over her shoulder, then back at Taylor. "But Laurel is still angry. She insists on being a lady every minute. She's a year older than I am, but she tries to be my mother!"

"My oldest sister was like that, too. I didn't think I'd miss her when she moved to Scotland with her husband, but I did."

"Are you sorry you're going to America?"

Taylor bit her lip. The Marstons had no idea she was running from James Rawlings. "It will seem strange living in a new world." What would she do there? How would she live? All she knew was that with God's strength and help she knew she'd survive. It was the biggest step of faith she'd ever taken in her life.

"I don't think I'm going to like it!" Kendra crossed her arms and looked very stubborn. The wind blew her long brown hair across her face, and she pulled it away and held it with her hand. "I'll like seeing Uncle Ward again. He is my very favorite uncle! He's fun and he always makes me laugh. One time he took me hunting with him. He shot a deer with a bow. I wanted to help him skin it, but I hadn't the heart for it. He didn't laugh at me or scold me, but instead he had me wait under a tree until he was finished." She bit her lip. "I hope he hasn't changed. Papa said living in America might have turned him into a barbarian."

"Does your Uncle Ward have a family?"

"No. Unless he married since we heard from him last." Kendra lowered her voice. "He left England six years ago because a girl broke his heart. He was all set to marry her and she married someone else."

"How terrible!"

"It was. I don't remember much of it, since I was too young. He must have been very sad though to leave like he did." Kendra brushed back her hair. "He seems happy now, though. He has a wonderful farm he calls Catawba plantation. He says there's room for all of us. One boundary of Catawba is as far from the other boundary as the village we lived in is to the next village. Can you imagine having all that land? He says we'll live in a three-story brick house as big as a castle."

"That's big," Taylor said with a laugh.

Kendra giggled. "He really didn't say as big as a castle. But he said it was huge and that Reid and I would have fun running and hiding in it. I think he's forgotten I'm practically a woman."

Just then Yates Marston walked past with Maida O'Dell.

Kendra sucked in her breath. "Papa has been spending too much time with Old Maid Maida. I don't like it a bit!"

Taylor frowned. She didn't like Kendra to be disrespectful, but it wasn't her place to correct her. "Your papa is lonely."

"Mama has been . . . been gone only six months. How can he forget her so quickly and take up with . . . with an Irish woman?"

"I like Maida."

"Even though she's Irish?"

Smiling, Taylor nodded. "You would, too, if you'd allow yourself to."

"If you say so," Kendra said, sounding unconvinced.

"I find her charming with a good sense of humor. And, by the way, her father was Irish, but her mother was English."

"You like everybody, don't you, Taylor?"

"Most people, yes, I do." Except James Rawlings, of course, but she couldn't tell anyone about that. Cammie had promised to keep James and all their problems a secret. Thankfully, Cammie could be very close-mouthed when she chose to be.

Kendra looked off across the vast sea. "Sometimes I have trouble liking my own sister. Isn't that awful? But I can't help it! She is too formal and never gets into trouble. Papa never has to scold her or punish her. Reid and I aren't always nice."

"I like your brother. He plays with Brooke and he's nice to Cammie."

"Papa told us we shouldn't talk to Cammie. Papa said slaves aren't like real people."

Taylor's dark brows shot up. "Does your father approve of slavery?"

"Yes! But I don't. Neither does Reid." Kendra motioned to Reid, who was talking excitedly to a sailor. "Do you know he taught Cammie how to spell her name? He's going to teach her to write it, too." Her finger pressed to her lips, Kendra leaned toward Taylor. "Don't tell Papa! He said slave owners say it's illegal for Negroes to read or write. Isn't that foolish?"

Taylor nodded. "How does your Uncle Ward feel about slavery?"

"Papa says he doesn't approve of it. But Papa says from what he read about running a plantation in South Carolina you must have slaves." Kendra shook her head and looked grim. "Taylor, it doesn't seem right to own other people, does it?"

"It's not right!"

"That's what I told Papa, but he shushed me and sent me to my room. He said in South Carolina I'll have to get used to having slaves. He said I'd even have my own! I don't like that at all, but there's nothing I can do about it," Kendra sighed, then changed the subject. "Where are you going to live, Taylor?"

Taylor's stomach knotted and she searched for an answer. "I'll know when I arrive. I'm led by the Holy Spirit."

Kendra's eyes filled with tears. "Is that really true?"

"Yes."

"Sometimes I forget God is with me."

Taylor patted Kendra's arm. "If it's agreeable to your father, I'll share the Scriptures with you daily. Your brother and sister, too."

"I'll ask Papa. I'm sure he'd agree. Anything so he'd have time with Old Maid Maida."

"Kendra, it's very disrespectful to call Maida that name. Please don't call her that. Besides, Cammie, Brooke, and I really do like her."

"I don't want her to marry Papa."

"She needs a home of her own, Kendra. Think of her and your father instead of yourself."

Kendra scowled. "I don't think I can!"

Across the deck Maida smiled at Yates. "I'm feeling much better today. I didn't expect to get seasick."

"I heard your aunt and uncle are still feeling delicate."

Maida sighed and nodded. "I'm to take them something to eat in a few minutes. I tried to convince them to come out on deck this morning and breathe the fresh air, but they wouldn't hear of it."

"Perhaps they will tomorrow."

"Perhaps."

But it was another week before they did. Maida helped them to the rail and stood with them as they tried to find their balance with the pitch and the roll.

"Isn't that better?" Maida asked in a cheery voice. Oh, it was so hard to be cheerful and polite with them! And it was getting harder every day. How was she going to make it through the rest of her life like this? Was there any hope?

"I suppose it is," Uncle Samuel said weakly. He'd lost weight and his clothes hung on him.

Aunt Erica sniffed, but didn't speak. She'd lost weight too, but she still looked as beautiful as a porcelain doll.

Just then the ship rolled and Erica fell to her knees. She cried out and struggled fearfully to her feet. She whirled on Maida, shaking a trembling, bony finger at her. "You should've held on to me! But you won't do anything unless I beg you to. You are an ungrateful wretch!"

Struggling to compose herself, Maida turned away. Her eyes locked with Yates Marston's. He had witnessed her humiliation yet again! Walking stiffly to the companionway, Maida refused to let the tears come while on deck. Once she reached her cabin, however, Maida flung the door open and let out a wrenching sob, tears streaming down her face.

Yates's heart went out to her and he hurried after her. She was a kind-hearted woman who didn't deserve the treatment her relatives gave her. Reaching her cabin shortly after her, Yates could hear her sobbing inside. Lifting his hand he knocked softly on the door. Inside Maida tried to control her tears as she opened the door slowly.

Her heart jerked. Yates Marston had followed her! Her eyes flashed as she looked up at him.

He saw the fire in her eyes and for a minute he couldn't speak. Finally he said crisply. "I will marry you. Today."

Maida gasped, her head spinning as she crumpled; but before she hit the floor he caught her, hauled her up, and held her tightly in his arms. He could easily pick her up and carry her off to his cabin. Ellen had been almost as tall as he was and he couldn't have picked her up if he'd tried. Now Yates felt a surge of protectiveness for Maida rush through him. He would never let anyone hurt her the way her aunt and uncle had in the past.

Maida felt his heart thud against her and saw the determined look in his eye. He was serious!

"Marry me, Maida, and you can leave your aunt and uncle. You can go to Catawba with us."

"But why would you want to marry me? What can I do for you?"

"Give me companionship. Mother my children. Share my bed. Catawba Plantation will be a lonely place for me."

Maida pressed her face against his chest. Here was her answer! She'd heard about Catawba until she felt she knew as much about it as Yates. But was this a dream? Would she wake up and find herself in the bunk above Taylor Craven?

Silently he held her. Was he doing something rash that he'd regret later? He didn't love Maida. After losing Ellen so recently Yates didn't believe he would ever be able to care for another woman again, but she'd meet his needs and he'd meet hers. That was better than loneliness for him, better than a hateful aunt and uncle for her.

After what seemed like a lifetime Maida lifted her head and gingerly touched Yates's cheek. It was strong with a hint of whiskers, and he didn't disappear in a puff of a dream.

She took a deep breath. "I will marry you. Now. This very minute." Was that really her speaking? Was she that brave? "Can I leave my aunt and uncle without a thought?" she said aloud.

"You can! Don't back out on me now, Maida. Wash your face, comb your hair, and let's go see the captain."

Maida trembled. "Do I have the courage?"

"Of course you do," he said with a grin. He tapped the tip of her small nose. "I'll wait right outside your cabin so you can't change your mind." He hadn't felt lighthearted in so long it took him by surprise.

Several minutes later Maida stood with Yates before the captain while he spoke the words that would unite them in marriage. Later with her hand in Yates's, she walked out of the captain's quarters. "We are married," she whispered.

He chuckled. "And I get the pleasure of telling your aunt and uncle."

Maida placed her hand on his arm. "They'll be very, very angry."

Yates laughed a great bark of a laugh. "I know. But you'll no longer have to be their slave!"

"It'll seem very . . . strange."

"You'll get used to it."

"What about your children? Will they be angry?"

Yates sobered immediately, sighed, and nodded. "They've been angry at me before. They'll get over it."

Maida bit her lip. "I hope so."

Yates grinned. "Shall we go tell your aunt and uncle?"

"I don't know if I can."

Yates gripped her elbow, and together they walked to Samuel and Erica Keech's cabin. Yates knocked firmly.

Maida tried to pull away, but she couldn't break free of his grip. "I can't face them," she whispered hoarsely.

"You can and you will." His voice was deadly calm and intractable.

The door opened and Samuel Keech stood there in his shirt-sleeves. He scowled at Maida. "I hope you have a good explanation for this intrusion."

Maida opened and closed her mouth, but no sound came out.

"A very good explanation, sir." Yates lifted his chin even higher than he was forced by the high collar of his shirt. "Your niece and I are wed. She is no longer your servant, but my wife. Tell your wife the good news."

Erica Keech poked her head around Samuel's arm. She screeched, "What's this? Married? I forbid it!"

"It's not for you to object, madam," Yates said coldly. He turned to Maida and smiled. "Shall we go?"

She nodded weakly, then clung to him to keep from fainting dead away where she stood. Leaning heavily on Yates, she walked beside him down the passageway. What a coward she was! Why couldn't she laugh in Aunt Erica's face?

"You'll be sorry for this!" Erica cried after them. "You've gone from the frying pan into the fire, you foolish girl!"

Maida gasped. Was that possible? Was she in a worse situation now than she had been with her aunt and uncle?

3

*T*aylor stared in shock at Maida. "You and Yates Marston are married?"

"Yes. About two hours ago." Maida rammed the rest of her things into her bag. Strands of black hair curled around her face. "I'm moving to his cabin." Her mouth felt bone-dry and her whole insides quivered so badly she didn't know if she could walk out of the room. They hadn't shared even a kiss, yet she was going to share his bed. Did she have the courage?

Taylor looked closely at Maida. Cammie had Brooke on the deck for fresh air, so Taylor felt she could speak freely. "Maida, is this what you want?"

"Yes!" Maida covered her face and burst into tears. "I don't know! I thought it was."

Taylor circled Maida's waist with her arm. "Marriage is a big step, but remember God is with you."

"I know." Maida sniffed, then dabbed her eyes with her white lacy handkerchief. She'd sat in on Taylor's Scripture reading and prayer time with Laurel, Kendra, and Reid. "My aunt said I went from the frying pan into the fire."

"She only wanted to frighten you."

"I know! She did a good job!"

Taylor grinned and tapped Maida's shoulder. "Put on a smile, Maida. You certainly made a change in your life. Now it's up to you to make it a good change."

Maida lifted her chin and dried her tears. "Yes! You're right. It is up to me!" She closed her bag and picked it up, then squeezed Taylor's arm. "And it's up to you! You can't really survive without someone's protection and you know it. Find someone to marry."

Taylor flushed. She'd given a passing thought to marrying Andrew Simons. She had a feeling he'd ask her if she gave an indication she'd agree. He'd hinted a couple of times, but she'd played dumb.

Besides, she had other responsibilities. "I have a baby. Who'd want me?" she asked dully.

"Then come with us to the Catawba Plantation!" Maida's face glowed. "Yes! What a perfectly marvelous idea! It would be wonderful to have you there with me."

"I don't know," Taylor said weakly. The end of the voyage was coming and she still didn't know what she was going to do. Should she accept Maida's invitation? After all she'd heard about Catawba and about Ward Marston she knew she'd like being there.

Still, she needed to consider it carefully, so she said, "I'll let you know."

"You do that. You could marry Ward Marston! Yates says he doesn't have a wife."

Blushing crimson, Taylor shook her head. When she was Kendra's age she'd dreamed about going to the New World and marrying a man with a fine sense of humor who worked the land, raised horses, and helped other people in need. She hadn't thought about the dream in years. Impatiently she pushed the beautiful memory away. She'd married Floyd and given birth to Brooke. Now she was a widow on the run with a slave. Her dream could never come true now.

"Maida, don't speak such nonsense!" she admonished.

Maida laughed. "Stranger things have happened. Look at me! Married to Yates Marston, part-owner of Catawba." Trembling on the inside, Maida hugged Taylor, said goodbye, and walked out into a new life.

Taylor sighed heavily. "Be happy, Maida," she whispered.

❦

Later, taking no notice of the roll and pitch of the *Falcon*, Taylor walked easily along the deck holding Brooke's hand. Andrew Simons had joined them and was telling her about the stately homes and wonderful people of Charleston. Often it was hard to hear over the snapping sails and creaks and groans of the merchantmen. The first mate shouted instructions to the sailors aloft. The stench of tar overpowered the smell of the sea.

Andrew stopped, leaned against the rail, and looked out across the unending ocean. He touched her hand and asked softly, "What will you do when you reach port?"

Cool wind ruffled her high-waisted green dress as Taylor faced him. She couldn't very well tell him she didn't know yet. And she didn't want to leave an opening for him to propose marriage to her. She kept a firm hold on Brooke to keep her from walking on. Over Brooke's chatter, Taylor changed the subject. "What are you going to do?"

"Visit a few friends." He didn't tell her he'd see one of his wives or that he'd ask if anyone knew James Rawlings of Virginia. If he could find enough money, he'd buy a trained blooded stallion, race it, then sell it for a higher price. "Now, suppose you tell me what you'll do." He liked the little games he played with her. Truth to tell, he liked her. She was delightful and pretty and made him laugh. He might decide to let her go without trying to make money off her. He did get impatient when he wanted time alone with her, however, and she wanted to have Brooke with her.

So he chided, "Don't keep me in suspense, dear lady. What are your plans?"

She glanced down at her black slippers peeking out from her dress's hem. "Walking on solid ground is all I can think about at present," she said with a weak laugh.

"You're a beautiful, desirable woman, Taylor." He'd thought about marrying her himself, but his other plans for her, the baby, and the slave would be much more profitable.

After all, a lot of people were willing to pay good money for an indentured servant. Why shouldn't he be the one to collect that money? Then, of course, Cammie would bring a very high price on the auction block since she was young and healthy. The baby was another matter altogether. He knew there was a demand for babies, but he was going to have to do some checking around. Surely there was a family in Charleston that would be grateful to him for bringing them such a beautiful little girl.

So his question was a careful one. "Do you have a man waiting for you there?"

She didn't want to answer him, but she didn't know why. She looked past the coils of ropes on the deck and two sailors deep in conversation toward the companionway. Turning to go, she answered lightly, "I must get Brooke down for her nap! Please excuse me."

"I'll walk you to your cabin." Pushing back the impatience he felt, Andrew took her arm and walked with her to the companionway. He knew a brush-off when he saw one. Just when he thought she'd tell him about herself, she pulled away again. She kept herself in tight control. At times he wanted to say, "I know James Rawlings. And I know you're running away from him along with his slave." What would she say to that? It would be very interesting to know. If she had money, she might be willing to pay him to keep quiet.

Just then Kendra Marston ran to Taylor. Sobbing, Kendra caught Taylor's hand. "I must speak with you."

Taylor pulled free of Andrew. "Excuse us, please, sir."

His jaw tightened. He wanted to send the girl back where she belonged, but he turned with a nod of his head and walked away.

With Brooke in her arms Taylor looked into Kendra's tear-stained face. "What's wrong?" she asked.

Her brown hair in tangles over her slender shoulders, Kendra plucked at her dress that had grown limp and faded during the voyage. "Papa married that Irish woman yesterday and told us just now!"

Taylor pulled Kendra close and patted her gently on the back. She smelled as if she needed to bathe. "There, there. It's not all that bad. You'll grow to love Maida."

With a cry of anguish, Kendra pulled away. Her blue eyes were wide and filled with pain. "No, I won't! Laurel and Reid said they won't either." Fresh tears filled her eyes and spilled down her ashen cheeks. "How could Papa marry so soon after Mama died?"

Taylor tried to comfort Kendra, but she was too angry and hurt to be comforted, so finally she tried a different approach. "I must put Brooke down for a nap. Would you like to go with me?"

Kendra nodded and as they walked her tears ceased. "Reid ran off to be with the sailors he made friends with." Kendra wiped off her cheeks in quick, impatient movements. "And Laurel is too upset to talk to me. I didn't know who else to turn to."

"I'm glad you came to me." Smiling, Taylor patted Kendra's shoulder. At sixteen every problem was overwhelming. But if she knew about James Rawlings, she'd think her problems were trivial.

Brooke squirmed to be let down and Taylor stood her on the deck, but kept hold of her hand.

Just then a short, ragged sailor with tattooes covering his thick arms grabbed Brooke, ran to the starboard rail, and swung up into the rat-lines.

Taylor screamed and ran to the rail and looked up. Brooke's white dress fluttered out, looking bright against the drab brown lines.

"Bring my baby back!" she shouted tearfully.

Kendra too yelled up at the sailor as he reached the first top. "Come back! Right now!"

"Please don't drop my baby!" Praying frantically under her breath, Taylor stretched out to grab the nearest deadeye to haul herself onto the rail, but she couldn't reach it. Frustrated to tears she screamed, "Somebody, help!"

Andrew Simons ran to Taylor and grabbed her waist and pulled her away from the edge. "Get back from there! What's wrong?"

She pointed up at the sailor with Brooke. Just then the sailor swung out to reach the next rat-lines, lost his footing, and almost dropped Brooke. Taylor's heart zoomed to her feet and she screamed. The sailor stepped onto the mainmast top while Brooke wailed in fear.

"Stand back! I'll save her!" Andrew caught the deadeye and sprang to the rail, then climbed the rat-lines almost as fast as the sailor had. Last year Andrew had learned to climb them just for the pleasure and daring of it. Now he could use his skill for his own ends. Somehow he had to make Taylor trust and rely on him. After all, this was part of the plan. He'd agreed to pay the sailor a month's wages to grab the baby and to keep his mouth closed even when he took a flogging for it later.

Taylor clamped her icy hand over her mouth and watched Andrew risk his life for Brooke.

Kendra clung to Taylor's arm and prayed with all her might.

Several sailors ran to the rail and watched, shouting to the sailor carrying Brooke.

Andrew reached the mainmast top and commanded in a forceful voice that he was sure would reach Taylor, "Hand over the baby!"

The sailor started up the main topmast shrouds, but Andrew caught him by the arm that wasn't holding Brooke and struggled to pull him back onto the mainmast top.

"Let me go or I'll drop the baby to the deck below!" the sailor shouted gruffly.

Taylor gasped and gripped Kendra.

"Give me the baby, and I'll tell the captain to lighten your flogging!" Andrew's voice was harsh.

The sailor shook his head.

"Don't be a fool, sir!" Andrew tugged on the sailor. "If you don't give the baby to me now, you'll be hung from the yardarm. Give up the baby now and you'll only get a flogging! You have my word on it!"

The sailor hesitated, stepped back on the mainmast top, and handed Brooke over to Andrew.

"He's got her! He's got her. He's got her." Taylor rocked back and forth.

Kendra sobbed and pressed her face against Taylor's arm.

The knot of sailors cheered. One of them said, "What got into Peeke?"

Gripping the shroud, Andrew held Brooke securely as he said in a low voice to the sailor, "Strike out at me. Make it look good."

Peeke grinned, showing rotted teeth. "Aye, sir."

Andrew started to turn away just as the sailor swung at him. He dodged, caught the sailor's foot with his, and flipped the sailor headlong toward the deck below. Andrew turned his face so he wouldn't see the sailor land, but he heard the thud of his body, the screams from Taylor and Kendra, and the cries of the other men.

"I couldn't have him telling my part in this, now could I?" Andrew muttered as he carefully climbed down with Brooke.

Sobbing, Taylor rushed forward and caught Brooke to her. "Thank God! Thank God!"

Turning her back on the grisly sight of the dead sailor as the others circled him, Kendra pressed close to Taylor and Brooke.

Without a backward glance, Taylor carried Brooke to the companionway and on to the cabin.

Captain Crawley ran to Andrew. "What's happening, sir?"

Sorrowfully Andrew shook his head and relayed the story as the others thought it to be. He wanted to go after Taylor to receive her thanks, but the captain wouldn't let him go. He wouldn't tell the truth of this story to the captain over a glass of brandy now or ever. Only the baby was a witness and she was too young to know what had really transpired.

❦

Several days later Taylor sat in her cabin alone for the first time since the sailor had carried Brooke up the rat-lines. The captain had said a few words over Peeke, explaining he'd gone out of his head, then they'd buried Peeke at sea. Kendra had been constantly at her side, but had finally agreed to go exploring again with Reid. Sighing, Taylor touched the wooden carriage. She had to decide her future. She was responsible for Brooke and for Cammie and even Cammie's unborn baby. Would it be wise to marry Andrew so he could take care of them? She trembled. So far she'd kept Andrew from broaching the subject, but after he'd saved Brooke she was giving it second thoughts.

She held her Bible to her and closed her eyes. "Father God, help me know what to do. Should I marry Andrew?"

As she prayed she felt deep inside it would be a grave mistake if she married Andrew. Relief washed over her. She had one answer —not to marry Andrew Simons even though he had saved Brooke. "Thank You, Father," Taylor whispered. God would continue to lead her and let her know what to do.

Suddenly the door burst open and Kendra rushed in. "Please come! Laurel is thrashing about in her bed, moaning with pain! She's burning with fever!"

Taylor laid her Bible on the bed and rushed with Kendra to the cabin the girls shared. At the door Taylor said, "Kendra, let me speak to Laurel alone. Find Cammie and tell her where I am. Help her feed Brooke, will you?"

Kendra nodded and walked away with bent shoulders. Laurel made her angry often, but she hated to see her in pain.

Taylor walked into the cabin and gasped at the closed-in stench. She left the door open in the hopes a little fresh air would drift in. She knew at a glance Laurel was weak and sick from not eating and not taking exercise. "Laurel, I've come to help you," Taylor said softly.

Laurel lifted her head. Her eyes were clouded and her hair was in dirty tangles. "I want to go home," she said weakly.

"Your new home will be Catawba." Taylor picked up Laurel's brush and started to brush her hair. "You told me you wanted to see your Uncle Ward. Remember?" Taylor knew talking of her Uncle Ward would get Laurel's mind off herself.

"I love Uncle Ward." Laurel sat on the edge of the bed and locked her thin hands together.

Slowly Taylor brushed Laurel's hair. "Tell me about him. Is he really as nice as Kendra and Reid said?"

"Yes. When I was a little girl I was afraid of almost everything. Uncle Ward knew it embarrassed me to be scared, so he said he'd help me conquer my fear." Laurel smiled.

Taylor tied Laurel's hair back with a blue ribbon that matched her dress. "What did he do?"

"I wanted to ride a pony, but I was too afraid. He took me off all alone where Kendra and Reid couldn't see, and he taught me to ride. It took days, but he didn't get impatient."

This new story of Ward Marston touched Taylor as much as the others had. Soon she'd meet the man himself. Would she be disappointed? She pushed the thought aside. "Can you still ride without being afraid?"

"Yes."

Taylor took Laurel's hand in hers. "I know how afraid you must feel about this new world that we're going to. I'm a little afraid myself since I've never left England before and that's where I had planned to stay all of my life. But now, here I am going on this adventure to South Carolina. You'll have your uncle there to show you around and help you over this fear."

Laurel sighed heavily. "But maybe he's changed like Papa said. Maybe he's become uncivilized and barbaric."

"From what your brother and sister have told me about him I think your uncle will always be the same."

"Papa changed after Mama died."

"I'm sorry. Maybe Maida will help him get over his grief."

Laurel's face hardened. "She will never make him forget Mama!"

"Of course not! But she can take away his loneliness." Taylor rubbed a finger along Laurel's thin hand. "I know you want your father to be happy again. Maida can help him find happiness." But even as she said it, she wondered if it were true. Maida had come to her in tears twice already because Yates had snapped at her when she'd tried to talk to him.

She brought her attention back to the young girl. "Can you try to love Maida?"

"It's too soon after Mama died!"

"Maida isn't trying to take your mother's place, Laurel. Learn to love Maida for herself as a part of your family. Do you think your Uncle Ward would like Maida?"

Laurel slowly nodded. "He would like her. But it's easy for him to like people. I'm more like my papa. It's hard for us to accept strangers."

"But he married Maida. He cares for her."

"He only wanted to take her away from her mean aunt and uncle."

"Is that what he said?"

"No, but I know it's true."

Taylor knew it wouldn't do any good to pursue the subject, so she suggested, "Wash your face and come on deck with me. The fresh air will make you feel better. I want to hear more about your Uncle Ward."

❧

A glass of brandy in his hand, Andrew Simons lounged in the chair in Captain Crawley's quarters. The captain sat behind his desk, a pleased smile on his face.

Crawley jabbed at the charts. "We'll reach Charleston tomorrow and put the nigger Cammie on the block shortly after. She's a handsome woman and should bring a good price."

"The Craven woman, too." What a shame his plan hadn't worked. Taylor still wouldn't tell him about herself nor give him an opening to speak of marriage. Little did she know she'd sealed her own destiny. "I got a list of people who want white indentured servants. And another list of folks who'll buy a baby—no questions asked." Simons leaned forward and said, "I was able to steal the receipt from Taylor Craven. She won't be able to prove she paid."

Crawley fingered a feather quill in his ink box. "I had a mind to ask Samuel Keech if he'd pay to have the marriage cancelled between his niece and Yates Marston, then thought better of it. Marston appears to be wealthy and is too well known in England. He could make trouble for us if we did anything against him."

"There are other voyages and other folks to buy and sell." Chuckling wickedly, Simons rearranged the folds of his collar. "One of these days I'm going to retire and settle down. But I'll have a devil of a time deciding what wife to choose." He slapped his knee and laughed harder. "I had in mind to marry that Craven woman, but she's a slippery one and wouldn't give me a chance to ask. She'll be right sorry, I'll tell you that."

❧

Her heart thundering, Taylor held Brooke tightly to her as she and Cammie walked on the crowded deck with the other passengers. The hot sun shimmered off the water and in the air over the sandy beach at Charleston. Ocean-going vessels vied for anchorage in harbor. The first mate shouted orders to the sailors.

"You stay close to me, Cammie," Taylor said in a low, tense voice.

Cammie shivered even in the heat. She'd heard spine-tingling tales of how much worse slaves were treated here than at Rawlings Plantation. "I stay real close, Miz Taylor."

Taylor smiled. It had taken the entire voyage for her to get Cammie to stop calling her Missy Taylor. The title was now used on Brooke, Laurel, and Kendra.

Brooke squirmed and said, "Down. Down." In the four weeks of the voyage she'd learned to walk and didn't like being held.

"No, Brooke. You must not get down. Look! See the land ahead? Soon we'll be on solid ground again." Taylor laughed and rubbed her face against Brooke's soft hair damp with perspiration. Taylor looked over Brooke's head to stare at the land with the bright blooms of flowers and bold green shrubs and trees. The flowers and trees and even the hot air were different from what she was used to.

"Oh, Brooke, will you know how to walk without the sway of the ship?" she sighed. Would she know how to walk on solid ground?

Just then Captain Crawley stepped up beside Taylor. He held his cap under his arm and looked very determined. "Madam, I must speak with you."

Taylor smiled and nodded. "I'm free to talk now, sir."

He settled his cap in place and squared his shoulders. "I have waited these many weeks for you to pay your fare."

Taylor gasped and the color drained from her face. What was he saying? "But I paid!"

He ignored her entirely. "If you can't pay it today, I'll be forced to get your passage fare by indenturing you."

Taylor thrust Brooke into Cammie's arms. "Hold her while I find my receipt. I do have a receipt!" Taylor's hands felt clammy and her body was almost too weak to support her light weight. She rummaged through her pockets, but she couldn't find the receipt.

"It has to be here." She had to calm herself and look again. She was shaking so badly she couldn't find the slits in her skirt that led to the pockets tied at her narrow waist.

Captain Crawley stepped closer to Taylor. His uniform was clean and neatly pressed. "I don't have it on my books that you paid. Please don't make it harder on yourself by purporting that you did."

Icy chills ran over Taylor. "I did pay, sir! Ask Andrew Simons! He took the money to you and brought the receipt back to me." Frantically she scanned the deck for Andrew and finally spotted him with Maida's aunt and uncle. He was dressed to the nines in a fawn-colored, double-breasted tailcoat cut away at the front and tight breeches tucked into high boots. The high collar of his white shirt lay in neat folds. He held his top hat in his hands. His blond hair was held back with a wide black cloth. Taylor caught his eye and urgently motioned to him, then turned back to Captain Crawley. "It'll all be settled in a minute. It will be."

A few feet behind Taylor, Maida saw Taylor beckon to Andrew and heard the conversation between her and the captain. Maida slipped around Kendra and Laurel and stopped just behind Taylor and beside Cammie and Brooke. "Is something wrong?" Maida asked in a low voice.

"Nothing that concerns you," Captain Crawley said impatiently.

Tears glistening in her eyes, Taylor gripped Maida's hand. "He says I haven't paid my way. He says he'll have to indenture me to someone to get his fee."

"I'll get Yates. Don't leave this spot." Concern for Taylor and anger at the circumstance rushed through Maida as she hurried across the deck to find Yates. Surely he'd deal with the situation. When she didn't see him on deck, she assumed he was still in their cabin.

Her breath lodged in her tight throat, Taylor waited for Andrew to thread his way through the crowd and reach her side. Wind ruffled his blond hair and the layers of his white collar. He looked every bit the gentleman.

He reached her side and frowned down at her. "Is there a problem that you should beckon me to your side in such an uncivilized manner?"

Taylor plucked at his arm. "Captain Crawley says I didn't pay him! And I can't find the receipt you gave me."

"Receipt I gave you?" Andrew looked at her as if he didn't know what she was talking about. "Madam, I don't understand why you're speaking to me about this. It's between you and the captain."

Gasping in unbelief, Taylor fell back a step and stared at Andrew. What was he saying?

Fear rushed through Cammie and she almost dropped Brooke. The man was as cunning as Master James!

Taylor finally found her voice. "Andrew, you paid the captain! You gave me the receipt."

"Lower your voice, madam." Andrew's tone was icy cold. "I have been a friend to you, but I refuse to listen to you fabricate such a lie."

Helplessly Taylor shook her head. "But I did pay! You did give me a receipt!"

"Pay your passage fee now." Captain Crawley held out his hand. "If you don't, we'll sell your nigger girl and your baby as well as yourself."

Taylor's head spun and she thought she was going to swoon. She didn't have enough to pay for their keep for more than two days, let alone to pay yet another voyage fee.

She forced herself to stay calm however. "Wait for Yates Marston. He'll have an answer for you."

Andrew's jaw tightened. He hadn't planned on Taylor finding help aboard ship. "Take her to your quarters, Captain. We'll settle it there."

Captain Crawley reached for Taylor, but she brushed his hand away.

"No! I'm waiting right here for Yates Marston! Don't touch me!"

Kendra stepped boldly to one side of Taylor while Reid stepped to the other side.

"Leave her alone," Kendra snapped. She believed Taylor and she would do anything to help her.

"Don't lay one finger on her!" Reid said with the authority he'd heard his father use. He knew Taylor didn't lie.

Tears of gratitude sparkling in her eyes, Taylor looked at them thankfully. She squared her shoulders and faced the captain and Andrew. She saw the anger in their eyes. She knew they weren't going to give up easily. How could she have been fooled by Andrew? Had he kept the money himself or was the captain involved in the terrible scheme? Silently she prayed for a way out of the situation.

The captain narrowed his dark eyes. "Either you go quietly to my quarters with me, or I'll have my mate shackle your darkie and keep her prisoner below deck."

Cammie trembled and Brooke whimpered.

Taylor's heart sank. What should she do? She couldn't let them harm Cammie in any way.

"Don't you lay a finger on Cammie!" Laurel Marston cried as she stepped to Cammie's side. Laurel's cheeks were bright red and she looked very determined. "You wait for our father."

Kendra gasped and stared in shock at her sister.

Reid looked at Laurel as if he couldn't believe his ears.

Taylor stood her ground and faced the captain squarely. "Don't touch me or mine, sir," she said in a deadly calm voice. "I have other friends in the crowd who'll come to my aid if I call for them." Taylor heard the other passengers whispering and knew they were wondering what was happening.

Fire flashed from the captain's eyes, but he didn't make a move toward Cammie nor did he order a command to take her. He couldn't afford to have anyone report his actions or he could lose his ship.

Taylor lifted her face to catch a cool breeze and waited for Maida to return with Yates.

❦

In their cabin Maida faced Yates squarely. He sat at a desk and was writing in a ledger. She'd told him about Taylor, but he'd refused to acknowledge he'd heard her.

"You must listen! And you must help her!" she demanded. "She's to be indentured if she can't prove she paid!"

"That's no concern of mine. Or yours, madam!" His voice had a hard edge she'd not heard before.

"I told her you'd go to her rescue." Maida tugged on Yates's arm. "Please! Come with me before the captain does something dreadful to her."

Yates shook her hand off. The cash money he had was to buy supplies for Catawba and slaves to work the land. He didn't have enough to help a stranger. So he answered her coldly, "I feel for the woman, but there's nothing I can do."

Maida stared at him in consternation. "Am I hearing correctly? You won't do anything for her? But she'll be sold. And if she is, what of Brooke and Cammie? What of them, Yates?"

He frowned thoughtfully. Cammie was strong; she could work for them. And Taylor seemed quite capable. There was a possibility he could buy Cammie and have Taylor indentured to him. But keeping the baby was out of the question.

"Please, Yates," Maida whispered. How could the man be so cold-blooded?

"If you insist, madam!" He yanked open the door and strode into the passageway.

It was getting harder and harder for Yates to ignore Maida. Since they had married she had been talking to him about things, but Yates wasn't used to that. Ellen had just agreed with whatever he had wanted to do. As far as he could remember they had never discussed anything. Now everything was different. But, as Yates reminded himself grimly, he was determined not to get so comfortable with Maida that he forgot all about Ellen.

Maida ran after him, lurching slightly at the roll of the ship. Yates didn't look back and didn't offer to take her arm. Tears burned her eyes. Was he sorry for marrying her so quickly? But it was too late now. Aunt Erica had been right—it appeared she had indeed gone from the frying pan into the fire.

❧

On deck Taylor forced back a cry of alarm as she faced Andrew and the captain. "Why are you doing this? I did pay and I do have the receipt."

"Then produce it, madam," the captain said coldly.

Scowling, Andrew stepped right up to Taylor. "Why are you making a spectacle of yourself? We could settle this alone in the captain's quarters."

"Don't go with him," Kendra whispered sharply as she gripped Taylor's arm.

Andrew glared at Kendra, but she didn't back away. He turned to the captain as if to ask him what to do now. He'd been positive Taylor would've done whatever he asked when she couldn't find the receipt, and since he'd secretly taken it from her cabin when no one was there, she was definitely not going to find it again.

Just then Yates Marston stopped beside the captain. "Is there a problem, sir?" he asked gruffly.

Taylor started to speak, but Yates silenced her with a look. She heard Brooke whimper and took her from Cammie.

"They's gonna do you wrong, Miz Taylor," Cammie whispered, shivering even in the heat of the South Carolina wind.

Taylor squeezed Cammie's hand reassuringly, then turned back to listen to Yates. The captain and Andrew were telling him their version of the story. Taylor watched Yates's face and her heart sank to her slippers peeking from under her too-warm wool dress. Then she remembered God was with her and she lifted her head higher. He would take care of her and Brooke and Cammie!

"Captain, I'm prepared to offer payment for Mrs. Craven and the black woman, but I have no time or use for the baby."

Taylor gasped and Cammie cried out.

Maida clamped an icy hand over her mouth. How could Yates be so cold-blooded after being so kind to her before they got married?

Kendra stepped to Yates's side, grabbing his arm as she insisted, "Papa, you must take the baby too! You can't leave her behind!"

Yates scowled at Kendra. Since when had she gotten so bold as to tell him what he must do? But the look of her was so much like dear Ellen's that his heart softened. Yates would do anything to appease the feelings of guilt that kept plaguing him for marrying Maida so soon after Ellen's death.

He turned to the captain with a sigh. "The baby will stay with her mother."

Tears sprang to Taylor's eyes and she clung to Brooke as if afraid the captain would snatch her away no matter what Yates said.

Cammie clamped her hand over her mouth and rocked back and forth. Master Marston owned her now. Would he whip her or worse yet force her to warm his bed? Soon her belly would be big and maybe he wouldn't be interested. Oh, dear Jesus, don't let him make me warm his bed.

Kendra smiled up at her father. "Thank you."

Maida bit her lower lip and tried to steady the wild beat of her heart. Would she ever see that warmth and love in Yates's eyes for her? She glanced across the deck to find Aunt Erica looking at her with a smug, knowing look on her face. Maida turned away, scalding tears in her eyes.

"We'll make the business transaction in my quarters," Captain Crawley said briskly.

Holding her breath, Taylor watched them walk away. What had happened to her receipt? She saw the insolent turn of Andrew's lip. Had he stolen the receipt? How she wanted to confront him and demand an answer, but she dare not do anything to make trouble for Yates. After they were on their way to the Catawba Plantation, she'd speak to him about it and sort it out. Surely he would never really make her stay an indentured servant to him. He couldn't be that kind of man or Maida wouldn't have married him.

After the captain and Yates were out of sight and Andrew was once again across the way talking to other passengers, Kendra squeezed Taylor's arm. "You're going to stay with us! I'm pleased!"

"Me, too." Reid smiled and tickled Brooke under the chin. "I'll teach you to ride a pony. Uncle Ward has the best horses in all of South Carolina!"

Maida beckoned to Taylor, who handed Brooke to Cammie and excused herself.

Taylor caught Maida's hands. "Thank you for helping us. I'll never forget it! You know I did pay my passage. Andrew lied for some reason."

"I know." Maida trembled. "Now I need your help."

"Anything! What?"

Giant tears welled up in Maida's sky-blue eyes. "Help me get away from Yates! I can't stay where I'm not loved or wanted."

Taylor frowned. "What do you mean? He just paid for Cammie and Brooke and me!"

"Only because I begged him to. He wasn't going to lift a finger to help! And you heard him say he wouldn't be bothered with the baby. Oh, Taylor, he seems to have locked his heart away where I'll never be able to reach it."

Taylor placed her arm around Maida. "With God's help you will. If you give him all the love you have, you'll begin to see the change in Yates."

"He doesn't care a pin about me!" Maida folded her arms and tried to stop crying. "How can I live with a man who doesn't love me and who is so hard-hearted?"

Shaking her head, Taylor looked at Maida sadly. "I can't help you leave him. You're married and that bond isn't to be broken. Just give Yates time to adjust to all these changes. Right now everyone is feeling caged up, and once we're on land you'll both feel better."

"I could find a husband here in Charleston," Maida spoke softly.

Taylor frowned. "But you have a husband."

Maida glanced quickly around to make sure no one was listening. "There is such a thing as . . . divorce."

Taylor gasped. "How can you even say the word? It's against Jesus' teachings. It's against the laws of the land."

Maida's face crumpled and she wept silently. "Then what am I to do?"

"As I said," Taylor said softly, "I'll be there to help you."

"Do you think we can still be friends—with you being a bond slave and me the master's wife?" Maida asked bitterly. "You know Yates won't allow that."

"But I'll get this all sorted out, Maida. I am not a bond slave, nor ever will be. Yates will understand once I've had a chance to tell him my story."

Maida shook her head. "He won't take your word over the captain's."

Taylor took a deep, steadying breath. "He must!"

But what if he didn't? What would she do then? She shivered and looked longingly toward solid ground. Surely she wouldn't step foot in free America as a slave, would she?

*S*oaked with sweat, Ward Marston pulled off his wide-brimmed hat and peered around the corner of the empty barn to see if the two men out to steal his money were still after him. They'd jumped him yesterday just after he'd received payment for the sale of a dozen of his best horses. He'd fought them off, sending them running away with bloody noses and black eyes, but not before one man had tried to stab him and instead had sliced his shirt wide open.

He'd thought he'd seen the last of them, but today he'd spotted them following him as he bought wagons and supplies. He touched the money belt under his buff-colored, big-sleeved shirt. The money was safely tucked away. And it'd stay there if he had anything to do about it!

"You men will be sorry you tangled with Ward Marston," he muttered. He was done with games and had led the men here to the edge of town to deal with them away from the crowds. He had other things to do. After all, he'd heard the *Falcon* was unloading and the passengers had come ashore. He was ready to see if Yates and his family had come as they'd planned.

Ward touched the pistol stuck in the waist of his leather breeches near the leather sheath that held his knife. A powder horn and bag hung from leather thongs around his neck. The trap was set, so he peered around the corner of the barn again.

The men were sneaking toward him. They were younger than he by several years, ragged and skinny. Two against one made it about even. Once they left the safety of the trees and then a shed, they'd have to cross the open area of the pen. Then he'd have them! He pushed back his shoulder length brown hair, clamped his hat on, and grinned.

If Yates were with him, would he be in the middle of the fracas? Or had he turned into an old man in the past six years? Ward shrugged. Yates wasn't here and he had business to tend. "I'm primed and ready," he said with a chuckle.

At the sound of a footfall Ward leaped into the open with the battle cry Pickle had said they used when he traveled with the Swamp Fox during the Revolutionary War. Ward punched the nearest man in the chin, sending him flying back to land with a thud on the hard-packed dirt. He jabbed the second man in the stomach, then followed with a quick blow to the face. The man crumpled unconscious to the ground.

It was over in a flash. Ward pulled his pistol and aimed it at the first man who was staggering to his feet. "Pick up your friend! I'm taking you to the magistrate," he ordered.

The man whimpered and awkwardly flung his partner over his shoulder. "We didn't mean no harm, sir."

Ward laughed. "I noticed that yesterday when you slit open my shirt with your knife. I liked that shirt. Now, walk!"

Several minutes later Ward left the two men behind at the jail with the magistrate and headed down the dusty street for the wagon he'd left at the blacksmith's. The smell boiling out of the soaphouse burned his eyes and clogged his throat. Two wagons and several buggies rattled past. Charleston was always crowded and noisy and Ward couldn't wait to leave it all behind and head up-country to Catawba.

Ward smiled. Soon Yates and his family would be at Catawba with him. His pulse leaped, as he muttered, "It'll be good to have family with me."

Just then Ward saw several boys ganging up on another boy. They were yelling and swearing like sailors. *Six against one. Now, that's not fair at all,* he thought. Shrugging, Ward walked to the knot of boys and shouted, "Stand back, boys!"

They fell away from the battered boy on the ground. Dirt and blood covered his face and clothes.

"He stole my knife!" cried a boy with long, shaggy hair.

Ward looked down at the boy on the ground. "Is that right?"

The boy barely nodded.

"Give it back."

The boy slowly stood, and then slowly held the knife out to the boy with shaggy hair.

Ward eyed the knot of boys. "Now, get!" He watched them

scamper away like rats in a grain bin. He smiled at the boy remaining. "What's your name?"

"Ben."

"Ben what?"

"Ben Bostwick, sir."

"I'm Ward Marston." He shook hands with Ben. "From up-country on Catawba. Do you live in Charleston?"

Ben shook his head. "My pa is delivering hogs. He got drunk and wandered off."

"I hope you find him."

"Me, too, sir."

Ward pulled his knife from the sheath at his side. "Here. Now you have a knife of your own."

Ben smiled in delight and surprise, but then sobered. "What'd I gotta do for it?"

"Nothing." Ward shrugged. "If you ever get up-country, come to Catawba. A job'll be waiting for you."

"Thank you, sir!" Ben sighed heavily and shook his head. "I got to take care of my ma. She's got five young 'uns back to home. I gotta get Pa and get on back."

"Let's get a bite to eat first. Then I'll help you find him." Ward rested his hand on Ben's thin shoulder and walked down the street toward the place where he'd eaten breakfast. Ben looked as if he could use a good meal and a helping hand.

❦

Her legs still weak as if she was aboard the weaving *Falcon,* Taylor stood with Brooke in her arms beside Yates Marston's family at the auction block. It was a scarred, raised wooden platform with enough room for about ten people. Yates stood only a few feet back from the block. The throng of men close around them were there to buy slaves. They stood or sat on horseback or inside buggies in a half circle out from the block.

Taylor pushed her face into Brooke's shoulder and longed to be miles away. She wanted to lay Brooke in the carriage, but she was too hot and fussy. Taylor felt hot and fussy, too. The blue lightweight wool dress was too hot for this weather. Her petticoats hung limp and damp with perspiration. She wanted to pull off her silver gray bonnet and let whatever breeze came along blow through her hair. Sand had gotten inside her slippers and hurt her feet.

Her stomach lurched at the smell of the slaves. It was a worse odor than the worst stench on the *Falcon*. The slaves were kept in a row of cages behind the auctioneer and brought out one at a time. Now a black man wearing only dark pants much too short for him stood on the block with shackles on his hands and feet. He was tall with lean hips, well muscled in his arms and shoulders, darker in color than Cammie, and a few years older. His ebony skin glistened with sweat. To Taylor's surprise, Yates was actually bidding on him against a man in a buggy!

"Turn the buck so's folks can see him real good," the auctioneer barked at the rumpled looking white man holding the slave's chain.

"Show them muscles, boy!" The man turned the slave slowly all the way around, then pulled up his upper lip and showed off his teeth. "Good, strong teeth."

Taylor felt Cammie flinch. This was the most horrible thing that Taylor had ever seen. How could these people stand by and watch this man sold like a piece of meat? Taylor wanted desperately to buy him herself just to set him free. If she had the money that's exactly what she would do. But Taylor's shoulders slumped as she realized that she was in the same position as that slave. She had been bought for the price of her passage and would be indentured for five years.

The auctioneer raked off his wide-brimmed hat, wiped sweat from his forehead, and dropped his hat back in place. His shirt was snug around his fat stomach and tucked in his tight tan pants. He waved a thick hand at the slave.

"This buck's name is Treet and he was owned by Baldwin Kilgore over in Georgia. He's well trained and knows his place. Only reason Kilgore is selling him is so as he can buy a blooded mare he wants to race. You know how much Kilgore likes to race." The men in the crowd laughed. "And win." The men laughed harder and the auctioneer slapped his thick thigh. "So this buck is worth more than you men are bidding. Up that price, then we'll start again."

Taylor moaned. From the corner of her eyes she saw Maida with her hand over her mouth and tears in her eyes. Laurel had her face pressed against Kendra's arm. With looks of horror on their faces too, Kendra and Reid watched everything.

Yates upped his bid, but the man in the wagon did too. Yates wanted to back down, but it had suddenly become a matter of pride. He'd already spent too much money on Taylor, her baby, and the darkie, but he had to have the strong Negro. Thoughts of what Ward would say about him purchasing slaves crossed Yates's mind, but he forced them away. Catawba was as much his as Ward's, so he had as much say as Ward.

Taylor turned Brooke away so she couldn't see the slaves. They should've been allowed to wait with the baggage, but Yates had insisted the whole lot of them stay with him. Taylor moved restlessly. Maybe Yates thought she and Cammie would run away from him. Taylor realized that they were in a much better place than if they had gone with James Rawlings. She would have already been married to James and Cammie probably would have been dead—by an accident, of course. Yes, Cammie, Brooke, and Taylor were definitely better off with Yates.

❦

Cammie's stomach knotted painfully as she remembered the humiliation of being sold with her mama the summer she turned ten. Master Carlton had insisted they be sold together, or she would've been separated from Mama. Master James had been determined to own Mama when he heard she was the best cook in the entire state of Virginia and so had paid a real high price for her. Cammie bit back a groan. Later when Master James took Cammie to his bed he'd said the price had been worth it. Sometimes she wondered if it wouldn't have been better if she'd been sold to someone else. But she guessed one master was the same as any.

She watched the man on the block and tears burned in her eyes. He was a fine-looking man and humiliated by what folks were calling out about him. She glanced at the slaves locked up, then looked quickly away. What would she do if she was behind the bars? What would she do if she had to stand on the block to be humiliated and sold to the highest bidder? She wanted to cover her eyes, but she studied the man up on the block above the crowd.

Just then he looked down and their eyes locked. A shock ran through her and she couldn't move. The white man holding Treet jerked his chain and forced him to turn again to show his back muscles. Cammie pressed her hand to her racing heart and tried to breathe again. What was wrong with her? Cammie felt as if she was going to faint dead away.

Maida tucked herself behind a tall man so she couldn't see what was happening on the auction block. If only she could block out the sounds! Everything seemed to be louder than usual. It was the chains that Treet wore around his feet and hands; every time he moved the rattle seemed to grate against Maida's nerve. Everyone in the crowd was trying to be heard so they all talked louder and louder. Clamping her hands over her ears Maida tried to close out the noise. How much longer could she endure this?

If she hadn't married Yates, she'd be in a carriage with her aunt and uncle driving to visit Adam and Ruth Brighton on their plantation. Aunt Erica had said the mansion had twenty rooms with big white columns in front and dozens of servants to wait on them hand and foot. Adam Brighton kept horses and had the most talked about stable in Charleston. They'd be free to ride as often as they wanted, she'd said.

Maida bowed her head. She had given all that up for this! What had she been thinking? Maida didn't even know where her new home was going to be. The Marston children always talked about Catawba, but they didn't say where it was located. Would they be close to Charleston or out in the middle of nowhere?

Yates raised his bid, and this time the man in the wagon sat quietly.

"Sold to the Englishman standing yonder!" the auctioneer cried, waving his arm at Yates.

Yates stood straighter and managed not to smile in triumph. He moved his head a fraction to acknowledge his win. He had won! This was just the beginning for what Yates had planned for Catawba. They were going to raise cotton and have slaves waiting on them hand and foot. His dream was finally coming true.

Suddenly, a deep sadness filled Yates's heart. If only his Ellen could be here to share in this joy. Things definitely didn't turn out the way they had planned them.

Maida pressed her lips tightly together. She could feel the anguish of Yates's children. How could he just ignore their feelings by making them watch such a disgusting display? Maida knew Yates would yell at her so she didn't insist they not watch this auction. Yates was unexpectedly too difficult to talk with, and Maida hated the times he got angry with her.

Taylor's arms ached from Brooke's weight. Carefully she eased her down inside the carriage, hoping she'd sleep since she was finally close to dozing. After all that had happened this morning, Taylor just wanted to sink into a nice soft feather bed and relax until all the kinks were out of her body.

Cammie gripped the carriage handle and longed to get far away from the auction block. She watched Master Marston's new slave Treet walk down the steps and stand beside the man Yates was paying. Cammie trembled. Would she and Treet become friends or would he ignore her? Would Treet hate her when he found out she was carrying Master Rawlings's baby?

Taylor eased over beside Maida, patted her arm, and whispered, "Are you all right?"

Dazed by all that had happened, Maida whispered, "I never knew he'd do this. He'd seemed so kind on the ship. I wouldn't have believed he could buy another human being."

"It's hard to understand his thinking—his wanting to buy a slave, but there's nothing we can do right now."

Laurel wanted to run off by herself, but she was afraid she'd get lost or abducted by the ruffians nearby. She should've found a way to stay in England! One day she would leave this wretched place and return to her beloved England. Laurel was determined to marry a proper English gentleman and not some colonial.

❦

Shivering even in the heat, Kendra inched her way out of the throng of sweaty bodies and back along the crowded dock. Ships were being loaded and unloaded. She knew she wasn't supposed to walk alone, but she just had to get away from the auction block. Here children ran along the sandy shore, shouting and laughing. Men called back and forth from two small boats nearby. The sounds were very different from the sounds in the small village in England where she'd lived with her family. Their village had been so quiet. Here in Charleston there were so many people moving around and shouting that you could hardly hear yourself think. She wanted to go to Catawba now, not wait until Papa was finished buying slaves!

Slowly Kendra walked from behind a pile of boxes, her head down, her eyes on the rough planks. Her skirts flapped about her ankles and her petticoats clung to her damp legs. Impatiently she pushed her bonnet off to let her hair blow free in the breeze.

Suddenly she heard a warning shout and jerked her head up. A large wooden barrel rolled toward her, rolling faster as it gained momentum on the incline. Her voice caught in her throat and she couldn't scream. Her feet felt rooted to the spot. But then strong hands grabbed her by the waist and swung her aside just as the barrel rolled past and crashed against a crate with a thud. She trembled violently. The hands tightened at her narrow waist. She looked up with her wide eyes. Her rescuer was a tall lean man with broad shoulders and strong muscles. He was dressed in leather breeches and a pale gray shirt with loose-fitting sleeves. His thick, dark red hair hung to his collar—too short to be pulled back and tied. His eyes were as green as the ocean. Suddenly he smiled and his eyes twinkled.

"I see no harm came to you."

"None at all," she barely whispered. His voice sounded English, but a little different from her accent. She realized her hands were pressed against his chest and she flushed. She felt his heart thudding against her palms and a strange feeling washed over her, leaving her weak. Sounds of activity around them faded to the background.

He smiled. "I have waited for this day—the day my dream would be in my arms and not just my imagination."

His words left her weak with a longing she couldn't understand. She knew she should move, but she couldn't.

Slowly he lowered his head and she knew he was going to kiss her. She wanted to leap away and cry for help, but she arched toward him and met his kiss with warm, hungry lips that had never been kissed. His arms tightened around her as the kiss deepened. She couldn't move or think—only feel.

Finally he pulled away from her and she moaned in despair. "I must go." He touched her cheek and she leaned her face into his hand. "I found you at long last, but I can't claim you—much as I want to."

"I'm Kendra," she whispered.

He bent his head and gave her a hard, swift kiss. "Goodbye, my Kendra." He then strode out of sight among the barrels and crates and boisterous workers.

She touched her lips and her eyes filled with tears. Could love come in such a swift unforgettable instant? Who was he? If only he'd told her his name! How could she find him again?

Frantically she rushed along the dock, searching for the tall lean man with dark red hair and laughing green eyes. A short, thick-set sailor bumped into her, clutched her arm, and leered at her. She jerked free of his filthy hands and leaped away. It wasn't fitting or safe to be on her own, but she had to find the man. She had to know his name!

Several minutes later she gave up and dejectedly walked back the way she'd come. She found the family standing near their piles of goods. Two wagons drawn by horses stood nearby.

Her blonde hair held tightly in place by her small bonnet, Laurel eyed Kendra closely. "What happened to you? You look different."

Her cheeks flaming, Kendra turned away. What would her family think if she told them about the man and the kisses? Papa would lock her up and starve her until she repented of her terrible actions.

Reid nudged Kendra's arm. "Did you have an adventure without me?"

Kendra managed a smile. "Yes. But you wouldn't have enjoyed it half as much as I did."

Reid shrugged and ran back to stand near the horses with Papa.

Just then a tall man with broad shoulders and skin the color of the leather he wore stopped a wagon beside theirs and jumped out. He strode up to Yates and clamped a hand on his shoulder. "Yates! You made it!"

Taylor's eyes widened in surprise. Could this really be the children's uncle, Ward Marston? After traveling with Yates these past weeks, Taylor had pictured in her mind another proper English gentleman. Ward Marston was far from the image she had in her mind. She heard the others exclaim in happy surprise. Even the horses jangled their harnesses and flicked their ears.

"Ward!" Yates grabbed the man in a bear hug. "Ward! I didn't know if you'd be able to meet us. It's good to see you."

Taylor bit her lip and her heart leaped. Ward was tall with broad shoulders, a wide mouth, and a prominent nose. His dark hair was not brushed back neatly and tied at his neck, but instead was cropped unevenly just above his shoulders. His loose-fitting shirt was stained with sweat. His boots were scuffed and dusty. He was a far cry from the English gentleman his brother Yates was! Taylor smiled and couldn't take her eyes off Ward Marston.

Ward stepped back from Yates and eyed him up and down. "I had forgotten what I once looked like." He tipped back his head and laughed, then hugged Yates so hard he lifted him off his feet.

Taylor glanced at Laurel, Kendra, and Reid. The girls looked shocked, and Reid seemed ready to burst with excitement. They wanted to run to their Uncle Ward, but they knew they had to wait until their papa had finished his greeting.

Maida bit her bottom lip—unable to believe the two men could be brothers. Would Catawba be as backward as Ward seemed? Maida trembled. She'd grown to like the Ward she had heard about from all Yates's stories about him. Could this Ward live up to the tales?

Her hands securely on the carriage handle, Cammie stepped closer to Taylor. Ward Marston wasn't at all what Cammie had expected. This man had a core of steel inside him, but maybe that's what it would take to tame the howling wilderness she'd heard stories about.

Finally Ward turned to scan the people around them. He first saw an attractive woman standing with a young black woman and a baby carriage, then another handsome but delicate looking woman, and finally two young ladies and a boy beside Yates. Ward turned with a frown to Yates. "Where're the children?"

Chuckling, Yates waved his hand at the boy and the young ladies. "There."

Ward raked his fingers through his hair and laughed. "They're all grown up!" He stepped up to Laurel. "Can you be Laurel? But you're a beautiful young lady, not a little girl!" He laughed a great booming laugh and slapped his thigh, sending dust flying. He reached to hug her, but she squealed and jumped away.

Kendra frowned in irritation. How could Laurel be so rude? This man had carried them piggyback and bounced them on his knee. He'd told them stories and sang to them. He looked strange and smelled sweaty, but he was their favorite, wonderful uncle—Uncle Ward.

Kendra stepped forward with a wide smile. "Hello, Uncle," she greeted. Her heart raced in anticipation. Would he hug her and say she was a beautiful young lady? Or had he forgotten all about her?

Ward clapped his roughened hand to his wide forehead and laughed again. His brown eyes twinkled. "Can this grown girl be my little Kendra? I whittled a doll for you." He hesitated, then reached for her. She jumped into his strong arms and he swung her high. Her long skirt belled out, and she giggled just as she had years before when he'd done the same thing. She hugged his neck and kissed his leathery cheek. Finally he set her down and stepped back from her, shaking his shaggy head and clicking his tongue. "You're not a child any longer, Kendra."

She flushed with pleasure. "I'll like the doll anyway, Uncle."

He winked at her, then looked at Reid. "As I live and breathe."

Reid grinned and thrust out his hand. "Uncle, I'm pleased to see you again."

Ward gripped Reid's hand, then hauled him close and hugged him hard. "You're a fine-looking boy, Reid Marston. And your muscles are growing strong. You'll fit well at Catawba."

"I mean to work hard just like you," Reid said with his chin high and his back straight. "I want to learn everything I can from you, Uncle Ward."

Grinning with pleasure, Ward slapped Reid on the back. "I'll be glad to teach you anything you wanna learn. And that goes for you girls, too."

Ignoring the noise of the crowd across the way at the auction block, Ward glanced at the two white women and the black girl, then down at the sleeping baby in the carriage. He raised his dark brows, then turned to Yates.

Yates flushed. Would Ward look down on him for marrying so soon after Ellen's death? Yates stepped to Maida's side, but he didn't touch her. He was ashamed of himself for marrying so soon after Ellen's death. He'd given in to his selfish needs and knew he'd live to regret it. He tried not to let it show in his voice, however, as he said, "This is my wife, Maida."

Maida held her breath. Would Ward brush her aside like the horses were doing the flies swarming around them?

Ward lifted a dark brow. "Your wife, you say?"

Yates nodded. He was older than Ward, but he'd always needed his approval. "Maida and I met and married aboard the *Falcon*."

Ward saw the fear in Maida's eyes and felt her tension, but she didn't back away from him or lower her eyes. Smiling, he bowed. "I'm happy to meet you, Maida." He took her hand. "I trust we will be friends. Welcome to your new home."

Maida liked the gentleness she saw in his eyes. Even in his rough attire he was a gentleman. She smiled and squeezed his hand.

"I'd like that," she said shyly. Ward seemed to be a kinder man than Yates. He didn't ignore her or look over her. Ward seemed to really care.

Taylor held her breath and waited for Ward Marston to ask about her. Her stomach fluttered. She didn't want to be introduced as a slave. She wanted Ward Marston to accept her into the family as easily as he had Maida. Frowning at her presumption, Taylor scolded herself for thinking that way. She wasn't going to be around long enough to become a part of this family. As soon as Yates and Ward heard her part of the story, they would let her go. She and Cammie would be on their way

Yates cleared his throat. "This is Taylor Craven, her baby, and the baby's nanny, Cammie. They belong to me."

Taylor flushed to the roots of her light brown hair. She wanted to sink out of sight in the sand under her feet.

Ward's brows shot to the hair hanging on his wide forehead. "Belong to you, Yates?"

"It's a long story. I paid for them."

Ward scowled. "You know how I feel about slaves."

"I thought you'd changed your mind by now." Yates cleared his throat. He didn't want an argument. In the past he'd always lost fights and arguments with Ward. "I've read how hard it is to make a living without free labor."

"I haven't changed my mind. I won't have slaves on Catawba!"

Taylor's heart plunged to her feet. Would they be sold yet again? Maybe this time they would sell Brooke away from her, and she'd never see her again.

Cammie ducked her head and began to pray silently. "Please, dear God, don't let them put me on that auction block to be sold. I couldn't bear for that to happen." And at that moment Cammie felt peace inside and knew that everything was going to be just fine. Smiling, she lifted her head to watch what was going on.

His dark eyes flashing, Yates stepped right up to Ward. This time he would not back down. "I own half of Catawba. I have every right to bring my own workers." His dream couldn't be fulfilled if he didn't have slaves.

Ward clenched his jaw. Yates had never stood up to him before. Finally he turned away. "Have it your way. Bring 'em to the wagons."

Her cheeks red, Taylor faced Ward. She had to tell him her story and make him know she was a free woman! "I am not a slave!" she shouted. "It's all a misunderstanding."

Ward saw the stubborn look on the woman's face. Had Yates taken on more than he could handle? Might serve him right if he had gotten saddled with a stubborn woman. Ward grinned. When a woman had her mind set, there would be no changing it and that's what this woman looked like.

Yates caught Taylor's arm and stopped her short. "You're not to speak unless you're spoken to."

"Sir!" Sparks shot from Taylor's eyes. "You know I am a free agent! I will not have you treat me like this." Jerking her arm free, Taylor stood her ground.

Yates narrowed his dark eyes. "The money gone from my person belies that statement, madam."

Ward frowned from Taylor to Yates, then turned his back on both of them and strode away. Reid and Kendra ran to either side of him and talked excitedly to him about the trip to Catawba. Ward patiently answered their questions but didn't look back at the woman Yates called Taylor.

Scowling, Yates turned to Maida. "Keep this woman in her place, madam."

Maida couldn't speak around her anger for a moment. "Taylor is my friend, sir."

"She is your servant! Treat her as such." Setting his top hat squarely on his head, Yates hurried after Ward. He could not have Maida talking back to him. He could already see that the children would do whatever Ward wanted them to do. Well, he was going to show them all that he was the one in charge. No one was going to dictate what he could or could not do.

Taylor's skin burned with embarrassment. She was less than nothing in Ward's eyes. The way he had walked away from her and not looked back had proved that. Now what was she going to do to prove her innocence?

Maida knotted her fists at her sides. The high neckline of her dress suddenly felt too tight. "It's not right! Taylor, you are my friend no matter what he says."

Taylor struggled against burning tears. "Don't make trouble for yourself. I'll talk to him when it's convenient and set it straight. I was duped by Andrew Simons and I must convince Yates of that."

From the far side of Maida, Laurel scowled at Taylor. "Call him Mr. Marston, as befitting your position."

Taylor gasped at Laurel, then looked evenly at her. "I am the same person I was on board the *Falcon*, Laurel. Please keep that in mind when you address me."

Laurel's face flamed and she wanted to take back her sharp words, but she had too much pride. Hurrying after her father, Laurel wished again that she was back in England. Things were too different here. A servant back in England would have never been allowed to speak to her in such a way. Laurel made up her mind right then: She hated this new world.

Taylor brushed a tear from her eye. "I hope I can settle this immediately. I will not be in service to Yates—Mr. Marston—for the five years the indenture paper says."

"You won't be," Maida said, but she didn't sound very sure, nor did she feel sure. She wanted to help Taylor, but she knew Yates would never listen to her.

Brooke cried and Cammie picked her up, found a biscuit for her to eat, then sat her back in the carriage. Cammie looked past the baggage as Ward Marston drove a wagon closer. Treet walked between Yates and Reid around to the back of the wagon. Cammie was surprised since she hadn't noticed when he'd arrived. She saw his muscles flex as he hoisted a trunk to his shoulder. He didn't say a word as he worked. What kind of a man was he?

Ward dropped to the ground and dust sprayed up on his boots. "I have another wagon coming, so that'll give us four. My man, Court Yardley, is driving." He motioned behind him. "Here he is now."

"Your man?" Yates asked sharply.

"Bond servant."

"And you talk to me about no slaves?" Yates cried.

Ward scowled at Yates, wondering why he was so upset. "He'll be working for me for three more years, then be free again. I paid his way from England a few years back."

"But that's how I got Taylor and Cammie."

"I see." Ward glanced at Taylor and Cammie, then back at Yates. "Why didn't you say so? An indentured servant is not the same to me as a slave."

Yates impatiently brushed away Ward's words. "You still need slaves to build up Catawba. With the plans I have we'll need a lot of slaves and I'm going to have them."

Ward snapped his mouth closed and motioned to Court Yardley sitting on the high wagon seat. "Court with Bard and Pickle back at Catawba are all I need. We get a lot of work done between us. You'll find that life here is a little more relaxed than in England. You're more respected around here for keeping your word than for how many slaves you own."

Kendra followed Ward's wave. Her nerves tingled. The man driving, the man he called Court Yardley, was the very man who'd saved her life—the very man who'd kissed her! A wide-brimmed hat covered his dark red hair, but she recognized him anyway. The color drained from her face and she locked her trembling hands tightly together.

She thought her heart would leap through her bodice when he saw her. Her breath caught in her throat. Did he recognize her with her bonnet on? What if he did and told her family he'd kissed her? Her legs trembled, but she stiffened her knees and her spine and stood with her head high. What could her family do, anyway, if they found out he had kissed her.

Court stopped the wagon and jumped to the ground. He didn't acknowledge Kendra with a smile or a nod of his head. He dare not until he learned who she was.

Ward waved a hand at his family and quickly introduced them all the way around. "This is Court Yardley. He works on Catawba for me along with Bard Keine and Pickle, a free black man."

Kendra waited for a reaction from Court Yardley when he learned she was Ward Marston's niece, but none came. He acted as if he'd never seen her before, let alone held her close and kissed her. She didn't know what to make of him. Did he go around kissing strange girls all the time? Was he that type of man? And how could she have reacted to him the way she did if he were? Kendra laced her fingers together and tried to stop trembling. If he didn't acknowledge her, then she was going to do likewise. But if only her heart would stop beating so rapidly, it would make ignoring him a whole lot easier.

His heart thundering, Court loaded the trunks into his wagon. He had fallen in love and kissed Ward Marston's niece! How could such an appalling thing happen? What could he do? He'd rip the love from his heart and erase the memory of the kiss! He was a bond slave and he had to remember that. Even when his time was up he couldn't consider marrying Kendra Marston. She was a Marston!

As he hoisted a trunk on his shoulder he silently prayed for the strength to put Kendra out of his mind and out of his heart. Court had never felt such defeat in all his life. The one woman that he had fallen for was out of his reach. How would he ever get through the next three years of being indentured? He would see Kendra, but never be able to talk to her or touch her again.

Taylor stood beside Maida and Cammie and watched as the men loaded the four wagons that would carry them and the supplies to Catawba, the place that would be her home until she set right the wrong done her. Her stomach tightened and she thought she'd burst into wild tears. But she refused to let her feelings show on her face. After all, at least here she was safe from James Rawlings.

Taylor shivered and darted a look around for Andrew Simons. He'd slipped away after Yates paid her fare and she hadn't seen him since. How she longed to force him to return her money so she could be free again! But she'd probably never see him again. He was out of her life—and so was her money.

ard led the way out of Charleston with Reid and Kendra on the high seat beside him. Yates with Laurel and Maida was next in line. Court with Taylor beside him was third and then Treet with Cammie and baby Brooke brought up the rear.

Ward had said, "In some places the pace will be slow. Other places we'll be able to cover several miles in a day. I plan to be home within a week. This first day we'll travel only about three hours—stopping just before dark, then make camp. It'll help ease you into the trip."

Taylor clung to the wooden wagon seat, trying to keep from falling against Court. They passed several stately homes with bright flowers of all colors and tall trees with huge shiny green leaves. Birds sang and flew from one tree to another. They passed other homes that were smaller with rundown out buildings scattered nearby. The smell of pine trees mingled with the sweet aroma of flowering trees. Along with the soft clip-clop of the horses' hooves on the sandy ground, the harnesses rattled and the wagon creaked.

"You'll learn to ride with the sway," Court said with a smile. The reins hung from his gloved hands and he drove easily as if he'd been doing it all his life. His hat blocked the sun from his face. He'd been trying to think of something to say to Taylor since they'd started, but nothing came to mind. He just wasn't used to conversing with a woman.

Taylor shrugged, then clung tighter to the seat. "I suppose if I became accustomed to walking on the ship without falling, I can learn to ride with the sway of the wagon," she admitted.

Court smiled and nodded. "How is it you came to be indentured to Yates Marston?" Alarmed at his boldness, Court glanced away from the horses to Taylor. "Or is my question too impertinent?"

"Not at all. I mean to tell it to Ward Marston the first opportunity I get. Maybe he'll talk Yates out of treating me like a servant."

"You get used to it."

Taylor flushed. "I'm sorry." How could she have forgotten that Court was indentured also?

"I was a cooper in England before I came here. Had my own barrel business." He looked longingly ahead to see if he could see Kendra through the dust, but he couldn't. If he was still in business, could he woo her? Probably not. After all, she was a Marston!

Since he didn't seem ready to continue, Taylor took a deep breath and told her story, leaving out the part about James Rawlings, but she told of Floyd's unexpected death and her decision to come to America. She finished with the comment: "I did indeed pay my way and Andrew Simons did indeed give me a receipt."

"There are scoundrels in all walks of life."

She thought of James and nodded. "I'm afraid so." She laughed lightly. "Now let me ask about you. Did you leave a family behind in England?"

"My father. He's a cooper. That's how I learned the trade."

"Did he mind your coming to America?"

"He wanted a better life for me." Court didn't want to think about or tell his entire story. Maybe someday it wouldn't hurt so much.

Taylor nodded. She could tell Court didn't want to pursue the subject, so she said, "Well, I want a good life for Brooke. Will she find it at Catawba?"

"There's plenty of room for a baby to grow. And she'll get a lot of attention from all of us. It'll be good having a baby around."

She wanted to ask if Ward liked babies, but she didn't. Instead she asked about the long-tailed birds flying across in front of them.

※

In the last wagon Cammie peeked over Brooke's head at Treet. He was wearing a baggy, light gray shirt with dark pants and heavy shoes. "You mind if I talk?"

Treet didn't speak for a long time. "No."

"I'm Cammie. I know you're Treet."

"You from Virginia?"

Cammie gasped in alarm. "How'd you know?"

"The way you talk. I been there. With my last master for a horse race."

Cammie stared at the ears of the horses pulling the wagon. Was it possible Treet knew James Rawlings? She dare not ask him!

"You scared about something in Virginia?"

"You see too much!"

"Then I won't look too close." Treet flicked the reins and guided the team around a branch in the road.

Cammie rubbed her cheek against Brooke's bonnet. "Did you leave a family?"

"No!"

Cammie sighed. "I wonder how it feels to be free to do what you want when you want."

"Don't you talk like that, girl! You could get the whip for them words."

Cammie lifted her head. "I still wonder."

"You that white baby's nursemaid?"

"Yes."

"I don't like no baby riding with me. When we stop you see if Missy Taylor will take her."

"I can't ask her to!"

"You find a way. I won't carry that baby all the way."

"How come you hate babies?"

Treet scowled straight ahead and didn't answer.

Cammie held Brooke close to her and sang her to sleep while they passed large fields, crops, and pastures full of cattle.

❦

In the second wagon Maida gripped the wagon seat. Laurel was in the back asleep. "Yates, why are you being so stubborn about Taylor? I told you the truth! She did pay her money to Andrew Simons. You shouldn't make her stay indentured to you. Set her free! She can stay with us—even help us at Catawba—not as a bond slave but as an equal!"

"Stop shouting, madam." Yates gripped the reins tightly. He wanted to do something to get back on good terms with Maida, but he would not take Taylor's word over that of Andrew Simons. He was, after all, an English gentleman.

Maida swallowed more angry words. It would not accomplish anything to continue the conversation about Taylor.

Yates watched the horses follow the trail, looked at the reins looped in his hands, and then glanced at Maida. His heart tightened. If he wasn't careful, he'd start loving her more than he had

Ellen. And that wouldn't be right. He'd married Maida for companionship and help with the children. Love wasn't supposed to enter into it.

He cleared his throat. "Ward says Catawba is a grand place. I'm impatient to see it for myself. I want it for my family—a big plantation that could stay in the family for generations to come."

Maida lowered her dark lashes. Would they have children? If so, would Catawba belong to them as much as to Laurel, Kendra, and Reid?

❦

In the lead wagon Ward held the reins easily, knowing the team would keep on the road. It was well traveled, but still only a one-lane dirt road that got too muddy when it rained and too dusty when it didn't.

"Have you been to Charleston before?" Kendra asked.

Ward nodded. "I brought horses to sell a couple of times and a load of lumber to a ship builder."

His blue eyes wide with excitement, Reid leaned around Kendra to Ward. "Will you teach me to train horses?"

"Sure will, Reid." Grinning, Ward nudged Kendra. "And you too, if you want to learn."

Kendra gasped and a thrill darted through her. "I do want to!" It was more than she'd thought possible. She'd become reconciled to learning to run a home—to train horses was beyond her wildest dream. With the thought that Court probably helped too, she felt color rise in her cheeks.

"I want to learn everything!" she asserted.

Reid nodded. "Me, too."

"Good." Ward turned back to watch the road ahead, satisfied with Kendra and Reid. Laurel might find life on Catawba too hard, but not Kendra and Reid.

Just before dark Ward stopped the wagons in a clearing at the side of a stream. Birds twittered in the trees. A bullfrog croaked, then was silent.

"Careful of snakes and alligators," he called as he jumped to the ground.

Taylor shivered as Laurel squealed. Taylor looked at the lush green weeds and shrubs. "How can we see the dangers?" she asked.

"The creatures are afraid of us and will hide." Court dropped to the ground, then reached up for Taylor. He swung her down easily.

Taylor's legs felt weak and shaky. "It feels good to be on solid ground again." She turned to check on Brooke.

Treet jumped to the ground and stepped away when Cammie started to hand Brooke to him.

Court hurried to the side of the wagon and took Brooke from Cammie. He smiled at Brooke, which caused Taylor to like him even more.

Clicking her tongue at Treet's rudeness, Cammie climbed down the wheel and shook her skirt in place. Something was mighty wrong with Treet's heart if he couldn't love a child—white or black.

Court swung Brooke high and made her giggle, then handed her to Taylor. "She's a pretty baby."

"Thank you."

"Get a fire going, Treet," Yates called.

"Yes, sir, master."

Yates pointed at Taylor. "*You* make supper."

Taylor froze. She wanted to protest at his sharp order but decided against it. She would've helped cook even if she wasn't an indentured servant. Her pride was trying to object and she wouldn't allow that. "Cammie, take Brooke again, please. Let her walk in the clear area, but be careful of snakes and things."

Laughing good-naturedly, Ward clamped a hand on Yates's shoulder. Ward hadn't liked the way Yates snapped orders at Treet or Taylor. "We all help with the work in America, brother. This is a whole different way of living. You're not in England now."

Yates flushed, but quickly hid his embarrassment with a chuckle. He'd wanted Treet to know he was his boss and not Ward. He'd snapped at Taylor to hide the guilt he felt. Buying her the way he had was not something he was proud of. But he couldn't let anyone know how he felt. "I'm new at this way of life. Just tell me what to do."

Taylor peeked through her lashes at Ward. Had he stepped in for her benefit? If so, she was thankful.

"Yates, you and Reid can fill the buckets with water." Ward motioned to the wooden buckets hanging on the side of the nearest wagon. A clear spring trickled over rocks and disappeared from sight among low branches of giant oaks.

"Let's do it, Reid." Yates lifted down a bucket and held it out to Reid, then carried the second on himself.

Leaving Brooke in Cammie's care, Taylor flipped back the canvas covering the cooking pots and food. All around her birds sang and flew through the trees. She smelled the stream gurgling beside the wagons, the sweat from the horses, and pine from nearby trees. She'd never slept outdoors before. She glanced around as Treet and Court unhitched the horses and led them to drink. Ward dropped a pile of wood beside what appeared to be an old campsite. In a few minutes Maida had a fire blazing.

Taylor set the cooking pots on the ground beside the fire and coughed from the smoke. She moved aside and her skirt belled out, brushing against the flames. The hem of her skirt smoldered and she jumped back with a screech. The smoldering burst into flames that quickly began to engulf her skirt.

Court leaped forward to help Taylor, but Ward reached her first, pushed her to the ground, and patted out the flames with his gloved hands. The smell of burned fabric filled the air.

Taylor lay on the ground while the others crowded around, exclaiming fearfully. Ward had saved her—if not from death, from horrible burns!

He pulled off his scarred gloves and gently lifted her skirts to check her ankles and the lower part of her legs. "You're not burned," he said softly as he tugged her skirts back in place.

Her heart racing from the near escape, she started to sit, but couldn't. She was too weak! What was wrong with her?

"Take it easy a minute." Ward snaked his arm around her and lifted her against his chest. He knelt on one knee and braced her against his other leg. He looked up at Yates. "See that supper is started, will you? The rest of you, please give Taylor some privacy."

"Thank you," she whispered against his chest. The sound of her name on his lips made her heart beat with a strange little jerk. She felt his heart thudding against her cheek and it sent tremors through her body.

Ward felt her trembling and tightened his arm around her. "You've had quite a fright."

She leaned against him, thankful for his strength. He smelled of sweat and leather. "You saved my life," she whispered.

He laughed softly. She heard the clamor of the others around her, telling the account to anyone who'd missed it, but their voices came from a great distance. She felt as if she and Ward Marston were alone in the entire world. It was a strange feeling She looked into his warm brown eyes and managed to smile.

"Thank you," she said softly.

"You're very welcome. Can you stand now?"

"I think so."

He helped her to her feet, and it seemed he kept his arm around her a bit longer than was really necessary.

She stepped away from him, still shaking, and longed to lean on him again. Embarrassed, Taylor turned away, reprimanding herself for acting like a schoolgirl.

Kendra peeked at Court. Was he sorry he hadn't been the one to save Taylor? Kendra had seen Court with Brooke and had heard him laughing with Taylor. Jealousy raged inside Kendra, and for one wild minute she wished Taylor had gotten burned.

Her cheeks flushed, Kendra turned away and walked slowly to the nearest wagon. How could she be so mean? Taylor was her friend!

Laurel touched Kendra's shoulder. "Is something wrong?"

Kendra shrugged. She dare not tell Laurel she loved Court Yardley! Laurel would tell Papa, and that wouldn't do at all.

"If you're worried about Taylor, don't be. Uncle Ward said she's all right."

"I'm glad." And she was, too!

Sighing in disgust, Laurel leaned against the wagon. "Do you know we have to sleep on the ground under the wagon tonight? What if an alligator bites us while we're sleeping?"

Court overheard that comment and chuckled. "We'll keep the alligators away," he said as he lifted a flintlock from the wagon. He kept his eyes on Laurel. He didn't dare look at Kendra, or she might read his feelings for her in his eyes.

"Are you a good shot?" Laurel asked. He was good-looking and not much older than she. Maybe it would be fun to flirt a little with him.

"I hit what I aim at."

Kendra grabbed Laurel's arm and tugged. "We're supposed to help make supper."

Smiling, Laurel looked over her shoulder at Court and waved. "Happy hunting."

Kendra pressed her lips in a thin hard line. Laurel flirted at every opportunity! "He is an indentured servant, Laurel! Don't speak to him!"

Laurel jerked away and stormed off to stand beside Reid at the fire.

Kendra glanced back and found Court looking right at her. By the look on his face she knew he had heard what she'd said. Her heart dropped and she opened her mouth to apologize, but Court turned and walked away.

Kendra pressed her hands to her burning cheeks and moaned.

Later Taylor sat in the circle with the others around the campfire. She gently rubbed Brooke's back even though she was already asleep in her lap. The night was warm enough that Brooke didn't need a cover over her. They'd eaten rabbit stew, rice, and cornbread with coffee to drink. A log snapped and tiny sparks flew out of the fire. The sounds of the night creatures formed a special background melody as Ward talked about Catawba.

"I knew it was for me the minute I saw it." Ward held his hat in his lap as he sat cross-legged. Shadows caused by the fire played across his face. "I was hunting deer. It was the way I made my living when I first came over. The woods were full of deer, and many a man made his fortune with the hides. When I saw Catawba, though, I decided then and there I'd settle down and make it my home."

"And ours," Yates said softly. He'd longed to be with Ward when he'd first seen Catawba, but he couldn't leave England. It would've broken Ellen's heart. Finally after six years of his longing to go, she'd agreed. But she hadn't lived to see it. A lump lodged in his throat. He felt Maida beside him and another wave of guilt washed over him. He felt heartless and selfish. Ward nudged a piece of half-burned wood into the fire. "I was wondering how I could work the place alone when I met Pickle, a short black man who can cook like nobody I know. I call him Pickle because he's short! He'd been a slave all his life. He fought in the Revolutionary War with the Swamp Fox, Francis Marion himself. After the war Pickle was set free and in his travels wandered onto Catawba. He told me about himself and I hired him on the spot."

Taylor liked the sound of Ward's voice. She felt her head droop and her eyes go heavy. She heard him tell about paying the passage for Court Yardley and Bard Keine, but she didn't catch it all. She must not embarrass herself by going to sleep and falling in the fire! But somehow she knew if she did, Ward would rescue her. Smiling, she closed her eyes and listened to his voice.

Ward saw Taylor's head droop and he jumped up. Why hadn't he realized how tired the others would be? "Time to call it a night," he said. He saw Taylor jerk her head up and he chuckled. He bent down to her. "Let me take the baby."

"Thank you," she said softly.

Her breath fanned his cheek and sent a tingle over him. He gently lifted Brooke and held her close as he turned away. If his face was red, the others would think it was from the fire.

Cammie pushed the carriage forward. "You can lay the baby in here, Master Ward."

Ward kissed Brooke's cheek, then gently laid her in the carriage. "She smells good," he said softly.

"I gave her a bath at the stream," Taylor said behind him. "It'll help her sleep soundly tonight."

Ward slowly turned until he faced Taylor. What was there about this woman that touched him so deeply? "I trust you will sleep well, too."

Taylor chuckled. "I am rather tired. I'm afraid I missed part of your story. Perhaps you'll tell it again sometime."

"I will."

Taylor said a soft good night and walked to where Cammie had wheeled the carriage. It had been agreed that the women would sleep under one wagon and the men take the other two. The men would take turns standing guard against wild animals and marauders.

"I done fixed your bedding, Miz Taylor." Cammie patted a mat on the ground under the wagon.

"Thank you." Taylor took off her shoes and gratefully stretched out. She pulled a cover over her and closed her eyes. Ward's voice played in her head as she drifted off to sleep.

As she slept she dreamed she was back in her home with Floyd and he was excitedly telling her about the man who'd stopped in to have three pair of boots made. He'd hugged and kissed her and said, "I love you, Tay. We have a good life, but I promise it'll be even better. I hired a boy to work for me today and that'll give me more time with you and Brooke. Maybe we can even take Brooke to the sea for a trip."

"And the circus," Taylor said.

Floyd pulled her close and kissed her. "I love you, Tay."

"I love you, too."

She felt his arms around her and his lips on hers. She smelled the special smell of leather from the shoes he made.

She smelled another smell and tried to place it. Wood smoke?

Her eyes popped open and she saw the glow of the campfire and saw the wagon above her head. Tears filled her eyes and ran down her cheeks. Floyd was dead and she was in the wilds of South Carolina!

A sob escaped, then another.

Court heard Taylor and he hurried to the wagon and knelt down. "Is there something I can do to help you?" he whispered.

"No. Thank you." She rubbed at her eyes. "I had a dream. . . . I was missing my husband."

"I'm sorry. If you need anything, let me know." He walked back to sit at the campfire.

Across the way Ward had seen Court go to the wagon and had heard the murmur of his and Taylor's voices, but couldn't hear what they'd said. Ward scowled and pushed himself up. Just what was going on between Taylor and Court? Ward walked to the campfire. "Anything wrong with Taylor?"

Shaking his head, Court jumped up. "She was crying over a dream about her dead husband."

Ward hurried to the wagon and knelt down beside Taylor.

"I'm really all right, Court," she said softly. "But thanks for caring."

"It's Ward," he said too sharply.

She sucked in her breath. "Oh. Did you want something?"

"Only to make sure you're all right."

"Thank you."

"Are you?"

Taylor bit her lip. "No, but there's nothing you can do."

"I'm sorry." Why couldn't he help her? He stayed there a while longer and said a silent prayer for her. "Sleep well, Taylor. Good night."

"Good night, Ward." His name slipped off her tongue easily and she flushed at her audacity. Would he think she was too forward? She wanted to apologize, but was afraid she'd make it even worse.

He slowly walked away from Taylor. Somehow his name sounded different on her lips. He slipped into his bedroll and closed his eyes.

Under the wagon Taylor lay awake a long time. The ground seemed to grow harder and harder. She saw Court's watch end and Treet's begin. Still she couldn't sleep. Tears filled her eyes again as she prayed, "Father God, I will sleep in perfect peace with my mind stayed on You."

She closed her eyes and let God's peace fill her as she drifted to sleep.

6

*T*aylor woke slowly. She felt the straw scratching her skin and smelled the pungent barnyard odor all around her. It was the third night, and Ward had stopped at a small farm where he always stopped on his trips to and from Charleston. Brooke whimpered in her sleep in the carriage beside Taylor. The women had slept in one stall of the barn, and the men in another one. Voices drifted in from the open barn door.

It was already daylight, but the sun wasn't up yet. Taylor wanted to close her eyes and sleep longer, but she knew the routine—up at daybreak, eat, and be on the road again. Would she ever get enough sleep? Would she ever be able to undress and sleep in her nightclothes in a soft bed?

Snores drifted from the stall where the men slept and up to the loft where pigeons cooed. Stifling a groan, Taylor pushed herself up. She slipped on her shoes, tied on her bonnet to hide her tangled, dirty hair, and stretched. Her dress was dirty and wrinkled, a far cry from her usual appearance. She felt about a hundred years old as she slipped out a side door to the necessary house between the barn and the cabin. On the way back she heard Yates talking to Eddie Norday, the owner of the farm. Yates sounded excited, and at the sound Taylor frowned. Last night Yates had snapped at anyone who even looked at him. Maybe the night's rest had done him good.

Back inside the barn Taylor changed Brooke's diaper as the other women silently put on their shoes and stood up. They'd all slept in their clothes as usual because there was no privacy for changing or for sleeping. By the snores coming from the other stall, Taylor knew some of the men were still sleeping.

Last night they'd arrived after dark and had eaten thick venison stew and heavy cornbread. Taylor had enjoyed the icy cold water straight from the well the most. On the trip the water they carried on the wagons was always lukewarm and sometimes tasted dirty.

Taylor handed Brooke a chunk of cornbread she'd saved last night, knowing how hungry the baby was on awakening.

Brooke cooed as she broke off a piece of cornbread. She studied it with great concentration, and then pushed it in her mouth.

Taylor smiled. "You're growing so fast, my sweet."

❦

Forcing back a smug smile, Yates stepped inside the barn and called, "Taylor, come here. Give the baby to Cammie and hurry out here."

The brilliant idea had popped into his head during the night. It was a good plan and he was going to follow it through no matter what anyone said, including Ward.

Taylor's stomach lurched. There was something about Yates's voice that troubled her. Still maybe it was nothing. He probably wanted her to make breakfast since the farmer, Eddie Norday, didn't have a wife.

"You watch careful-like, Miz Taylor," Cammie whispered as she took Brooke. "I didn't like the way that old farmer man looked at you last night."

Taylor shivered. She'd been so tired last night she'd thought it was her imagination when Eddie Norday had paid extra attention to her. He was over fifty years old, unwashed, and had yellow teeth.

Yates motioned impatiently to Taylor. "Step outdoors." He couldn't look at Maida, but he felt her eyes on him. He'd told Treet to keep the others away from the front of the barn until his business was completed.

Taylor slowly walked toward Yates. She glanced over her shoulder trying to find Ward. Why would she think of him? He wasn't her protector just because he'd saved her from being burned and had been kind to her on the trip. Or was he?

Her nerves tight but her head high, she walked outside with Yates. Pleasantly cool wind rustled the leaves on the trees. A rooster crowed and another answered. To the left of the barn was a large field planted with cotton. To the right of the barn were four shacks and a large vegetable garden. Smells of frying bacon and brewing coffee drifted out the open door of the cabin and into the yard. Eddie Norday stood between the barn and the cabin with two of his strongest slaves, Young and Dancer. They were about Treet's age and size and wore ragged pants and ragged gray shirts. Taylor remembered seeing Cammie talking to them last night.

Leering, Eddie Norday stepped right up to Taylor. He wore the same dark pants and light shirt he'd worn yesterday. He rubbed his hands together and almost smacked his lips. "You get a good night's sleep, Miz Craven, ma'am?"

She barely nodded. Exactly what was happening here? Eddie Norday was looking at her as if she was his breakfast after a week-long fast.

Yates jabbed her between the shoulder blades. "Answer the man!"

Her heart racing, Taylor pulled away from Yates and crossed her arms. "Yes, sir."

Eddie Norday pulled off his floppy brimmed hat and held it between dirty hands. His hair and beard looked as if they hadn't been washed or trimmed for a year. "Do you like me good enough, Miz Craven, ma'am?" he asked, squinting at her.

Taylor's mouth turned dust dry. Why was he asking? "I don't know you, sir," she said weakly.

"She'll learn to like you soon enough," Yates snapped. Eddie Norday was poor even though he was a landowner. With only his few slaves to tend the cotton field he'd never get rich. Yates's jaw tightened. Not him! He would not grub out a living! He planned to become wealthy beyond his wildest dreams! But to be rich he needed slaves. He jabbed his finger at Norday. "You ready to trade, Mr. Norday?"

Taylor gasped and stumbled back away from Eddie Norday. What was Yates doing?

"Sure am, Mr. Marston." Eddie Norday licked his lips and giggled.

The color drained from Taylor's face and icy chills ran over her body as she finally grasped what Yates was planning. Was this a nightmare?

"I'll take Young and Dancer in an even trade for Taylor." Yates motioned to the slaves, then at Taylor.

Helplessly Taylor shook her head.

"I'll write out a paper saying so and you make your mark." Yates knew Eddie couldn't read or write, but as a gentleman he wouldn't cheat him. Yates eyed the slaves. They were worth more to him at Catawba than Taylor ever would be. Maida would be angry, but she'd just have to get over it. Ward might object too, but once the paper was signed, it'd be too late.

Eddie called the slaves over. "Say your goodbyes and report to your new master, Yates Marston."

Yates smiled in victory. Inside he was trembling, but he wouldn't let guilt stop him from doing what he wanted. He had dreams to fulfill.

Taylor's head spun and she stared at Yates in horror. Was she dreaming this dreadful nightmare because she was so tired? Was he really trading her for two slaves?

Yates scowled at Taylor. "It won't do you any good to look at me that way. My mind is set." Yates motioned to Treet in the barn doorway. "Help hitch up the wagons."

Chuckling, Eddie Norday reached for Taylor and she leaped away from him. "Get over here, girl!"

❧

Inside the barn Ward looked around for Taylor. He enjoyed just watching her work and taking care of Brooke. When he couldn't find her he wandered over to Cammie. "Have you seen Taylor?"

"Yes, sir. Your brother made her go outside with him. I have a terrible feeling something bad is going to happen to her."

A frown creasing his brow, Ward walked to the doors of the barn. Stepping out into the sunlight Ward glanced around at the people standing together. Taylor was standing apart from the men with her hands clenched into fists.

"I will not stay here with him, Yates. You can't make me." Taylor's blue eyes flashed in anger.

"What's going on here, Yates?" called Ward as he looked around the group.

Taylor turned the full force of her anger on Ward. "Yates is trying to trade me for two slaves."

"What?" Ward's eyes flashed. "Yates!" Ward knotted his fists at his sides and glared at Yates. "You can't trade Taylor! What's wrong with you?"

Yates faced Ward squarely. This time he wouldn't cower before Ward. "I have her papers. I have every right!"

"What about her baby?"

Taylor bit back a wail.

"You take her," Yates growled. "Eddie doesn't want a baby getting in the way."

"No! Ward, stop him!" Taylor gripped Ward's arm. "Don't let him do this!"

Yates glared at Taylor. "You have no right to say anything. Get to the cabin and finish making breakfast."

Ward covered her hand with his. "Stay where you are," he commanded. Forcing back his anger, he turned to Yates again and smiled. "You can't do this, brother. It's not right. And you know it."

"I'm going to do it anyway." Yates was tired and discouraged and ready for a fight. Nothing had been going right for him since Ellen had died. "I'm getting my own way this time, Ward."

"But why?"

Taylor gripped Ward's arm so tight her knuckles turned white.

Yates stood with his booted feet apart and his chin thrust out. "We need those slaves in order to make a profit growing cotton, and we don't need Taylor."

She groaned.

"We won't raise cotton. I've been doing good with horses and selling trees for lumber."

"Horses! Lumber!" Yates brushed them aside as if they were nothing. "I've been reading up on cotton. It'll make us rich! I will raise it at Catawba, Ward!"

"Then raise your cotton, but I won't let you trade Taylor off, Yates." Ward couldn't leave Taylor behind—especially with Eddie Norday. The thought of it sent a chill down his spine.

Taylor's spirits soared. Ward was going to save her again!

Yates waved Taylor's paper. "I'll give this to Eddie and the transaction will be finished."

Ward grabbed the paper.

Yates tried to get it back, but Ward easily held it out of Yates's reach. "Don't be a fool, Yates!"

"Give that back!" Yates shouted, his face red with anger.

"I'll buy her papers. Cammie's and the baby's, too."

Taylor's mouth dropped open. God had sent her a miracle—a bigger one than she'd ever expected. "Thank You, Father God," she whispered brokenly.

"I want the money now." Yates thrust out his hand. "I intend to have those two slaves!"

Ward opened his money belt and pushed the correct amount into Yates's hand.

"What about me?" Eddie Norday growled. "I want that woman for myself."

Shivering, Taylor moved closer to Ward.

"She's mine now." The words struck Ward to the heart. He'd

said the same thing of Audrey Smythe, but she'd married someone else. Impatiently he pushed the thought aside. This was entirely different. Taylor Craven was his because he'd bought her and not because he loved her.

Taylor sighed a great sigh of relief. "Thank you," she whispered.

Ward smiled and patted her hand on his arm. "You have nothing more to fear."

She smiled and reluctantly released him. She had nothing more to fear. The thought of James Rawlings flashed through her mind, but she pushed it aside. He was probably in Virginia at his home and would turn his attention on someone else for a wife.

"For Dancer and Young." Yates held the money out to Eddie Norday. "Take it or leave it. I can always buy slaves elsewhere."

Eddie snatched the money from Yates and stuffed it inside his shirt. "Write out the paper for 'em, and they're yours."

Taylor ran to the barn, took Brooke from Cammie, and hugged her close.

An hour later with Brooke in her arms, Taylor sat on the high wagon seat between Court and Cammie as they slowly drove away from the Norday farm. Dancer was driving the second wagon for Yates, and Young rode with Treet. The strained silence between the brothers set the tone for the rest of the trip.

❧

Three days later in the mid-afternoon they stopped the wagons side by side in the shade of a giant magnolia tree in the yard at Catawba. Pigs squealed and grunted near the barn and a dog ran into sight, barking and wagging its bushy tail.

"Quiet, Musket!" Ward shouted with a laugh.

Musket stopped barking and leaped up to try to lick Ward's hand.

Taylor looked around for the fine home like the ones she'd seen around Charleston. She saw two light-colored log cabins near a well with a square stone foundation, a necessary house, a low log barn with an extended roof supported by four heavy posts, and two weathered-gray shacks. Maybe the house was off in the trees in back of the cabins or out past the split-rail fence.

Cammie's mouth dropped open. She'd thought Catawba would be grander than Rawlings Plantation. Instead Catawba looked like the back section of Rawlings where the slaves lived.

"This is Catawba!" Reid shouted happily as he jumped out of the wagon and raced around as wildly as the dog had done. Inside he

wanted to cry as loud as Brooke sometimes did. He looked around
for something that matched what Uncle Ward had said. He spotted
horses in a pen behind the barn, raced to the split-rail fence, and
leaned against it. The horses were beautiful all right.

Knowing how Reid was feeling, Court followed him and leaned
against the fence beside him. "They're some of the best horses I've
seen."

Reid turned thankfully to Court. "The rest of the place looks
rather . . . unfinished."

"You're right." Court grinned. "You're here now to help finish
it."

Reid thought about that a while, then smiled and nodded. Yes!
He'd help build Catawba! He'd be more a part of it for doing so.

His hat in his trembling hand, Yates dropped to the ground. This
Catawba wasn't what Ward had described to him. The woods were
there and the barn, but nothing fancy. "Where's the house, Ward?"
Yates asked.

Laughing, Ward strode to Yates. "Right before your eyes,
brother!"

"The cabins?"

"Yes." Ward laughed and slapped Yates on the back. "Built
sturdy and strong by me and my men a short time ago!"

Laurel cried out at the thought of living in such an uncivilized
place and Kendra hushed her.

Stunned, Maida slowly climbed from the wagon and walked to
Taylor's side. They stared at the cabins. What had happened to the
mansion that was practically the size of a castle?

Brooke cried and squirmed to be let down. Cammie stood Brooke
on the ground and she ran after a chicken, giggling and waving her
arms to keep her balance.

Yates forced back his anger. He'd expected something different,
but he should've known better. Ward always dreamed big and often
he spoke of his dream as a reality. "I thought the house was already
built," was all he could say.

Ward clamped his hand on Yates's shoulder. "We'll get it done in
no time. In the meantime we'll make do. The cabins are comfortable and roomy. You and your daughters can take one and Taylor,
Cammie, the baby, and I'll take the other. The darkies will occupy
one shack and Court, Bard, and Reid the other." Ward had sorted it
out as he'd driven. He could've put Taylor and Cammie in a shack,
but it was important for him to keep Taylor close and to make her
as comfortable as possible.

Just then Taylor saw Brooke starting into the woods and she ran after her, walking her back to stand with the others near the wagons. This was going to be a whole new way of living!

Ward called for everyone to gather round. After waiting for Reid, he faced them and smiled. There'd only been four men living at Catawba, now there would be five women, a baby, a boy, and eight men. It would take some getting used to.

He pulled off his hat and began, "Welcome to Catawba! Yates, you'll never know how happy I am to have you here." Ward's voice broke and he couldn't go on for a while. He'd spent many lonely days working to make Catawba a home, but even Catawba couldn't be a home without family. Ward cleared his throat. "We'll get things running smooth as soon as we can. Court, see that the wagons are unloaded and the horses taken care of. Treet, Young, Dancer, and Reid, you take orders from Court."

Yates frowned. It certainly wasn't right for Ward to order his son and his slaves around. He'd take it up with him later and get it settled.

Ward waved a hand and called, "Follow me and I'll show you where the house will stand." He led Yates and his family and Taylor off to the side of the cabins away from the garden, up a small hill, and into a clearing in the woods. Piles of bricks lay in a row near stacks of lumber. Dirt was piled near the area where a part of the foundation had been dug.

With a flourish Ward indicated the placement of the house. "This is it! It'll be three stories high and big enough for the lot of us."

"Are we going to build it ourselves?" Yates asked with a shudder as he walked close to the surveyed area.

"I thought we could, but we won't have the time. We'll hire the housewright in Darien, and he can get to work as soon as he's available."

Maida looked at the mess all around and her heart sank. It would take years to build the house! Could she live in close quarters with a man who didn't even care for her? If only she could break down the walls Yates had put up around himself.

Taylor watched a mockingbird fly from one tree branch to another. A gentle breeze swayed the leaves. She and Cammie and Brooke were safe from James Rawlings at last. He'd never be able to find them in such an out-of-the-way place.

"I even have a piano on order," Ward told her confidently as he led them back to the cabins. The men had unloaded the wagons and put the luggage and supplies away.

Just then two men walked into the yard with flintlocks over their shoulders and dead rabbits dangling down their sides. The tall white man had neatly combed brown hair, brown eyes, and a cleft in his chin. He wore leather pants and a loose-fitting blue shirt. The black man was short and slight with a scar that ran from the corner of his left eye down to his jaw.

Ward hailed them in a hearty voice. "Bard, Pickle, come say hello to everyone." When they stopped beside Ward, he said, "Pickle's the cook and handyman—the man who fought with Francis Marion, the Swamp Fox, in the Revolutionary War."

Pickle stood proudly. He saw Reid looking with interest at him, so he smiled. He'd have a whole new audience with whom to share his adventures.

"Bard's my other worker I told you about. He once lived in London and he saw the King on several occasions."

Bard flushed. It hurt his pride to stand before the Marston family in old clothes with dead rabbits hanging from his belt. He'd been a lawyer in London and had dressed the part. He'd never carried dead rabbits from his belt!

As Uncle Ward talked, Kendra glanced around until she caught sight of Court. Not once in all the days it took to get here had he let on that they'd kissed. What was wrong with the man? Did he go around kissing every girl in sight, then put it out of his mind?

Taylor lifted Brooke into her arms and slowly walked with the others to the cabins. She looked inside the cabin Maida and Yates would share with their children. It smelled of fresh-cut logs.

"It has a bedroom and a loft," Ward said proudly. "Most cabins around here have only one room, but I wanted more for us." He touched the windows. "Real glass." He tapped the floor with his toe. "We made wooden floors so you wouldn't have to contend with dirt floors like in the shacks."

Looking down at the split-log floor, Maida pressed her hand to her throat. She had given up luxury for this! She stopped in the middle of the room beside a trestle table with a chair at either end and a bench on either side. A black bearskin rug lay near a stone fireplace with a cooking pot hanging in it. A ladder pegged to the wall led up to the loft, and to the side of the ladder was an open door.

She peeked inside at the bed that almost filled the small room. This was the room she'd share with Yates. Could she endure having him touch her now that she knew how mean-tempered he could be? But what choice would she have? She was his wife and to him that meant he owned her. Tears pricked her eyes, but she quickly blinked them away before anyone noticed them.

In the other cabin Taylor sank to a chair with Brooke on her lap. The others were listening to Ward tell the good features of the cabin and the story of how he'd killed the bears that were now rugs in front of the fireplaces in both cabins. Finally he turned to Taylor. He saw the disappointment on her face and it made him wish he'd pushed harder to have the house built.

"You and Cammie and the baby will sleep in the loft and I'll keep my bedroom." Ward motioned to the room in back of him.

Taylor nodded. If she tried, she could make this into a comfortable home for Brooke. It was better than being forced to marry James Rawlings even if he did live in a large house with several slaves to take care of it. Handing Brooke to Cammie, Taylor walked past the spinning wheel and the loom to the window to look out at the other cabin. What if Yates forced Maida and the children to treat her like a servant? That would hurt.

She watched Court walk toward the barn with a milk bucket in his hand. He'd become a friend on the way. She'd almost told him about James, but had decided against it. He'd told her about his life at Catawba and that he had three more years before he was free. Having him here would make her life happier. They could be friends and Yates Marston would have no reason to forbid it.

Across the room Cammie looked up the ladder and smiled even though she was so tired she could barely hold her head up. "I gonna like it here," she whispered.

Later Pickle fixed rabbit stew and cornbread for everyone. They all ate together crammed in Ward's cabin which was lit by several lamps. The room was warm from the fire and smelled of stew and unwashed bodies. Taylor yearned for a bath and clean clothes, and she imagined the others felt the same.

Yates moved restlessly. He'd talk to Ward about eating with the slaves and servants; it just wasn't fitting. Ward should have remembered his good manners. Reid especially was prone to imitate Ward and he couldn't let that happen. He'd promised Ellen he'd raise Reid to be a fine English gentleman even if they did move to Catawba.

At long last Taylor wearily climbed the ladder after Cammie. Brooke was already asleep in her carriage. Soon they'd have to make a bed for her and put the carriage away. She'd outgrown it on the voyage.

In the darkness Taylor yawned as she peeled off her clothes and thankfully slipped on her nightdress for the first time since they'd left the ship. Below she heard Ward moving about. The smell of supper still hung in the air. A cricket chirped. Outdoors a wolf howled, or maybe it had been Musket. Across the small loft Cammie settled down on her mat with a loud sigh. Yawning, Taylor stretched out on her straw tick and pulled a light cover over herself. It wasn't a bed, but it was home until she could tell Ward her story and he'd let her go on her way. She frowned. She had no money. Where could she go? She'd have to stay here. But she couldn't stay and be treated like a bond servant. She'd gladly work for him until she knew where she wanted to go, but she would not be called a servant!

" 'Night, Miz Taylor," Cammie whispered.

"Good night, Cammie. We're here and we're safe."

"We sure are, Miz Taylor. Thanks to Jesus."

"Yes." Taylor smiled. She closed her eyes and silently thanked God for bringing them safely to Catawba.

In the other cabin Laurel whimpered as she stretched out on the straw tick. Kendra shared the loft with her and Reid had been sent to sleep in the shack with Court and Bard. Reid had been happy, not upset at all the way Laurel felt he should've been.

"How can we live like this, Kendra?" she pouted.

Her eyes closed, Kendra said, "Would you rather sleep in the barn?"

"It wasn't fair of Uncle Ward to tell us we'd have a big house to live in."

"But we will have one." Kendra moved and the straw rustled. "This is better than sleeping in the ship or under the wagon or in that barn."

Laurel sighed. "Oh, I suppose you're right."

Downstairs Maida turned to Yates and shook her head. Inside she was quivering with fear, but on the outside she looked very determined. "I don't want to share a bed with you."

He felt as if he'd been struck. Moments before he'd planned to tell her he was going to sleep in the shack with Reid because he'd made a mistake marrying her, but he'd been unable to find the words. But to have Maida say it to him was a blow to his pride. How could she tell him she wouldn't share his bed? She had no right! He gripped her arm and looked sternly into her face. "We are husband and wife, and we will share a bed."

Her eyes flashing, she pulled away from him, but without another word, walked to the bedroom.

❧

The next morning Ward found Yates leaning against the fence near the barn. The men had already done the morning chores and were working with the horses.

"Ward, I want to get a few things settled." Yates watched Ward to catch his reaction. "I plan to raise cotton."

"Go right ahead, brother." Ward had given Yates's idea about raising cotton some thought and had decided it was a good plan. "There's a couple of fields that'll work just fine for it. I intend to keep raising horses. And as long as I can, I'll sell trees to be lumbered and sold to the ship-building company." Ward looked toward the horse pen thoughtfully. "I see your man Treet knows horses. How about letting me use him part of the time?"

"Of course. As long as I can use your men when I need them." Ward nodded.

Yates looked down at his boots, then up at Ward through narrowed eyes. "I want Taylor to help Maida when she needs it."

Ward frowned. "I paid for Taylor! I won't have her working for Maida and your girls. They seem well able to do a good day's work."

"Taylor and Cammie are servants! My wife and daughters aren't."

Struggling to keep from snapping at Yates, Ward leaned against the split-rail fence. He didn't want Taylor to work for Maida and the girls. But finally he said, "Cammie can help your family when they need it."

Yates forced back his anger. "Why not Taylor?"

Ward didn't know. "Because I said that's how it'll be," he snapped.

Yates was quiet a long time. He watched Treet run a horse around inside the pen. Someone laughed. "Do you plan to make her your woman?"

Ward shot away from the fence. "I could never do that to her or myself! It's wrong in the sight of God."

Yates flushed. "You're right, of course. But how about taking her as your wife?"

Ward sucked in his breath. It had been a long time since he'd had to explain his actions to anyone. And he didn't like it one bit. "I'm not in the market for a wife."

"You can't still be hurting over Audrey!"

"Can't I?"

Yates thought of his undying love for Ellen and finally he nodded. "Yes, I suppose you can. We Marstons love only once in our lives."

Ward glanced toward Yates's cabin. "Does Maida know that?"

"She didn't marry me for love," Yates said sharply. "She wanted to be free of her aunt and uncle."

In the cabin Maida slowly awoke. For the first time in weeks she'd slept the night through and felt rested. Last night Yates had kept to his side of the bed without speaking for a long time; then he'd apologized for forcing her to share the bed. He'd pulled her close and kissed her. She smiled. If Yates would include her in his life, maybe she could find a way to be happy.

In Ward's cabin Taylor smelled bacon frying and she sat up with a start, making the straw rustle. Was Ward cooking breakfast? She peeked down the ladder to see Pickle and not Ward. She sighed in relief. After this she'd fix meals for them and leave Pickle free to cook for the others.

Longing for a bath, Taylor dressed in clean clothes, brushed her hair, and pinned it in a loose knot at the back of her head. Cammie and Brooke were still asleep. She'd let them sleep. Cammie had to take care of herself in order to have a healthy baby.

Holding her skirts carefully, Taylor climbed down the ladder and onto the floor. She smiled at Pickle. "Good morning."

"Mornin', Miz." Pickle rubbed a hand over his big apron that almost covered his entire body. "Did my noise wake you?"

"No. The smell of bacon frying did." She sniffed deeply. "Mmmmm. It's delicious. Is there anything I can do to help make breakfast?"

Pickle shook his head hard. "Master Ward done told me to cook. You sit right down and I'll pour you a fine cup of coffee."

"I want to make a trip outdoors first, then I'll have a cup of tea instead." She started for the door, then turned back. "I'd like to take a bath later." She flushed painfully. Talking to a man about taking a bath was most embarrassing. "How will I manage it?"

"Master has a tub, Miz Taylor. I'll heat up water and set the tub up in master's room where you can be nice and private."

Taylor smiled in relief. "Thank you!"

Later, after a trip to the necessary house and a wash and drink at the well, Taylor spotted Ward alone near the barn with his back to her. He wore a fawn-colored shirt that hung over his leather pants. Pulling together all her courage, she walked toward him. "Mr. Marston, may I speak with you?"

He turned and smiled. He was pleased to see her looking rested. "Of course."

She stood with her hands at her sides, the tips of her slippers showing from under her gray dress. "I felt you should hear the truth about my indenture."

"Tell away." He leaned against the fence and watched her. She was quite pretty.

Taking a deep breath, she told him what had transpired on the *Falcon*. "So, I am not a servant, but a free woman."

Ward nodded. "I can see that." And if he had Andrew Simons before him, he'd thrash him until he told the truth and returned the money.

"Thank you! It's a relief to me." She took one step toward him, her eyes dancing with excitement. "Will you be so kind as to tear up the indenture paper?"

"Yes." He wanted to do that very thing, but if he did, she'd leave. He couldn't have that. "As soon as you pay me what I paid Yates."

Taylor gasped. She'd thought Ward Marston had a heart. "But I have no money!"

"Then work for me until you pay it off."

"Don't you understand?" Tears sparkled in her eyes. "I will not be anyone's slave!"

Ward was quiet a long time. He understood how she felt. "Look at it this way, Taylor. You have a home for yourself and your child. You're working a job. You have food, clothing, and shelter. What more do you need?"

"To be free! To come and go as I choose!"

"Where would you go?" He waved a hand to take in the woods and the yard. "We're a couple hours' ride from the nearest town. There's nothing there for you to do to earn a wage." He held his hand out to her. "You can work willingly for me or unwillingly. It's your decision."

She turned away, her head down and her shoulders bowed. His words rang in her head. "You can work for me willingly or unwillingly. It's your decision."

Ward's nerves tightened. Had he hurt her so much she'd treat him like a stranger after this?

Silently she prayed for help. From deep inside she heard the Lord's still, small voice, "I'm with you. Work willingly for him."

She spun around and lifted her head high. Her eyes shining, she proclaimed, "God is with me, Mr. Marston! I'll work willingly for you!"

Ward's heart jerked strangely. Here before him was a woman of faith. This was the kind of woman he needed as a mate. Impatiently he pushed the thought aside. Marriage wasn't for him. "Tell Pickle you'll take over his job in the cabin after today."

"I will." Taylor walked to the cabin with light steps.

Ward ran his hand through his dark hair. Had he made a mistake by having her stay?

Inside the cabin Taylor told Pickle what Ward had said. "I would appreciate it if you'd show me how to cook in the fireplace."

"I can do that sure enough, Miz Taylor, ma'am." He grinned and looked proud.

She motioned to the spinning wheel and the loom. "Do you know anything about them?"

"Sure do, ma'am."

"Would you teach me to use them?"

He nodded. "Sure will, Miz Taylor, ma'am!"

"I'll need to know about gardening here at Catawba since it's different from England. Will you teach me?"

"I planted a fine big garden that needs tending in a careful way." Pickle laughed.

Taylor laughed along with Pickle as she sat at the table. "Now that that is settled, I would love that cup of tea."

7

When Taylor stepped outside the cabin to get Brooke for her evening bath, she stopped and laughed under her breath as Ward chased Brooke across the yard before scooping her up high in his arms. His hat flew off and landed on the ground. Musket sank down beside it and watched Ward.

Brooke giggled and hugged Ward around the neck. They'd become friends in the past two months since they'd come to Catawba.

He nuzzled her cheek, then held her out and spun around with her. Her face glowing, she laughed in delight.

Taylor's eyes filled with tears, and pain stabbed her heart. Floyd had played with Brooke the very same way. It was so sad that Brooke had probably forgotten it—and her father.

Taylor turned aside and quickly brushed away the tears with the tail of her apron. After being here only two months she'd come to realize what a wonderful home Catawba was for Brooke. Everybody loved her and played with her except, of course, for Yates and Treet. Since it was a little late in the season, Yates was preoccupied with getting the ground ready to plant cotton. Treet just acted as if he didn't like babies.

With a tremulous smile Taylor walked toward Ward and Brooke. As they headed out to help Yates in the cotton field, Court called to Young over the sound of a horse whinnying. A bluebird flew from behind the cabin to a tree near the barn. The clatter of the spinning wheel and the smell of baking bread drifted from Maida's cabin.

Ward saw Taylor coming and he held Brooke high. "Your mama is coming to get you," he whispered. "Tell her you're going with Uncle Ward to get Reid."

"Weid, Weid!" Brooke shouted.

Laughing, Taylor stopped with her hands at her waist. The sleeves of her muslin dress hung just below her elbows and her apron had flour on it. "And just where is Reid?" she asked.

"Fishing for our supper. Want to go with us?"

"I'd like that. Let me tell Cammie I'm going." Taylor ran to the cabin and stuck her head through the doorway. Cammie looked hot and tired as she stood at the table rolling out crust for a berry pie. Her apron couldn't hide her rounded stomach. Taylor smiled. "I'm going to the river with Ward and Brooke to get Reid."

Cammie grinned. "I do think Master Ward has his eye on you, Miz Taylor."

She flushed. "Don't say that!"

"I seen him watching you, Miz Taylor." Cammie giggled. "You know, you could get out of your indenture by marrying up with Master Ward."

Taylor gasped. The same thought had crossed her mind, but she'd never said it to anyone. What if Cammie mentioned it? Without thinking, she snapped, "Don't you ever say that to me again. Or to anyone! You hear me?"

Giant tears filled Cammie's eyes. "I didn't mean no harm, Miz Taylor."

Taylor hurried to Cammie and wrapped her arms around her. "Oh, I know. I'm sorry I snapped at you. Please don't cry."

Cammie sniffed and pulled away. "It 'pears like I cry over everything lately. I knows you barked at me 'cause you been having them same thoughts. Only you didn't want nobody to know it."

Taylor bit her lip. Cammie was entirely too observant! "It's not right for me to even have those thoughts, but they keep coming. And to have you say my thoughts right out loud frightened me—that's all."

"What thoughts are those?" Ward asked from the doorway with Brooke on his shoulders chattering happily. He'd come to see what was taking so long.

Gasping, Taylor spun around, her face burning with guilt and embarrassment.

Cammie giggled. "Get on with you, Master Ward! Miz Taylor can't go telling all her thoughts to every person who comes around."

"I'm ready to go." Taylor hurried to the door, thankful for Cammie's quick remark to Ward. Taylor tickled Brooke's chubby leg. "Are you ready to get Reid?"

"Weid, Weid!" Laughing, Brooke pounded on Ward's head.

Chuckling, Ward caught her hands as he walked away from the cabin.

"Don't hurt Uncle Ward, Brooke," Taylor gently reminded.

In answer, Brooke snuggled down to him and kissed the top of his head.

"She's a charmer." Ward grinned at Taylor. "Have you noticed how she can get her way with almost everybody?"

Taylor sighed. "I'm afraid so. I do hate to see her so spoiled."

"We love her." Ward whistled to Musket, who ran to his side. "And don't worry, none of us let her get by with doing anything wrong or hurtful."

"Yes, I suppose you're right about that."

They walked out of the yard, through the trees, and past the field where all the men were planting cotton seeds. Ward had ordered his men to help Yates's men, so Pickle was working in the field even though he'd objected when Ward first mentioned it.

"I'm surprised Yates doesn't have Reid working too," Taylor said.

"He did, but I told Yates we needed fish for supper."

"Because Reid was tired out?"

Ward grinned and nodded. "Yates knew it too, but he didn't let on. My brother is determined to have a crop this year even if it's small."

Brooke squirmed and cried, "Birdy! Birdy!"

Taylor looked in the sky at ducks flying over. "Ducks. They're ducks, Brooke."

Ward walked in silence for a while. He glanced at Taylor, then at the path that led to the river. As usual, he had to watch out for snakes. Musket was good about spotting danger, but Ward liked to keep a lookout himself.

As they walked along, he decided to open the subject that concerned him. "Taylor, I need to ask you a delicate question."

She stiffened. What was it? Last night she'd been laughing and talking with Court and Ward had frowned at them. Was he going to forbid her to be friends with Court? "What is it?" she finally asked.

"Is Cammie getting fat or is she . . . is she going to have a . . . baby?"

Taylor flushed to the roots of her light brown hair. "She's going to have a baby."

"Who's the father?"

A shaft of fear shot through Taylor. How could she answer that without telling him about James Rawlings? "Does it matter?"

"Did you take her away from her husband?"

"No!" Taylor stopped short and stared at Ward in dismay. "I would never do that!" She bit her lip and locked her fingers together. "She was never married. The man forced her to be with him."

"Why couldn't you stop him?"

"It was before she was with me."

Ward started walking again with Taylor on one side of him and Musket just ahead. "How'd you come about getting her? You said she wasn't your slave."

Taylor's head spun with what to say. "Does it matter?"

"I don't want to be taken by surprise if some angry man comes looking for a runaway slave."

Taylor gasped. She'd never thought about that. What if James Rawlings did come looking for Cammie? He'd find Taylor and Brooke as well!

Ward frowned at Taylor. "Is she a runaway?"

Her eyes wide in alarm, Taylor pressed her fingertips to her mouth.

"Taylor, answer me!"

Helplessly she shook her head. "Don't make me. Please!"

Ward sighed and shook his head. "I guess you'd better not. Just tell me if I need to watch for someone from here in South Carolina."

Taylor shook her head.

"Then maybe she'll be safe and so will I." He smiled and shrugged. "We won't go looking for trouble, will we?"

"No," Taylor whispered.

"Let's get Reid."

"Weid, Weid!" Brooke waved her arms and laughed.

They walked in silence a while, then Ward said, "You may not know this, Taylor, but helping a runaway slave is serious business. A person can be hanged for it."

Taylor shivered. Would she be considered a runaway, too? If so, could Ward be punished for taking her in? She shivered again even in the heat around her. "Then it's best if a person doesn't get caught, isn't it?"

Ward looked steadily at Taylor. "Or doesn't help runaways," he said sternly.

Taylor ducked her head. She couldn't promise that to Ward, but she would be very careful.

"Weid, Weid!" Brooke cried, waving her arms frantically.

Taylor looked up as Reid ran toward them, a string of catfish in one hand, a fishing pole in the other. His skin had tanned to the color of leather and he'd had Taylor cut his hair short enough so he wouldn't have to pull it back in a tail. He looked as if he belonged in the wilds of South Carolina.

"Good catch, Reid," Ward said with a broad smile. "You'll have to clean them yourself unless you can talk Laurel into helping you."

Reid chuckled. "I don't think she's ready for that. Why can't Kendra help?"

"She's working with the horses."

"I'll help you clean them," Taylor said brightly. "I'm good at it. And fast. I learned it from my papa."

Ward studied her as she talked to Reid while they walked back toward the cabins. New questions buzzed inside his head about Taylor. He knew her husband had died, but he knew nothing about her family or why she'd chosen to come to South Carolina. Why was she so closed-mouthed about herself?

At the cabin Ward handed Brooke over to Cammie and he helped Reid and Taylor skin, clean, and fillet the fish on a worktable Pickle had built near the well. Ward told about fish he'd caught and Taylor told about hooking herself with a fish hook when she was a child. She even showed them the tiny scar at the base of her thumb.

A few minutes later Taylor carried the fish to the cabin where Cammie was working. "I'll give Brooke a bath while you fry the fish for everyone," she suggested.

Cammie grinned and took the fish. "My mama taught me how to fry fish fit for the King of England. I'm gonna have everyone's mouth watering with just the smell of this here fish."

"Good." Taylor quickly bathed, fed, and tucked Brooke into bed for the night; afterward she stepped outdoors for fresh air. The smell of frying fish was strong in the cabin. Soon the men would come in from the field, tired enough to drop and hungry enough to eat everything in sight.

❦

Maida stood by the well looking toward the field which was hidden from sight by several trees. Sometimes she felt like a totally different woman from the one who'd waited hand and foot on her aunt and uncle. She'd never worked as hard as she had the past two months! She had to do the washing, mending, sewing, cooking, and cleaning. Pickle had taught her to make soap and candles and chop wood. Kendra gladly helped with everything, but Laurel would only sew and at times cook. Maida had spoken to Yates about her, but he had said she didn't need to work like a slave since she wasn't one.

Smiling, Taylor stopped beside Maida. "I'm glad the heat's gone from the day."

"Me, too." Maida leaned against the stone foundation of the well near the wooden bucket. One end of a rope was tied around the bucket handle and the other end was around a windlass. She'd learned the first day how to drop the bucket in and turn the crank to lower the bucket into the water and to crank the bucketful back up.

Maida sniffed the air. "The fish smells good."

"Cammie's frying it for everyone."

"That's nice."

Taylor moved restlessly. It sometimes was hard to talk to Maida because of Yates.

Just then Musket lifted his head and barked toward the road that ran along the trees at the edge of Catawba.

Taylor stiffened, thinking again of James Rawlings.

Ward hurried from the barn, calling, "Company's coming."

Maida brushed back loose strands of hair and tugged off her apron.

Taylor whipped off her apron, but soon remembered it didn't matter if she left hers on. She wasn't the lady of the house; still, she didn't tie it back on. She brushed back her clean, shiny brown hair and tucked it in the knot at the nape of her neck.

Her face flushed with excitement, Laurel rushed from the cabin and ran to Maida's side. "I hope there'll be a girl my age to talk to about clothes and parties and gossip of all kinds!"

"It's probably Alden Bromley to shoe the horses." Ward stepped to Taylor's side and said in a low voice, "Bromley hunts runaway slaves no matter what state they're from. Have Cammie tend Brooke in the loft."

Perspiration popped out on Taylor's forehead and her blood ran cold. Ward wouldn't warn her if he wasn't afraid for Cammie. "I'll be right back." Taylor hurried to the cabin where Cammie waited in the doorway. Taylor urgently tugged Cammie inside. "Grab something to eat, then you wait in the loft with Brooke until the visitor leaves or until Master Ward or I call you down."

"Am I in danger?"

"You might be. Now, hurry!"

"I can't eat. Dear Jesus, dear Jesus, don't let nobody come take me." Cammie trembled, and then ran to the ladder and scrambled up.

Taylor swung out the arm of the fireplace crane that held a pot of food so it wouldn't cook while she was outdoors. Four platters of fish sat under a cloth on the table. Whoever was coming would probably stay for supper. She wiped her damp face with a towel and hurried outdoors to stand beside Ward. He looked at her with a cocked brow, but she barely nodded.

Just as Kendra and Reid ran up looking dusty from working with the horses, a wagon pulled into sight with two riders flanking it. The back of the wagon was covered by a tarp.

"Alden Bromley is on the right on the big bay," Ward said in a low, tight voice. "I don't know the slave."

Her nerves taut, Taylor studied Bromley. With hands bigger than both hers put together, he was about Ward's age with bulging muscles in his arms and chest. Tangled brown hair hung well below his tricorn hat. A powder horn and bag hung over his open buckskin vest and gray shirt that looked ready to burst at the seams. Taylor watched him look at all of them. His gaze stayed on her the longest, and her stomach knotted painfully. Unconsciously she moved closer to Ward. Finally Alden Bromley looked past them at the cabins. Was he hoping to catch a runaway?

Smiling, Ward stepped forward. "Good evening, friends."

Bromley swung from the saddle as the wagon and the other rider stopped in the shade of the magnolia tree. "Marston, good to see you again. This is Jacob Ferguson. He stopped by my place and said he was looking for you, so I said I'd ride along with him."

"Good to meet you, Mr. Ferguson." Ward waited for him to climb down, then shook hands with him. "I heard we had a new neighbor to our south. Could that be you?"

"Surely is, Marston. And a fine place it is, sir." Ferguson was heavy set with reddish brown hair, a broad smile that showed off a gold tooth, and a Scottish burr to his speech. He pulled off his hat and bowed to the ladies. "I have a fine daughter who'll be pleased to learn of your young ladies."

Ward made the introductions, pleased the women had good manners as they each greeted Mr. Ferguson. "Supper is almost ready. We'd be proud to have you stay," he invited.

"I'd be honored." Jacob Ferguson smiled, then turned to the black man driving the wagon. "That's my man Blake. Can he water the horses?"

"Of course." Ward motioned to Reid. "Help him, Reid."

Blake stepped out of the saddle. He was tall and thin with baggy clothes and scuffed boots. "Careful of this horse, Master Reid. He bites if you turns your back on him."

Reid chuckled. "Then I won't turn my back."

Ward motioned to the pen where he kept his horses. "We'll look at the horses before it gets dark. Did you have anything particular in mind?"

"Surely do." Ferguson nodded as he walked with Ward. "A well trained gelding, but with plenty of spirit for my daughter Marissa."

"Marissa," Laurel whispered with her hands clasped at her throat and her eyes sparkling. "I wonder what she's like. I hope Papa will agree to let me call on her even if she is a Scot."

With that comment, Maida saw a way to gain Laurel's acceptance even if not her affection. "I'll tell your papa I'll go with you since he's too busy. And you could go too, Kendra. We'll ask Court if he'll escort us."

Kendra forced back a blush. She really didn't want to meet Marissa Ferguson, but if Court was going, then she'd definitely go, too.

"Mr. Ferguson didn't say anything about a wife," Maida said as she watched Ward, Jacob Ferguson, and Alden Bromley lean against the fence to look over the horses.

Taylor stiffened. She didn't want to hear what she knew Maida was thinking—here was a chance to find a husband. "I'd better put more potatoes on to cook. Maida, is there enough yeast bread or should we bake some cornbread?"

Maida chuckled. "Don't think I can't read your mind, Taylor. But by all means, let's bake cornbread so we don't run out of food. Mr. Ferguson looks like he has a healthy appetite."

"So does Mr. Bromley," Kendra said, making a face. "I don't like that man. He looked at me funny."

Laurel tugged Kendra's hair. "Look how dusty you are from working with the horses. How can you get so dirty, Kendra? You look like a bond servant yourself."

A few minutes later Yates and the other men walked tiredly from the field. Yates washed while he considered if he wanted to meet Jacob Ferguson. Shrugging, Yates decided Scotsman or no, the man was their neighbor.

Maida called to Court. "After you've washed, have the men carry the tables outdoors so we can eat out here."

"Yes, ma'am." Court motioned to Treet and Dancer. "Get the table from Master Ward's cabin. Young, you and Bard get the one from Master Yates's.

"I can carry a chair," Kendra said softly.

Court's heart jerked, but he didn't let it show. "If you want, Miss," he answered nonchalantly.

Color flamed in Kendra's cheeks, and she rushed inside away from Court. How could he act as if they'd never shared that precious time together? Had he really forgotten about the kisses? She touched her lips but soon dropped her hand to her side. If that's how he was going to be, then she'd forget about it too! She sighed. If only she could.

Pickle walked into Ward's cabin as Taylor put more potatoes on to boil. "Get that Cammie girl to do that, Miz Taylor."

"I sent her to tend Brooke. I said I'd do this." The heat from the fireplace quickly turned her face red, and she wiped her hair back with her hand. "If the others ask about Cammie, you tell them she's with Brooke."

"That's what I'll tell them, Miz Taylor. I sure will tell 'em that."

Taylor darted a look at Pickle. Was he suspicious? Taylor forced herself to keep working as if her nerves weren't tight enough to snap.

Later the yard seemed full of people as everyone gathered in front of the cabins to eat. Ward had asked the blessing on the food and the meal began. Several feet away Pickle set up a spread of food for the slaves. Laughter rang out from time to time, especially when Mr. Ferguson told a wild tale. Taylor sat at the table only because Ward had told her to. Later she'd tell him she was thankful for not making her an outcast like Court and Bard when he easily could have. Court and Bard weren't allowed to eat with the blacks or the free whites; instead they sat near the well with food from the table.

Kendra looked over at Court and wondered if he was embarrassed having to sit away from everyone else. She thought it was very unfair of Papa not to let Court and Bard sit with them, but she didn't say so. It would only make Papa angry if she spoke up.

Taylor glanced at Ward, then quickly away. Why had he told her to sit at the table? Taylor wished he would decide how he was going to treat her. One minute he acted as if she was a servant, the next like a member of the family. It just got too confusing wondering where she stood here at Catawba.

Ward set his water goblet back in place and smiled at Jacob Ferguson. "Jake, you made a fine choice in that black mare. If your daughter's not pleased with her, you bring her back."

"Marissa will like that beauty, you can bet your boots she will."

"I shoed that mare a while back and her hooves are in good shape." Alden Bromley looked proud of himself. "I'll be by your place regular-like to check 'em, Mr. Ferguson."

"I got a couple of more for you to shoe, Bromley," Ferguson said as he lifted another bite of cornbread to his mouth.

Taylor ate in silence without appreciating the fried fish that was usually her favorite. She felt Alden Bromley's eyes on her too often. Had Ward noticed? He sat at the head of the table and she sat on a bench between Kendra and Laurel. Ward probably didn't notice her discomfort. And why should he? She shouldn't expect him to deal with all her difficulties.

After the visitors left and Ward was still outdoors talking to Yates, Taylor softly called Cammie down. "There are leftovers if you want to eat now."

Cammie looked past Taylor at the open door. "Is the danger over?"

"Yes. Thank God!"

"I sure did pray up there in that loft!" Cammie lifted the cloth on the platter of food. "And I do want to eat a piece of fish. I got powerful hungry from smelling it."

"I'm sure you did. I'm going back out for a breath of fresh air before I retire for the night."

"I can see something's making you all jittery inside, Miz Taylor. What can I do to help you?"

Taylor shook her head. "Nothing. But thank you, Cammie."

"Is you lovesick after Master Ward?"

Taylor gasped. "Cammie! Don't say such a thing!"

Cammie hung her head. "I'm sorry, Miz Taylor."

Her cheeks flushed, Taylor walked outdoors and stood in the shadows with stars twinkling high in the sky. She heard the frogs croak and an owl hoot, even the screech of a panther. She shivered. Court had told her about shooting a panther several weeks ago when it was after a pig. As she stood there she heard Yates tell Ward good night and watched Yates go into his cabin as Ward headed for the barn.

Just then someone moved near the well. The movement seemed stealthy. Her skin tingling with fear, Taylor peered through the darkness. Who was at the well? She waited, without moving, without breathing. It had to be one of the workers. Soon the person crept around to the side of the well in full sight of Taylor. It was a woman! But it couldn't be Maida or the girls. Yates never allowed them out alone after dark.

The woman beckoned to Taylor. Trembling, she hurried across the yard. It was light enough for Taylor to see the woman was young and black.

"Who are you?" Taylor whispered.

She ducked down and whispered, "I Sippy, Missy Taylor. Don't let nobody know you seen me, please. Not even Master Ward."

"He's coming from the barn," Taylor said in a low tight voice, but she didn't know if she could keep this from Ward.

"Master Court say you'd help me."

Taylor sucked in air. Was the woman a runaway?

Sippy inched around the well away from Taylor and where Ward couldn't see her.

"Taylor," Ward said in surprise. "I thought you turned in."

"I needed a breath of fresh air." Could he hear the quiver in her voice?

Ward leaned against the well and crossed his arms. "I saw the way Bromley looked at you tonight. I'm sorry you had to be put through that, but I couldn't say anything to him. It would've been too awkward."

"I understand."

"Yes, I suppose you do." He didn't have anything else to say, but he liked standing beside her in the starlight. She was a peaceful woman to be with—not like some others he'd known.

The silence stretched on and on until Taylor couldn't stand another minute of it. She snatched at a chance for conversation, knowing Sippy waited for her. "Do you think Yates will let his girls and Maida visit Marissa Ferguson?"

"I suppose. But he won't take time to go with them."

"Maybe you could go."

"I suppose, but I'd rather not."

"You could send Court. Or Bard."

"I could. Would you go too?"

"No. It would be . . . awkward."

"I suppose it would. I'll send Court." Ward rubbed a hand against the cold stone. He'd send Court as long as Taylor didn't go. He didn't like seeing Court and Taylor together. They were getting too friendly and that could lead to. . . . Court was younger than Taylor, but it didn't seem to matter to either of them.

"Court's a fine man."

Ward clenched his jaw. "Yes. So is Bard."

"I haven't talked to him much. I understand he studied before he came here. It seems he was forced out of London because he spoke for the wrong man."

"So he said."

"He could study American law and be of more value to you as a lawyer. Don't you think?"

"You're right, but first he must finish out his time. He's a good worker and a fine man."

Taylor moved uneasily. Was Ward waiting for her to go inside? But she couldn't until she knew what Sippy expected of her.

Ward looked up at the stars. "They never seemed so bright in England."

"Maybe you were too busy to look at them. Or too young to care."

Ward chuckled. "You're probably right. I'm glad I can enjoy them now."

They stood in silence again. Taylor's nerves tightened more. "Don't feel you must wait for me, Ward. I like the solitude."

He shot a look toward the shacks. Was she waiting for Court? If so, she'd have a long wait! "I think I'll go talk to my men before I go to bed. Good night, Taylor."

"Good night, sir."

He frowned. "Taylor, can you just call me Ward?"

"It's not fitting."

"It is to me. And isn't that what counts?"

"Yes. You're right."

"You call me Ward from time to time anyway." She flushed. "I know."

He chuckled. "Make it all the time and I'll be happy."

"Then I will," she said brightly. Why wouldn't he leave?

"I'll get going." He walked slowly toward the shack. He had nothing to say to the men, but he'd be sure to keep Court from going to Taylor—if that's what he had planned.

At the well Taylor whispered, "Sippy, what do you want of me?"

"Food. And a paper that say I is free."

Taylor pressed her hands to her cheeks. "Did Court say I could make the paper for you?"

"He sure did, Missy Taylor. He done say he would, but he don't got no paper."

Taylor thought of the paper on Ward's writing desk in the corner of his bedroom. Dare she get a piece and use his quill and inkhorn? She'd have to hurry. "Can I get the paper for you tomorrow?"

"Yes, Missy. Court say I could hide in the barn. He say he'll wake me early."

"I'll get you food now and bring the paper to you tomorrow."

"Thank you, Missy Taylor."

Taylor hurried to the cabin and filled a napkin with fish and cornbread, then rushed back out to Sippy. Just as she handed her the food, she saw Ward walking from the shack. "Ward is coming," Taylor whispered weakly.

Without a word Sippy crept around the well to the back side where Ward couldn't see her.

Frowning, Ward stopped beside Taylor. Court had already fallen asleep. Was Taylor perhaps waiting for Bard?

"Taylor, I'm surprised you're still out here," he said evenly.

Could he hear her heart thundering or feel her tremble? "I . . . I was just ready to walk in."

"I think I'll have a drink first."

Taylor jumped for the crank. "Let me draw up fresh water for you." She couldn't take a chance on his seeing Sippy.

"That's not necessary, Taylor."

"I want to do it." She lowered the bucket, dipped up water, and cranked it up. She pulled the bucket toward her and rested it on the side of the well, dipped in the dipper, and handed it to Ward. As their hands brushed, sparks flew. Her heart racing, Taylor jerked her hand away.

Ward trembled and almost spilled water down his shirt. What was wrong with him? He could touch a woman's hand without his nerves tingling, couldn't he? Angrily, he flung the remainder of the water onto the dirt and hung the dipper in place. "I'll go in now."

"Me, too." Taylor walked beside him, her ears tuned to the slightest sound behind them. What would Ward do if he knew she was helping Sippy escape?

Ward shortened his steps to equal Taylor's. Maybe he was wrong about her meeting Court. Maybe she had waited for *him*.

Taylor shivered.

"Are you cold?" Ward asked softly.

"No," she whispered, shivering again.

Ward reached out to touch her, to comfort her, but he drew back. Instead he said, "Cammie is safe here. You have my word on that."

"Thank you. And thank you for allowing me to eat at the table tonight." Her voice broke and she slipped past him into the cabin.

At the ladder she turned and managed a smile. "Good night."

He wanted to keep her a while longer, but he smiled and nodded slightly. "Sleep well."

Her legs weak and shaky, she climbed the ladder into the loft to join Cammie and Brooke.

*F*eeling all thumbs, Taylor made Ward's bed, fluffed his feather pillows, and dropped them in place. She heard Cammie humming as she cleared off the table from Ward's breakfast of biscuits and sausage gravy. Thankfully Ward was already out of the cabin for the morning. He usually was out training the horses or chopping down trees from daybreak until noon, then in for an hour for dinner, and back out until dark. Finishing with the bed, Taylor peeked out the window in time to see the sun brighten the leaves on the trees.

Shivers running up and down her spine, Taylor pulled a paper from the box in the top desk drawer and dipped the quill into the inkhorn. She stopped, her heart racing. Dare she disobey the law to forge a paper for Sippy? Taylor pushed the quill back in the inkhorn and pressed her hands to her breast. Why had she agreed to do it? Last night she could've told Sippy she wouldn't help her. But could she let Sippy be beaten or, worse, killed, because she wanted to be free? Taylor bit back a moan. Just this morning she'd spoken to Court at the well. He'd confirmed that there was danger at Bromley's plantation.

"I must help her," Taylor whispered. "I must!"

Trembling, she pulled the quill from the inkhorn and held it over the paper. Court had told her what to say. Disguising her handwriting, she wrote that Sippy was free because she'd saved her master from a burning house. The law stated a slave was to be freed if he saved someone from death or if he fought in the Revolutionary War. Court suggested this as a believable reason, for Sippy had fresh burns on her wrist from a punishment from Bromley.

Taylor signed the paper with a flourish, using her own dead father's name, Adam Hetherington, and dated it 22 June 1800. She stuck the quill in place and blew on the ink until it was dry, folded the paper, and pushed it into the pockets tied at her waist over her petticoat.

She touched her pocket and closed her eyes. Did she really want to do this? It wasn't too late; she could tear up the paper and burn it in the fireplace. She could tell Court she couldn't help Sippy no matter how much danger she was in.

Taylor bit her lip. How could she not help Sippy?

As Taylor turned away from the desk, she heard Ward's voice at the door: "Where's Taylor, Cammie?"

Taylor leaned weakly against the bed. What if he'd caught her writing out the paper for Sippy?

"She's making your bed, Master Ward," Cammie said.

Praying for strength, Taylor walked out of the bedroom. Was guilt written all over her face?

"Did you want me?" she tried to keep her voice steady.

He stood beside the table, his hat in his hand. His hair was combed neatly and his face fresh shaven. "I must drive in to Darien, and I wondered if you need me to fetch anything."

Her head was so full of Sippy she couldn't think of mundane things. Helplessly she looked at Cammie. "Can you think of anything?"

Cammie pursed her lips. Taylor stood rooted to the spot. Fire popped in the fireplace; outdoors Yates called to Treet. Both were silent until Cammie's eyes lit up.

"Maybe that muslin for a dress for Brooke since she growing so fast," she suggested.

"Muslin?" Ward obviously had no idea what it was.

Taylor rubbed her sleeve that reached just below her elbow. "This is muslin. But I can cut down one of my dresses for Brooke. I don't expect you to provide for her."

"I'll get muslin." Ward peered closer at Taylor. "What's wrong?"

She flushed. She felt as if the paper in her pocket was in full view even though it was hidden by her dress.

"Are you still worried about Bromley? I told you I'd take care of him."

"I know you did. I'm fine. Honestly I am." But she wasn't. Her insides were quivering.

"Then it's decided," said Ward with a grin. "I'll be ready to leave in just a few minutes. Does that give you enough time to get yourself ready?"

She felt too flustered to answer. He wanted her to come along?

The paper felt heavy in her pocket and the responsibility to get it to Sippy even heavier.

"I see she gets ready directly, Master Ward." Cammie giggled and turned away to keep from catching the murderous look in Taylor's eye.

His hat in his hand, Ward thoughtfully frowned at Taylor. "Don't you want to go?"

"Of course, I do! But maybe you should take Maida and the girls. It would be more . . . fitting." Did the excuse sound as foolish to him as to her?

His eyes flashed and he clamped his hat back on. Did she want to stay behind to spend time with Court? They'd been pretty cozy this morning at the well. "Be outdoors as soon as you can," he ordered. "I have Court hitching the wagon now."

The color drained from Taylor's face. "Is Court . . . going, too?"

"No!" Ward stalked out of the cabin. "If she thinks I'm going to throw her and Court together, she has another thing coming," he muttered under his breath.

In the cabin Taylor looked at Cammie questioningly. "What was that all about, Cammie?"

Looking at Taylor innocently Cammie said, "I figured you could do with Master Ward's company. Don't worry none about Missy Brooke. I can take good care of her when she wakes."

"Cammie, what am I going to do with you?" Shaking her head, Taylor turned and quickly climbed the ladder, and quietly so as not to wake Brooke, she changed into her green traveling dress and bonnet. She folded Sippy's paper twice more and stuffed it up her sleeve. She'd try to pass it to Court since she wouldn't be able to see Sippy.

With a silent prayer for help Taylor climbed down the ladder, told Cammie goodbye, and hurried into the yard where a hot August breeze fluttered the leaves on the trees. Ward waited in his wagon, the butt of his flintlock stuck out from the scabbard on the side of the wagon. A powder horn and pouch hung around his neck. Musket ran up and, wagging his tail, whined up at Ward, but Ward ordered him away. Court stood at the head of the team buckling a strap.

"Good morning, Court," Taylor said, her cheeks flaming red. How could she pass the paper to him without Ward seeing?

Court turned with a smile on his lips and a question in his eyes as he pulled off his hat. "Morning, Taylor. Don't you worry about

Brooke. I told Master Ward I'd keep an eye on her and on Cammie. On everything important."

Taylor knew Court was saying he'd tend to Sippy.

Ward tightened his grip on the reins. The look he saw pass between Court and Taylor made his stomach knot.

Taylor's brain whirled with a way to get the paper to Court as she walked closer. All at once the way to do it was clear. She inched out the paper and held it pressed to her palm. As she reached Court, she stumbled and caught herself on his arm. She dropped the paper into his hat and looking flustered, pulled away from him. "I'm sorry. How clumsy of me."

Court eased the paper into the sweat band of his hat and clamped his hat back on. "Don't worry about it at all." Smiling, he took her arm and helped her into the wagon.

Her heart hammering wildly, Taylor adjusted her skirts and carefully sat down. She felt the tension in Ward and darted a look at him. Why was he frowning at Court? Had Ward seen the paper? Surely not! She smoothed her skirts over her knees and took a deep, steadying breath.

"I'm ready when you are, Ward."

He impatiently flicked the reins on the horses and the wagon jerked forward. With a gasp, she gripped the seat to keep from falling against him. She slowly relaxed and at last released her hold on the seat and folded her hands in her lap. It was a very pleasant day for a trip to town—even better because she no longer had to be concerned about Sippy. Court would get the paper to her and send her on her way. Silently Taylor prayed for Sippy's safety.

On the road to town a wayward breeze carried the smell of pine as well as the aroma of the lacy pink flowers covering a tall bush. Trees lined both sides of the road for a long way, then opened into a wide valley. The bright blue sky was dotted with mounds of whipped meringue-like clouds. In the distance Taylor saw a three-story brick house, a huge white barn, and at least a dozen outbuildings. Inside a split-rail fence a herd of cattle and several horses grazed the lush green grass. Big fields of cotton flanked the farmyard.

"That's Austin Grand's place. You'd like his wife, Lady."

Taylor grinned. "Lady?"

"I don't know if that's really her name or a title everyone has given her. They have six children—four girls and two boys."

"That's a fine big family."

"I'd like lots of children, too," Ward said wistfully. He hadn't missed having children of his own until Brooke had come. And Reid, too.

Taylor flushed. The topic suddenly seemed too intimate. "It looks like they must have several slaves to keep their place," she said carefully.

"They do. Austin said he's not for slavery, but he was forced to use them, so he made a pact with his workers—he'll never sell them away. So, they marry and raise families without fear of being torn apart."

"That's nice, I suppose."

"I told Yates that's what I expect from him since he's determined to keep slaves." Ward sat with his gloved hands resting on his knees and the reins looped between his fingers.

"What about Alden Bromley? Does he have a pact with his slaves?"

Ward darted a look at Taylor. What a strange question. "No, no, he doesn't. In fact, he's a harsh taskmaster."

Taylor's heart lightened. If Ward ever learned what she'd done, maybe he'd understand she'd felt forced to help Sippy.

They rode in silence for several minutes, then Taylor asked, "Do you think Negroes have the capacity to learn like we do?"

Ward laughed. "I don't know another woman aside from Kendra who'd ask that question."

Taylor flushed. "I want to know what you think."

"I don't see why they couldn't. They're no different from you and me except for their color. But I'm probably one of the few who actually believes that."

"Reid taught Cammie to spell and write her name during the voyage here."

Ward lifted his brows and shook his head. "Don't ever bring the subject up with Yates."

"I know. I heard him scold Reid and Kendra when they tried to."

"Let's talk about something else, Taylor. You can get in a powerful lot of trouble discussing the rights and wrongs of keeping slaves."

"Shall I tell you how the garden is growing?" she asked sharply.

He laughed. "It's a safer topic."

"Then I can discuss gardens!" She looked straight ahead at the horses' ears. "The beans are ready for picking and the corn has ears. In a few days all the plants will be ready to harvest, even the speckled beans and the okra." She took a deep breath and hurried on. "We had no flower seeds, so we couldn't plant flowers."

"Don't be angry, Taylor. It's not worth it."

"I know." She smiled and felt a little better. "Slavery is a very touchy subject with me. And I can't discuss it with anyone anymore it seems!"

"Maybe we can discuss something less volatile. Like religion." He laughed, enjoying his own joke.

Taylor chuckled softly. "My dear Floyd got in many scrapes talking about religion."

Ward leaned toward Taylor to hear every word she said. Maybe she'd reveal more of her past.

"Floyd believed in living the way Jesus taught, but many so-called religious men didn't want to hear they had to be born again to enter the kingdom of heaven." Taylor dabbed a tear and couldn't go on. "I'm sorry. The memory of Floyd is still very painful."

"I'm sorry for your loss."

She nodded and brushed away another tear.

Just then a man on horseback leaning low in the saddle raced toward them. A cloud of dust billowed out behind him. Ward urged the team closer to the edge of the dirt road to give the rider plenty of room. Quickly Taylor covered her mouth and nose with her handkerchief to block out the dust. But the rider slowed and stopped in a flurry of dust in front of the wagon, forcing Ward to pull up the team.

"It's Alden Bromley," Ward said in a low voice.

Taylor stiffened and coughed. She daintily shook dust from her handkerchief as her stomach fluttered nervously. Was Bromley looking for Sippy?

"Morning, friend Ward." Bromley pulled off his hat and bowed slightly to Taylor. "Miz Taylor, you're looking real pretty today."

"Thank you." The words hurt her throat and she wanted to urge Ward to continue on. She hated the way Bromley looked at her. It would certainly not be safe to meet Bromley on the road alone.

"It's a fine day for a trip to town." Ward managed a smile even though he wanted to rip Bromley's eyes out for leering at Taylor. "But you're heading in the wrong direction, sir."

Bromley's face hardened. "I'm after a runaway—Sippy, the young slave I bought last year from Carter Logan."

Taylor willed herself not to flicker even an eyelash. Could Ward hear her heart thundering or feel her tension? The horses moved just as a crow cawed, then all was quiet.

"Maybe she ran back to the Logan plantation. I heard you bought her away from a husband and a young daughter." Ward kept his voice light, but he wanted to snap in anger for such a dastardly deed.

Bromley chuckled and slapped dust off his pant legs. "That Sippy sure put up a fight, but it didn't do her no good." The smile vanished and Bromley leaned forward, his eyes narrowed into angry slits. "I checked with Carter Logan. She didn't show up there and even if she had, it wouldn't do no good. Her child died two months past and her husband was sold to a man in Georgia." Bromley peered closely at Ward. "You sure you didn't see her?"

"I haven't." Ward squared his shoulders and looked Bromley in the eye.

"I know you got a soft heart for slaves."

"Dare you question my honesty, sir?"

Bromley flushed. "Sorry, Ward. I surely don't." He turned his gaze on Taylor. "What about your woman? Did she see my Sippy?"

Before Taylor could speak Ward said sharply, "This is Taylor Craven! She works for me and is not *my woman*! I resent the implication."

Bromley laughed in a low, seductive laugh. "That's mighty good news to me, neighbor Ward." Bromley eyed Taylor up and down. "Maybe I'll be calling on Miz Taylor. I'm looking for a wife and she fits the bill."

Taylor's heart plunged to her feet. Surely Ward wouldn't allow Alden Bromley to pay her court!

Ward scowled at Bromley. "The woman is in my service and can't consider marriage to anyone."

"Indentured, is she?"

Ward barely nodded to acknowledge it.

"Then I'll be glad to pay what's owing and take her home as my woman."

Taylor gasped in horror.

Bromley's horse danced away from the team. He brought it up short with a sharp command and a tug on the reins. "You ready to talk business, Ward?"

Anger at Bromley's disgusting offer raged through Ward. He kept his voice light as he said, "I have no time for foolish talk. I'm going to town and must be on my way."

"Maybe I won't take no for an answer." Bromley chuckled as he slapped his hat back in place. "I'm on my way to your place now to check on Sippy. Maybe I'll wait there for you to talk business."

"There's no need," Ward said firmly.

Bromley chuckled. "I don't mind waiting a bit." He tipped his hat to Taylor. "Until another day, Miz Taylor."

She moaned and moved closer to Ward.

"You see my Sippy, let me know. She's in for a whipping for sure!" Bromley urged his horse forward and raced away.

His nerves tight, Ward flicked the reins and the team stepped forward, their harness jangling and the wagon swaying and creaking. "That man is trash!"

"I don't want him calling on me!"

"Nor do I! He is a most determined man. Once he was after a mare of mine that I knew he was too heavy-handed for. He stopped by Catawba every day until I sold the mare to someone else." Ward grimly shook his head. "He surely is determined!"

Taylor trembled. "Well, I won't speak to him if he does visit! I'll find a way to turn him away."

Ward glanced at her and saw the determined set of her shoulders. What did she have in mind? Marriage to Court? Ward flicked the reins harder and the team jumped ahead, swaying the wagon so violently Taylor fell against Ward. His heart leaped and he found he liked the feel of her soft body against him. Suddenly he realized he wanted the right to have her close to him at all times, but in a proper way. If he was married to her, he could keep her from both Bromley and Court. Or any other man who wanted her along the way.

Ward's pulse leaped at the idea. He couldn't say he loved her, but he certainly respected and admired her. And since he couldn't love anyone but Audrey Smythe, maybe he'd marry Taylor. It was a perfect plan—one he should've considered from the first day he saw her and admired her.

Flushing, she pulled away and mumbled an apology. Just how long could Ward protect her from Bromley and men like him? She peeked at Ward, but he was so deep in thought she didn't speak.

❧

At Catawba, in the barn, Court handed a bundle of food to Sippy. He also opened the paper Taylor had written and read it for Sippy.

"You must remember what it says so nobody can trick you into saying you're a slave," he told her.

"I remember. That paper say I saved my master from a fire and he set me free 'cause of it." Sippy nodded. "Tell Miz Taylor I won't never forget her."

"I'll tell her. Now, you slip out among the trees and stay hidden until you're past Bromley's place."

Sippy nodded as tears dampened her eyes. "I won't never forget you either, Master Court. Thank you for helping me be free."

"You're welcome. Godspeed." Court watched her slip into the trees and disappear from sight. He'd met Sippy just after Bromley had bought her. She'd been sick with grief, but even so Bromley had worked her until she fell in the field. He beat her daily and wouldn't feed her regularly. Now Bromley wouldn't be able to lay a hand on Sippy ever again.

A grin spread across Court's face. Oh, how he wanted to be there when Bromley discovered Sippy was gone. He wished he could tell Bromley that he was the one to help Sippy, but of course he couldn't. At least he could sit back and watch Bromley's anger mount when he couldn't find Sippy; that would have to be enough.

With a chuckle Court slipped from the barn and out to the horses where Reid and Kendra were going to meet him later.

❧

Bromley stopped at Austin Grand's home and asked about Sippy, but they said they hadn't seen her. He knew they wouldn't give him the freedom to search their place, so he rode away. He'd stop at Catawba, get a free meal, and talk to the women without Ward being there to stand in his way.

At Catawba Bromley tied his horse in the shade of the barn and called Pickle to water him.

Without saying a word Pickle filled a bucket and set it down for the horse. Pickle knew his being a free man rankled the man, since Bromley thought all blacks should be slaves.

Bromley stood in the shade of the magnolia and waited for the women folk to offer him something to eat. Surely they would; it was only polite and neighborly.

With Laurel beside her, Maida walked from the cabin with a forced smile on her face. Kendra had stayed behind in the cabin and refused to come out. Now Maida wished Yates would come in from the field, but she knew he wouldn't. Pickle had taken dinner to the men and had just returned before Bromley had arrived. So she was forced to be hospitable. After all, the man was a neighbor.

"Good afternoon, sir," Maida said as politely as she could.

"Afternoon, ma'am." Bromley passed over Maida to look in delight at Laurel with the sun shining in her blonde hair. She was a beauty all right. Idly he thought he could carry both of them off without straining a muscle. But he might as well get his eyes off Laurel—for Yates Marston would never approve. With Taylor Craven, however, it was different. She wasn't in the Marston family.

"How do, Miss Laurel. You're both looking well. Have you settled in Catawba just fine?"

Kendra heard and saw from the cabin and she doubled her fists. The man was a lecher!

"We're settling in slowly." Maida sat with Laurel on the bench they'd brought to the shade tree earlier. "What brings you here?"

"My slave Sippy ran away. I came to see if any of you have seen her."

"We haven't." Maida hoped he'd never find Sippy.

And Kendra wanted to shout, "I hope all your slaves run away!"

"Why did she run?" Laurel asked.

Bromley chuckled. "Who knows what them blacks are thinking? You know they aren't like we are. Why, they don't bleed when they're stuck. They got no feelings at all."

Laurel's eyes widened. "Is that true?"

Kendra frowned at Laurel's question. Good grief! How could it be true?

"Sure is! Them coloreds don't have the thinking capacity like we do. They're more like animals that way." Bromley liked the sound of his own voice. He liked having pretty women listen to him and believe what he said. He smiled and talked on and on.

ard parked the wagon outside the general store in Darien. Along with the magistrate's office and a bank, the town had a general store, harness shop, carpenter shop, ten homes spread far apart, and a small stone church with the parsonage beside it. The smell of freshly cut lumber drifted from the carpenter shop. Ward jumped to the dusty street and lifted Taylor down. He wanted to pull her close and promise he'd always keep her from danger, but he reluctantly released her. Should he tell her of his idea to marry her? No, for the time being, he decided against it. If he waited until the last minute to convince her that this was the answer to the Alden Bromley problem, she wouldn't have enough time to be afraid of marrying him.

Keeping his voice normal, Ward said with a smile, "You go in the store and get what you want. I have business and will be back shortly to pay for your purchases." He wanted to set a time for the housewright to build the house and see the pastor about a marriage ceremony.

Taylor smiled and walked slowly through the open door into the small, crowded store. The smells of coal oil, leather, tobacco, bolts of fabrics, and dill pickles in a barrel blended together to make a fascinating odor. Shelves filled with various items lined the walls and a line of counters ran down the center of the room. A pudgy man with a red beard and mustache sat behind a counter at the side of the store on a tall, round stool. He looked over the top of his newspaper at Taylor and slowly slid off the stool. He was shorter than she was, with friendly blue eyes and a smile that lit up his face. Cammie had been right. She had needed to get away from Catawba and into town.

"It's right good to see you, ma'am. Beautiful day, don't you think?"

"Very nice—not too hot even though the sun is shining."

"You're from England!" He noticed quickly.

Taylor smiled and nodded. "I've been here over two months though."

"It's a pleasure to meet you. I'm Ian Travis."

"Taylor Craven."

He beamed happily. "Do you live hereabouts?"

"At Catawba Plantation."

"With Ward Marston!"

Taylor nodded. She talked several more minutes until the pleasantries were over and she could state her business without being offensive.

"I need two lengths of muslin, please."

"Right this way. Buttons? Needles or pins? Maybe ribbon?" Ian Travis showed her a roll of pink ribbon and another of blue.

"They're lovely, but I can only purchase the muslin. Thank you kindly, sir. Give me a few minutes to decide the color." Taylor knew she'd get the blue, but she wanted a chance to take in all the fabrics. She'd forgotten the smell and the feel of a store.

Later Ian measured out the blue muslin she chose and folded it carefully. "Very good choice."

"Thank you. I'm making a dress for my little girl, Brooke. She looks pretty in blue."

Just then Ward strode in, greeted Ian, and said, "I'm paying for the cloth, Ian." Ward shook hands with the man and talked about the weather and crops and the horses he'd sold last month. Ian told Ward how his business was doing and about the good health of his family.

While they talked Taylor looked at the ready-made clothes. She saw a shirt that would be nice for Ward since she'd noticed his were wearing thin. She caught her breath in delight at a dress of soft yellow cotton that was embroidered at the neckline and hem with blue and pink and yellow flowers with green leaves. Oh, how she'd love to have the dress!

Ward saw her face as she looked at the dress. "See if it fits and buy it, Taylor."

Her eyes widened in surprise, then pleasure. She looked until she found one to fit her. She'd never bought a ready-made dress. It made her feel strange to have Ward pay for it, but she allowed him to do it.

"Here's the bonnet to go with it." Ian held up a small bonnet with the brim embroidered with the same flowers.

Breathlessly Taylor took the bonnet, removed hers, and tied the new one in place. It made her blue eyes sparkle and her skin glow.

Ward wanted to tell her to leave it on, but he didn't want to arouse her suspicions. He turned back to Ian. "I need twenty-five pounds of flour and sugar, and some flower seeds." As Ian walked away to fill his order Ward turned to Taylor. "I noticed you don't have heavy shoes for walking in the woods. See if you can find a pair that fits. Later we'll have a pair made for you."

Taylor shook her head and said in a low voice, "You've already done too much for me, Ward. I don't need heavy shoes."

He grinned and nodded. "Yes, you do, so get them. If I pick them out, they might not fit."

She could see he was serious and so she hurried to the rack that held a few pair of dark brown leather shoes in an average size for women. She measured them to her feet until she found a pair that fit. It would be nice to wear them while she worked in the garden.

She held the shoes to her, suddenly remembering the shoes Floyd had made for her. For the past four years she'd only worn shoes he'd made for her. Tears scalded her eyes and she blinked them away before she carried the shoes to the counter. She didn't want to have Ward think she was ungrateful for the shoes or the dress and bonnet.

Ward paid the bill, they said their long goodbyes to Ian Travis, and walked outdoors to the wagon. Being in town was exciting. Three women walked past and spoke; a man Ward knew stopped to talk. Finally Ward handed Taylor into the wagon and drove to the church. His stomach fluttered nervously. Maybe he should forget his plan. He glanced at Taylor and suddenly knew he didn't want to.

"Why're you stopping here?" Taylor asked before she could stop herself. She flushed. "I'm sorry. I didn't mean to be impertinent."

"You're not." Suddenly he felt as if he'd let a swarm of bees loose in his stomach. How could he think his idea would be acceptable to her?

She saw the uncertainty in his eyes and frowned. "Is something wrong?"

Ward steeled himself to say what he had to say, what he'd discussed with the minister, Seth Keppel, after he'd left Taylor at the store. "I'm worried about Alden Bromley." And Court, but he didn't say that. "And I have devised a plan to thwart his attention."

"Thank you! I knew you would. I am very relieved!" Taylor

smiled, glad that Ward had once again come to her rescue. "What is it?"

Ward saw the anticipation on her face, and he forced back a groan. Was he going about this correctly?

"What is it, Ward? Surely you can tell me."

"I have given this considerable thought, Taylor." Ward looked down at her hands clasped in her lap, then back into her face. She trusted him! Should he continue?

She smiled and waited patiently for him to continue. Her gaze took in several children who ran past on the street, laughing and shouting. The team moved restlessly, rattling their harness.

"Taylor, I am going to marry you."

She gasped and drew back from him. Had she heard correctly? "Marry me? But I'm married. To Floyd."

"He is dead, Taylor," Ward said softly.

"I know. I forgot. I was thinking about him when I got the shoes. He was a cobbler." How she was rattling on!

Ward barely nodded. He took her hands in his. They were icy cold. "I don't want you to forget him. I want to be your friend and protector."

She looked at their clasped hands, his large and tanned from the sun, hers almost white. Her hands fit into his as if they were made to. "Why?" she whispered unevenly.

"I care for you! And Bromley won't call on you if you're already my wife."

Taylor trembled. "I don't want Bromley calling on me."

"And Yates will allow you to be equal to Maida." Ward quickly added, "I know you are equal, but Yates won't admit it because I bought you from him."

"I would like to be back on the footing I was with Yates and Maida while on the voyage."

"Will you marry me?" Ward waited, barely breathing. If she refused, would he force her? He pushed the thought aside. He'd deal with that if he had to.

She sat quietly a long time until she could assimilate what he'd said. She silently prayed for the right answer until deep inside she heard the still, small voice of the Lord, "I am with you. Marry him."

Ward rubbed his thumb across her hand. "If you marry me, I'll tear up the indenture papers and you'll be a free woman."

"I will marry you," she said softly.

His heart turned over and he couldn't move or speak. Finally he smiled. She'd agreed only after he'd said he'd tear up her paper.

Disappointed, he had hoped she'd agree because she wanted to marry him. But that was ridiculous. She had agreed; now they needed to make it a reality. "I spoke to the minister and he will perform the ceremony now," he quickly told her.

Taylor waited for a rush of panic to attack her, but she felt calm and confident. "Good. May I wear my new dress and bonnet?"

Ward laughed. How could she be so calm? He certainly wasn't! "Of course. I told Pastor Keppel you might want to change and he said you could use his house."

"Thank you."

Ward jumped to the ground and helped her down. He kept his hands at her waist and looked into her face. "I will make a good father to Brooke."

Her heart jerked strangely. "I know."

His mouth suddenly felt bone-dry. "And to . . . our children."

She stiffened. Was she ready for that? Finally she nodded. "Yes, and to our children."

He felt light enough to float in the air as he lifted out the bundle that held her dress and bonnet. Maybe he should wear something more appropriate. He wanted them to look back on this day and remember it in a special way.

Later Taylor stood beside Ward at the altar with Pastor Keppel and his wife. Ward had borrowed a buff-colored double-breasted tail-coat, cut away at the front to wear over his white shirt and buff colored pants. He looked very handsome. Taylor was glad she'd changed into her new dress and bonnet. Mrs. Keppel had picked a bouquet of pink and yellow roses to decorate the altar. The aroma wafted around Taylor. And she knew from this day forward when she smelled roses, she'd remember the vows she'd spoken with Ward Marston.

Against her will she thought back on the day she'd married Floyd Craven. Her parents had been there to witness the joyous occasion. Floyd had longed for his cousin James to come, but of course he'd refused because she'd turned down his own marriage proposal. Taylor had been glad then; James would've ruined the day. And thankfully Floyd hadn't known the reason James refused to attend.

She remembered the glorious kiss she and Floyd had exchanged at the end of the ceremony. How she'd loved him! And he had loved her as much. Now, tears pricked her eyes. Could she accept a kiss from Ward when she'd never been kissed by any man but Floyd?

Ward felt her pull away from him and into herself. What had

caused it? So before Pastor Keppel could tell him to kiss his bride, Ward said, "Thank you for a fine ceremony."

"Yes, thank you," Taylor said, quickly holding her hand out to the pastor and his wife before he could step in to tell Ward to kiss her. Had Ward stopped the pastor from telling him to kiss the bride on purpose, or didn't he know it was part of the ceremony?

"It was a beautiful wedding," Mrs. Keppel said, dabbing at her eyes.

"It was." Pastor Keppel nodded and smiled. "We'd like you to stay for tea."

Ward shook his head as he slipped off the tail-coat. "We must hurry so we can reach Catawba before dark. Thank you for the use of the coat. Come visit us at Catawba when you can."

"We will." Pastor Keppel laid his Bible on the altar and took his wife's arm.

"If I may, I'd like to change my clothes," Taylor said, brushing her hand down her dress.

"Of course." Mrs. Keppel started for the door. "Come with me."

Several minutes later Taylor sat in the wagon beside Ward as they drove out of Darien toward Catawba. Suddenly Taylor laughed.

"What?" Ward asked with a laugh. He was relieved that she wasn't in tears over their hasty marriage.

"It was a surprise when Maida married Yates aboard the *Falcon*. Think what a shock it'll be when we announce that we're wed!"

"It might take Yates a while to get accustomed to it. I had forgotten how he hates change."

They talked about how each one would react to the news, but neither brought up Court Yardley. Ward couldn't bring himself to mention Court's name just in case Taylor might show she cared deeply for him. Taylor didn't mention Court because she didn't even think of Court as a suitor. If she had she might have wondered if Ward even liked Court.

They reached the spot where Alden Bromley had stopped them as they headed into town and Taylor trembled. Her worries flooded in on her. Had Sippy left Catawba? Was she far enough away that she could make it to freedom?

Ward felt Taylor tremble. "Don't worry about Bromley. He won't dare look at you in that odious manner again, or he'll have me to answer to."

"I was thinking of the slave he was chasing."

"Sippy. I talked to her a few times. Nice woman. She'll never get away from him, though. No matter how far away she runs, he'll go after her and return her—even if it's just to kill her."

Taylor bit back an anguished cry. If Bromley did find Sippy, what would happen if they traced the paper back to her? Maybe she should tell Ward what she'd done. But somehow she couldn't bring herself to do it. He might feel he had to tell Bromley.

Just then a rider galloped toward them. Taylor grew rigid. Was it Bromley on a different mount?

Reading her mind, Ward covered Taylor's hand with his. "It's not Bromley. Relax." Ward narrowed his eyes. "If I'm not mistaken, that's the horse I sold to Jake Ferguson for his daughter Marissa."

Taylor sighed in relief, but still slid a little closer to Ward.

He smiled at Taylor. His pulse leaped as she slid close enough to touch him. He hadn't made a mistake by marrying her! Now he had every right to protect her—and touch her and be touched by her!

The rider came closer and called a cheerful greeting. It was a woman and she was riding sidesaddle. Long blonde hair hung below her black hat and touched the shoulder of her black riding habit.

❦

"You must be Ward Marston," she said, her brown eyes sparkling. "I'm Marissa Ferguson. Papa told me all about you. And is this one of your nieces?"

Taylor flushed. Niece, indeed!

Ward pulled to a stop and stared at the woman, his breath caught. Marissa Ferguson looked enough like Audrey Smythe to be her sister!

Taylor looked questioningly at Ward. Why was he staring so intently at Marissa Ferguson?

Ward flushed painfully. "Sorry, Miss Ferguson. You remind me of someone."

"A ghost perhaps?" Marissa laughed, making her even more beautiful.

"Perhaps." Ward moved enough that Taylor was no longer touching him.

She tensed. Why had he done that?

"I am Ward Marston." Ward felt his throat close over, but he forced himself to continue. "This is Taylor Craven. My wife."

Marissa's brows shot up. "Wife?"

Taylor smiled. "Yes. Taylor Marston, actually."

"Yes," Ward said, flushing again. What was wrong with him? "How do you like your mount?"

"Very much! Well-trained, thanks to you." Marissa turned her gaze on Taylor. "Do you ride?"

"No," Ward said.

"Yes," Taylor said.

Ward looked at Taylor in surprise. "I didn't know that."

Taylor shrugged. "You'll learn all about me in time." Turning a little pale Taylor wondered if he would ever learn about James Rawlings. And what would Ward think of her if he did find out?

Marissa lifted her hand in a wave. "It was nice seeing you both. Please come visit Papa and me at Red Oaks."

"Thank you," Ward managed to say in a normal voice. "Please stop in at Catawba to visit."

"I will." Marissa rode away with her laugh floating back behind her.

Taylor waited for Ward to urge the team ahead, but he didn't. "Is something wrong, Ward?" she asked.

He frowned. "Why?"

"Who did Miss Ferguson remind you of?"

"I'd rather not say." His hands icy in his gloves, Ward flicked the reins and the team jerked ahead.

A chill ran down Taylor's spine. Kendra had said Ward had left England because the woman he loved had married someone else. Did Marissa Ferguson look like that woman? If so, it meant Ward still loved her, a thought that sent a shaft of pain through Taylor.

Ward gripped the reins as agony—and memories—filled him. He'd wanted to marry Audrey for years before she'd given him an indication that she felt the same way. He'd been the happiest man alive when he'd proposed marriage and she'd agreed.

"I want a long engagement, Ward," Audrey had said with her arms around him. "Do you mind?"

"I do mind. But whatever you want, sweetheart." He'd kissed her, feeling as if the world was his at last.

During the two years of their engagement he'd set aside money he earned for overseeing his father's estate, money for the house they wanted to build near Yates and Ellen. Ellen and Audrey were best friends even though Audrey was several years younger. Then just a few weeks before the wedding he'd gone to see Audrey only to find her in tears.

He pulled her close. "Audrey, what is it? Did someone die?"

She touched his cheek with her fingertips. "You know I care for you, don't you?"

"Of course! We're going to be married soon."

Audrey cried harder and shook her head. "I am sorry, Ward, but I can't marry you! I can't!"

"But why?" His heart had stopped.

"I should have told you sooner, but I couldn't find the courage!"

"Tell me now." Despite her words, the truth had not dawned on him. Whatever the problem, he was sure he could convince her they could still wed.

But her words ended all that. "I have fallen in love with someone else. And I plan to marry him in a fortnight."

His world had shattered. A few days later he took the money he'd earned and the inheritance his father left him, and set sail for America. Now, after seeing Marissa, all the memories were back, along with the pain.

Taylor touched Ward's arm. "Can I help?"

He couldn't look at her as he shook his head. "It's something I must deal with on my own."

She bit her lip and moved further away from him. Now she knew why he hadn't kissed her at the church. He couldn't stand the thought of kissing someone besides the woman from England.

"Why did you marry me?" Taylor asked stiffly.

Ward sucked in his breath. Yes, why indeed? At the time it had seemed the only answer. Now, it didn't. "To protect you," he finally answered.

"I am indentured to you. That gives you the right to protect me."

"Not from the likes of Alden Bromley." Ward forced the pain back where it had been hiding and thought again of Bromley's persistence. "Bromley wants you, but he won't have you as long as I'm here to stop him."

Taylor relaxed slightly. "Thank you."

He looked at her sharply. "Did you ever love anyone but your husband?"

Taylor gasped. What a question! "No," she whispered as she shook her head.

Why couldn't Audrey have loved him and only him? "Were you engaged long?"

She flushed. "No. We didn't want to have a long engagement."

He nodded, his jaw set. Why had Audrey been so insistent on a long engagement? Had she suspected she'd fall in love with another man?

"We were very happy," Taylor said, her eyes on the road ahead. "We'd hoped to have children immediately, but we were married three years before Brooke was born."

Audrey wouldn't talk about children. He had, but she'd always managed to change the subject. He hadn't realized that until now.

Taylor watched birds fly among the trees they were passing. She caught a movement in the woods and made out a deer. She nudged Ward. "There's a deer."

He jumped. "Oh. Yes. A deer."

Taylor leaned toward Ward. "Don't let a memory ruin your life. You are a blessed man. You have Catawba and your family there with you."

Ward slowly nodded, then laughed. "You're right! I am blessed. I have Catawba and my family." He looked into her eyes. "And a wife."

She barely nodded. A wife. Her!

10

*T*aylor glanced at Ward as he turned off the main road and onto the narrow road between tall oaks and pines that led to Catawba. In the semi-darkness she saw his strong legs, gloved hands holding the reins, a loose-fitting shirt, strong chin, a nose too large for most men but on Ward just right, and his hat pulled down on his forehead. He was her husband.

"Husband," she mouthed. She was going to share his bed tonight! Deep inside she started trembling. She tried to stop it, but the trembling spread out and out until she was quaking so badly she had to grip the seat to keep from falling off. Tears welled up in her eyes and rolled down her cheeks. A sob escaped, then another and another. She must get herself in hand! She brushed at her eyes, but the tears fell faster. The trembling grew worse. She remembered the same thing had happened to her the day she'd started labor to deliver Brooke.

Taylor shivered harder even though the evening air was warm. It had been warm in their cottage that day, too. She'd started having pains that morning after Floyd had left for his cobbler shop where he made and repaired shoes all day long. When he returned after dark she'd said calmly, "Floyd, the baby is coming." He'd shouted for the neighbor to get the midwife, then suddenly she'd started trembling so hard she couldn't stand. Tears had gushed from her eyes.

"Tay, what's wrong?" Floyd had cried.

"I . . . don't know!"

"What can I do to help you?"

"I don't . . . know!"

He had pulled her close and had held her tight in his arms, then had prayed for her until she was calm again and the trembling had stopped. The midwife arrived and soon after Brooke was born—a healthy, beautiful baby girl.

But now Floyd wasn't with her to comfort her or pray for her. Her hands ached from gripping the wagon seat, and her heels made a steady tap-tap on the wagon bed. A sob tore through her tight throat and seemed loud even over the creak of the wagon and the calls of night birds.

Alarmed, Ward pulled back on the reins. Was Taylor crying? Had a tree branch struck her and hurt her? He looped the reins around the brake handle and turned to her in concern. She was crying! Her entire body was shaking as if she had the palsy. Fear stung his heart.

"Taylor, what's wrong?"

"I . . . don't . . . know!" Each word was an agony to force out. "I'm suddenly so frightened!" She sobbed harder.

"Frightened of what?" he cried, feeling at a loss.

She gulped hard. "I am so sorry, Ward. Honestly I am."

"Did you hear a panther? Or see a bear?" Ward peered closely at her. She was scaring him, scaring him more than when he'd almost been struck by a rattlesnake the size of his arm.

Taylor brushed at her tears, but they continued to fall and wet her face and her hands and the front of her dress. "I was sure the Lord said to marry you." The words were muffled between the racking sobs and Ward helplessly leaned closer to hear her. "I was sure I was doing just what God wanted of me." Another sob escaped and she couldn't go on. Quickly reaching into the cuff of her sleeve Taylor pulled out her handkerchief.

Ward reached out to touch her, but gripped his thighs instead. Touching her might make it worse. "I don't know what to say, except I know God is with us both. Always."

"I know." She wrapped her arms about herself and rocked back and forth as tears continued to stream down her face. Even the seat shook with her tremors. "I think perhaps I heard Him wrong."

Ward shook his head. "You didn't! It is right that we wed."

"I am suddenly frightened . . . to share your bed."

He pulled off his hat and rolled the brim tight. What could he say? "I'm nervous, too. But we're married."

"Without love!"

Biting back a moan he looked up at the sky where three stars twinkled. Then he turned to her. "You're my wife."

At a sudden thought she grabbed his arm. "We could have the marriage dissolved since it hasn't been consummated."

He clamped his hat back on. "No!"

"Then what shall we do?" she wailed.

Awkwardly he patted her icy hand. "You're tired and it makes your fears worse. Please, please stop crying and we'll sort it all out."

She took a deep, trembling breath that sounded like Brooke at the end of a long cry. "Are you sure we can . . . sort it out?"

"Yes. I'm sure." He wanted to hold her close and comfort her, but he was afraid she'd start crying again. What was expected of him? This was all new to him. Dare he ask Yates what to do?

"I'm sorry," Taylor whispered.

"I know." But was she? Had she suddenly remembered Court? Was this a hoax to keep him from being a true husband to her?

"I think I'm all right now." The shivering had lessened. She brushed tears off her face and breathed in deeply. "I am quite embarrassed, sir. Quite."

"Don't be." Ward caught up the reins and slapped them against the team. "We'll get home and you can rest."

She sat in silence several minutes. Without looking at him, she said, "Would you mind if . . . if we didn't tell the others of our . . . marriage. In case we do have it dissolved."

He snapped, "I don't want it dissolved."

"Oh," she said in a tiny voice. "Then what shall we do?" She locked her hands together and braced her feet to keep from falling against him. "I don't want the others to . . . know."

He looked grimly ahead at the lamplight glowing from the windows of the cabins. By *others* did she mean Court Yardley? Ward couldn't bring himself to look at her. "I refuse to keep it a secret!" The words sounded harsh, so he added, "Besides, the pastor and his wife have spread the story all over by now."

"Oh."

He had to say something to get them back on an even footing. "It's been a strange day, hasn't it?"

"Yes."

The events of the day flashed through Ward's mind, striking his funny bone. Suddenly he laughed and it rang up into the branches of the trees that lined the road. "A very strange day indeed!"

A laugh broke from Taylor before she knew it was coming. She shook her head. "I never dreamed when we left this morning, we'd return . . . married."

He smiled at her as they neared the cabins. "I'm glad you're feeling better. You gave me a scare."

"I'm sorry. I suddenly became very frightened. Very frightened indeed."

"Look ahead and be prepared." He nodded at the family and

servants gathered to meet them. Lanterns lit the yard. Musket barked a happy greeting, then was quiet.

But Taylor thought of Sippy and shivered. Anxiously she looked around for Court. She had to know if Sippy was gone or if she'd been caught.

Ward stopped the wagon amid glad shouts of hello. For Taylor's ears alone he said in a low voice, "Are you all right now?"

"Yes. Thank you." She still quivered inside, but she'd stopped crying and shaking. She could easily face the others with a calm exterior now. Her eyes were probably puffy and red, but it was too dark even in the light of the lanterns for anyone to notice. Once again she looked for Court, but she couldn't find him.

Ward glanced at her and saw her looking around. Was she longing to catch a glimpse of Court? Ward snapped the reins around the brake handle as Yates stepped forward.

Yates motioned and called, "Treet, unload the supplies. Dancer, Young, drive the wagon to the barn and unhitch the team." Then Yates smiled up at Ward. "What's the news from Darien?"

His stomach doing flip-flops, Ward caught Taylor's hand in his and announced in a ringing voice, "Taylor and I were wed today."

In the dead silence Cammie giggled, but clamped her hand over her mouth and backed away before Taylor could frown at her.

Suddenly Yates, Maida, and the children all spoke at once. Yates turned to his family. "Hush! Give Ward a chance to explain himself."

Kendra glanced around for Court and saw him near Taylor's side of the wagon. Kendra bit her lip. Oh, why couldn't it be Court announcing he'd married her? She flushed crimson and lowered her eyes. What a daring thought! She must not think of Court Yardley in such a manner!

Ward had jumped to the ground, trying to reach to help Taylor alight before Court could. Ward circled Taylor's slender waist with his arm and faced his family, answering more of their questions while Treet quickly unloaded the few supplies and Dancer drove the wagon to the barn. An owl hooted at the edge of the woods.

Reid held his lantern high. "Uncle, Mr. Bromley was here today for his slave Sippy."

Taylor stiffened and felt Ward's arm tighten around her. She sought for Court, found him near the well, and tried to read a message in the way he stood, but couldn't.

"We saw him on the road," Ward said grimly.

Cammie laced her fingers together. Bromley had almost caught her in the garden picking beans, but thanks be to Jesus she'd slipped into the cabin and to the loft where Brooke was taking her nap.

"We'll discuss Mr. Bromley later, Reid." Yates moved restlessly. He wanted to hear if Ward was joking with them or if he was serious about marrying Taylor Craven. After all, they didn't look like happy newlyweds to him. But then neither did he and Maida. At least she was better off with him than with her aunt and uncle. Maybe one day he and Maida could be content being together, but that was something that Yates wasn't going to worry about right now. He had a fortune to make first and then maybe he could take time for his family.

Taylor wanted to break away from Ward and run to Court for word of Sippy, but she didn't dare.

Yates wagged a finger at Ward. "Tell us if you're having a bit of a joke at our expense."

Ward felt Taylor's tension and he forced a smile. He didn't want them to think he'd coerced her into the marriage. And she certainly wasn't acting as if she'd been a willing partner. "We are husband and wife. How better to create a dynasty here at Catawba?"

Taylor's legs trembled and she leaned heavily on Ward to keep from falling.

"Welcome to the family." Maida hugged Taylor and kissed her lightly on the cheek. "We'll talk tomorrow," she whispered in Taylor's ear.

Yates shook hands with Ward, then brushed Taylor's cheek with his lips. He couldn't bring himself to say he was glad she was in the family. He'd just worked out a scheme this morning after he'd visited Ferguson's plantation Red Oaks that would've made Catawba into an empire—Ward would marry Marissa Ferguson and when she inherited the Ferguson plantation, it would become part of Catawba. When he'd seen how much Marissa looked like Audrey Smythe he'd thought Ward would be more than willing to comply. Now, that couldn't happen. Hiding his sudden anger, Yates turned away to let Laurel and Reid congratulate Ward and Taylor.

Finally Court and Bard stepped forward to offer their regards. Court tried to think of a way to get Taylor away from Ward's side, but he couldn't.

"God's best to you both," Court said, smiling.

"Thank you," Taylor whispered.

Ward nodded. What was the look that passed between Court and Taylor?

His hat under his arm, Bard tipped his head slightly and the lantern light turned his blond hair gold. "May your lives together be happy," he said, smiling.

Several minutes later Ward led Taylor to the cabin. Cammie had already gone to the loft, leaving a lamp burning on the table and the fire banked carefully for the night. The smell of cornbread drifted out from a covered pan on a shelf beside the fireplace.

Hanging her bonnet on a peg, Taylor glanced across the room to the open bedroom door. Suddenly the strength left her legs and she started to sink to the floor.

With a low cry Ward caught her and lifted her in his arms almost as easily as he did Brooke. Tears gushed down her cheeks and she shook like a leaf during a windstorm.

Ward stood in the middle of the floor and looked helplessly down at Taylor in his arms. Her face was wet with tears and her eyes were closed tightly. Did he frighten her this much? Or was this to keep him away from her? He inched a chair away from the table with his foot and sat down with Taylor in his lap. She buried her face into his chest and clung to him.

"There, there," he whispered hoarsely as he cradled her close and patted her back. What should he do? Was he so undesirable and frightening that she couldn't tolerate sharing his bed? He cringed at the terrible thought.

She sobbed against his shirt—sobbed because she was afraid of sharing his bed; because Floyd was dead and James had killed him; because she'd been forced to flee to South Carolina without money to provide for herself, Brooke, and Cammie; because she had been forced to marry to keep Alden Bromley from looking too closely at her or Cammie; but mostly because deep in her heart a flame of feeling for Ward Marston was flickering when Floyd had been dead only these few short months and Ward still loved a woman from his past.

"There, there," Ward whispered again. He wanted to take away her fear and pain and bring a smile back to her lips and a sparkle to her eyes. It was beyond him to do that, but he knew the God of miracles. "Comfort her, Holy Spirit," Ward said against Taylor's hair. "Fill her with peace until there's no room for fear and anguish."

Taylor felt Ward's heart beating against her face and she heard his quiet prayer. Slowly the trembling stopped and her tears dried. But she didn't move. It felt good to be held as if she were a child again. For a while she could forget she was a mother to a year-old daughter, that she was responsible for Cammie and her unborn baby, that she had written a note to say Sippy was a free Negro, and that she was in danger from James Rawlings.

Ward rubbed his cheek against her soft hair. She fit in his arms as if she was made for them. "Are you all right now?"

She brushed at her wet cheeks. "I guess so." Still she didn't move off his lap.

His arms tightened around her and he moved his head until his lips brushed her hair. He felt the jolt through his entire body. He wanted to lift her face and touch his lips to hers. The desire surprised him. He'd thought his feelings were dead after Audrey Smythe. But maybe his feelings had nothing to do with love, but with a natural desire to hold a woman and kiss her.

Taylor lifted her face and met Ward's eyes. "Thank you. I should be all right now."

"Good." He smiled slowly, but didn't release her.

She looked at his lips and a yearning for him to kiss her rushed through her, startling her. She pushed against his chest. "I'm too heavy to sit on your lap! I'm not a child."

"You most surely are not." He grinned and slowly, reluctantly set her free.

She stood and wriggled her skirts in place. "I can make supper for you." How could she speak of such mundane things when she was wondering how it would feel to have him kiss her?

"That'd be fine." He liked the way her hair had come loose and hung down on her shoulders. Slowly he stood. This woman before him was his wife. And she wasn't Audrey Smythe. He tried to bring up a picture in his mind of Audrey, but he couldn't find her in his memory right now. He brushed a strand of hair off Taylor's damp cheek. "Cammie has something on the shelf. That'll be enough."

Taylor wanted to step into Ward's arms and lay her head against his chest again. "I smell cornbread."

He wanted her in his arms again. "I like cornbread."

Just then Yates hammered on the door and shouted, "Ward, Pickle's gone!"

Ward leaped to the door and flung it wide. "When did you see him last?"

"Just before you drove in. He probably ran. Bromley says they all do if you don't show them they're slaves."

"Bromley's a mean-tempered man without a heart." Ward rushed out the door. "Pickle's an old man and he's not a slave. He could have collapsed and been hurt."

Taylor ran out after Ward and caught his arm. "Pickle told me he saw a panther after one of the hogs last night."

Ward turned Taylor toward the cabin. "Get back inside where you'll be safe."

Frustrated, Taylor hurried back inside. Cammie was standing at the door wringing her hands. Taylor closed the door and faced Cammie. "Do you know where Pickle is?"

"Last I saw he was working in the garden. He weren't near no pigs for no panther to get him."

"Then what happened to him? Tell me, Cammie!"

She closed her eyes and moaned. A log snapped in the fireplace.

"Cammie?" Taylor said sternly.

Cammie lifted her head and she looked ready to faint. "I don't want to make trouble for nobody."

"I know."

"Missy Laurel done sent Pickle out after some honey. She wouldn't let him wait till morning like he wanted to do. She got real uppity like she sometimes does and she said he had to do what she said when she said or she'd have him whipped."

"Whipped? What has come over Laurel?"

"She listened to that mean Bromley man!"

Taylor nervously brushed back her hair. "Why didn't Pickle speak to Court? He would've told Laurel to wait for the honey."

"I say it weren't no business of mine, Miz Taylor." Cammie bit her lip. "Missy Laurel don't like me butting into her affairs. She told me that, Miz Taylor."

"I'll take care of it." Taylor rushed outdoors to the sounds of night bugs. Stars twinkled overhead while lantern lights bobbed in the trees. The sound of voices drifted back to the yard.

˜

Kendra stood on the edge of the trees watching the men starting the search for Pickle. Kendra longed to run after them to help but she knew that would be forbidden. There was too much danger in the forest after dark. With so many wild animals and swamps a person could be lost forever. Sighing, Kendra turned toward the cabins and started walking back. Her thoughts were on Court, wondering where he had gone. He wasn't with the others as they had left and Kendra figured he had gone a separate way. Her head down, deep in thought, Kendra suddenly came to an abrupt stop as she collided with something solid. Strong hands closed around her arms and she looked up. Court.

"Excuse me, miss." Court hadn't been looking where he was going when Kendra had bumped into him. His mind had been full of Pickle. Quickly Court turned and started walking past Kendra.

"Court, wait." Kendra turned to face him, placing her slender hand on his arm. "Can I go with you? I really would like to help search for Pickle."

Looking at her with shock at such a suggestion, Court stepped back and Kendra's hand fell away from his arm. He couldn't have her touching him. Seeing Kendra every day was difficult enough, but to have her touch him when Court knew no one was around was too much. All he wanted to do was clutch her in his arms and kiss her.

"No, you cannot go," he snapped.

"But what if something happens while you're out there by yourself? You could get hurt and no one would be able to help. Please, Court, let me go with you." Kendra looked up at him with pleading eyes. "I couldn't stand it if something happened to you."

That was the last straw. Pulling her hard against his chest Court lowered his head and captured her lips. This is what he had been dreaming of since that first day on the dock. Moaning deep inside, Court knew that they could never be together. He surrendered his heart completely to Kendra with this last kiss. They could never let this happen again, but she felt so good in his arms that Court couldn't let her go yet.

Kendra couldn't believe this was happening to her. All her dreams were coming true. Court still loved her or he wouldn't be kissing her right now. Clinging to him, Kendra returned his kiss with all the love that was bottled up inside her. This was where she belonged—in Court's arms.

Pulling away abruptly, Court looked deep into Kendra's eyes with a longing that frightened her a little. Kendra gasped as if she had been running for hours. Was it always like this when you kissed a man?

"Go back to the cabin, Kendra." Court turned abruptly and started stalking off. Running his hand through his hair, Court wondered what man would be allowed to marry his Kendra.

Watching Court walk away, Kendra felt a sudden panic. What was happening? Could Court just turn his love on and off so easily? With a whimper Kendra turned and started back to the cabins.

❦

Taylor ran to the other cabin and knocked and called, "Maida! It's me—Taylor."

Maida opened the door and gripped Taylor's arm. "Maybe Pickle took a gun and is going to kill us all in our sleep!"

Taylor frowned and pulled back from Maida. "Where did you ever get such an idea?"

Maida pressed her hand to her heart and shivered. "That Alden Bromley told us about a slave who got a gun and shot every member of the family that owned him, then ran away. They never caught him to this day."

"Maida, this is Pickle we're talking about. Pickle! He taught us both how to spin and weave, cook in the fireplace, tend a garden. Pickle, Maida! He's a free man! He cares about all of us."

Maida sank to a chair and groaned. "I don't know what's wrong with me, Taylor. I've changed! I am a totally different woman from before when I was with my aunt and uncle. I sometimes don't even like myself!"

Taylor hugged Maida. "We'll talk later. Right now I must speak with Laurel."

"She's in the loft."

Taylor glanced toward the loft, then back at Maida. "Kendra? Reid?"

"Reid went with Yates and Kendra is somewhere outdoors. She wanted to go search too, but Yates wouldn't let her. I tried to keep her inside, but she has a mind of her own."

"She'll be all right. I must speak with Laurel." Taylor ran to the ladder and called, "Laurel, come down, please."

Trembling, Laurel lifted her head from her pillow. "I'm tired."

"Laurel, I know about the honey. Come down now!"

"What honey?" Maida asked, frowning.

Laurel scrambled down the ladder. Her face was as white as her lacy nightcap and her eyes were red-rimmed. "It's not my fault he didn't come back!"

"We must tell your father so he'll know where to send the men."

Laurel pressed against the ladder and shook her head. She hated when Papa got angry and she knew this would make him very angry. Everyone, especially Bard, would detest her. He already thought she was worthless. "How do I know where Pickle went?"

"You told him to get the honey. You know where it was."

Maida groaned. How could Laurel do such a thing?

"Tell me," Taylor said in a kind, but firm voice.

Laurel finally nodded. "Near the swamp on the other side of the cotton field."

Maida gasped and leaped up. "Near the swamp? You know Court warned all of us about going near there! He said the snakes are dangerous when it gets so hot during the day."

Laurel burst into tears. "I know. But I thought Pickle couldn't be hurt by a snakebite. That Mr. Bromley said Negros aren't like real people no matter what we've been told. They don't have feelings and don't even bleed if they get hurt."

Gently Taylor pulled Laurel close. "He's wrong, honey. Remember when Cammie cut her arm when we were on the *Falcon*? It did bleed and it hurt so badly she cried. She cried real tears."

"I guess I forgot." Laurel clung to Taylor. "I am sorry, Taylor! I know you're right. I don't know what's wrong with me! My heart feels dead inside."

"I'll tell Ward where Pickle went," Taylor said.

"Shall I go with you?"

Taylor kissed Laurel's cheek. "No. Stay here. And you remember this—your heart isn't dead at all. You ask Jesus to melt that stony heart and fill you with love again."

"I will." Laurel brushed at her tears. "I'm really sorry about Pickle."

"I know." Taylor hurried out, leaving Maida to talk with Laurel. Soft wind blowing her hair and her skirts, Taylor stopped near the well. She could see only one lantern light flashing among the trees.

Just then Kendra ran across the yard to Taylor. "I want to help look for Pickle! They wouldn't let me go, Taylor!"

"I know. I just learned where he went. Where's your papa or your uncle?"

"Out there somewhere. But Court's there." Kendra pointed at the light, then pressed her hand to her fluttering heart. She'd begged him to take her, but he'd refused.

"I'll tell him." Taylor ran for the woods, wishing she had her new shoes on. She stopped just inside the woods and shouted for Court. She saw the light come into full view and she called again. Dare she walk further into the woods?

"I'm going with you," Kendra said from the edge of the trees.

"No! Your father will be very angry if you do. Wait in the yard!"

Kendra sighed heavily and walked slowly back to stand beside the well. "I am not a child, no matter what they think," she said under her breath.

Taylor hesitated, then hurried deeper into the woods. She couldn't get lost as long as she saw Court's light. An owl hooted and she jumped. Did snakes come out at night? What if she stepped on a poisonous one? She lifted her skirts and tried to watch where she put her feet. It was too dark. She stopped again.

"Court, come here!" she called.

"Taylor, what are you doing out here?" Court responded as he hurried toward her.

"Laurel said Pickle went to get honey near the swamp on the other side of the cotton field."

"He'd never go there this time of night."

"She ordered him to."

Court stopped beside Taylor and said in a low voice, "I know this isn't the time to speak, but I must. I gave the paper to Sippy and she left. She said to tell you thank you."

"I'm glad Mr. Bromley didn't catch her."

"He'll keep looking and he'll send word out on her." Court sighed heavily. "You get back to the yard and I'll see if I can find Pickle."

"But it won't be safe for you!"

"I can't leave him out there."

"I know." Taylor turned, then frowned. "Where're the cabins?"

Court turned her part way around and pointed. "You keep your eye on that light you see through the trees. If you can't see it, you're going in the wrong direction. Then you stop and look until you see it again."

"Thank you! You be very careful, Court."

"I will. Now, get going, so I can be on my way."

Taylor kept her eye on the light and ran as quickly as she could back into the yard.

Kendra caught Taylor's hand. "Is he going after Pickle?"

"Yes."

"Oh, what if he gets caught in the swamp?"

"He has a gun and a knife."

"I wish he'd come back and wait until morning!" Kendra burst into tears. "I don't want him to get hurt!"

Patting Kendra's shoulder, Taylor said, "You care for him very much, don't you?" Kendra nodded her head. "Then let's pray for him. And for the others. Especially Pickle."

"Yes! Let's do!"

Taylor clasped Kendra's hands and she prayed for a safe return of the men and for special protection for Pickle and Court.

Kendra brushed at her tears. "Mama would've prayed for them too, Taylor. But I didn't think to. Why didn't I?"

"Because you're thinking of other things more than you're thinking of God. Tomorrow we'll start meeting together again to have Scripture reading and prayer like we did on the *Falcon*. It'll help us all."

"I'd like that. Um, Taylor, you won't say anything to Papa about Court and me, will you?"

Taylor slipped an arm around Kendra and walked her back toward her cabin. "I won't say a word, and if you start being afraid again, you pray for the men."

Kendra hugged Taylor tightly. "I am glad you married Uncle Ward! You're much nicer than Audrey Smythe."

Taylor looked at Kendra curiously. "Who is she?"

"The girl Uncle Ward was going to marry. She married a duke instead. It broke his heart. Laurel says Marston men only love once in their lives, but she was wrong. Uncle loves you." Taylor felt numb all over. So Marissa Ferguson had reminded him of Audrey Smythe. Taylor bit back a moan. They had married knowing they didn't love each other. But she had thought she could learn to care for him after a while. What about him? Was it possible he'd never love anyone but Audrey Smythe?

"Is something wrong, Taylor?"

"Nothing that concerns you. I must speak to Laurel before I go to my cabin." Taylor hurried Kendra to the cabin and they stepped inside. The lamp and the log burning in the fireplace cast a soft glow over the room. Maida and Laurel sat at the table with cups of tea.

"Yes?" Laurel said eagerly. It was a whole passel of questions lumped in one word.

Taylor rested her hand lightly on Laurel's shoulder. "I sent Court after Pickle."

Laurel sighed in relief. "I'm glad."

Kendra shook her finger at Laurel. "Why are you glad? Court could get hurt! It's dangerous out there at night!"

"Girls, girls," Maida said tiredly. She held up the teapot. "Would you two like a cup?"

Kendra shook her head and ran to the ladder. "I don't have the stomach for food or drink! Excuse me, please."

Taylor watched her climb up and disappear. Laurel stood up and walked toward the ladder to follow Kendra.

"I'll talk to her," Laurel said.

Taylor started for the door. "I must get home to see Brooke. I missed her today."

"I saw her running around the garden by herself this afternoon," Maida said.

Taylor stopped short. "What?"

"It made me rather nervous."

"Where was Cammie?"

"Talking to Treet."

"I'll speak with Cammie about this!" Taylor excused herself and ran to her cabin. Cammie was waiting near the fireplace where a cricket sang loudly.

"Cammie, Maida said you let Brooke run around the garden by herself while you talked to Treet!"

Cammie hung her head. "I'm sorry, Miz Taylor. I turned my back for just a minute when Treet stopped to talk and she was off and running before I could stop her."

Taylor forced back her fear of what could've happened if Brooke had wandered alone into the woods. "Please be more careful in the future."

"Yes, ma'am. I watch her real close. I promise!" Cammie sighed heavily. "There just be something about that man Treet. My heart goes pitter-pat when he walks by."

Taylor sank to a chair. "Does Treet know you're going to have a baby?"

Cammie shrugged. "He never asked and I never told him, but he'd have to be a blind man not to know."

"You know he doesn't like children."

"I know, Miz Taylor." Cammie sank back weakly against the log wall. "I don't know what's wrong with that man."

"Don't fall in love with him, Cammie. He'll break your heart when he won't marry you because you're having a child."

"It's too late, Miz Taylor. I loved him from the minute I seen him on the block down in Charleston."

"Cammie, Cammie."

"I been praying for him. Jesus can fill him with love—so much love it'll spill right over on me and my baby."

Taylor smiled. "That'd be nice, Cammie."

"I been praying the same for Master Ward—that love fill him till it spills over on you and baby Brooke."

"Cammie!" Taylor helplessly shook her head. Was it possible for Ward to love her and Brooke since he still seemed to be in love with Audrey Smythe? "I'll go up and see Brooke."

"I done brought your things down and put them in Master Ward's room."

Taylor flushed. "Thank you." She climbed the ladder and looked down at Brooke on a mat on the floor. Her cheeks were flushed and her baby-fine hair mussed. "Good night, sweet baby," Taylor whispered. She kissed her fingers and touched Brooke's warm cheek. "God is with you."

Slowly Taylor climbed back down. Tonight she'd sleep in a bed again, but far from the circumstances she'd planned.

"I'm going to bed now. Good night, Miz Taylor." Cammie giggled and climbed up the ladder.

Taylor stared into the fireplace at the log glowing against the back stone wall. Finally she turned the lamp low and walked slowly to the bedroom. She changed into the nightdress Cammie had laid out for her, then crept into bed. When would Ward return?

She heard the log snap and Brooke whimper in her sleep. Outdoors an owl screeched and indoors a cricket sang its cheery melody. Taylor's eyelids drooped and she felt as if she was sinking lower and lower into the bed.

Much later Ward walked quietly into the room. His heart fluttered seeing Taylor asleep in his bed. He wanted to crawl in beside her, but he couldn't until Court was back. Maida had told them where Court had gone to find Pickle. Ward had wanted to go after them both, but had decided it wouldn't be wise. If anyone could bring Pickle back safely, Court could.

Taylor moved in her sleep.

Ward smiled down at her, but quickly turned away and hurried outdoors. Musket pushed his wet nose into Ward's hand. Slowly he walked to the well and leaned against the stone foundation. Musket sank at his feet. Quietly Ward prayed, "Father God, take care of Court and Pickle. Bring them back safely."

When Ward heard a slight sound, he turned to find Kendra standing nearby.

"Could I wait with you, Uncle?" she whispered.

"Yes." Ward held out his hand and she gripped it tightly.

11

*H*is gun hanging down his back, Court carried Pickle into the yard as easily as he'd carry an armload of wood. He recognized the night sounds around him and knew he had nothing to fear.

Holding the lantern high, Ward ran forward with Kendra beside him.

"Is he hurt?" Ward asked.

What Kendra wanted to do was fling herself against Court and ask if he was safe. However, she had to be content just to look at him and listen to him.

"Bees stung him, but with care he'll be fine." Court eased Pickle to the ground beside the well, set the bucket that held the honeycomb and honey next to the well, and filled a dipper of water for Pickle—a dipper used only by the slaves and servants. It wasn't proper for them to drink out of the same dipper as the master and his family, or so Master Yates had said when he'd put out the second dipper. At the time Court wanted to smash the dipper and leave only one, but he didn't give in to his anger.

As Ward knelt and talked to Pickle, Kendra grabbed the opportunity, stepped close to Court, and asked in a strained voice, "Are you all right?"

Court's pulse leaped. Did she care? His eyes searched for an answer while he whispered, "I'm fine." He just couldn't say more to her without his voice giving away the strong emotion he felt. He smelled the clean aroma of her hair and heard her quick breathing. Why wasn't he free to show her how he felt?

Kendra tried to see Court's face to know for sure if he was all right, but his hat kept it in shadows. She wanted to touch him, to have him reassure her. Instead she tried to use the words to say what couldn't be said. "Thank you for bringing Pickle back safely."

Court shrugged. "I'm glad I found him."

"I'm glad you're safe." Then blushing at her boldness, she ran through the darkness to the cabin before she said something more embarrassing.

Court didn't want to watch her leave, but he couldn't help himself. When she disappeared inside the cabin he forced his racing heart back to normal and knelt beside Ward and Pickle.

"I smeared cold damp dirt on him to draw out the poison," Court said.

Ward nodded. "That should help."

"I ain't never been stung by so many bees." Pickle swallowed another drink of water. "My eyes done swole right shut and I couldn't tell where I was."

"It was a good thing you stopped where you did," Court said to Pickle, then turned to Ward. "He was almost in the swamp."

"I done got the honey," Pickle said.

Ward's jaw tightened. "It was too dangerous to go out no matter what my niece said. You know that, Pickle."

"I know that and you know that, but that little miss wouldn't listen to me."

"We'll talk about it tomorrow. Court, take Pickle to bed and I'll tend him after I set the honey inside." Ward picked up the bucket and started to walk away.

"No need to watch over me. I'll be just fine." Pickle eased himself up.

"If he wakes up, he can call Treet," Court said.

Ward finally agreed. "I'm thankful you're both back safely."

"Me, too," Pickle said as Court picked him up again.

"Good night. Sleep well." The bucket in hand, Ward slowly walked to his cabin. Tomorrow he'd speak to Laurel about her high-handed manner, no matter how angry Yates might get.

Ward set the bucket on the table and peeked in at Taylor. Her lashes long against her rosy cheeks, she was sleeping soundly. He wanted to wake her, but he was afraid she'd be so frightened again she'd burst into tears. He sighed as he undressed and slowly slipped in beside her. He lay awake a long time listening to her breathing.

Yates turned his back on Maida and burrowed his head into his pillow. "I don't want to hear another word about Laurel."

Maida raised up on one hand and frowned down at Yates. "If Pickle would've died, Laurel would be to blame. Doesn't that distress you at all?"

It did, but he couldn't admit it to Maida. "Leave me alone. I'm too tired to talk about anything tonight."

Maida flopped back down and sighed loudly. "You should talk to Laurel about her behavior. It's not my place to say anything."

"Will you keep quiet?" Yates snapped. "How can a man get to sleep?"

Maida moved away from Yates and as close to the wall as she could get. Why had she married this terrible man? She lay with her eyes open, staring at the shadows from the fire.

❦

In the loft Kendra jabbed Laurel's arm. "How dare you put Court and Pickle in danger!"

"Be quiet!" Laurel rubbed tears off her cheeks. She'd been feeling terrible since she'd been so mean to Pickle, but she couldn't very well say so.

"Pickle almost went in the swamp! What if Court had?"

"I don't care! Leave me alone!"

Kendra flopped back on her pillow with a long, ragged sigh. Something was wrong with Laurel. She'd always been too prissy, but she'd been kind-hearted. Now she was mean. "I don't like you at all," Kendra whispered. And she hoped Laurel had heard.

❦

The next morning Taylor woke with a start to the smell of porridge. Daylight streamed through the window, and Cammie was humming in the kitchen. Where was Ward? Taylor touched his pillow. He had come to bed! But he hadn't awakened her! Had he wanted to or had he been relieved to find her asleep?

Taylor slipped out of bed and grabbed her robe. "Cammie, did you see Ward this morning?"

"No, but I done seen a beautiful bucket of honey so sweet it makes your toes curl."

"That means Court came back with Pickle!" Taylor's hand trembled as she tried to tie her robe in place. "Cammie, look out the door and see if you see anyone."

Cammie grinned. "Master Ward be that anyone, Miz Taylor?"

"Cammie! Just look out the door." Taylor pulled her emotions into line, smiled, and added, "Please."

Smiling, Cammie opened the door, letting in a rush of pleasantly cool fresh air and the sound of a rooster crowing. "Master Ward and Master Yates both out there by the well. And they look real mad."

"I'll get dressed." Trembling, Taylor hurried to the bedroom.

§

Outdoors Ward faced Yates squarely. Ward stood almost a head taller than Yates and they were both dressed for outdoor work. "I tell you, it's Laurel's doing that Pickle's laid up and in pain! She must learn to respect others, Yates," Ward insisted.

Yates reared back. "Respect a darkie?"

"He's a man the same as we are!"

Yates growled deep in his throat. Ward always had been hard-headed. "How will making her nurse Pickle help teach her that?"

"You know how. You can object all you want, but Laurel will indeed tend to Pickle until he's well. That's my final word!"

Yates jabbed a finger into Ward's chest. "And why should you have the final say, brother? You're younger than I am. Laurel is my daughter. And half of Catawba is mine—so half the say is mine."

Looking away to calm down, Ward watched a crow fly into a tree and heard Bard singing as he milked the cow. "Yates, we have to decide what we want for Catawba."

"I know what I want!" Yates waved his hand to take in all he could see. "I want a grand house like we saw in Charleston. I want acres of cotton to make us wealthy. I want our neighbors to look in awe on us."

Ward shook his head. "Brother, you didn't say a word about helping others like you always did before. What happened to caring? That was all part of your dream before."

Yates knotted his fists and his eyes were filled with pain. "I lost my wife and my baby! I lost everything!"

"But you have three children. You have Maida. And you have me." With that, Ward thumped his own chest.

Yates brushed the words aside. "You asked what I wanted of

Catawba and I told you. I didn't expect a sermon or a lecture. Suppose you tell me what you want?"

"I want Catawba to be a big plantation known far and wide for its hospitality and, of course, its horses. I want to continue to breed and train horses. I don't mind raising cotton as long as I can pay the workers and not keep slaves. If I must raise less crops, then I must."

Just then Court hurried toward Yates and Ward to tell them about Pickle's condition. As he approached, Yates's eyes flashed. "I plan to marry my girls to wealthy landowners to assure their futures."

Yates's announcement brought Court up short. How could Yates marry off his girls for wealth instead of love? Would Kendra and Laurel agree to it? Court knew the answer. They would because they'd been raised to be obedient English ladies. The thought of Kendra with another man brought a flash of anger to Court's eyes.

Yates scowled at Court. "Did you want something?"

"Yes, sir."

"What? Speak up!"

"What is it, Court? Did Pickle take a turn for the worse?" Ward asked.

Court nodded. "The swelling around his eyes is worse. And it's hard for him to swallow."

"Bring him on his pallet out here under the magnolia tree where he'll get fresh air. It'll be better than the dusty shack. I'll get Laurel." Ward strode to Yates's cabin and thumped on the door.

Maida opened the door and frowned slightly. She was already dressed, but her hair still hung down on her shoulders. The smell of porridge drifted out. "What's wrong?"

"I need Laurel out here now. Pickle is worse."

"I have some tea that'll help. I'll brew it while Laurel's getting dressed." Maida hurried across the room and called up to Laurel.

"I'm still sleepy," Laurel said even though she was wide awake, unlike Kendra who was sleeping soundly.

"I have a job for you," Ward said sharply.

"Uncle Ward?" Trembling, Laurel peeked down from the loft. "What is it?"

"Pickle is bad off from bee stings. I want you to nurse him back to health."

"You don't have to do it," Yates snapped from behind Ward.

Laurel thought about refusing, but decided against it. She was to blame and she had to do something to assuage her guilt. "I'll get dressed and be there shortly."

"I don't want you to nurse that slave!" Yates's face was dark with anger.

The shout woke Kendra and she sat up, her eyes wide in alarm.

"But Papa, it was my fault. I want to do it." Laurel's statement surprised herself as much as the others.

"And he's not a slave!" Kendra shouted down. "He's free! He helped fight in the war with the Swamp Fox and he's a free man because of it!"

"Stop it," Yates growled. His face dark with anger, he glared at Ward. "You've done this to my girls! They were good English girls before they came here. We should've stayed where we belonged!"

"You belong here," Ward said softly.

Yates frowned at Ward, then stormed out of the cabin.

"I'm sorry," said Maida, almost in tears.

"I'll settle it with him later." Ward smiled. "Don't worry about his leaving. He wasn't serious."

Maida turned away with her head down. At times like this she didn't know if she'd ever set it straight with Yates. Since that was such an unpleasant thought, Maida's mind drifted in another direction. One day, surely, she and Yates would be content with being together, wouldn't they?

Ward smiled up at Laurel. She looked like the little girl he remembered in her white nightcap. "Court will show you what to do and Maida is making special tea for him. Hurry out now."

"I will, Uncle."

Ward excused himself to Maida, and emerged from the cabin in time to hear Yates shout to Dancer, Treet, and Young to follow him to the field they were clearing to be ready for cotton for next year.

Yates swung the grubbing hoe to his shoulder without acknowledging Ward and hurried out of the yard. It was hard work to grub out the roots Ward had left behind when he chopped down the trees to be lumbered for the shipbuilder, but once the ground was readied, it would be perfect for cotton. "And I will buy more slaves and raise acres of cotton!" he proclaimed under his breath, but it felt as if he'd shouted it until folks in the next county heard.

A herd of deer leaped across the field and out of sight in the woods. Yates lifted his grubbing hoe and swung it hard into the ground. He'd work himself to the bone if need be to have a good crop next year. But when he had enough slaves, he'd take care of business the way a gentleman did and never again dirty his hands with physical labor.

He glanced up and watched the slaves working nearby. They were hard workers. As soon as he could he'd have a dozen of them. He frowned. He should've thought to have Reid come grub out stumps instead of train that sorrel gelding for Ward. Reid had to learn Yates was his father, not Ward.

❦

Standing outside the cabin, Taylor watched Ward stop at the well as Court and Bard hitched the team to the wagon to go chop down trees in the woods. They wanted to fill the four wagons with trees to take to the mill to be lumbered and shipped north.

Ward glanced toward the cabin, wishing Taylor had woken before he left. He saw her standing there and his heart jumped. Slowly he snapped the lid of his canteen of water and walked toward her just as she started toward him. He liked the way her dress fit snug at her waist and belled out down to her feet. Her shiny, light-brown hair hung to her shoulders and down her back. He wanted to tell her to leave it that way, but of course he couldn't. It was too personal.

They met in the shade of the oak and smiled hesitantly at each other. She noticed he hadn't shaved, but he still looked handsome. He noticed how clear and bright her eyes were and how rosy her cheeks were. Had she been this beautiful yesterday?

"Good morning," Ward said softly.

Taylor flushed. "Good morning. How is Pickle?" Safe topics were better this morning, although she wanted to ask why he hadn't awakened her when he came to bed.

He wanted to ask her if she'd have been frightened if he'd awakened her last night. Instead he said, "He'll be fine with care. He was stung bad, but he got the honey."

"Yes. Cammie showed me." Taylor saw flecks of gold in his brown eyes she'd never noticed before. "I tasted it and it's very good."

"I'm sure it is." Tonight would she burst into tears and start shaking again?

"Have you spoken to Laurel?" Why was it suddenly hard to speak?

Ward nodded. What would Taylor do if he took her in his arms and kissed her? "She'll be tending Pickle until he's well again."

"I know she was sorry for her actions." So was she! Why had she suddenly been terrified last night to share his bed?

Ward nodded. "Yes. Yes, she was." He heard the wagon creak and the harness rattle, but he didn't want to leave Taylor. "What are you going to do today?"

"Pick beans, churn butter, do some mending, and of course, tend Brooke." And she'd take a bath and wash her hair before bedtime.

"Could you keep an eye on Reid? He and Kendra are working the sorrel I've been having trouble with."

Taylor nodded. Today it felt different when he asked her to do something. Today she was no longer a servant, but a wife.

He heard the horses snort and shake their harness. "I have to go."

"Be careful."

He smiled. "I always am."

She laughed. "Yes, I suppose you are."

"See you for dinner."

"For dinner."

He smiled and she smiled, then he reluctantly turned away. She watched him walk across the yard and climb in the wagon with Court and Bard, then she slowly walked back to the cabin. Tonight she would not be frightened to have him make her his true wife!

In the wagon the old jealousies surfaced when Ward glanced at Court. Would Taylor rather be married to Court? He clenched his fists as he realized the depth of his feelings. He was Taylor's husband, not Court, so she was going to have to learn to accept it.

❦

The sun warm on her back, Laurel knelt on the grass beside Pickle's mat and gently rubbed the baking soda paste on Pickle's swollen eyelids and face. "I am very sorry for sending you out after that honey," she whispered around the lump in her throat.

"I should'a used smoke on 'em. But I got in a hurry so's to get back before pitch dark."

"I'm glad you didn't . . . sink in the swamp and die."

"Me too, Missy Laurel." Pickle laughed, then grimaced and groaned from the pain.

Tears burned Laurel's eyes. "Lie quietly, Pickle. I'll take care of you."

"Old Pickle can fend for hisself, Missy Laurel. You get back inside and do what you do."

She smeared the salve on the stings on his arms. "I really don't do much of anything, Pickle."

"That's 'cause you need to know you're home here at Catawba."

She dipped her finger in the salve and frowned thoughtfully at him. "I don't know what you mean."

"You're always wishing to be back in England and back with that boy you love so much."

"That's right!"

"Once you done told yourself this be your home and you'll be happy here even without that boy, you'll find joy bubble right up inside." Pickle's words came with another grimace as the ointment was rubbed in harder.

Laurel bit her lip to hold back a guilty cry. "Try to go to sleep. I'll watch over you."

"When I'm better I could teach you to shoot. If you ready to learn, Missy." He'd already taught the others, but Laurel had refused to learn.

Laurel remembered watching Kendra shoot and it had frightened her. She shook her head. "I don't think I want to learn."

Pickle lifted his head. "I don't never want anything to happen to you, Missy Laurel. I want you to know how to shoot if you ever have to protect yourself or Catawba."

Laurel shivered. "Do you think I can learn how?"

"You can do anything you sets your mind to, Missy Laurel."

She squared her shoulders. Nobody had ever told her she could do anything she'd set her mind to. "Do you really think so?"

"I know so, Missy."

"Then I'll do it!" She felt strong and determined, not at all herself.

Pickle lay his head back and smiled. "I sure would like to hear some singing, Missy."

"Oh, no, I really can't do that."

"Old Pickle don't have no right to expect you to sing to him. Even if you do got a voice of an angel, Missy Laurel. I heard you sing a time or two when you was sewing."

She laughed. "All right. I'll sing." She looked around to make sure nobody, especially Bard Keine, was near enough to hear her. To her relief, none of the men were. And Maida and Taylor liked her singing. Kendra and Reid might tease her, but it really didn't matter.

Taking a deep breath, Laurel sang "Rock of Ages." The words

reached deep inside her and softened her stony heart. Healing tears slipped down her face and splashed on Pickle's arm.

🍃

Taylor leaned against the split-rail fence and watched Reid ride the sorrel slowly around the enclosure. Still, the gelding wouldn't obey the commands Reid gave him.

"Use a lighter hand," Taylor called. Before she'd married Floyd she'd helped her friend Gladys train her horses.

Reid loosened his hold on the reins and stopped using the crop. Soon the gelding was turning, walking, and trotting at Reid's command. Reid reined in and slipped easily to the ground. His face was red from the heat and wet with sweat. "Where'd you learn that, Taylor?"

"From my friend Gladys in England. She had one of her horses win several of the local races."

"You don't talk much about your past." Reid looked questioningly at Taylor. "Why is that?"

Taylor forced a laugh. "What is there to say? Isn't the present more interesting?"

Grinning, Reid nodded. "And the future. I mean to raise horses just like Uncle Ward. Papa thinks I'll raise cotton with him, but I don't want to."

"Why can't you do both?"

Reid shrugged. "Maybe I can."

Taylor patted the gelding, then had a sudden desire to ride. It had been a long time. "Do we have a sidesaddle?"

"No. Why?"

"I want to ride." Taylor laughed. "But I can't let not having a sidesaddle stop me, can I? Turn around, Reid, so I can fix my skirts."

Shaking his head, Reid turned around. "Uncle Ward won't like this at all."

"He won't mind, I'm sure." Taylor lifted her skirt, untied her pockets and pulled them off, then tied them on the outside of her dress. She reached between her legs, pulled the tails of her skirts through, and tucked them in the band that held her pockets. "It looks funny, but nobody but you and I will see," she said to Reid with a laugh. She and Gladys had done this very thing when they wanted to ride astride.

"Can I turn around?"

"Yes."

Reid gasped at the sight Taylor made.

"I know it's most unladylike, but I don't care. I want to ride!" Taylor walked into the pen and easily swung into the saddle. It felt strange after such a long time. She urged the sorrel forward around the pen, then stopped near Reid. "I want to take him for a run."

"But he isn't trained well enough to be taken out!"

"I can manage." Taylor laughed. She wanted the freedom to go for a run in the open. "Honestly I can, Reid."

Finally he opened the gate and let her out. "Don't be gone long or I'll be worried about you."

"No need to worry, but I won't be long." She nudged the sorrel toward the trail Ward used when he took the horses out for a run. She knew it led past the area where he was chopping down trees, but she wouldn't go that far. She didn't want him to see her riding in such an unladylike manner. Besides, she was sure it was a far cry from the way Marissa Ferguson rode!

Holding the reins easily, Taylor urged the sorrel to a run. The trees on either side of her whipped by. The pins flew from her hair and her hair whipped out behind her. She was free! Finally she pulled back on the reins. She dare not go any further or she'd be in the area where Ward was working. The sorrel kept running. She pulled back harder and shouted, "Whoa!" But the sorrel raced on, his mane flapping and his tail flying out behind him.

Taylor's heart lurched and her face flamed. She'd been positive she could control the sorrel. She pulled back harder and shouted louder. Suddenly the sorrel stopped, and Taylor flew over his head and landed with a thud in the path. The world spun as she struggled to catch her breath. When she moved, a twig stabbed her in the back. She saw the sorrel standing a few feet away chomping grass at the side of the path. She heard the ring of an axe and the call of birds. She smelled mold and dirt and her own sweat. Could she get up? Could she walk?

Slowly, carefully, she eased herself to a sitting position. The world spun, but finally righted itself. The sorrel lifted his head and nickered.

Just then Court stepped around a tree and caught the reins, then tied them onto a low branch.

Taylor moaned and her face flamed. Why didn't the ground open up and swallow her?

Court leaped to her side and knelt beside her. Her hair hung in wild tangles around her head. Her skirts were in tangles around her legs. "Are you hurt?"

"I don't think so," she whispered.

"I saw you ride past and was afraid the horse was out of control."

Her eyes widened and she clamped her hand to her mouth. "Did Ward see?"

"I don't think so." Court circled her waist and gently helped her stand.

She groaned and leaned against him. "I can't believe I fell off!"

"It happens to the best of us. Do you think you can get back on and ride back by yourself?"

"I ache all over, but I think I can."

He kept an arm around her as he walked her to the gelding. "Keep him at a walk and you'll be fine."

Smiling, she said, "Thank you, Court. Please don't say anything to Ward about this."

"I won't."

"Please turn your head so I can fix my skirts again."

Laughing, he turned his head. "We'll have to get you a sidesaddle."

"I suppose so." Her cheeks flaming again, she tucked her skirt in place again. "All right. I'm ready."

He easily lifted her into the saddle, then stepped back. "See you at dinner."

She nodded and smiled as he handed her the reins. She looked off into the woods and the smile froze. Ward was looking right at her! Had he seen her take the tumble? How humiliating!

She turned away and urged the gelding to a run. She could not abide the slow pace of a walk when she was sinking to the depths of humiliation.

❦

After supper Cammie found Treet sitting alone with his back against the wagon wheel. He looked deep in thought and weary. Beads of water glistened in his black curls. The smell of fresh-cut trees overpowered the aroma of fresh manure in the barnyard. Cammie nervously twisted her toe in the dirt. "You wants company, Treet?"

He didn't look up or smile. "No."

Ignoring him, Cammie awkwardly sat beside him. "I been wondering about you."

"Don't bother. I's nothing to wonder about." He picked up a pine straw and studied it as if it was interesting.

"Treet, why don't you likes babies?"

He turned his head and scowled at her. "That's a dumb question, woman."

"No, it's not! I see how you get away from Brooke if she tries to play with you."

"I'm no play toy."

"I didn't say you are! Is it 'cause she be a white baby?"

"White babies don't get sold from their mamas," he said roughly.

"Brooke almost got sold from Miz Taylor."

"But she weren't!"

Cammie didn't respond immediately. Instead she watched Laurel sitting with Pickle and Ward at the well talking to Court and Bard. Suddenly, with her hand on her stomach, Cammie turned to face Treet. "I won't never let my baby be sold from me."

"You won't be the one to choose. It's up to your master."

Cammie rubbed her rounded stomach. "It's up to me," she whispered fiercely.

Treet caught her hand and held it so tight she almost cried out. "I had me two baby boys and they growed to be seven and nine. My woman died birthing Joe. Last year Master ups and decides them boys would be a good wedding gift for his daughter." Treet moaned. "Master never asked me. He never even told me until them boys were going away. I cried and I even begged. It done no good. Them boys rode away crying for me to save them. But I couldn't!"

"I sorry, Treet." Tears rolled down Cammie's cheeks.

"I sorry too, but that don't bring my boys back." His jaw tight, Treet sat back against the wheel. "I done made myself a promise that day—that I would never have more children and I would never care for another child."

Cammie lifted his hand to her cheek while tears rolled down her face. "Jesus can help take away the loneliness and bitterness in your heart."

Jerking his hand out of Cammie's hold, Treet growled. "Don't preach to me, woman. When my boys were taken away from me I stopped caring for anyone or anything. That includes the God you talk about." Treet stared at Cammie, his eyes full of anger and pain. He quickly turned on his heel and stalked away.

Cammie sighed and prayed silently, "What can I do, Lord? He needs Your love to fill his heart and take away all the pain inside. I know You're able to do it, but Treet needs to know." A small grin began to spread across Cammie's face. "Watch out, Treet, you can't run from God."

ಌ

Taylor paced the floor in the light of the lamp and the fireplace. The smell of venison still filled the room. Ward had stayed away from her at dinner and again at supper. Now Cammie was already asleep in the loft with Brooke. Why wouldn't Ward come in? Was he that angry at her for riding the sorrel in such an unladylike manner?

Taylor touched the huge bruise on her thigh. It was going to be black and blue a long time. On her return she'd taken a hot bath to help ease her sore muscles, but a few places still ached.

The door opened and Ward stepped inside, his mouth a firm, straight line, and his eyes flashing. His anger had been building since this morning and now he didn't care what he said. He would have the truth.

"Why would you have a clandestine meeting with Court right where you knew I'd see you?" he ground out.

Taylor's eyes widened in surprise. "What are you talking about?"

"I saw you on the trail with him! You know I saw you!"

"I know you saw us. But what do you mean by meeting with Court?" she asked. "I was so embarrassed that anyone saw me."

"Embarrassed? Is that all?"

Forgetting to question him further about her meeting Court, Taylor lifted her head. "Is *humiliating* a better word?"

Ward forced himself to keep his voice down. "Humiliating doesn't begin to cover it."

She sank to a chair. "I should've listened to Reid, but I was so sure I could control the sorrel."

Ward frowned. What did she mean?

Ward shook his head in confusion. "The sorrel?"

"Yes. I should've stayed in the pen, but I wanted to take a run. I didn't think I'd fall."

Ward's heart stopped. "You fell?"

She shook her head. "Isn't it embarrassing? Court helped me up and back on the sorrel."

Ward suddenly laughed. Court had helped her after she fell! They hadn't been meeting secretly. Maybe they weren't in love. Ward sobered quickly. He lifted Taylor to her feet and kept her hands in his. Ward was relieved when he realized Taylor seemed to have forgotten about his accusation. How could he have thought she was meeting Court in the woods behind his back?

"Are you all right?" he asked.

"Yes. A little bruised and mortified."

"Why aren't you in bed?"

She looked down at their clasped hands, then into his face. It was suddenly hard to breathe.

"I was waiting for you."

*T*aylor wiped perspiration off her forehead with the back of her gloved hand and pulled a weed she'd somehow milled. This morning she and Kendra had planted the flower seeds in two rows in the garden at the sunny end of each cabin, and they then had picked a basket of beans to can.

Just a few minutes ago, Kendra had gone to get a drink from the well, leaving Taylor alone at last to remember last night with Ward. He'd been hesitant, but loving and gentle. Taylor bit her lip and sighed. Not once, however, had he said he loved her. But then, she hadn't been able to say the words either. Would love come later? Or was it impossible for both of them? With a moan she pushed the thought away.

In the distance Taylor heard the ring of an axe. Ward, Court, and Bard were cutting trees again. They had three wagons loaded with logs. When the fourth was finished, they'd take them to be lumbered and shipped north to Philadelphia, bringing back more materials to build the house. Ward had reminded all of them that, though not a mansion like those around Charleston, the house would be large enough for the entire family. As he said, folks in their area didn't build big and showy like the people in the low country.

Taylor gazed up the hill at the wide cleared area where the house would sit. It was to be a three-story brick, Federal-style house with four rooms on each floor plus large center halls with open stairways wide enough three people could walk abreast. It would be a far cry from the two-room cabin and a loft with a ladder. Actually, Ward had said each room would be bigger than an entire cabin. Taylor laughed just thinking about living in such a house, but sobered as she realized she'd be considered the mistress of the house along with Maida. How would Yates feel about that?

She wrinkled her nose. Yates had certainly become a hard man since she'd first met him on the docks of Liverpool. At that time he'd seemed lost in grief, but now he was encased in a shell too hard to crack. Today he'd taken Reid and the men to clear the stumps and had told Pickle to carry dinner to them so they wouldn't have to take time to return to the house. So that meant a few hours' reprieve from the harsh looks and words.

Just then Taylor caught a movement in the trees to her left. Her nerves tightened. Could it be an animal ready to spring on her and eat her alive? Frantically she looked for a weapon, found the hoe and picked it up, ready to use it if need be. As she watched, a black man she had never seen before peered around a tree right at her. Her heart lurched, and she stifled a scream.

"What do you want?" she asked in a strained voice.

He darted a look around, then stepped into plain view. He wore a ragged shirt, dark baggy pants, scuffed shoes, and a red bandanna around his curly head. He looked scared and half-starved. He opened his mouth, closed it, and opened it again, but no sound came out.

Taylor gripped the hoe. Should she shout for help? Kendra would come running with the flintlock if she did. "What do you want?" Taylor asked again, this time in a firm voice.

"I is looking for Sippy."

The color drained from Taylor's face. Sippy! Why would the man even know to ask her about Sippy? Taylor took a step toward the man, then stopped. "Did you ask Mr. Bromley?"

"No, ma'am."

"Then you should."

The man was quiet a long time. He rubbed at his ragged sleeves and looked ready to collapse. "Sippy said she run away. She say ask here when I wants to find her."

Taylor's mouth turned dust-dry. Was this another man wanting a paper saying he was free? Should she help him or send him on his way? He looked pitiful. She couldn't just send him away, could she? Silently she prayed for the right thing to do and say.

She opened her mouth to offer him help when deep inside she felt a check. She knew she wasn't to help the man. She didn't know why, but she knew she couldn't go against that inner answer. "I have food you can eat and water you can drink, then you must be on your way."

"I need Sippy!" he said urgently.

"You'll have to talk to Mr. Bromley," she insisted.

With a low chuckle Alden Bromley stepped from behind another tree. "I thought I was gonna catch me a nigger-lover."

"Mr. Bromley!" Taylor leaned weakly on her hoe and stared in horror at the man. He had set a trap for her! And if it hadn't been for God, she would've fallen right into it! "How dare you! I will call Ward and Yates this instant and they'll send you on your way!"

Bromley pulled off his tricorn hat, leaving his hair sticking every which way. He slapped the black man on the back with his hat and ignored her, directing his comments to his slave. "Fetch me a drink of water, Elmer."

Elmer ducked his head and ran around the edge of the garden toward the well.

Bromley grinned at Taylor. "The food and water you offered Elmer is for me, too, ain't it?"

"Of course." Taylor wanted to send him on his way immediately, but she kept her angry words locked inside. She had to be polite. "Shall we walk to the yard?" She motioned for him to join her.

Grinning, he tucked his hat under his arm and tried to rub his hair in place as he hurried toward her. "For some reason I thought you might know where my Sippy is. Being new in the area, as you are, I figured you wouldn't know no better than to help a runaway slave. I guess I was wrong."

Taylor lifted her chin and quickened her pace.

Chuckling, he fell into step beside her. "You're a mighty pretty lady. Next time I plan on offering Ward Marston twice as much for you as is owing."

Taylor stopped short and faced Bromley. "Mr. Bromley, you are wasting your time!"

"That's for me to decide, darlin'."

Flags of red flew in Taylor's cheeks and fire shot from her blue eyes. "I will not permit you to be so familiar with me!"

"You won't, huh? I plan on getting more familiar than that. Because I've decided to take you to be my woman no matter what Ward Marston says." Chuckling wickedly, Bromley caught her arm and pulled her toward him.

She broke away, leaped back, and lifted the hoe as a weapon. "Don't touch me again!"

"You got no say, madam," Bromley said hoarsely.

Taylor trembled, but she didn't loosen her grip on the hoe. "If you take one step closer or even try to touch me, I'll use this! Besides, I'm Ward Marston's wife now."

Anger flashed in Bromley's dull blue eyes. "I don't believe you. You are acting mighty uppity for a bond servant."

His face without expression, Elmer stepped between Bromley and Taylor with the dipper of water in his hand. "Here's your drink, master."

Bromley struck Elmer's arm, sending the dipper of water flying through the air. Then he yelled, "Grab that woman and take her to my horse!"

"What, master?" Elmer asked in a shaky voice as if he hadn't heard.

Taylor backed away, her eyes wide in alarm. Would Bromley try to steal her away?

Bromley shoved Elmer aside. "I'll do it myself."

Bromley was serious! "Kendra!" Taylor screamed. "Bring the gun!"

Bromley darted a look around. "There's no call for that."

"Kendra, bring the gun!" Taylor shouted even louder and more frantic. "Bring Maida and Laurel!"

"Now, now," Bromley said as he clamped his tricorn hat on. "There's no call for that. I'm a lonely man and I want you as my woman. There's nothing wrong at all about that."

Elmer stood to one side, his head down.

"I am not your woman, nor ever will be! I am Mrs. Ward Marston!" Taylor stood her ground, the hoe raised.

"We're coming!" Kendra shouted, the heavy flintlock in her hands. Kendra spotted Bromley and the black man and shouted over her shoulder, "Maida, Laurel, hurry!"

Taylor breathed a sigh of relief. Let Bromley try to take her with the others there to see it all!

Kendra ran to Taylor's side and aimed her flintlock at Bromley's heart. Bromley began to back up.

Soon Maida and Laurel joined them. They didn't know what was wrong, but they planned to help Taylor at any cost.

"There's no call for this, ladies," Bromley said nervously as he edged away from them.

"What did he do?" Kendra asked, never lowering the rifle.

"He tried to take me with him against my will," Taylor said in a flat voice.

"No!" Maida cried, shaking her head.

Laurel clamped her hand over her mouth in shock.

"He won't take you now," Kendra said grimly.

Elmer hid a smile and silently backed away so Bromley couldn't reach out and whack him out of pure meanness.

Taylor slowly lowered the hoe. "Mr. Bromley, if you ever come to Catawba again, you speak to the men, never to me."

"Or me," Maida said sharply even though inside she was icy with fear. "Or Laurel or Kendra."

"I didn't do no harm," Bromley said uncertainly, looking at the angry women facing him.

"If you want to see Ward or Yates, go find them. If not, leave now," Taylor said in a calm but firm voice. She felt suddenly strong inside and knew she could face down Bromley with God and the women of Catawba at her side.

Bromley grumbled under his breath as he turned away, shouting angrily, "Elmer, get the horses!"

Elmer ran into the woods and came back leading two horses. Bromley leaped into the saddle and rode away at a gallop. Elmer turned to the women and said softly, "Sorry for that, ma'am."

Taylor nodded.

Elmer swung into the saddle and followed Bromley's trail of dust.

Suddenly Taylor laughed and turned to the others. "Thank you! We women of Catawba can't be beaten!"

❧

Later Laurel stood before Pickle, the flintlock in her hands. It felt heavier than two buckets of water and smelled like gunpowder. "I'm ready to learn to shoot."

He grinned. "You sure looks it, Miss Laurel."

She told him about Bromley's visit. "If he comes back and tries anything again, I'll know how to shoot."

"It's not easy to shoot a man dead, Miss Laurel," Pickle said gently. "Don't you never do it 'less you be backed in a corner."

"I'll remember that." She flipped back her blonde hair and raised the stock that was polished until it looked like a tortoise shell to her shoulder. A well-fitted brass plate protected the butt. On the right side against the butt plate the wood had been hollowed out and fitted with a hinged brass cover to hold a lump of patch grease and bullet patches.

"Don't shoot anybody here," Pickle said with a laugh. He eased the rifle from her hands and stood it down beside him. It was less than five feet long with an octagonal barrel. A hickory ramrod, scorched with dark bands for looks, was held in place in a long recess in the underside of the stock. "We'll go out in the woods where I showed the others how to shoot."

Excitement flashed in Laurel's eyes. "I want to shoot well enough to kill a deer or a rabbit for supper."

"Old Pickle can teach you. But it won't be tonight's supper you be bringing home."

Laurel hung the powder horn and the bag around her neck and walked with Pickle to the spot he'd chosen.

❦

Later Kendra finished milking the cow and turned her out in the pen next to the horses. She carried the milk to the cabin for Maida to strain it and share it with Taylor. As she came into the cabin, Maida sat at the table with a faraway look on her face.

"Here's the milk," Kendra said when Maida didn't move or look up.

"Milk?" Maida finally looked at Kendra, then jumped up. "Is it that late?" The churn sat beside her with the cream barely turned to butter. "I've been sitting here for hours!"

Kendra nodded. She'd noticed how Maida had been doing that more and more. "I'll be outdoors if you need me."

Maida nodded and absently looked at the bucket of milk on the floor beside the table. The fire was almost out in the fireplace and she knew she'd have to put a log on soon. Since sometimes she had a hard time starting the fire with flint and steel, she found it much easier to get hot coals from Taylor.

Kendra walked slowly back outdoors. The men would be returning soon and she wanted to be the first to tell them what Bromley had done to Taylor. Maybe Court would be so proud of her that he'd say something besides "good evening."

She walked to the three wagons loaded with logs, then past the shacks where the men slept, and back to the well. She filled the dipper with water and drank before she realized she'd used the wrong dipper. She shrugged. It didn't matter to her like it did Papa. Besides, Court used that dipper. Absently she stroked it and wondered if Court's lips had touched the same spot hers had.

Finally she heard a wagon coming through the woods. As she ran to meet it, she saw Uncle Ward driving, Bard on a log in the back, and Court walking behind. Her heart leaped. Now was her chance to speak to Court alone! She started toward him, but drew back. He would think she was too forward if she ran to him in such a manner.

Impatiently she waited until Uncle Ward stopped the wagon beside the other three, then she ran to him. "Something simply awful happened today!" She saw Court from the corner of her eye. He was listening, so she quickly told the story.

"Is Taylor safe?" Ward asked sharply.

"Yes!" Kendra told about her holding the rifle on Bromley. "I didn't let him near her!"

Rage rushed through Ward. He wanted to jump on his horse and ride to Bromley's place and tear him limb from limb. But he knew he had to wait until he was calm, or he wouldn't go with a clear mind, ready for any kind of attack.

Kendra saw Bard's anger also before he unhitched the team. She turned to Court, who was looking toward Taylor's cabin with a worried expression on his face. Unknown to her, his thoughts were directed at her. What if something had happened to his Kendra? His Kendra? No, he couldn't think of her that way. She would never be his.

Tentatively Kendra walked over to Court. "Hello, Court."

Looking at her with eyes full of anguish, Court couldn't answer right away. Quickly he pulled his emotions under control. "I'm glad nothing happened to you."

Happiness began to coarse through Kendra's body. Maybe he did care about her. "Me, too. I was a little frightened, but I didn't let Mr. Bromley see it."

Seeing Kendra's smiling face, Court wanted to pull her to him and kiss her until the sun set on the horizon. He had made a vow that he would never touch her again, though, and he had to keep it. Turning quickly away from Kendra, Court mumbled something about having work to do and walked away. Kendra was left standing there, staring after him.

What had she said to make him leave like that? Did he not care for her, could that be it? Kendra's shoulders sagged in defeat. Kicking a clump of dirt, she watched it fly across the yard.

❦

After supper Cammie sat on the bench under the tree and sighed heavily. She'd tried to talk to Treet again, but he'd sent her on her way. She watched Pickle get a drink and hang the dipper back in place.

"Hey, Pickle," she called.

Grinning, he walked to her. "You look ready to bust open."

She rubbed her stomach. "I feel ready. You sure you know about bringing babies into this world?"

Pickle nodded. "I brought many babies into the world, squalling and slippery."

"I ain't never had a baby before."

"You listen to old Pickle and you'll do just fine."

Cammie watched the fireflies at the edge of the woods. "You hear what that Bromley done to Miz Taylor today?" she remarked.

"I heard," Pickle said grimly. "Laurel told me. Then she had me teach her to shoot."

"Good. You and Laurel are getting along real good now."

Pickle nodded.

"I wish me and Treet could."

"Treet gots a lot of pain inside him. When he lets that pain go, he can love again. Not before."

Cammie caught Pickle's hand and held it tight. "You a wise man, Pickle."

He chuckled. "I am. That's for sure. But I had lots of years to get this way."

"Sometimes I feel old as them old men in the Bible. Then other times I feel like a chile who wants to play with dollies." She rubbed her stomach again. "I wants this baby to grow up wise and strong and loving Jesus."

"He will here at Catawba."

"If we gets to stay," she whispered.

Pickle looked at her sharply. "Why wouldn't you stay, girl?"

She shrugged. She couldn't tell even Pickle about James Rawlings.

❦

After Laurel and Kendra were asleep in the loft Maida paced the cabin, glaring at Yates as he again wrote the figures to show how much money he'd make if the cotton yielded what he expected.

Suddenly, she stopped and hissed angrily, "Doesn't it make you want to go kill Bromley after what he did to Taylor?"

"Ward will tend to it."

"Don't you even care?"

"Leave me alone," he said tiredly.

She stamped her foot. "Don't you have a heart?"

Yates leaped to his feet. Though not a tall man, he towered over Maida. "Ellen never once questioned my actions! Why must you?"

Pain stabbed Maida. She'd known all along Yates had compared her to Ellen, but he'd never said it aloud. She lifted her chin and spat out, "I am not Ellen and never will be. If you want to live in this house in peace, you're going to have to stop comparing me to her. Besides, Ellen would've questioned you if you'd acted this way around her!"

Yates shuddered at the blow, knowing it was true. But still he couldn't back down from Maida. "You could never take Ellen's place in my life. She was the perfect wife. Ellen knew how to love me the way I am. You can't tolerate me! You peck at me on every turn! I can see why your aunt and uncle despised you." Even as the words came from his mouth, he wanted to take them back, but it was too late. He'd said them and they'd remain spoken. He would not, could not repent.

Maida burst into tears and ran to the bedroom. She slipped into bed and covered her head to hide her sobs from Yates. How could she go on with a man that could never let go of his dead wife enough to care for her? Realizing the full extent of unhappiness that lay ahead of her, Maida sobbed even harder.

Yates sank to his chair and covered his face with his hands. What had he become? He could hear Maida in their bedroom crying her heart out, but Yates couldn't go in to comfort her. He seemed to have forgotten what was important in life. He was neglecting his family and only thought of making money and the respect that would bring him. Not knowing what to do and shaking his head to clear his mind, Yates stood and walked outside to get away from Maida's tears.

❦

His hat in his hand, Ward strode into the cabin. Taylor sat on a bench at the table sewing a dress for Brooke by the light of the lamp. Brooke was asleep for the night and the fire had already been banked.

Ward stopped behind a chair and forced his voice to stay steady. "Kendra told me about Bromley's visit today."

Taylor bit her lip and carefully laid the dress on the table.

Ward gripped the back of the chair. When Kendra had finished the story he was ready to ride to Bromley's plantation and break him in two. He hadn't, of course. He'd waited for Taylor to tell him at supper, but she hadn't. He'd gone off alone to pray until he was calm enough to confront Taylor without shouting. "Why didn't you say anything to me?"

Taylor was thankful for Ward's control. She didn't like to deal with anger. She shrugged and even managed a smile. "We sent him on his way."

"So Kendra said." Ward hung his hat on the peg with his powder horn. With his back to her he asked, "Did you tell him we're married?"

She touched the needle and the tiny stitches in Brooke's dress. "I tried, but he didn't believe me. I suppose it would carry more weight if you told him."

"I'll tell him." Ward sounded grim. "We go past his place tomorrow with the logs."

She looked up in surprise. "You're leaving tomorrow?"

He turned to face her. "Yes."

"How long will you be?"

"Less than a week." Did he detect relief in her eyes? "I'm taking Bard, Court, and Reid." Reid had begged to go and Ward had decided to let him drive one of the wagons. He'd learned to handle a team of horses well. Ward watched the shadows play across Taylor's face. He'd chosen to take Court to keep him from Taylor. What would she say if she knew? But he pushed the thought aside and continued, "Yates will be here to deal with Bromley if he tries anything again. And, of course, Pickle and Yates's men will be here, too."

"I'm sure we can manage." Taylor lifted a fine brow. "Could I get you a cup of tea?"

"No. I must get ready for the journey."

Taylor jumped up. "I'll pack clothes for you. I repaired your white shirt."

Ward's heart beat strangely. "Thank you."

"I'll get a length of cotton fabric from the store in Darien when we go next and make you a new shirt."

Ward smiled. "You do sound like a wife."

She flushed. "Yes. I suppose I do."

"I like it." He wanted to reach out and touch her hair, but he turned away to gather food for the trip. "We're pulling out at first light."

"So early!"

Ward set a bag of cornmeal on the table and nodded. Was she

going to miss him? Quickly changing the subject, Ward said, "Laurel did a fine job with Pickle. I was afraid she wouldn't stick with it until he was all right."

"He did look much better today."

Ward nodded. "I've seen a man swell to twice his size and live." What was he doing? Why couldn't he say what he felt like saying—that he'd wanted to rip Bromley to pieces for daring to look at her or touch her? "Pickle's healthy and his faith is strong."

"I know. We talked a lot while he was teaching me to do all the things around here."

Frowning, Ward turned away to get flour and baking powder. Why was it Taylor could talk easily to Court and to Pickle, but not to him?

Just then Brooke wailed at the top of her lungs, filling the cabin with her cries.

Taylor ran to the ladder. "She's been teething. I'll settle her down."

In the loft Taylor lifted Brooke and held her close. She smelled hot and was burning up with fever. Frantically Taylor called down the ladder, "Ward, could you get Cammie to bring up a cup of cold water? She's outside at the bench."

"I'll get it." Ward filled a cup from the bucket of water and climbed the ladder. "Is something wrong?"

"She has a fever, I guess, because of her teeth." Taylor took the cup and held it for Brooke.

She drank, then pushed the cup away. She spotted Ward, whimpered, and held her arms out to him.

Taylor flushed. "No, Brooke. Ward must get to sleep."

"I'll take her." Ward sat on the loft floor and held Brooke close. He kissed her flushed cheek and brushed back her damp hair. "Maybe you should have her sleep with you downstairs where it's a little cooler."

"No, I'm sure she'll be fine. She'll stop crying." Taylor reached out to touch Brooke, but her hand brushed Ward's instead. Her stomach tightened and she jerked her hand back. "Look. She's stopping." Her voice sounded strange even in her own ears.

Ward rocked Brooke gently a little longer, then carefully laid her back on her mat. "She needs a bed. I'll get one built for her."

"Thank you. I'd feel better if she had one."

Ward rubbed Brooke's back, then bent down and kissed her head. "Sleep tight."

Taylor smiled at the tender picture. Floyd had been good with Brooke, but he never had much time to spend with her. She was usually asleep when he left each morning and in bed when he returned at night. Sometimes Taylor had even kept Brooke awake just so Floyd could see her.

"I'll go down and finish," Ward said softly. He touched Taylor's hand. "Stay with Brooke. I can get my own clothes ready."

"No, I can help you. Cammie will be in soon to help with Brooke."

Later, just as Taylor set Ward's pack of clothes next to the supplies, Brooke started crying again. Taylor hurried to the ladder and called up, "Cammie, how's her fever?"

"She's burning up, Miz Taylor."

"Bring her down and let me sponge her off." Sighing, Taylor turned to Ward. "I'm sorry. I don't think you'll get much sleep with her crying."

As angry as he was at Bromley, Ward didn't think he'd get much sleep anyway. "I'll hold Brooke." He took her from Cammie, sat down, and rocked her in his arms.

"Thank you." Taylor smiled at him, then wiped a damp cloth over Brooke's hot face.

"You needs my help, Miz Taylor?" Cammie asked as she leaned tiredly on the ladder.

Before Taylor could answer Ward said, "No, we don't. Go up to bed, Cammie."

She smiled and slowly, awkwardly climbed into the loft.

Taylor leaned down and kissed Brooke's cheek. Her hair brushed against Ward and he closed his eyes. She was his wife and Bromley would never get her!

❦

The next morning Ward woke at dawn and slipped quietly out of bed, leaving Taylor with Brooke on her shoulder to sleep. He hesitated, then leaned down and kissed Brooke, then Taylor.

Taylor's eyelids fluttered. "Floyd?"

Ward's blood froze. Floyd! "No, it's Ward!" he said quietly.

Taylor mumbled something and slept on.

Slowly Ward walked out of the cabin, his gear in his hand, his heart heavy. She still loved Floyd. Ward sighed. In his heart he'd known that, but somehow he'd pushed the knowledge away. Birds twittered in the trees as he hurried to the shack to get the men and

Reid. No sense wasting more time this morning grieving. He'd best be on his way, and later he'd deal with Taylor.

❦

At Bromley's plantation Ward jumped from his wagon and faced Bromley squarely. Pigs squealed and grunted in the pigpen. A rooster sat on the top of the split-rail fence and crowed loud and long. Bromley had a pleasant smile on his face and his hat pushed to the back of his head. Ward had left the others waiting in their wagons on the main road while he went alone to see Alden Bromley. Court had offered to ride with him, but Ward wanted to deal with Bromley alone.

"What brings you here, neighbor Ward?" Bromley knew exactly why Ward Marston had stopped in, but he had to stall for time enough for Elmer to fetch his Pennsylvania long rifle.

Ward wasn't in the mood for pleasantries and he was too angry to be polite. Ward forced back the desire to punch Bromley in the face. It took all his willpower to keep from pulling his pistol and putting a ball in Bromley's heart. Instead he said grimly, "I stopped by to tell you Taylor and I are married."

"Married?" Bromley's eyes widened. So it was true. He had his mind made up—to get Taylor any way he could. Was Ward Marston speaking the truth, or only saying that to thwart his plans? Aloud, he let his frustration show. "What kind of game are you playing?"

"No game." Ward's muscles tightened, ready to spring if Bromley tried anything.

Bromley knew Ward was ready to fight him, so he grinned and waved a hand for Elmer to stay back with the long rifle. No sense killing each other when he could talk his way out of almost anything. "Seems I missed my chance for a fine woman." Bromley shrugged. "But I'll live." He pulled his hat off and frowned. "The true reason I stopped by your place was to ask about Sippy."

Ward cocked his brow in surprise. Kendra hadn't said anything about Bromley looking for Sippy—nor had Taylor.

"I know Miz Taylor has a soft spot for colored folk and I thought she might've helped Sippy get away from me."

"Leave my wife out of the hunt for your runaway," Ward snapped. Had Taylor helped Sippy get away? Why hadn't he thought of that? Taylor might do that very thing. Well, he'd find out when he returned.

"Surely will, neighbor." Bromley smiled, but anger was building on the inside. It was degrading to have Ward Marston warn him away from Taylor. To distract him Bromley motioned to the logs in the wagon. "Looks like you're taking another load to the mill."

Ward nodded. "I'll be gone for a few days, but my brother and his men are still at Catawba."

Bromley caught the warning and felt his anger rising. It wasn't right for Ward Marston to treat him in such a manner. The English had a way of rubbing salt in an open sore. Being defeated in the war had sent them running back across the ocean where they belonged! Bromley bit back a chuckle. He'd helped defeat the Tories and the English and he'd find a way to get even with Marston—maybe shoe a few of his horses in a way to ruin their hooves. Or maybe burn down his cabins. As an even better idea started formulating in his mind Bromley smiled, holding out his hand. "I'm mighty sorry for the trouble I brought to you and yours."

Ward hesitated, then shook hands with Bromley. "I accept your apology. Feel free to come by Catawba. When I'm there."

Bromley nodded. The anger burned even hotter.

Glad he'd dealt with the problem, Ward climbed in the wagon and drove back down the road to the main road, the wagon swaying and the harness jangling. Now he could deliver the logs with a clear mind.

Bromley's face hardened. "That Taylor woman will rue the day she rejected me," he muttered.

13

Listlessly Maida walked from Catawba to the main road. Her limp skirts clung to her legs and her bonnet flapped against her back where it had fallen, but she didn't notice. She'd had to get away from the girls and Taylor before she'd lost control. How could they be so pious and holy and act as if they actually liked living at Catawba? Maida groaned deep inside. Why hadn't she been content to stay with her aunt and uncle? Life with them had been miserable, but not as bad as at Catawba with Yates. She had thought he was the answer to all her problems. But all Yates did was yell at her for trying to talk to him and work from dawn till dark clearing out stumps. If only he would take time for her and care for her just a little bit. Living in a cabin away from the city was miserable. She hadn't left the place since they'd arrived over two months ago! With her aunt and uncle she'd gone daily to the stores and the shops.

Maida lifted her skirts and walked faster even though the sun was hot against her. She was oblivious to the beauty around her. Butterflies flitted from flower to flower and birds sang in the trees. Behind her she heard Musket bark. He was with Pickle, who was near the barn splitting firewood.

Her hand trembling, Maida pushed back a stray strand of black hair. Maybe she should've told Taylor where she was going. But the past four days that Ward had been gone Taylor had been occupied with Brooke because she was teething, making it hard to speak to her about anything. Taylor couldn't have helped anyway. She would never help her leave Catawba. With a small groan Maida wished again that someone—Yates in particular—would care about her.

Frowning thoughtfully, Maida walked slower, careful to watch where she stepped. She knew the dangers, but somehow maybe it would be better to have a poisonous snake sink its fangs in her and kill her. Her mind wandered from topic to topic, anything to keep from thinking of her problems.

"I wonder why Taylor won't talk about herself?" Maida muttered. Even Cammie told selected bits of her life, but Taylor didn't. Had she led a secret life? Maybe she hadn't really been married before—maybe Brooke had been born out of wedlock. Her hand at her throat, Maida gasped. Could that be Taylor's secret?

Yates certainly had no secrets! He loved Ellen and always would.

Maida brushed at a tear. She didn't care any longer. She was trying to keep her heart from caring for Yates and the children. She'd even stopped questioning Yates about his work or his thoughts. She'd even considered telling him to sleep in the barn, but Maida couldn't stand for anyone else to know how miserable their marriage was. She brushed away another tear.

Unknown to her, a man waited in the woods with a gunny sack in his hands. He'd followed the woman from the yard at Catawba. Each step she took was making his job easier. Alden Bromley had said to steal away Taylor Marston. The man grinned. This job was simple. Why hadn't Bromley done it himself?

When the woman stopped at the main road he crept from the cover of the trees and with one quick movement jerked the heavy sack down over her head and shoulders and arms.

She screamed frantically, but the scream was muffled inside the hot, smelly sack. Dust choked her and strangled the scream in her throat. She tried to break free, but she was held too tight. Perspiration soaked her skin. What was happening to her? Why would anyone do this to her?

The man flung her over his shoulder like a sack of grain and hurried to the horse he'd left hidden among the trees at the side of the road. The job had been easier than he'd thought. He could get her to Bromley and be on his way with the pay in his pocket before the morning was gone.

Blood roaring in her ears, Maida again tried in vain to struggle but she couldn't move more than her fingers. She felt dizzy. Dust from the sack settled on her damp skin, leaving it gritty. Who would do this to her? And why? Icy chills darted up and down her spine and fear stung her skin. Would anyone from Catawba know where to look for her? Was she going to be sold as a slave? Pickle had told them many stories of men snatching free folks to make them slaves.

Soon the man sat her on the front of the horse, mounted himself, and clamped a strong arm around her middle.

She groaned. She felt wind on her leg and she knew her skirts were hiked up. How mortifying! She tried to kick them down, but couldn't move enough to. She swayed with the move of the horse and wondered how long the trip would be.

Much later the man stopped the horse and said gruffly, "Here she is. Just like you wanted. Pay me and I'll be on my way."

Maida cried out, but her voice was muffled. She felt her feet touch the ground and someone drag off the sack. She swayed and her captor caught her and righted her. The sunlight hurt her eyes.

"You got the wrong woman, fool! Lock her up inside while I think what to do."

Maida kicked the man holding her and jerked free, then faced the other man. Alden Bromley! Her head spun and she thought she'd swoon on the spot.

"Sir, what is the meaning of this?" she cried.

Bromley looked her up and down, then chuckled. He liked the spunk in her. She was short and slight with eyes the color of the summer sky and hair as black as a crow's wing. Maybe he could keep her as his woman. It would still spite Ward Marston even if she wasn't Taylor—after all, she was a relative of his. This woman had fire and beauty, and she didn't seem as aloof or as controlled as Taylor.

"Maida, ain't it?" he leered.

"Yes!" She brushed at the grit on her cheek. "Now take me home this instant!"

Bromley crossed his arms and looked her up and down again. His thoughts moved slowly. Maybe this had happened to show a greater power was in control of his life. He'd thought he wanted Taylor, but this woman had come and she was better. She was for him; if that weren't so, she wouldn't be here.

When he reached this conclusion, he smiled gently. "This'll be your home from now on."

She gasped and stared in horror at him. "That's impossible! Yates is my husband!"

"No matter. I'll keep you hidden when anyone but my people come here. You and me can have a fine time of it."

Fear raced through her and she locked her knees to keep from sinking to the ground. "Yates will come after me."

"He won't find you." Bromley laid an arm around Maida, but she leaped away from him.

She faced him with her fists doubled at her sides. Even from the distance she could smell his sweat. "He'll find me and then he'll kill you."

Shaking his head, Bromley laughed. "He won't find you and he won't kill me. Don't you worry none about that. You and me'll have us a real fine time. You're a little bitty thing, but you got fire inside you."

Across the yard Elmer watched and listened to Master Bromley and Miz Maida, then turned back to hoeing the garden. Served Master right to get the wrong woman, he thought. Miz Taylor was safe. Then Elmer stopped. Could be Miz Taylor would want to know Master Bromley had Miz Maida. Elmer bent down and pulled a weed too close to the spinach plant. Should he put himself in danger by trying to help Miz Maida? He'd have to think on that.

❦

At Catawba Kendra ran to Taylor beside the well where she was giving Brooke a drink of water. Kendra wiped sweat off her face and tried to stop trembling. "Taylor, have you seen Maida?"

"No. But I've been occupied with Brooke." Taylor stripped Brooke down to her diaper and shift and sponged her hot face with a cloth wet from the cool well water. "Her fever is down a little. I'm sure once her teeth break through, she'll be fine again."

Kendra rubbed her hands down her apron. She should not have sassed Maida this morning when she'd asked her to mix up the bread.

And now that she needed to apologize, Maida couldn't be found. "I asked Laurel and Pickle. They haven't seen Maida since this morning."

"She must be around somewhere. She knows not to walk in the woods alone." Taylor was more concerned for Brooke than for Maida. Taylor held Brooke to her shoulder and patted her back. "Maida would never just wander off."

"I know, but I have looked everywhere! I've called and she hasn't answered." Kendra trembled. "You know she's been acting melancholy."

"I know." Taylor stood Brooke to the ground, but instead of running around the yard she clung to Taylor's leg.

Kendra wrung her hands. "I am rather worried."

Taylor wasn't really concerned about Maida, but for Kendra's sake, she suggested sending Pickle out. Maida was probably hidden away somewhere to be alone.

"I hope nothing's happened to her," Kendra said again with a worried frown. "I'm afraid I was rather rude to her this morning."

Taylor finally saw just how worried Kendra was and she patted her arm. "I'll leave Brooke with Cammie and we'll look for Maida together. If we can't find her, then we'll send Pickle out to look for her."

"Thank you." Relieved, Kendra squeezed Taylor's hand.

Several minutes later Taylor hurried to Pickle and explained how they'd looked all over, but couldn't find Maida. "Would you please go look for her? Maybe she went to watch Yates work."

"I don't think so," Kendra said, shaking her head. She knew Maida was upset with Papa and with her whole way of life.

"Check anyway, Pickle." Taylor heard Brooke's sharp cry and turned toward the cabin. "I must tend Brooke." Lifting her skirts, Taylor ran to the cabin.

Kendra clasped her hands together as she begged, "Let me go with you, Pickle. Please."

"You be mighty good company, Missy, but I best go alone. I can travel faster. Musket will go with me." The dog wagged his tail and whined.

Pickle stepped inside the barn and picked up the flintlock Laurel had been shooting. He hung a large and a small powder horn and a bag around his neck. A knife was already buckled on his skinny hip. He was proud Master Ward trusted him with weapons. He wasn't a slave, but he was black and it took a lot for a white man to trust a black one with weapons.

Laurel burst out of the cabin and ran toward the barn, her blonde hair flying out behind her. "Pickle, where do you think you're going?"

"To find Maida," Kendra said sharply.

Laurel clutched the flintlock and tried to pull it from Pickle's hands. "You're not strong enough to wander all over the place."

Pickle chuckled. "I plenty strong, Missy. Don't you worry your head none about old Pickle."

"What if you collapse? Or run into more bees?"

Kendra pulled Laurel away from Pickle. "Let him hunt for Maida, will you? He's got to look now before dark."

Laurel shivered. "Oh, all right! But you be careful, Pickle!"

"I be very careful, Missy."

Laurel glanced around. "I wonder where she is?"

"I can't imagine." Kendra frowned as she looked around the yard again. Kendra bit her lip and shivered. "What will Papa say if she's not here when he returns?"

"Old Pickle will be going." He smiled at the girls. "Jesus knows where Miz Maida is."

Laurel nodded and stepped closer to Pickle. "Take me with you. Please."

Kendra gasped in shock. Perhaps Laurel had really changed.

Pickle grinned and shook his head. "You best stay here, Missy Laurel. You and Missy Kendra and Cammie and Miz Taylor gots to take care of each other and little Brooke."

"I suppose so." Laurel sighed heavily and reached for Kendra's hand. They stood side by side and watched Pickle walk away with Musket running beside him.

Just before dark Yates and his men walked into the yard and directly to the well. They were dirty and sweaty and hungry. Kendra and Laurel ran to Yates, but before they had a chance to say anything Pickle and Musket returned.

Yates drained the dipper dry, then said sharply, "Any sign of Maida?"

"Not a one, Master." Pickle rested the rifle against the well and pulled off his hat. He was dripping with sweat. He'd stopped in the field to tell them Maida was missing. "It be like she disappeared in thin air."

"But she couldn't." Yates raked his fingers through his hair. It was his fault she'd walked away. He'd been too preoccupied with work and he'd snapped at her if she tried to talk to him. He never could bring himself to take back the cruel words he'd said to her. But he'd never considered that she'd run away.

Kendra gripped Yates's arm. "What'll we do, Papa?"

"We'll have to look again."

"But it's dark!" Laurel cried. "You can't go looking now!"

Yates's stomach knotted. He should've stopped working when Pickle came to the field looking for Maida. "Pickle, you're the only one who knows the area. Would it do any good to look now that it's dark?"

"No, sir, it won't, 'specially since none of you knows where it's safe to walk and where it ain't." Pickle patted Musket's head. "If Miz Maida be out there, Musket here would've found her."

Kendra whimpered and shook her head.

"We can't wait for Uncle Ward to return!" Laurel cried. "Something dreadful could happen to Maida by then."

Weary to the point of collapsing, Yates leaned against the well. "Pickle, what would Master Ward do to find Miz Maida?"

Pickle rubbed his tight curls and frowned. "I thinks Master Ward would get Master Bromley to bring his dogs and hunt her down."

"Then that's what we'll do." Yates turned to Young and Dancer. "Saddle two horses and bring them here. With Pickle to guide me I'll go see Alden Bromley and get him to come help us." Yates shook his head and thought, I hate to get help from that man, but I must set aside my pride. He bit back a sharp laugh. This would be the first time he'd ever set aside his pride. Hopefully it was not too late.

❦

Much later Yates and Pickle stopped outside Bromley's stone and wood three-story house. Lights shone from four windows on the main floor. Across the yard near a shed dogs barked frantically.

His long rifle in his hands, Bromley stepped into the lantern light on the porch. "You dogs, quiet!" he shouted. Then he said in a sharp voice to the riders, "Speak your business and be on your way!"

"It's Yates Marston. And Pickle. We need your help." It almost choked Yates to ask for Bromley's help.

Bromley tensed and his finger itched to fire. "Help with what?" he asked in a polite, neighborly voice.

"To find my wife Maida. Have you seen her?"

Bromley forced back a laugh. "No."

Pickle peered around, taking in all he could from the back of his horse. The smell of wood smoke swirled around in the air.

Yates wanted to ride away without another word. "Did any of your workers see her?"

Bromley shrugged. "No."

Yates brushed aside his pride even more. "Could you bring your dogs and come look for her?"

Pickle wanted to tell him not to bother, but he knew they'd say he was stepping out of bounds.

Bromley relaxed a little. Marston didn't suspect Maida was inside locked in his bedroom. "Why should I help after the way them women at Catawba treated me?"

Yates bit back a sharp retort. "My wife is gone. She could be lost in the swamps or be lying hurt and defenseless. I'm not a man to beg, but I beg of you to help find her."

Pickle touched the gun stuck in his pants. He could kill Bromley where he stood. Pickle moved his hand to the pommel of the saddle and waited.

Bromley forced back a snicker. It was grand to have a Marston beg him! "Be on your way! I won't help you find any of them women of yours!"

With a low growl Yates swung his mount around and rode away from the house.

Pickle hesitated, then followed. He could see the dark form of Master Yates ahead of him. Up above stars twinkled in the sky, but neither of them noticed.

At Catawba Taylor paced the yard with Kendra and Laurel and prayed for Maida. "It's hard not to be able to go look for her," Taylor said as she sank to the bench under the tree. "Praying for her will help."

Her icy hands locked together, Kendra walked to the well and back, praying under her breath.

Catching back a sob, Laurel sat beside Taylor. "I didn't think I'd miss Maida, but I do. I was quite mean to her." Laurel's voice broke and she nervously rubbed her skirts at her knees. "I will never be mean again if she comes back!"

Taylor remembered Maida's unhappiness with Yates. Had Maida walked to the main road and caught a ride into Darien? If Yates wouldn't go there tomorrow to check, she'd go herself!

"Maybe she went to visit the Fergusons," Laurel said. "She's been wanting to go, but she couldn't."

"Your father will check before he returns, I'm sure," Taylor responded.

Just then Brooke cried in pain again and Taylor ran to the cabin to help Cammie with her.

Three hours later Yates rode in with Pickle just behind him. Laurel and Kendra were in the yard before he had a chance to dismount. Taylor waited at the bench, Brooke in her arms, and Cammie almost asleep beside her.

"No sign of her," Yates said tiredly as he dismounted. He handed the reins to Pickle.

"I'll do it," Laurel said quickly. She took the reins and walked beside Pickle to the barn.

"Did you check at the Fergusons'?" Kendra asked anxiously.

"Yes. And two other places. Nothing." Yates shook his head. "I'll ride into Darien in the morning and ask there. She could've flagged someone down and asked them to take her to town." She might even be in Darien right now, sleeping soundly in a comfortable bed she didn't have to share with him—a thought that sent a shaft of pain knifing through him. "Get to bed, girls. You too, Taylor. And Cammie," he added as an afterthought.

Slowly Yates walked to the cabin. Tonight he wouldn't have to listen to Maida's sharp tongue and he'd have the bed to himself. A great sadness welled up inside him and tears burned his eyes. Why couldn't things have been different between him and Maida? Now it was probably too late to give their marriage a chance. Surprised, Yates realized that he no longer felt guilty for wanting their marriage to work. When had he let go of Ellen? Moaning deep inside, Yates finally realized that he wanted nothing more than to have Maida there talking to him.

❧

Two days later, just before dark, Ward drove into the yard and stopped the team outside his cabin. His men and Reid were following in their wagons with others coming behind them with some of the building materials for the house. He'd come ahead at a faster clip to reach home first in order to see Taylor. Ward jumped to the ground just as Taylor rushed from the cabin. Ward's pulse leaped at the sight of her there to greet him. He pulled off his hat and without hesitation took several steps forward to meet her. "Taylor!" He wrapped his arms around her and pulled her to him.

Deeply concerned for Maida, Taylor didn't consider his action nor hers. She lifted her face to say something, but he thought she was lifting it for a kiss. His heart soared. She'd run into his arms and she wanted his kiss! He kissed her eagerly and fire leaped through his veins.

Alarmed, she tried to push against his chest to get away from him, but he was holding her too tightly. Her eyelids fluttered shut and to her own surprise she returned his kiss with a passion that matched his own. Thoughts of Maida flew from her head as the kiss went on and on. He lifted his head, looked deep into her eyes, and smiled.

"I missed you," he whispered. Before she could speak he kissed her again.

She slipped her arms around his waist and clung to him as if she'd never let him go.

"What a nice homecoming," he whispered as he heard the other wagons drive into the yard.

She gasped and pulled back. "I must tell you! Maida's gone! She disappeared three days ago and we've looked everywhere for her!"

Fear shot through Ward and the romantic thoughts vanished. "Did Yates get Bromley to bring his dogs to track her?"

"He tried, but Bromley wouldn't come."

Ward's nerves tightened. Perhaps he knew why he hadn't come. "I'll go see him," he promised.

"He's probably upset because I ordered him away," Taylor said. "Maybe if I beg him he'll help."

"I won't have you beg him for anything!"

Taylor laid a hand on Ward's arm. "Not even to find Maida?"

"She's probably dead by now."

"Oh, Ward!" Trembling, Taylor pressed her hand to her throat. "Where's Yates?"

"In the field working. He and his men looked for Maida all day yesterday. They took Musket with them, but he didn't find anything. Pickle said if she was out there, Musket would've found her."

"He's right."

"Then why would we need Bromley and his dogs?"

"It would make me feel better. His dogs are used to tracking. They might find something Musket didn't." Ward looked around with a frown. "Where are Kendra and Laurel?"

"In the field with Yates. He said they had to help him since he was behind after yesterday."

Ward scowled. "Did Yates leave you and Cammie here alone?"

Taylor nodded. "But we're fine. I have a musket that Pickle taught me to shoot."

Ward smiled. "Is Brooke feeling better?"

"Yes. Finally."

"Good." Ward pulled Taylor close. "I missed you."

She flushed and pushed him away. The feelings he'd evoked in her had alarmed her. She wanted to sort them out before he held her and kissed her again. Besides, the men were drinking at the well.

Ward lifted a brow questioningly. Why was she pushing him away after such a warm greeting? He glanced around and spotted Court at the well. Was he the reason?

Ward forced thoughts of Taylor aside and hurried to show the drivers where to unload the materials.

Taylor hurried to Court, Bard, and Reid and told them about Maida. They asked her questions and she answered them the best she could before Ward called for them to help unload the wagons.

Ward saw Taylor with the men and frowned. Well, Taylor hadn't rushed to Court for a kiss. Ward stopped short. Or perhaps Taylor had not rushed to him for a kiss but to tell him about Maida being gone. And slowly he felt the pleasure in the kiss slip away.

Taylor followed the wagons up the incline to the building site and watched them unload. It looked like there was enough material to build ten houses.

Later she hurried to the house to help Cammie fix supper. When Yates and the others returned they'd be hungry.

After supper she looked out the window and saw Ward talking earnestly to Yates on the bench under the tree. After Yates went to his cabin Ward walked slowly to his. He reached to open the door, then let his hand fall to his side. How could he face Taylor?

Ward stood outside his cabin long after dark. Truth to tell, he was afraid to go inside and learn the truth from Taylor. Had he forced his kisses on her? Had she clung to him only to keep from a worse fate?

Inside Taylor sat at the table, her hands idle for once, her ears tuned for Ward's footstep outside the door. Cammie and Brooke were already asleep. The fire was banked in the fireplace to keep from going out in the night, yet not give off a lot of heat.

Why had Ward kissed her the way he had? She blushed just thinking of her response. Would he think she was too forward? She moaned and covered her face. How could she want him to hold her and kiss her so soon after Floyd's death?

Impatiently she jumped up. Ward was her husband! She couldn't consider the past any longer even though she'd loved Floyd with her whole heart.

She stopped at the door. Where was Ward? Had he decided to spend the night in the barn? She had to know. She couldn't wait all night to see if he was going to come inside.

Her heart in her mouth, she opened the door. Ward stood there and she jumped in surprise. "I was coming to find you," she said weakly.

"You were?" For a minute he couldn't move, then slowly he walked into the house and shut the door. He looked deep into her eyes. "Taylor, are you sorry you married me?" he asked just above a whisper.

She barely moved her head to show him she wasn't. "Are you?" He smiled and reached for her. "No."

ॐ

In Virginia at Rawlings Plantation James Rawlings eyed Andrew Simons suspiciously. He looked the picture of a dandy like the drawings in the newspaper.

"Sir, how do I know what you've told me is true? You're asking a big reward for information I doubt," he drawled.

"I traveled the *Falcon* from Liverpool to Charleston with Taylor Craven as well as Yates Marston and his family. I know Mrs. Craven went with Marston to the Catawba Plantation near Darien in South Carolina. It's between the low country and the up country. I checked." Andrew had run into a man who'd bought horses from Ward Marston to learn the exact location of Catawba, then he'd asked around until he found someone who'd been to Darien within the past few weeks. He knew he couldn't approach James Rawlings without proof. "I know she's there."

"And my Negra Cammie was with Taylor Craven?"

Simons nodded. "She helped with Taylor's baby. And Cammie's in a delicate condition herself."

James's stomach tightened, but he didn't let his shock show by even a flicker of movement. His offspring, his slave, and his future wife were at Catawba when they should have been with him at Rawlings Plantation! He looked carefully at the man before him and said, "Simons, go with me to this Catawba Plantation, help me get back what's mine, and I'll pay you twice what you're asking."

Andrew Simons thought for a minute and agreed. It would give him a chance to take revenge on Yates Marston for paying for Taylor, the baby, and the colored girl when he had had other plans for them. Plus, he could use the money. He'd lost a horse race he had been positive he'd win. He smiled and nodded. "When do you want to leave?"

"In two days."

"I'll be ready."

"We'll chart the quickest route and take it." James opened his study door to see Simons out. "You may stay here until we leave." James motioned to Darla who was dusting the china figurines on a round mahogany table. Since Cammie was gone Darla was his bed warmer. She filled his arms more than Cammie had and she served him well, but she wasn't Cammie.

"Darla, Mr. Simons will be with us two days. Show him to the blue guest room."

"Yes, sir." Darla smiled politely and led Simons across the great hall to the grand stairway. She hoped Master wouldn't give her to Simons tonight as he had when other visitors stopped by.

James walked slowly to the window and looked out across the wide stretch of green lawn with bright beds of flowers and several shade trees. He clenched his fists. He'd built the mansion and had the lawn landscaped for Taylor. He'd amassed a fortune for Taylor. How could she refuse what he had to offer?

His voice was low, but threatening. "First she rejected me to marry Floyd, then she ran away to South Carolina to get away from me. No more! I will destroy Catawba and I will get back what belongs to me."

14

*H*er heart an icy stone inside her breast, Maida sank lower in her chair beside Alden Bromley. The cook had served fresh garden okra, string beans, and carrots. She'd set three meats on the table—venison, rabbit, and turkey along with gravy and cornpone. Maida had only picked at it while Bromley wolfed down most of it, drowning it with a mug of rum.

"You can't go without food the rest of your life, woman," Bromley said good-naturedly as he wiped his calloused hand across his mouth.

Maida stared at her plate. She had used up her tears in the first few days.

"They won't be coming for you." Bromley gently patted her hand. She didn't pull away or seem to notice he'd touched her. "They don't care you're gone. If they cared they would've stopped in to ask for my help." He'd said the same thing to her every day since she'd come to live with him. He didn't tell her Yates had come the first night or that Ward had come last week to ask for his help. He'd acted real sorry and had taken his dogs to Catawba, but the dogs hadn't found a thing.

He took a long swig of rum. He'd acted real sorry and had offered to take the dogs out again just in case they'd missed something. "I got tracking dogs and everybody knows it. Folks from far and wide that need runaways or lost folks found call on me. Nobody from Catawba said one word about you being missing. Nobody. That seems real heartless to me." He stroked her arm. "I tell you they don't care." He lifted her hand to his mouth and kissed each finger. "But I care. I will always care." Bromley knew that eventually she would have to start believing him. He would be patient and wait for her.

Maida heard what he said, but she didn't acknowledge it. At first she'd argued with him. Now she believed him. They didn't care. Nobody did. Not her aunt and uncle, not Taylor, not Ward, and certainly not Yates and his children.

"I would've gone to offer my help, but you know I'm not welcome at Catawba. That Taylor thinks too much of herself." Bromley leaned over and kissed Maida's cheek. "But not you. You're a real lady—one like I always wanted—with black hair and blue eyes." He rubbed a hand on the sleeve of her yellow dress. "Ginny sewed a real fine dress for you." He could trust Ginny not to say a word to anyone about Maida. A few months back as punishment for telling Elmer something he didn't want told outside the house he'd sold Ginny's oldest youngster. No, Ginny wouldn't breathe a word about Maida for fear of losing her other child.

Bromley lifted Maida's hand to his lips again and kissed it. It was soft and smelled like bayberry. "You're a mighty pretty lady. I plan to keep you forever because I love you. I'm not like them folks from Catawba." He nuzzled her neck, then turned her face and kissed her lips. She'd fought him at first, but she didn't any longer. He didn't mind because soon she'd return his kisses with a fervor. She'd give him the children he'd always planned to have once he found the right woman. He leaned his head against hers. Fate had handed the right woman over to him and he'd hang on to her forever.

He pushed back his chair and stood, then gently lifted Maida. "Let's sit in the other room now so Ginny can clear the table. Would you like a cup of tea?"

"No, thank you." She walked with him to the sitting room and sank weakly in the big maroon chair where she always sat after supper. It hugged her body and made a half circle around her shoulders and head. Alden liked to talk after they ate even if she didn't listen. Alden! She trembled. When had she started thinking of him in that way? What did it matter? She'd be here the rest of her life.

"I heard they're building the new house at Catawba. Next thing you know, Yates will be getting himself a new wife." Bromley kissed Maida on top of her head, then sat in a matching chair beside her. "He won't find one as fine as you, I can tell you that."

Maida studied a rough spot on her thumbnail. She snagged her skirt each time she moved her hand. "My aunt made me keep her fingernails perfect," she said idly. "She said it was important for a lady to have nice-looking nails."

Bromley smiled. Finally Maida was talking! He settled back and listened. He liked the sound of her voice.

Maida touched her neatly arranged hair. "I did her hair every day. She liked it piled like this on top of her head with a few loose strands and if I did it wrong, she wouldn't allow me to eat that day."

Bromley frowned. "You're better off without her."

"She promised I could go to a Christmas party when I was twenty. I had a red and white dress and red shoes. I piled my hair on my head and tied it with a red ribbon."

"I bet you were the prettiest woman for miles."

"I looked in the looking glass." Maida smiled at the memory. "I was very pretty."

"Did you have fun at the party?"

"I hated to walk away from the looking glass for fear I'd turn ugly." Maida touched her cheek and her hair, then smoothed her dress. "Aunt Erica called me and I didn't hear her. I looked awfully beautiful. I turned and twisted so I could see as much of myself as possible." Maida's face puckered and she shivered. "Aunt had to send the maid after me. Aunt was so angry she gave my dress away and wouldn't let me go to the party. I cried." She brushed at her eyes, then lifted her chin high and looked smug. "But I didn't shed a tear for Aunt Erica to see. I wouldn't give her the satisfaction of seeing me cry." Her lips quivered. "I cried almost all night."

Bromley's jaw tightened. "If I ever see her, I'll cut her heart out!" He stroked Maida's arm. "Forget about your aunt and think of your future. You'll have children to love."

"Yates doesn't want children. He has three and he says that's enough."

Fire flashed in Bromley's eyes. "Forget Yates! You're with me now. We'll have children. All the children we want."

"Two girls and four boys. I always wanted two girls and four boys. My aunt said I'd never marry." Maida's voice broke and for a minute she couldn't speak. "She kept the suitors away. But I fooled her—I married Yates Marston. He's a fine man with possibilities."

Bromley lifted her hand to his lips again. "Yates Marston doesn't care for you. He never even looked for you. He kept working his cotton field. Cotton is his love. He wants to grow cotton so he can be wealthy."

"He was rude sometimes and cruel, too. I didn't know he could be cruel. Aunt Erica said I went from the frying pan into the fire. She was right."

Bromley knelt at Maida's chair and took her hands in his. "Look at me, Maida!"

"I tried to get Taylor to help me out of the marriage, but she wouldn't. She said a wife belongs with her husband. She married Ward. We were all surprised." Maida pulled a hand free and brushed a strand of hair off her ashen cheek. "I don't think she likes me."

"She doesn't. She never once looked for you."

"Neither do Laurel and Kendra. Reid does, I suppose."

A chill ran down Bromley's spine. Did Maida even know he was there? He stood and lifted her to her feet. He'd show her he was there! He wrapped his arms around her and kissed her passionately. She didn't pull away or lean against him. She stayed as straight as a ramrod. He looked into her eyes. It was as if she'd left, leaving only her body behind. Gently he kissed her again. "I'm real sorry, dar-lin'. One day you'll come back and when you do, you'll love me like I love you."

❦

At Catawba Taylor leaned back against the cabin beside Ward and watched the builders working on the new house. Piles of materials sat all over. A housewright from Darien had come with his workers the day after Ward had arrived home and had worked each day since. They said it would take months to finish the house.

"I wish Maida was here to see this." Taylor turned to Ward. "I feel so terrible about her!"

"I know. Yates is working himself even harder to keep from thinking about her. He blames himself."

Taylor glanced toward the well where Yates and the men were filling canteens before heading back out to the field after eating dinner. Yates had lost weight and looked gaunt. "Do you really think she's dead?"

Ward nodded sadly. "We checked everywhere. If she'd gone to Darien someone would've seen her."

"You're right, I suppose."

Ward was quiet for a while as he watched the men dig the foundation. "Bromley's coming to shoe the new mares I brought home a couple of days ago."

Taylor stiffened. "I don't want to see him!"

"You won't have to." Ward squeezed Taylor's hand and smiled.

He wanted to pull her close, but he couldn't in front of the others. "Court will have the bed finished for Brooke today."

"I'm glad. Brooke will be, too. She's growing so much!"

Ward watched Yates and his men walk away from the yard toward the field. Just as they disappeared from sight Musket barked and looked toward the road leading to the main road. "Someone's coming." Ward pushed away from the cabin. "It's probably Bromley. Go on inside now."

"I have some wash to bring in." She'd hung clothes out to dry that morning and in the heat they were already dry. "Don't worry about me. I'll stay out of sight until Bromley's in the pen with you."

"Good." Ward squeezed her hand, then hurried toward the barn. As soon as he could, he'd hire someone else to shoe his horses. He didn't want Bromley on the place.

Taylor peered around the edge of the cabin as Elmer drove Bromley's wagon beside the pen of horses. Bromley and Ward greeted each other as Elmer jumped to the ground. He darted a look around until he spotted Taylor. She started to step out of sight, but stopped. He was motioning to her, trying to give her a message without Bromley seeing. Was it about Sippy? Oh, surely not! Bromley shouted to Elmer and he immediately stopped motioning to her and looked as if he didn't see or hear anything but his master's voice.

"Curious," Taylor muttered. She'd find a way to speak to Elmer. What if he wanted her to write a paper for him saying he was free? What if it was another trap? She began to pray.

Just then Pickle walked around the corner carrying a large basket full of corn to be shucked for supper. His wide-brimmed hat shaded his face and shoulders.

"Pickle, find a way for me to speak to Elmer without Master Bromley knowing," she asked.

Pickle's eyes widened and he set the basket down so hard two ears of corn tumbled out. "You sure, Miz Taylor?"

"He wants to speak to me. I'm curious to know what it is all about."

"What if he's got orders from Master Bromley to hurt you or something? I can't let nothin' happen to you, Miz Taylor." He couldn't let her be left alone in the company of Bromley's slave. If she was so determined to talk to him, then Pickle was going to be right there to make sure she was all right.

"Now, Pickle. There is nothing to worry about. Please see that I can talk with Elmer without Master Bromley knowing."

"Yes, ma'am," Pickle said gruffly. He could see that nothing he said would change Taylor's mind.

"I'll take the clothes off the line and wait inside for you to get me."

Pickle shook his head. "I don't like this one bit, Miz Taylor."

"I know, but I feel this is important." She hoped Elmer wasn't going to tell her Bromley had found Sippy and killed her and was now looking for the person who'd written the paper.

Later Pickle led Taylor into the woods away from the house-builders and away from Bromley and Ward. Elmer was waiting behind a tulip tree about three feet around and over a hundred feet tall. High in the tree three squirrels flipped their tails, leaped to another tree, and chattered excitedly.

"I got to see you alone, ma'am," Elmer said in a low voice with his head down. He knew he was in grave danger by just talking to Miz Taylor. If Master found out, he'd kill him dead on the spot.

Pickle glared at Elmer. "I staying right here!"

"No, Pickle." Taylor shook her head. "Please leave us alone."

Pickle forced back the words of argument on the tip of his tongue and slowly walked away, his feet silent on the thick leaves.

Taylor turned to Elmer. "What is so important?"

"Miz Maida," Elmer whispered frantically.

Taylor frowned. "She's gone. She disappeared about two weeks ago."

Elmer finally lifted his eyes to Taylor, then looked quickly down at his feet again. "Master Bromley has her locked in his house."

"What?" Taylor glanced around to make sure nobody had heard her outcry and was coming to check on her. She lowered her voice. "Are you sure?"

Elmer nodded. "I done told you 'cause of what you done for Sippy. But I's got to get back before Master Bromley finds me gone. Don't tell even Master Ward I told you about Miz Maida."

Taylor hesitated. Dare she make that promise? She already had too many secrets from Ward. Throwing all caution to the wind, she nodded. With that promise she knew she'd have to rescue Maida without help from Ward or Pickle. "I won't tell Ward or Pickle. I promise."

"You gets her away so's nobody sees you. Master Bromley will kill anybody at his place that helps you."

Taylor nodded. "You go back now. And don't worry. I won't let him kill anybody!" She managed a smile. "Thank you for telling me."

Nodding, Elmer ran back toward the pen in back of the barn.

Praying silently for the direction to take, Taylor slowly walked toward the house. Before she reached the edge of the woods Pickle joined her, looking concerned.

"What'd he want, Miz Taylor?"

"It's private."

"Don't trust him, ma'am. Don't trust nobody of Master Bromley's."

"You're a kind man, Pickle, but I can't tell you what he said." Taylor's head whirled with ideas on rescuing Maida. Was Elmer telling the truth? Could this be a trick to get her to Bromley's place. "Pickle, how long will Master Bromley be here?"

"On to dark most likely, ma'am."

Suddenly Taylor had a plan. "While he's here I am going for a ride with Laurel and Kendra."

Pickle's nerves tightened. He didn't like the sound of that one bit. "Takes me with you, ma'am."

"No, Pickle. We're safe since Bromley's here." Taylor smiled. Her plan had to work. "Tell Master Ward we're going for a ride and we'll be safe."

"You take a weapon."

"We'll take a gun. You get a wagon ready for us now."

Pickle wanted to argue further, but he knew Miz Taylor had set her mind and no words would change it. "Yes, Miz Taylor, ma'am," he said as he stalked off, muttering to himself.

Taylor ran to her cabin to tell Cammie she'd be gone for a while; then she hurried to find Kendra and Laurel. They were finishing washing and drying dinner dishes. "I need you both to help me, but I can't tell you what we're going to do until we're on the way. Please, no questions. Hurry fast. Kendra, bring the musket and Laurel, bring the pistol."

"Taylor!" they cried, shocked that she'd take both a musket and a pistol.

She put her finger to her lips. "Not a word until we're away from here."

Several minutes later Taylor drove the wagon away from Catawba. She'd dropped a folded blanket and a pillow in the back of the wagon. The pistol in her lap, Laurel sat on Taylor's right; Ken-

dra sat on her left, the musket in her hands. A powder horn and bag
hung around her neck down onto her dress.

Kendra had a dozen questions on the tip of her tongue, but she
didn't voice any of them.

Laurel's stomach fluttered nervously. What was the adventure
Taylor was taking them on? Maybe she was only trying to get their
minds off Maida's disappearance.

At the main road Taylor stopped, her nerves tight. Dust settled
around them. With her bonnet shielding her eyes from the sun she
looked right, then left. Which way to Bromley's? Why hadn't she
asked Elmer?

"What's wrong?" Kendra asked sharply.

"Don't you know where we're going?" Laurel rested her hand on
the pistol in her lap.

Taylor searched for the right words to say to the girls. She'd been
going over and over in her mind what she would say, but somehow
the first sentence to start it all eluded her. Finally she blurted out, "I
think Maida's being held a prisoner at Bromley's. We're going to see
and to get her out if she is. And we have to get there and back
before Bromley leaves Catawba."

The girls were speechless as Taylor explained her plan. Finally
Kendra said, "Uncle Ward said Bromley lives off the road going to
Pine Bluff where the sawmill is."

Taylor slapped the reins on the horses' rumps and turned left.
How long did it take to get there? They had to be back before dark.
If they didn't have any trouble, surely they could do it.

She drove along the narrow road with trees on both sides, around
a swamp, and past a valley where they saw some deer. "Why is it
taking so long?" Taylor muttered as chills ran up and down her
spine.

❦

At Catawba Bromley wiped sweat off his face with a big dirty
handkerchief, then stuffed it in the leather apron around his thick
waist. He was dirty and smelled like a horse. "I can't shoe two of
them mares today. They got split hooves. I'll trim 'em and do what I
can, then shoe 'em on my next trip." Inside he was laughing like a
wild man. Here he was at Catawba, working and talking like all the
other times. Ward Marston had no idea Maida was hidden away at
his place and learning to like it better every day.

"I have a couple of others for you to check." Ward pulled off his hat to let the breeze cool his head, wiped sweat off the sweatband, and put it back on. "Looks like you'll get done quicker than you thought."

"Sure does." Bromley chuckled under his breath. And Maida would be waiting with open arms.

Elmer heard what they'd said and his blood ran cold. What could he do to delay Master? Elmer's head whirled with ideas, but not a one would work. No matter what he tried, he'd get a whipping for it, and Master would still go home early.

❦

In the distance Laurel spotted a three-story house and outbuildings. Smoke drifted from the chimney up into the bright blue sky. She pointed and said, "Maybe that's Bromley's place."

"We'll stop and ask." Taylor's mouth felt cotton-dry. Had she taken on a job too big for her? No! God was with her!

Kendra touched the rifle in the scabbard at the side of the wagon. It was primed and loaded if she needed to use it.

Several minutes later Taylor drove into the place. Dogs barked in a frenzy in a pen by a shed. She drove past the barn and around the house. The dogs continued to bark wildly. No one was in sight and no one checked to see why the dogs were barking. She stopped the team near the back door of the house.

"I'll go ask," she said quietly. She climbed down the wheel to the ground, steadied her thundering heart, then knocked on the back door. No one answered and she knocked again, harder this time.

The door opened a crack and a black woman peered out. It was hard to judge her age. She looked tired and sad and her gray dress hung loosely on her plump body.

"Does Alden Bromley live here?" Taylor asked, keeping her voice light.

"He do, ma'am, but he's not to home." She started to shut the door, but Taylor stuck her foot in it.

"We're coming in." Taylor waved to the girls and they jumped to the ground, their guns ready. Taylor pushed the door wide and the black woman threw her hands into the air and shrieked.

"We came to get Maida Marston," Taylor said firmly. "If you do what we say, we don't hurt you."

"Bless Jesus! I prayed somebody would come get that sweet lady! Master Bromley had no right to keep her here. Miz Maida be asleep in the rocking chair in there." The black woman pointed to a nearby door, then wiped her face with the tail of her gray apron.

"Lead the way," Taylor said.

Kendra kept the musket pointed at the black woman's back.

Laurel's hand shook, but she kept the pistol aimed the best she could.

In the front room the curtains were drawn and the room was pleasantly cool and in perfect order. Maida sat rocking with her head back and her hands folded in her lap. She looked very peaceful.

"Miz Maida, they done come for you." The black woman gently shook Maida's shoulder. "Wake up, ma'am. You can go home now."

Maida opened her eyes, but she didn't seem to see Taylor or the girls. "Tell Aunt Erica I will be right up to fix her hair, Ginny."

"I sure will, Miz Maida."

Taylor's heart stood still and she couldn't move. Maida had slipped over the edge. "Who else is here, Ginny?" Taylor asked sharply.

"Only me and Miz Maida. The others be working a cotton field way out yonder." Ginny wrung her hands. "Master Bromley say he'll sell my child if I does something he don't like. He won't like this one tad!"

"Master Marston will deal with him," Taylor said grimly.

"Aunt Erica wants her hair fixed," Maida said as she walked in circles, wringing her hands.

Taylor caught Maida's arm. "Come with me."

"Aunt wants me."

"Oh, my," Laurel whispered.

Kendra bit her lip and looked ready to cry.

"I'll take care of everything, Maida." Taylor walked Maida through the house and outdoors to the wagon. "Climb in the back and lie down."

Maida obeyed as if she were a child.

Taylor covered her with the blanket. "You stay down until I say you can get up. And keep the blanket over you. We don't want anyone to see you."

"I'll sit back with her," Laurel said as she climbed in the back. Her chin quivered, but she didn't cry.

Kendra braced her feet as Taylor drove around the house and down the lane to the road. Kendra looked back at Maida. She looked so tiny under the blanket. "Will she be all right?"

"Yes! She has to be! We'll pray for her and tend her together and she'll come back to herself." Or at least she prayed it would happen.

❦

At Catawba Bromley shook hands with Ward and climbed in the wagon Elmer was driving. "I'll look in on them mares in a few days to see if I can shoe 'em yet."

"Thank you." Ward nodded a goodbye and stepped away from the wagon.

"Get me home quick, Elmer," Bromley said with a chuckle. "I got my little darlin' to see."

Elmer's nerves jangled and it was hard to keep from looking frightened. They'd meet Miz Taylor on the road. Then what? He'd have to do something to keep Master from killing all of them.

❦

Taylor slapped the reins hard on the team. The wagon bucked and swayed and she was forced to slow the team. She took a deep breath to calm herself. They'd made good time. Surely they'd get back to Catawba before Bromley left.

She drove down the tree-lined road and past the valley. As they topped a hill Kendra shouted and pointed. A wagon was heading toward them.

"Is it Bromley?" Laurel cried.

"We don't know. I can't take a chance on meeting anyone." Frantically Taylor looked around for a place where she could pull off the road. She saw a grassy spot that led to a clump of trees that would easily hide them. She turned the team and drove them across the grassy area and behind the trees, then stopped. Sweat soaked her skin and she trembled.

Her eyes wide, Laurel leaned against the seat. "What'll we do?"

"Wait until we hear the wagon pass." Taylor pulled off her gloves to cool her hands as she glanced back at Maida. She was lying quietly with her eyes closed.

Kendra rocked back and forth. If only Court was with them, then she wouldn't be so frightened!

Taylor sat with her head up, listening intently for the wagon. Finally she heard it pass. She flicked the reins and the team pulled forward, but the wagon didn't budge. She'd pulled into a swampy area and the wheels were stuck.

Kendra gasped. "We're stuck! We have to get out before Bromley reaches home and finds Maida gone!"

"What'll we do?" Laurel cried.

Taylor bit her lip and groaned. On the trip from Charleston to Catawba she'd watched the men get the wagons out of mire and back on the road. Could she and the girls do the same thing? "Girls, get down and push!"

Laurel peeked over the edge and shivered. "What about snakes?" she whispered.

"We must get out of here!" Taylor cried, suddenly feeling desperate. "Laurel, you drive and I'll push."

"I don't know how!" But when she got back, if she ever did, she'd have Pickle teach her!

"Be brave, Laurel." Kendra hesitated, then climbed to the ground. Her shoes were heavy leather, but not high on her foot. Water seeped into them, making a squishy sound when she moved.

Laurel reluctantly dropped to the ground. Her feet sank down and the bottom of her skirts were soaked immediately.

"Push, girls!" Taylor waited until each girl was on a back wagon wheel with their hands on the spokes to try to turn them as the horses moved. Taylor slapped the reins down hard on the horses' back and shouted, "Get up!" The horses leaped forward, their muscles bunching as they tried to pull the wagon.

Mud flew from under the wheels, spattering the girls. Laurel whimpered, but Kendra didn't make a sound.

"Again, girls!" Taylor slapped the team again and shouted to them. The horses leaped forward, moving the wagon a few feet. Again and again Taylor slapped them and shouted to them while the girls grabbed the spokes and rolled the wheels. By now the girls were spattered with mud from head to toe.

Suddenly the horses reached solid ground and with one last mighty effort pulled the wagon from the mire, sending Laurel sprawling to the ground on her stomach. Kendra ran to her and helped her up.

"Hurry, girls! Climb in!" Taylor shouted. Her arms ached and her hands felt raw even though she had on leather gloves. They'd lost a lot of time getting back to the road. Had Bromley reached his place and discovered Maida was gone?

The girls climbed into the back and sank exhaustedly beside Maida. She hadn't moved at all nor opened her eyes.

Taylor hurried back onto the main road and headed for Catawba. Was she going in the right direction or was she heading right back to Bromley's? Trembling, she pulled back on the reins and stopped the team.

"What's wrong?" Laurel cried.

The mud already drying on her from the hot sun, Kendra scrambled up beside Taylor. "Why are you stopping?"

"I don't know if I'm going the right way to Catawba!" Frantically Taylor looked up and down the road.

"You're going right." Kendra pointed back at the grassy spot where they'd turned off. "See your tracks going in, then coming out?"

Taylor sighed in relief and weakly flicked the reins and shouted, "Get up!"

Several minutes later she came to a fork in the road and she again slowed the team. Why hadn't she noticed the fork on the way? She glanced at Kendra. "Which way?"

"I don't know," Kendra said hesitantly.

Laurel jumped up and clung to the seat. "Are we lost?" She'd heard many stories about the dangers of wild animals and swampy areas that could swallow a whole team and wagon.

"Go that way!" Kendra pointed. "I'm sure that's the right way. I think."

Taylor tugged the reins so the team would go where Kendra pointed. A pleasantly cool breeze blew up, taking the heat from the sun and bringing the smell of pine. With a sigh Taylor settled back, the reins looped through her fingers. They'd be back soon and could get Maida home where she belonged.

❧

At Bromley's Elmer stopped the wagon near the house. The dogs recognized them and didn't bark. Elmer's nerves twitched like crazy as he waited for Master to jump down and walk into the house. Had Miz Taylor picked Maida up yet, or had they got lost?

Bromley sprang out of the wagon, calling, "Ginny, bring my darlin' to me!" He ran up on the porch, expecting the door to open wide. But the door remained closed. He opened it and stepped inside. The house seemed unusually silent. No smells of supper cooking filled the room. He scowled, then ran to the sitting room where Maida spent her day. It was empty! He fell on his knees at her rocker and with a great roar slammed his fists onto the seat. "Maida! Maida, where are you?"

He leaped to his feet and ran to the kitchen. Ginny would know.

Maybe she'd taken Maida out for a walk. But the kitchen was empty and the fire out. He picked up a butter crock from the table and flung it hard to the floor. It exploded into dozens of pieces.

"Ginny?" He ran to the door and shouted even louder, "Ginny!"

Elmer heard the shout and almost dropped the heavy harness. He hung it carefully, then led the horses to the trough to drink. He peeked around as Master ran back in the house, still shouting for Ginny. "They gots Miz Maida," Elmer whispered, then whistled as he led the horses to the pen.

"I ought to shoot the nigger," Bromley snarled, hunting for his long rifle. He remembered it was in the wagon and he shouted out for Elmer to bring it.

Bromley ran upstairs and looked in each room. He finally found Ginny on the third floor curled on her bed with her head covered. He jerked off the quilt and hauled Ginny to her feet. She shivered and looked ready to collapse. "Where's Maida?" he shouted.

"They break in and steal her away," Ginny said in a weak voice.

He slapped her and she would've fallen had he not held her arm so tightly. "Who took her?"

Ginny shivered and kept her head down as she said in a quivering voice, "Them Catawba womenfolk."

With a roar Bromley flung Ginny away and stormed out of the room. He ran down the stairs, almost fell, and caught the banister to right himself. He sped outdoors and leaped the porch steps in one bound. "Elmer, bring my horse! And the long rifle!"

Elmer saddled the horse and stuck the long rifle in the scabbard. "Something be wrong, Master?"

"Them Catawba women took my Maida. I mean to get her back."

Hiding his fear, Elmer stepped back and watched Master ride like a whirlwind out of the yard.

"Jesus, take care of them Catawba women," Elmer muttered. Then he grinned. He'd left the powder out of the flash pan. When Master pulled the trigger, the gun wouldn't go off. He couldn't kill nobody with that long rifle of his unless he loaded it again. And them Catawba women wouldn't give him a chance to do that.

❦

Taylor looked at the sun ready to go down and she groaned. They had been traveling long enough that they should've been home by now. They must have taken the wrong fork several miles back. Fear pricked her skin and for a moment she couldn't think.

Her brows cocked, Kendra touched Taylor's arm. "Taylor?"

"What's wrong?" Laurel cried, jerking up.

Taylor sighed heavily. "We must have taken the wrong turn. We'll have to backtrack to it."

"But Mr. Bromley will know we took Maida and be after us!"

Taylor nodded. "But maybe the wagon we hid from wasn't Mr. Bromley."

Laurel shuddered. "I hope not!"

Taylor found an easy turnaround and maneuvered the team and wagon around and headed back the way they'd come. She snapped the reins to hurry the team. They had to get home before dark!

15

*H*is head almost touching the horse's neck, Bromley raced down the road toward Catawba. Blood roared in his ears along with the thundering hooves of his horse. He'd kill every last one of them Marstons and take Maida back! She belonged to him no matter what they said!

Taylor wanted to send the horses running along the road, but she knew the wagon would sway and rock so much it could flip over, so she kept at a steady pace, the horses clip-clopping at a fast walk. "How's Maida?" Taylor called back to Laurel.

"She seems all right." Laurel nudged Maida. "Open your eyes and talk to me."

Maida closed her eyes tighter. She couldn't think of anything but getting to Aunt Erica to fix her hair. If she was late, her aunt might give away all of her clothes and lock her in her room until she was an old woman.

Kendra braced her feet to keep from tumbling over and tried to brush the dried mud off herself. What if Court saw her this way? She moaned. It would be worse if Bromley saw her and killed her, killed all of them.

Taylor leaned forward, her face intent. Sweat darkened the horses and flicked off them as they walked. A hawk shrieked in the blue sky and dove for its prey. Taylor shuddered. They were Bromley's prey! She had to get the others back to Catawba before Bromley swooped down and caught them. Her hair whipped out behind her. A chill ran down her spine as if danger was near. She looked back and her eyes widened in alarm. A rider was racing toward them. Was it Bromley? She shivered. "Is the rifle primed and ready to fire?" she shouted to Kendra.

"Yes!" Her feet braced against the wagon, Kendra pulled it from the scabbard and clutched it fiercely.

Laurel gripped the pistol as she watched the rider bearing down on them, a dust cloud billowing out behind him. Was it Bromley? Who else would ride so fast after them? She looked down at Maida, then up toward heaven. "Oh, Jesus. Oh, Jesus. Help us, Jesus. Help us, Jesus," she prayed.

❦

At last Bromley recognized Taylor in the wagon ahead of him and he laughed a great triumphant laugh. The rush of wind caught the laugh and flung it behind him along with lather from his horse. He pulled the long rifle from its scabbard and held it across his lap. If them women thought they could take what belonged to him, he'd show them they couldn't. They'd rue the day they ever crossed Alden Bromley!

❦

Taylor narrowed her eyes as she once again looked back to see the rider coming up hard behind them. He drew closer and she saw it was Bromley! "Hang on tight!" she shouted. Leaning forward, she slapped the reins on the horses. They leaped ahead, making the wagon sway dangerously, and almost pulling her arms from their sockets. The creak and rattle filled the air, but over it came the sound of pounding hooves. She slapped the reins harder and the team lengthened their stride.

❦

Low in the saddle, Bromley whipped the ends of the reins against his horse's neck and shouted at the top of his lungs. He'd get Maida and take her home where she belonged! Wind whipped off his hat and left his hair in tangles. It whistled past his ears and the thundering hooves sounded even louder. He squinted to keep dust from his eyes. He was drawing closer. The rattle and creak of the wagon was louder. They could never outrun him!

❦

Taylor's arms ached and her lungs felt on fire as if she'd run an hour without stopping. She wanted to see if the others were safe, but she didn't dare take her eyes off the road at this breakneck speed. The horses' ears were laid back and their muscles bunched and lengthened, bunched and lengthened.

Kendra whimpered and with all her might clung to the seat with one hand and the rifle with the other. Would she be able to aim the rifle at Bromley and shoot him? She'd shot a wild turkey once and watched it bleed and twitch and flop around. She shivered.

Laurel gripped the back of the seat to keep from being bounced until she was black and blue all over. Her teeth rattled in her head. Wind whipped her blonde hair in tangles around her head. Could she shoot Bromley? She'd tried to shoot a squirrel and couldn't bring herself to take its life. Could she take Bromley's life to save theirs? A bitter taste filled her mouth and she shivered.

Maida groaned and clung to the blanket. The wagon bed tossed her up, caught her, tossed her again, caught her again. Each toss seemed higher, and each landing hurt worse than the first.

🦋

Bromley saw the back of the wagon in a blur, then rode along beside it. Slowly he gained on it. He passed Taylor whipping the reins and shouting. He raced around the wagon and grabbed the neckstrap of the lead horse and ran side by side with the team, gradually slowing them. "Stop the wagon!" he shouted.

Kendra wanted to shoot him, but it was impossible to shoot true with the bumping and swaying of the wagon. And if she did shoot, the shot would go wild and she'd have to reload. That meant she'd have to measure a charge from the powder horn into the muzzle, set the patch with a ball on it on the muzzle, and with both hands shove it to the bottom of the bore with the ramrod, prime the lock with a little powder, close the pan cover over it, and then cock the lock. Pickle said it should take less than a minute, but it took her longer. She'd have to wait to shoot until she could take careful aim.

Laurel moaned and wanted to release the wagon enough to pick up the pistol. She clung tighter and her knuckles turned white and pain shot up to her elbows.

Her stomach knotting painfully, Taylor pulled back on the reins. They had to stop running and face Bromley head-on. She didn't want to, but he could easily outrun the team and wagon. Silently she cried for God's miraculous help. Now she wished she had told Pickle or Ward where they were going so they would be on their way to rescue them!

At last Bromley released the strap of the lead horse and gripped his long rifle still across his legs. His eyes glistened triumphantly. He had them! It would be easy enough to swing up his rifle and get a shot off before Kendra could shoot him. He then saw the pistol in Laurel's hand and scowled. If he shot Kendra, Laurel would be sure to shoot him. Oh well, he'd just have to talk his way out of this situation just like he had many others before.

He kept the rifle across his legs and even managed a smile. "Ladies, you have something of mine."

"She's not yours," Taylor said grimly. "Get out of the way and let us pass!"

Kendra aimed her musket at Bromley's heart. "Get off your horse."

"Now!" Laurel snapped with the pistol aimed at Bromley.

Bromley thought fast. If he wasn't careful, he'd end up dead on the road. Still he chuckled and shook his head. "There's no reason for any of us to get killed. Give me Maida and you can be on your way."

"You know we won't do that." Taylor didn't take her eyes off Bromley. She didn't trust him as far as she could throw him. Chuckling, Bromley wagged a finger at them. "Now, ladies, you don't want no bloodshed, do you?"

Just then Maida raised her head. "Alden? Is that you?"

Bromley's heart leaped. His Maida! She'd called for him! "I came to take you home, darlin'. Climb out of the wagon and come with me."

Maida started to obey, but Laurel caught her and pushed her back down. "Stay there!" she hissed.

Rage rushed through Bromley. He could shoot Kendra, duck to miss Laurel's shot, grab Maida, and ride home. Once he was there he could barricade himself and Maida inside and nobody, not even the Marstons could get him out.

"Be ready, Kendra," Taylor said in a low voice.

Kendra kept her eyes on Bromley. If he so much as moved a finger, she'd fire and kill him on the spot.

In one quick movement Bromley raised his long rifle and fired point blank at Kendra. The gun clicked but didn't fire, sending terror licking through Bromley's veins. In the split second before Kendra could shoot Laurel took aim and fired. The shot plowed into Bromley and knocked him off his horse, which shied away from the shot.

Moaning like a hurt animal, Laurel sank to the wagon bed and dropped the pistol beside her.

Her hands icy, Kendra slowly lowered the rifle. Her finger had frozen on the trigger and she hadn't been able to fire. What had happened to her? She'd thought she was brave enough to protect them, but instead she'd turned into a coward.

Taylor looped the reins around the brake handle and leaped to the ground. She ran to Bromley and stared in horror down at him. Blood spread over his broad chest, soaking his shirt. She shivered. "I think he's dead," she whispered.

The girls gasped, but Maida didn't make a sound or even look out of the wagon.

Taylor caught Bromley's horse, tied it to the back of the wagon, then drove the wagon around Bromley and stopped again. "We'll take him to Catawba. Ward will know what to do." Was that calm voice hers? Inside she was shaking so badly her bones ached. She willed herself to move. Slowly, she turned and climbed back down the wheel.

"I can't touch him," Laurel whispered, shaking her head. Pickle had been wrong. It had been easy to shoot Bromley, but it was hard to accept that she had.

"You must help," Taylor said sternly. "He's too heavy for Kendra and me."

Shivering, Kendra pushed the rifle in the scabbard and dropped to the ground on legs almost too weak to hold her. The terrible incident played again in her head. What had happened to her? When she'd seen Bromley pull the trigger, she couldn't move. If his gun would've fired correctly, she'd be dead at the side of the road. She swayed, but got control of herself. She thrust the horrible thought aside and walked to Bromley with her head down. She couldn't look at his face or his bloody chest. She kept her eyes on his boots. "I'll take his feet."

Taylor touched Laurel's arm. "We need your help, Laurel. Please."

Laurel whimpered, but she finally climbed out. She moved as if she was in a dream. She reached out to take an arm, then jerked back. Bile filled her mouth and she was afraid she'd vomit. Pushing back her agony, she took an arm while Taylor took the other. Kendra wrapped her arms around his legs.

"Lift on the count of three," Taylor said as if they were moving a log off the road. "One, two, three, lift." She heaved the dead weight at the same time the girls did. They lifted him high enough to get him to the edge of the wagon, then shoved him all the way in. He landed inside with a thud. They leaned weakly against the wagon, breathing hard. The horses nickered and moved restlessly.

Laurel rubbed her hands down her dress, but she couldn't rub the dirt or the feel of Bromley off.

Kendra stared at her muddy feet. Bromley's boots had been dusty, but not muddy.

"Let's go." Her strength almost gone, Taylor nudged the girls, climbed wearily to the high seat, and took up the reins. Could she drive with her arms feeling so feeble?

Laurel and Kendra sat beside her, leaving Maida in the back almost under the seat and Bromley further back. Maida kept her eyes closed. Bromley's were wide open, but he couldn't see anything.

❦

Before dark Taylor drove up to Yates's cabin door. Every muscle in her body screamed with agony. She looped the reins around the brake handle, yet could only sit there in the great silence after the noise of the wagon and harness. When she saw Pickle start toward them, she called, "Get Ward. And Yates. We found Maida!"

Pickle stopped short for a moment as he considered the best way to reach them. Then he raced to get a horse to ride to the field. It would be quicker.

Ward heard the shout and ran around the barn to the wagon as Pickle, riding bareback on a gray gelding, headed toward the cotton field for Yates. Ward saw the pallor of Taylor's face and climbed up to her.

She wanted to lean against him and have him hold her until she forgot what had transpired. Instead, she motioned behind her.

Ward looked back and saw Bromley in a heap with his blood spilled on the floor of the wagon. "What happened?" Before Taylor could speak he caught sight of Maida under the blanket with only her head showing and her eyes closed. "Is she dead?" he asked in alarm.

Taylor shook her head.

Slowly Kendra and Laurel climbed out of the wagon. They sank to the ground and just sat there.

"What's happened, Miz Taylor?" Cammie cried as she ran toward the wagon with Brooke on her hip.

"Stay back!" Taylor shouted. "I don't want Brooke to see!"

Cammie froze with her heart in her mouth and Brooke trying to squirm down. Something dreadful had happened, but she'd have to wait to see what it was.

Ward scrambled into the back of the wagon and picked Maida up wrapped in the blanket. He climbed from the wagon and walked into the cabin. Taylor ran after him and turned the covers down on the bed. Ward gently laid Maida down and flipped off the blanket. Her face was as white as the pillowcase. The pins had come out of her hair and it lay in a black mass down her face and over her shoulders.

"I'll see about Bromley," Ward said crisply. He hurried out as Kendra hung the musket, the powder horn, and the bag in place.

Laurel walked in as if she was walking in her sleep and laid the pistol on the table. She had killed a man with it. She'd have to tell Pickle just how awful it was.

Kendra took Laurel's hand and they walked slowly to the bedroom to look down at Maida. "She's not dead at least," Kendra whispered.

Laurel's voice was locked inside her throat.

"She's been through a lot." Taylor smoothed Maida's hair off her forehead and cheeks. "Maida, you can open your eyes now. You're home safely."

Maida opened her eyes, looked around at the log walls, the muslin curtains at the window, the bright quilt over her, before closing her eyes again. Her voice was soft. "Aunt Erica will be very angry with me for coming here instead of fixing her hair."

The girls looked at each other.

Taylor patted Maida's hand. "No, she won't, Maida. Someone else is fixing her hair." Taylor turned to Laurel. "See if Cammie has some soup you can feed her. She doesn't look like she's been eating."

Laurel walked out in a daze.

"Do you suppose she went there of her own free will?" Kendra asked.

"Never!" Taylor shook her head hard. "She felt about Bromley like we do. She'd never walk into his house unless she was forced!"

"Maybe he offered her a ride that day she left here and she decided she'd rather be with him." Kendra bit her lip. And after the way she'd acted, she wouldn't blame Maida if she wanted to live somewhere else.

Taylor shook her head again. "She'd never go with him willingly. She'll tell us the whole story when she's in her right mind." Taylor sat on the edge of the bed and held Maida's hand. "In the meantime we'll treat her as if she's healthy and strong. We'll feed her and tend her as much as we have to, but we'll try to get her to take care of herself. We can't make a cripple out of her."

Taylor had seen it happen to Aunt Victoria. Her babies had died in a fire and she'd slipped over the edge. Everyone had treated her like an invalid and she grew worse daily. Finally Aunt Moira came along and stated that things would be different. "Treat her like she's useless and she'll be useless. Treat her like a whole person, and she'll be a whole person," she had said with such authority everyone believed her and did as she said. She got Aunt Victoria back on her feet in no time.

Laurel returned with a bowl of soup and coaxed it down Maida. Taylor gave her a sponge bath and dressed her in clean clothes. They helped her to a chair and sat her down. In the lamp light Laurel brushed her hair and braided it for the night.

"Alden said he cares for me." Maida folded her hands in her lap and looked into space. "He said nobody else does. He saved me from people who hate me."

Taylor pressed her lips together in a hard, straight line. Bromley was good at talking people into believing what he said.

"I must go with Alden. He wants me with him." Maida pushed herself up and started toward the door.

Taylor caught her and gently sat her back in the chair. "You belong with us, Maida. We love you and want you here with us."

"Alden cares for me."

Taylor knotted her fists. "You girls stay with Maida while I speak to Ward." Taylor ran out the door to the wagon where Ward was looking into the back. Soon it would be too dark to see. "Is he dead?"

Ward nodded. "He doesn't have a heartbeat. Cammie put a looking glass under his nose to see if he was breathing even a little. He's not." Ward sighed heavily. "We'll take him to Josiah Pardee in the morning." Ward took Taylor's hand and walked to the bench where they sat side by side. "Tell me everything that happened. Josiah will need to know."

Taylor took a deep breath. Musket licked her hand and laid at her feet. She tried to find a place to begin and finally just started talking.

Ward's eyes widened in shock.

Taylor finished as quickly as she could between his cries of alarm and disgust and his questions.

"Yates will want to hear this." Ward looked toward the field and saw Yates riding fast toward them.

Yates's ears rang and his insides fluttered alarmingly. Pickle had said Maida was back! Covered with dust and bone-weary, Yates slid off the horse and raced to Ward. "Is she all right?"

Ward swallowed hard. She was a long way from all right! "She's home. Bromley had her locked up in his house."

With an anguished cry, Yates ran into the cabin. Maida sat at the table looking relaxed and healthy in the glow of the lamp. His heart leaped. It couldn't have been as bad as he'd thought. "Maida!" Smiling in relief, he reached for her.

She flung out her hands with the palms out to keep Yates back. "Don't touch me!" she cried.

"What's wrong?" he asked hoarsely.

Laurel and Kendra slipped out of the cabin and joined Ward and Taylor on the bench.

Maida slumped in the chair and closed her eyes. "I am Alden's woman. Nobody can have me but him."

Yates gasped and backed away. "Bromley's woman?"

She rocked back and forth with her arms cradled against her body. "He cares for me. He saved me from people who hate me."

His face full of anguish, Yates cried, "What has that man done to you?"

"He cares for me. Nobody else does."

Yates knotted his fists. "I'll kill him! I swear I'll kill him!" He ran from the cabin. "Ward, I'm going after Bromley. I swear I'll kill him!"

"He's already dead," Laurel said in an expressionless voice. "I killed him."

Yates stumbled back and stared at Laurel as if she'd lost her mind as Maida had.

Ward clamped a hand on Yates's arm. "Sit down and listen to what happened."

Before Taylor could begin, Pickle and Reid ran into the yard. The others followed close behind.

"Maida's back!" Reid cried as he ran into the cabin. He hugged her before she could stop him, then jumped back when she saw how dirty and sweaty he was. "I'm happy you're home, ma'am," he said softly.

She looked at him vacantly.

Shivers running up and down his spine, Reid backed away and ran to Taylor to learn what had happened.

In the light from the lanterns Ward had lit, Taylor told the story again with help from Kendra. Laurel caught Pickle's hand and gripped it. She didn't want to think about shooting Bromley.

Court doubled his fists and forced back a cry of pain as he watched Kendra. He wanted to hold her close and keep her from all harm.

Ward wrapped Bromley's body in a tarp and left it in the back of the wagon near the barn. In hushed silence the men washed, then ate the supper Cammie and Pickle had prepared for them. In the cabin with Maida, Taylor and the girls managed to eat a little. Maida nibbled on a raw carrot. She hadn't spoken since she'd talked to Yates.

A few minutes later Taylor helped Maida prepare for bed, then tucked her in. Taylor kissed Maida's pale cheek. "God is with you, Maida. He'll give you a peaceful sleep."

Taylor hugged first Laurel, then Kendra. As she did, she caught their hands and bowed her head to pray. "Heavenly Father, thank You for Your protection today. Comfort our hearts and give us all peaceful sleep. In Jesus' name. Amen."

Slowly the girls climbed to the loft to their straw mats.

ಌ

Outdoors Yates and Ward sat on the bench in the dark. The men and Reid had gone to bed. The night sounds filled the air. Yates could barely hold his head up, but he was too tense to sleep. And when he did go to bed, where would he go? Maida wouldn't let him in bed with her. He shrugged. He could always fix a pallet on the floor. Maybe that's where he'd sleep the rest of his life.

"I made a mess of things, Ward," Yates said just above a whisper. "I never should have treated Maida the way I did. She deserved better."

Ward patted Yates's back. "You can't go back in time, brother. You have to do the best with the way things are."

"She says she's Bromley's woman." Yates groaned from deep inside. "How can I live with her, knowing she's been with him?"

"Remember God is with you. His strength is yours."

Yates shook his head. "Not even God's strength can help with this."

Ward stared at Yates in surprise. "You know better than that!"

"I don't need a sermon, Ward."

"You need to rely on God, Yates. Don't run from Him when you're in pain. Trust Him; cry out to Him; depend on Him to help you."

Yates wearily pushed himself up. "I have to get to sleep. Thanks for trying to help me."

Ward caught Yates close in a bear hug. "Sleep well, brother."

In her cabin Taylor kissed a sleeping Brooke and slowly climbed down from the loft.

Looking anxious, Cammie tapped the chair. "You sit down and rest, Miz Taylor. I made you a cup of tea just like you like."

"Thank you." Taylor sank to the chair and sipped the sweet, hot tea. "You sit down too, Cammie. You look worn out."

Cammie sank awkwardly to a chair. It was getting harder and harder to sit down. "That Brooke run my legs clean off today."

"I'll be here to help with her tomorrow." Taylor sighed. "Laurel has to go to town with Master Ward to see the magistrate about Mr. Bromley's death."

Cammie shivered. "That was one bad man. Almost as bad as Master Rawlings." Cammie gasped. "I sorry, Miz Taylor."

Frowning, Taylor shook her head. "You have to push all that to the back of your head and never think about it. Please don't ever say his name again!"

"I won't. I have my child to think of from now on. That's all that's important to me."

❦

The next morning Laurel stood beside Pickle as Ward talked to the men about the day's work and Dancer hitched the team to the wagon. Flies buzzed around the tarp covering Bromley's body. Her face as white as the clouds in the blue sky, Laurel forced herself to turn away from the wagon.

"You done what had to be done," Pickle said softly.

"It was awful!" Laurel pressed her trembling hand to her stomach. A new thought made her gasp. "Will I have to go to jail?"

Pickle shook his head. "Your Uncle Ward won't let that happen."

"I didn't plan to shoot him dead," Laurel whimpered.

"You was backed into a corner. What else could you do?"

"I aimed at his arm just to make him drop his rifle, but I hit him right in the chest."

"I know. I know."

"I won't ever, ever shoot another man as long as I live!"

Pickle nodded. He'd made that same vow after he killed a soldier who was trying to kill him.

"Ready, Laurel?" Ward called from across the yard.

Laurel took a deep breath. "I'm scared, Pickle."

"Jesus is with you, Missy."

She nodded, lifted her chin, and walked toward the wagon.

❦

Yates sent the men on out to the field and slowly walked into the cabin. Kendra stood at the fireplace and Maida sat at the table with a bowl of porridge in front of her.

"She won't eat," Kendra said in a tired voice.

"Aunt Erica hates porridge," Maida said, pushing the bowl away. "I must fix her something she likes."

Yates's heart sank. He'd hoped Maida would be herself after a good night's sleep in her own bed. He walked out without another word.

In the field Yates listlessly swung the grubbing hoe. What had happened to his life? He'd had such wonderful plans. Pictures of Maida with Bromley flashed through his mind, sending rage through him. He swung the hoe harder as if each stump root was Alden Bromley. Yates chopped until his muscles ached like never before, but the anger burned hotter inside him. After a long time he sank to the ground, drenched with sweat and too tired to lift the hoe over his head.

Reid ran to Yates and dropped on his knees beside him. "Papa? Did you hurt yourself?"

With his head down and tears burning his eyes, he whispered, "Leave me be, son."

Reid draped his arm around his papa and pressed his forehead into his arm. "Take away his pain, Jesus," Reid whispered.

❦

Maida walked out of the cabin into the bright sunlight. She had to get to Aunt Erica before she sent a maid after her. "I'm coming, Aunt," she called.

Musket ran to Maida and licked her hand. She gasped in horror and pulled her hand away. She looked all around at the strange trees, the log cabins, the shacks, the barn. She heard someone whistling off in a clearing in the woods where men were building something. The thought that these people hated her came clear in her mind. She had to get away from them.

Lifting her skirts, she ran out of the yard to the road. Birds flew up from the trees in a rush of wings.

Just then Taylor stepped out of her cabin. She saw Maida running away. "Cammie, take care of Brooke. I have to help Maida."

Breathing a prayer, Taylor lifted her skirts and ran past the magnolia tree and the oak tree to the tree lined road. She wanted to call to Maida, but was afraid she'd run faster, or even dash into the woods and get lost if she did.

At last Taylor caught up to Maida and said as they ran, "I came to join you."

Maida frowned. "Aunt Erica won't let anyone help her dress but me."

"She asked someone else to help her, Maida. You don't have to. You can help me churn butter. Would you?"

Maida stopped and so did Taylor. "Are you sure Aunt Erica doesn't need me?"

"I'm sure." Taylor smiled and took Maida's hand. "Come with me and we'll gossip about all kinds of things and work together."

Maida shrugged, then finally nodded.

Sighing in relief, Taylor smiled and walked Maida back to the cabin. They were going to have to watch her closely to keep her from wandering off. How long would it take before Maida really returned to Catawba?

ates walked listlessly around the building site without hearing the pounding of a hammer or the calls back and forth of the workers. Somehow a grand house didn't seem as important as it once had. As he walked around the outside edge of the garden he didn't notice the flowers or Pickle working hard.

With a deep sigh Yates walked to the bench under the shade tree and sat down. This was the first day he hadn't gone to the field to help. Work didn't seem as important either.

Taylor watched Yates as she hung clothes on the line to dry. In spite of how mean he had been, she hated to see him so dejected. Slowly she walked to the bench. "May I join you?" she asked softly.

Yates looked up vacantly and shrugged. "I'm not good company."

Taylor sat down and smoothed her skirts. Her hems were coated with dust and a few pine straws. She brushed loose strands of hair from her damp cheek. "May I say something, Yates?"

He sighed and nodded.

"I know some of the feelings you've been having about Maida." Taylor bit her lip and couldn't continue for a minute. "You see, I've had the same guilt."

He turned to her, his brow cocked questioningly.

"My husband Floyd died a short time before I boarded the *Falcon*. I didn't plan to marry again. But I did. So did you. Your Ellen loved you and she'd want you to find love again. Don't feel guilty for loving Maida."

Yates gripped his hands between his knees as he leaned forward. "I lost Ellen and the baby! How could I let myself consider my needs so easily and so soon after Ellen was gone?"

"You weren't just considering yours and the children's needs. You were thinking of Maida. You truly wanted to save her from the miserable life she led."

He barely nodded. It all seemed so long ago. He had wanted to save her, though little good it did him.

"You must release your guilt and leave room in your heart to love Maida as you should."

"Don't you see? I can't!"

"Yes, you can. Not in your own strength, but in God's. He is your refuge, your fortress, your Heavenly Father! I know Jesus is your Lord and Savior, so don't push Him away when He is longing to help you. And help Maida."

A yearning to cry out to God rose inside Yates as Taylor talked. He'd been so foolish to try to deal with his problems in his own strength. Now that he considered it, why had he ever thought he was being disloyal to Ellen by marrying Maida? Ellen would indeed have approved of Maida.

"We don't have to carry our sins around. We can turn them over to Jesus and be free of the guilty load." Taylor couldn't tell if she was being of any help to Yates, but she knew God's Word was powerful and could bring healing to his heart if he'd accept it. Her words were soothing as she tried to reach him. "Yates, I know how much you love your children. God loves you even more than you love them. He desires for you to turn to Him for help and comfort. He wants to take care of you even more than you want to take care of your children." Finally she stopped talking and sat quietly beside him.

He cleared his throat and blinked back tears. "Thank you, Taylor. I'll consider what you said."

He thought over her words as he walked to the cotton field they'd planted in June. The plants were high and the yield would be good. Even that didn't seem to matter at this point.

With a groan he knelt beside the cotton field and lifted his face to heaven. "Father, You are my strength and my refuge. Forgive me for pulling away from You when I needed You so badly. I accept Your love even though I feel unworthy. I know Jesus makes me worthy."

Tears ran down Yates's cheeks as he continued to pray. A peace settled over him and at long last he smiled. He prayed for Maida's health to be restored, then he said in a low, hoarse voice, "Help the beginning of love for Maida blossom inside me so that I love her as a husband loves a wife." His voice broke. He waited for the guilty feeling to return, but it didn't. He smiled and said, "Father God, help Maida to love me as a wife should love a husband."

Yates pushed himself up and wiped his eyes and face dry. From now on things were going to be different. He'd help make Catawba into a powerful plantation, but more importantly, he'd teach his own family how to love God and one another. In time he and Maida would find love for each other. But how long would it take? He needed her and her love more than he'd thought possible.

❦

Taylor gently brushed Maida's hair just as she had the past two weeks since they'd found her. "Maida, God's strength is yours." She'd told Maida the same thing each day the past two weeks. She'd read promises from the Bible to her daily. "You hold on to that thought while you're helping me today."

Maida tried to stand. "I must shop for fresh meat for Uncle Samuel's dinner before he gets angry at me."

"You're going to sit outside and work, Maida." Taylor kissed Maida's pale cheek, then prayed, "Heavenly Father, in Jesus' name restore Maida's mind. Heal her pain. Help her to know she's here at Catawba with people who love her."

Maida walked listlessly outdoors to the bench to snap beans. As she sat down to work, once again Musket licked her hand and laid at her feet. This time she smiled at the dog, thankful to have him beside her; he'd protect her, she knew. She frowned. Protect her from what? But her mind shied away from the answer.

Taylor sat beside Maida with another basket of string beans beside her to snap and can. Behind the barn she heard Kendra and Ward working with the horses. Reid and Yates were still clearing the field with all the other men. Inside Laurel helped Cammie make jam. Shouts and laughter floated across the yard from the builders. The stone foundation was already laid and the massive timbers were jointed and pegged together and kept square with stiff braces in vertical angles.

Musket stood, looked toward the road, and barked.

With a shriek Maida leaped up, spilling the beans, and looked wildly around.

Taylor slipped an arm around her. "You're safe, Maida. Nobody can hurt you."

"Alden can."

Taylor looked sharply at Maida. Usually she thought her aunt was going to. "He can't hurt you any longer, Maida. He's dead."

"Dead?" Maida trembled.

Josiah Pardee rode into sight in a red-wheeled trap pulled by a team of gray mares. Pulling back on the reins, he called, "Whoa!" He plucked off his hat and slapped dust off his dark pants and loose-fitting blue shirt.

Just then Ward strode into the yard with Kendra running to keep up. They both were dirty and sweaty. With a sharp order for Musket to sit, Ward pulled off his hat and gloves and wiped his face with his big handkerchief. He and Laurel had told Josiah Pardee about Bromley the day after she'd shot him, and Josiah had come to Catawba to question Taylor and Kendra about the incident. Josiah had said Laurel wouldn't have to go on trial and Bromley's place would be sold to pay his debts. Yates had wanted to buy the slaves, so Josiah had said he'd let him know if he could at the first opportunity. Maybe Josiah was coming to say Yates could buy them.

"How do, Marstons!" he said louder than was necessary as he climbed out of the trap.

"Nice day for a ride, Josiah." Smiling, Ward tied the team to a post. "You know my wife and my sister-in-law. And my niece Kendra."

"Sure do. Sure do." Josiah tipped his hat, showing graying hair, and smiled. "Miz Maida, you're looking fit as a fiddle if you don't mind me saying so. Much better than when I was here last."

Maida ducked her head and pressed close to Taylor.

"She is better," Ward said.

Josiah turned sharp brown eyes on Taylor. "And you, Miz Taylor? How're things with you?"

"Very well, thank you, Mr. Pardee." Taylor's nerves tightened at the look he gave her. "Could I get you a glass of cold buttermilk?"

"No, thank you, ma'am." Josiah looked toward the well. "But a dipper of cold water would wash the dust from my throat."

"I'll get it, sir." Kendra ran to the well, drew up a bucket, and filled the dipper. She carried it to Josiah.

He took it with thanks, drank noisily, and handed it back. He turned to Ward with a smile. "What is more pleasing to a man than to have a daughter such as this one?"

Forcing back a flush, Ward nodded. He'd been thinking of how good it would be for him and Taylor to have children, but he hadn't said anything to her. They didn't talk of such intimate things. Ward frowned slightly. Come to think of it, they didn't talk about anything much at all since Bromley's death. He forced his attention back on Josiah. "What brings you out here today? Will Yates be able to buy Bromley's slaves?"

Josiah nodded, then nodded again. "Sure can. Sure can. You tell him to pick up them slaves and see me next time he's in town and I'll take care of the paperwork."

"I will." Ward started to ask Josiah if he wanted to take a look at his new stallion, but the words died in his throat as Josiah pulled a paper from a pack around his thick waist. So Josiah had other business to tend to. He saw Josiah dart a look at Taylor. Ward's heart stopped, then thundered on. Josiah had official business, and it had something to do with Taylor! Had Josiah learned something about Cammie?

As unobtrusively as he could, Ward walked to Taylor's side. He felt her tension, and his own nerves tightened to the breaking point.

"Josiah, how about a piece of cornbread? My other niece Laurel made a pan that beats any you've ever tasted."

"Sounds mighty good, Ward, but not this time." Josiah tapped the paper on his gloved hand. "I got a little unpleasant business to tend to with your wife."

Taylor gasped. She wanted to glance toward the cabin to see if Cammie was in sight, but she didn't dare. Since Bromley's death they hadn't made her hide each time someone rode in.

Ward slipped an arm around Taylor and pulled her tight to his side. "You deal with me, Josiah."

"If that's how you want it, Ward."

Taylor bit back a cry of anguish as she silently prayed for help.

"I do." Ward motioned to the paper in Josiah's hand. Ward turned to Kendra. "Take Maida inside, please, and stay with her."

Kendra desperately wanted to stay to hear everything, but she obediently ushered Maida into the cabin. Still Kendra left the door ajar in hopes of hearing what was happening.

Ward narrowed his eyes as he looked from the paper to Josiah. "What's it all about, friend?"

Josiah blew out his breath and looked uncomfortable. "A man came to me yesterday and said he had proof you got his runaway slave and his bond woman here at Catawba."

Taylor's eyes widened in alarm. James? Had James found them somehow? But Josiah couldn't mean her. She wasn't a bond woman to James.

"Who is this man?" Ward asked sharply.

"James Rawlings from Virginia."

Taylor's knees buckled and she would've sunk to the ground if Ward's arm hadn't been around her. She forced the strength back in her legs. She started to speak, but Ward silenced her with a quick look.

"Let me see the paper." Ward reached for it and Josiah gave it to him. The words blurred before Ward's eyes. He finally managed to focus on the paper and read the date James Rawlings had bought Cammie along with her description. His heart sank. He looked at the other paper and read of Taylor's indenture to James Rawlings for ten years, starting 18 April 1800. Taylor's signature was at the bottom. For a long time Ward couldn't find words to speak. How could Taylor do this? Was this the real reason she'd married him?

His hat in his hand, Josiah moved from one foot to the other. On the ground at Ward's feet, Musket whined and swept his tail across the ground in a wag.

Ward finally looked up. "Did you tell this James Rawlings Taylor is my wife?"

Josiah nodded. He didn't tell Ward how angry Rawlings had become over that bit of news. "He doesn't care. He wants Miz Taylor and his slave Cammie."

Taylor bit her lip and whimpered.

"I'll pay him what she owes him."

Josiah named the sum and Ward gasped.

"May I speak?" Taylor asked in a low, tight voice.

"Speak away," Josiah said with a wave of his thick hand.

Taylor looked into Ward's set face and waited for his answer. Finally he nodded. Taylor moistened her dry lips with the tip of her tongue. "It's a long story. May we sit?"

"By all means!" Josiah clamped his hat on and headed for the two benches in the shade.

Taylor sat on the bench facing Josiah and smoothed her skirts over her knees. Where should she start? Would it do any good to tell the truth now? Ward looked as if he wouldn't believe a word she said. Taylor locked her hands together in her lap and took a deep breath. "I am not indentured to James Rawlings. I didn't sign the paper. He probably forged my signature."

"He says you are his bond servant," Josiah said.

Taylor shook her head and locked her icy hands together. "James was a cousin to my husband Floyd. Because of bad business dealings Floyd was in debt to James. When Floyd died I became responsible for the debt and James said he'd consider it paid if I returned to Virginia with him just to see his plantation. I thought it was an unusual request, but I was forced to agree because I had no way to pay him."

"Yet you came to South Carolina instead of Virginia," Ward said gruffly.

"I know." Taylor took a deep, steadying breath. She could almost feel the cold wind at the Liverpool docks and hear the shouts and bustle all around and the terror she'd felt when she'd learned the truth. "I overhead James telling the captain of the ship he planned to marry me and wanted the captain to perform the ceremony just after we boarded. I had refused to marry him before because I loved Floyd and also because James has an uncontrollable temper. I knew if I boarded the ship with James he would force me to marry him no matter how much I objected. So, I ran away."

"Where does Cammie come into all of this?" Ward asked.

Taylor glanced toward the cabin where she knew Cammie and Laurel were working. "Cammie witnessed James killing Floyd."

"What?" shouted Ward, jumping off the bench.

"Well, that's mighty interesting. Sit down, Ward, so the lady can finish the story," said Josiah. He hadn't liked the look of this James Rawlings when he had first seen him, and now he knew why.

Taylor continued. "James was driving the coach that hit and killed Floyd. I thought it was an accident until Cammie told me what she saw. James had this whole thing planned before he even came back to England for his visit. Cammie knew that James wasn't going to let her live since she had seen this, so she ran away. She hid at the Liverpool dock to warn me about him and that's when I asked her to come with me."

Josiah whistled in surprise.

Ward frowned. Could this be true?

"A man, Andrew Simons, helped us board." Taylor frowned as she remembered Andrew and his deceitful ways. "He took my money to pay the passage, but when we arrived, he said I didn't give him any money and the captain said I didn't pay. That's why Yates paid my fair and I became indentured to him." Taylor shuddered as she relived the horrible day.

Josiah leaned toward Taylor with a thoughtful expression on his round face. "This Andrew Simons—is he a light-haired, tall, and well-dressed Englishman?"

"Yes."

"He's in Darien with Rawlings."

Moaning, Taylor helplessly shook her head. "Mr. Pardee, can't you see? They're working together to force me to go with James!"

Ward scowled at Taylor. "Why didn't you tell me this story before?"

"I didn't want to put Cammie in danger."

"So, Cammie does belong to James Rawlings?"

"Yes. But she can't go back to him! He'll kill her!" Her eyes wide with pleading, Taylor gripped Ward's arm. "Don't let James take her! He will indeed kill her!"

Inside the cabin Kendra heard the story. She had to get Papa and the men to help save Taylor and Cammie! Leaving Maida at the table with a cup of tea, Kendra slipped out the door and around the cabin. When she was out of sight of the yard she ran faster than she'd ever run before to the field where they were working. Dust puffed onto her shoes and skirts. Just before she reached the field she spotted Court walking toward her. With the last burst of energy in her she flung herself at him. "Court! Oh, Court!"

His heart racing violently he pulled her against him. "Kendra, what's wrong? Did someone get hurt?"

She clung to him with her head on his chest and her eyes closed. Why couldn't she stay there forever? But she couldn't think of herself.

She quickly lifted her head. "Court, Josiah Pardee brought a paper saying he could take Taylor and Cammie away and give them to a man named James Rawlings. We have to stop them! I must tell Papa!"

"Yes. Tell the others." Court knew he should drop his arms and step back from Kendra, but he couldn't find the willpower. Oh, but she felt good in his arms!

She saw the look in his eyes and it melted her very bones. Standing on tiptoe Kendra kissed his warm lips, then jumped away, flushed and flustered. Shock registered across both their faces, but then Court pulled her to him and kissed her again with all the love he had. All thoughts of Taylor and Cammie flew from their minds as they shared the kiss.

Reluctantly, Court brought his head up and stared into Kendra's eyes. "I couldn't stand it if anything ever happened to you, Kendra. You're the only girl for me and I will love you forever."

Kendra gasped, her hand flying to her throat. What could she say? All rational thought left her and she could only stare at Court.

Seeing her shock, Court quickly said, "I'm sorry. I should never have said such an improper thing. Please forgive me." Stepping around Kendra, Court began to walk away, but Kendra whirled around and grabbed his arm.

"No, you can't leave me like this." Kendra tried to appeal to Court with her eyes. How could she tell him her true feelings?

Not understanding how she was feeling, Court took Kendra's hand in both of his. "I know you can't feel the same way about me. One day you'll marry a fine English gentleman that your father picks for you and live happily ever after." Those were the hardest words Court would ever have to say, but he couldn't let Kendra make a mistake about caring for him.

"I am not going to marry a fine English gentleman, Court. I could never be happy with anyone but you. You're the one that I care for, but these feelings are so strong they scare me." Blushing a deep red, Kendra lowered her eyes. She had finally put into words the feelings from her heart.

With a whoop of joy Court swung Kendra around and around in his arms. Finally lowering Kendra to her feet, Court smiled into her eyes. "If you're sure that you love me, then nothing can stand in our way. I want to marry you, Kendra. Not right away, but once I have my free papers. Will you wait for me?"

"Oh, Court, yes. Yes, I'll wait for you." Kendra flung her arms around his neck, hugging him to her fiercely.

"I know your father won't like this, but with God on our side his heart will change. One day he'll accept me as his son-in-law and be very proud of us."

"When can we tell everyone the news?"

"We better wait until it's closer to the time for me to become free. I don't want anyone to question my love for you. And I want you to be proud of your husband."

Realizing how long they had been together, Court quickly stepped back from Kendra. "I think you better go tell the others what's happening at the house and I'll see if I can do anything."

Kendra didn't want to leave without Court by her side, but she knew that Taylor and Cammie needed their help. "All right, but I shall miss you terribly. It will be so difficult to keep our love a secret. I want to shout it from the roof—I love Court."

Smiling proudly, Court kissed her one more time on the cheek. "Get going, love. I'll see you later."

❧

Running as fast as he could, Court came rushing to the cabins, his face wet with sweat. "Kendra told me what's happening."

Ward reached to push Court back, but stayed his hand with a

new, pain-wrenching thought—if Court had been the master of the plantation, would Taylor have married him?

"We'll get it sorted out, Court." Taylor smiled through tears of gratitude.

"What can I do to help?" Court asked.

"Nothing." Taylor patted his arm. "Thank you for caring."

Court stepped back and frowned at Josiah. "What are your plans, sir?"

Ward scowled at Court. "It's not your concern. Wait at the barn. I'll call you if I need your assistance."

Court flushed in humiliation and frustration. Oh, to be a free man! His back stiff and his fists doubled at his sides, he strode away. He would find a way to make money to pay for his freedom before his indenture was up if it was the last thing he ever did!

Taylor slowly stood. "Mr. Pardee, what do you expect of me? James Rawlings lied to you. He killed my husband."

Josiah rubbed a hand over his graying hair. "Miz Taylor, I don't know what to say." He turned to Ward. "What do you say, sir?"

"We could talk to Cammie."

Josiah frowned. "Talk to a slave? Who would believe her?"

"I would!" Taylor cried, tapping her chest with her fingers.

"Get Cammie," Ward said sharply. "I want to hear her story."

"I wouldn't believe a colored girl's story over a white gentleman's," Josiah said softly.

Taylor squared her shoulders and lifted her head high as she looked Josiah in the eyes. "Did you believe my story?"

Josiah shrugged. "James Rawlings is a gentleman of wealth. Why would he need to kill your husband or forge your name on this indenture paper?"

Taylor flushed painfully. "He wanted me as his wife, but I married his cousin instead. James hates losing and he wants revenge."

Thoughtfully Josiah tapped the papers against his hand again. "I'll listen to Cammie. Send your man for her, Ward. I don't want Miz Taylor out of my sight."

Taylor bit back a sharp retort as Ward yelled for Court to get Cammie. Taylor turned to Ward to convince him she was telling the truth, but he wouldn't look at her. She stepped closer to him and whispered, "Don't you believe me, Ward?"

His eyes were full of pain as he looked at her. "We'll discuss this later, Taylor."

She fell back as if he'd struck her. She'd believe any story he told her if he said it was true. Suddenly she realized she loved him. She loved him with a passion she'd never felt for Floyd Craven! When had it happened? It had crept up on her and overtaken her. She loved Ward Marston with her whole being! She loved him! The realization left her weak. She wanted to fling herself into his arms and declare her love for him, but she stood quietly at his side as if everything was as it had been moments before.

Just then Court walked from the cabin with Brooke in his arms. Her hands against her stomach, Cammie waddled beside him.

"She's expecting a child?" Josiah asked and blushed.

"Yes." Her cheeks red with embarrassment, Taylor said, "James forced himself on her. She couldn't refuse because she was his slave."

Josiah sighed heavily. "He has every right, but it ain't proper in my eyes."

"Nor mine," Taylor said.

Ward knotted his fists. If Rawlings was standing before him, he'd beat him until he couldn't speak or move.

Her eyes wide, Cammie stopped beside Taylor. "Something wrong, Miz Taylor?"

"Yes. James Rawlings is in town."

A cry of fear burst from Cammie and she shook her head. "I won't go with him! He wants me dead!" She pressed her hands to her stomach. "He'll kill my baby!" Suddenly fluid gushed down Cammie's legs and onto her feet and the ground around her. She cried out and doubled over. "This baby coming, Miz Taylor!"

Just in time to hear Cammie's screams, Kendra and Yates and his men hurried into the yard. Treet ran forward and caught Cammie up in his strong arms.

"Take her inside and put her on my bed," Taylor said, forgetting her problem and Josiah for the time being.

Josiah rubbed his head and clicked his tongue. "We got us a real difficult situation, Ward. What do you say we do?"

Before Ward could speak Yates snapped, "You can get off Catawba and tell Mr. James Rawlings that Taylor and Cammie are staying here where they belong." Kendra had told the story as they'd hurried in.

"Take it easy now, Yates," Josiah said. "This is a matter of the law."

"Jail the man for his crime!" Yates snapped.

"I would if I could, Yates, but I got no authority since the crime was done in England. Besides, it's his word against a nigger girl's word. There's no case."

Ward finally found his voice. "Josiah, you talk to James Rawlings and tell him the situation. Tell him Taylor and Cammie are staying right here. Tell him I won't let them go with him because he killed Taylor's husband." Taylor's husband. Ward frowned. He was Taylor's husband! He often forgot she'd been married before he'd met her, but suddenly it was very real.

"I'll tell him, but he won't like it at all." Josiah clamped his hat on. "I best be heading back."

"Maybe I should ride in and have a talk with James Rawlings and Andrew Simons," Ward said grimly.

His jaw set firmly, Yates stepped forward. "I'll go with you. I want this settled with Andrew Simons."

Josiah shook his head. "I don't know, men. We don't want a bunch of dead bodies laying around Darien."

Kendra dragged her eyes off Court holding Brooke and dashed to Taylor's cabin. She knew Taylor would want to know what Ward and Papa were planning. Treet stood just outside the cabin door, a nervous look on his face. Kendra stepped around him and hurried inside. The smell of grape jam filled the room as Laurel patiently funneled it into jars even though she wanted to be where the activity was. Kendra ran to Taylor in the bedroom with Cammie.

Taylor looked up in relief. "Kendra, get Pickle. He said he'd deliver the baby when it was time."

"Is it time?"

Cammie nodded.

Taylor patted Cammie's arm as she spoke to Kendra. "She didn't tell me she started labor this morning. You run and get Pickle. Please!"

Kendra nodded. "But first I must tell you Uncle Ward and Papa are going to town to confront James Rawlings and Andrew Simons."

Taylor gasped. "No! They can't!"

"They'll both be killed for sure," Cammie said in alarm.

Taylor ran for the door and said over her shoulder, "Kendra, stay with Cammie. I'll be back as soon as I can." Just outside Taylor almost ran into Treet. "Get Pickle fast and tell him it's time for Cammie to have her baby!" Not waiting to see if Treet obeyed, Taylor lifted her skirts and raced toward Ward as he strode toward the barn. "Ward! Yates! Don't go! It's too dangerous!"

Maida heard Taylor's cries and she ran from the cabin up to them. "Taylor, what's wrong? Is Bromley back?"

Ward and Yates turned at the same time. They looked at each other, then at Maida. Yates took her by the arms. "Maida, Bromley is dead. He can't hurt you or us ever again."

"Yates?" Maida looked confused, then pulled away. "You don't like me. Don't touch me."

Yates clenched his jaw. "Go back to the cabin, Maida. I'll see you when I get home."

"Where are you going?"

"To Darien to see a man who wants to hurt Taylor."

Maida grabbed Taylor's arm. "I won't let anybody hurt her! I won't!"

Taylor peeled Maida off her and said gently, "I must speak to Ward. Would you wait in the cabin for me?"

Maida nodded. "Don't go away, Taylor."

"I won't."

Ward waited impatiently for Taylor. He wasn't going to let her talk him out of going. He had to deal with Rawlings and Simons face to face.

After Maida walked away Taylor took a deep, steadying breath and said to Ward, "James is a cruel, deceitful man. He'll tell you I'm lying and that Cammie is lying. Please don't let him take us. Please!"

Ward's face was dark. He had too much to sort out before he could answer Taylor. "I can't talk now." Ward turned away and hurried to the horse that Bard had saddled for him.

Taylor bit her lip and slowly walked toward her cabin and Cammie.

❧

Dressed in a white shirt and fawn-colored breeches, James Rawlings sat astride his bay gelding hidden among the trees at Catawba with Andrew Simons hidden alongside on a dappled gray. James chuckled and said in a low voice, "The law is on my side. I'll have Taylor and Cammie back within the hour."

He'd said nothing to Simons or Josiah Pardee about murdering Floyd Craven to get Taylor to do his bidding. He thought he heard someone coming and he tensed. "Be ready for anything."

Simons dabbed perspiration off his face. He hadn't counted on hiding like a common criminal in the heat of the woods. He wanted revenge and he'd get it even if it meant going against Rawlings's orders. But he'd rather do it in a civilized place.

James tensed as the bay gelding pricked his ears. "Someone is coming!"

Simons held his dappled gray in check and waited.

A few minutes later Josiah Pardee drove past with Ward and Yates on horseback behind him.

Anger rushed through James. He should've expected such a thing, but he hadn't. He'd expected to see Taylor and Cammie shackled in the backseat of the trap.

Simons rested his hand on the butt of his pistol. He could easily kill Yates Marston and be done with him, but shooting a man in the back wasn't sporting at all.

James ground his teeth and muttered under his breath, "I'll find a way to get Taylor and Cammie myself. The law is on my side." He chuckled under his breath. Even if the law wasn't on his side, he'd get them. Then he'd decide just what to do with them.

17

With one mighty, pain-searing push Cammie delivered her child into Pickle's hands.

"You gots yourself a boy child," Pickle said as he cleared out the baby's mouth and held him by his heels. The baby squeaked first, followed by a lusty cry that the others waiting outside the cabin could hear.

Taylor blinked back tears as she recalled Brooke's birth. When the midwife had delivered the tiny girl, Floyd had forgotten he'd ever wanted a boy. Taylor watched Pickle cut and tie off the umbilical cord. Would she ever have another child, perhaps a boy who looked just like Ward?

Later Cammie lay in the clean bed with her baby washed and dressed in her arms. Laurel had finished the jam and left, but the smell stayed on. Cammie touched the baby's cheek. "My own son."

"What will you name him?" Taylor asked. The baby looked so much like James she found it hard to look at him.

Cammie had given a name for the baby much thought in the past several weeks. She was thankful to Taylor that she'd be able to give the baby a name of her choice, unlike other places where the master picked the name. Cammie smiled. "His name be Daniel. An angel kept Daniel from being ate by lions and an angel will keep my Daniel free."

Taylor brushed tears from her eyes. "Daniel. Daniel Marston." They'd already agreed he'd take the master's last name as was the custom.

Pickle walked back in from dealing with the soiled bedclothes in time to hear the baby's name. Proud that he'd delivered the baby, Pickle smiled down at Cammie and the baby. "Daniel be a fine strong name for a fine strong boy."

"Thank you. Pickle, I won't never forget you for doing such a fine job. I'll tell Daniel the story so he won'ts never forget you either."

With tears in his eyes, Pickle kissed Cammie's forehead.

Cammie lifted her head off the pillow. "Miz Taylor, I want Treet to come in to see me. And Daniel."

"I'll see if he will."

Pickle grinned. "He's still standing right outside the door."

Reluctantly Taylor walked away.

Pickle stroked Cammie's head. "I best be going and leave you with Daniel. If Treet say something mean to you, you tell me and I'll take care of him." Pickle scowled but stopped when he caught sight of Cammie's face. He kissed Cammie and Daniel and walked out just as Treet stepped inside.

Her heart fluttering, Cammie covered Daniel's face with the corner of the small soft blanket.

Steeling himself, Treet walked to the bedroom. He didn't want to see the baby and be reminded of the births of his sons, but he did want to make sure Cammie was all right. He pushed back his fear and looked down at Cammie. Thankfully the baby was covered and he didn't have to deal with that. "You look mighty pretty lying in a white woman's bed like you queen or something."

"I feel better than a queen. My baby boy is healthy and strong. And he's gonna grow up here on this beautiful Catawba land."

Treet's heart sank. Cammie didn't know she had to go back to James Rawlings. And the baby would have to go with her.

"I named him Daniel. Want to see him?"

Treet shook his head. "I can't. You know that, Cammie."

She flipped off the blanket.

Treet's eyes filled with a great sadness. Would he be able to watch Cammie's baby boy grow up without the pain of losing his own sons welling up inside? Cammie saw the look in Treet's eyes and reached out and took his hand. "Treet, Jesus can take away that pain that I see in your eyes and fill you with His love. Will you let Him do that, Treet? Please."

Treet squeezed Cammie's hand, trying to release some of his own tension. Slowly he knelt down beside the bed and rested his head on the edge while Cammie circled his neck in a hug. "Cammie, I don't know if I can let go of my boys. They're all the family that I have left and the only way I can seem to hang on to them is by keeping this pain locked inside me."

"Just because you let go of the pain doesn't mean you're going to forget your own boys. When you think of them you won't be hurting and you'll be able to pray for them to come home to you."

Treet looked at Cammie. "I don't want to live with this pain anymore, Cammie girl. I want to be able to love you and your baby boy." Shyly Treet looked straight into Cammie's eyes trying to read her reaction to his words. If she rejected him now he would never be able to face her again. "Will you let me love you, Cammie?"

Her eyes filling with tears of love, Cammie wrapped both her arms around Treet's neck. "Yes. Yes. Yes. Yes. I've been praying for you so long and now the Lord has answered my prayers. I love you, Treet. I have from the minute I laid eyes on you."

Treet smiled more broadly than Cammie had ever seen. He was the luckiest man around. "Miz Taylor said not to stay too long, that you need your rest. I have to get back to work anyways so I'll see you later." Reluctantly Treet untangled Cammie's arms from around his neck and stood up in the doorway. Glancing at her one more time Treet smiled and walked out of the cabin and headed for the barn.

❦

Outside the cabin Taylor turned to Maida, Laurel, and Kendra. Taylor had told them about Daniel. Laurel and Kendra wanted to see Cammie and the baby, but Maida wasn't interested.

"You can go see them, but don't stay long. Cammie needs to rest," Taylor directed.

Talking excitedly, Laurel and Kendra hurried to the cabin.

Maida looked around with a frown. "Where is Yates? Did Bromley kill him?"

Taylor patted Maida's arm. "Bromley is dead." How many more times would she have to say it before Maida understood? "Yates and Ward went to town to see two men on business. They'll be back by dark."

Sighing, Maida walked slowly into her cabin and shut the door. She had to see Yates for herself to know he wasn't dead. But what did it matter? He didn't want her. He didn't love her. And all Maida wanted was just someone to love her.

❦

At the edge of the trees near the lane James tied his mount to a branch and crept forward. He'd told Simons to cover him from the safety of the trees. They'd both impatiently waited until the builders had driven away and the yard was empty except for Taylor getting a drink at the well. The slaves and Ward Marston's two indentured servants were in back of the barn. Josiah Pardee had already told him about them.

Holding back his anger, James walked boldly into the open. If he could reach Taylor before she spotted him, well and good. If not, he'd still grab her and carry her away on his horse. Nobody could stop him! Taylor was his!

Taylor drank the last drop in the dipper, enjoying the cold water soothing her dry throat and quenching her thirst. She was not going to be concerned about James Rawlings any more! Ward would send James right back to Virginia where he belonged.

Just at that moment James touched Taylor's shoulder. She turned with a smile, expecting to see Kendra or Laurel. But it was James, looking at her in triumph! She flung the dipper at him and screamed at the top of her lungs.

He grabbed her around the waist and growled close to her ear, "Shut your mouth!"

Simons ran into sight, his gun out, ready to shoot anyone who came to Taylor's aid.

Taylor screamed again and struggled to break free.

James tried to hold her, but she was stronger than she looked.

Just as the men ran into sight, Maida flung the cabin door wide and stepped out, the flintlock cocked and aimed right at James Rawlings. "Let her go!" Maida cried, the rifle steady against her shoulder.

James shoved Taylor aside and pulled his pistol.

Maida fired and James cried out. His pistol flew from his hand and he fell hard back against the well.

Simons aimed at Maida and fired, but missed. He swore under his breath and started to run back into the trees, but he was stopped dead in his tracks by a black man blocking the way. "Step aside!" Simons shouted, striking out with his pistol.

Treet knocked the pistol from Simons's hand and punched him hard in the stomach. The breath wooshed out of Simons and before he could defend himself, Treet rammed his fist into Simons's face. Blood spurted from his nose. Treet jerked Simons's arm up behind him and forced him to walk to where the others had gathered around Taylor, Maida, and James Rawlings.

With a mighty yell from deep inside Taylor leaped at Andrew

Simons and shrieked, "You dare to show yourself at Catawba after what you did to me?"

"Get her away from me!" Simons cowered back from Taylor but she pummeled his face and chest. He'd never expected a woman with such control to turn into a raving maniac.

Maida caught Taylor's arm and tugged her back from Simons. "Taylor! Taylor! Stop!"

Taylor sank to the ground on her knees and sobbed into her hands.

Maida knelt beside her and wrapped her arms around her. "You're safe now. I won't let anyone hurt you or take you away."

Kendra and Laurel knelt with Maida and Taylor, offering their comfort.

James Rawlings groaned and gingerly rubbed the back of his head where he'd struck the well. He felt a big knot and pulled his hand away to find it covered with blood. He tried to move, but pain shot through him. He looked down and saw blood gushing from his thigh. He was going to bleed to death if someone didn't help him, so he pleaded, "Help me! Taylor, by all that's holy, get some help for me!"

Taylor heard him cry and slowly walked to him, her face wet with tears and her fists doubled at her sides. She stood over him and glared down at him. "You killed Floyd!"

"Help me, Taylor. Can't you see I'm in pain?"

Taylor dropped on her knees beside him and pushed her face right into his. "You killed my husband without a shred of remorse!"

"No. No, he was run over by a carriage." James shook his head. He frantically searched the faces of the others looking down on him. They all believed Taylor. Wouldn't anyone help him? He could always find someone to help him. He finally looked back at Taylor. "Please, look at my leg. I'll bleed to death."

Taylor grabbed his hair and yanked it hard. She wanted to snatch him bald!

He cried out and tried to pull her hands loose, but he was too weak. "I'm hurting bad, Taylor. Help me."

Taylor slowly stood, brushed strands of his hair from her hands, and looked down on him. What should she do now that she had him before her? Her eyes cold, she folded her arms. "Nobody will help you until you confess to the murder of my husband Floyd Craven."

"No." James shook his head.

"Then die where you sit!"

"I didn't do it. He was my cousin! How could I kill my own cousin?"

"Cammie saw you," Taylor snapped.

"Who'd believe a nigger over me?"

Taylor thumped her chest. "I would." She waved her hand to take in the others. "They would."

James groaned. "Forget about Floyd. Help me. Can't you see I'm bleeding to death?"

"Bleed to death, then!" She started to walk away.

"Taylor! How can you do this to me? You are a woman of God!"

"I am a woman of God and I demand to hear the truth about Floyd from your own lips." Taylor bent down and thumped James on the head. "I refuse to go to Virginia with you." She kicked his leg. "I refuse to allow you to take Cammie. But the law says Cammie must go. The law even says I must go. Until I know Cammie and I are safe, no one is going to stop the bleeding in your leg."

"That leg of yours looks real bad," Pickle said, clicking his tongue. "I seen legs like that cut right off during the war. I even sawed a leg off myself."

James shuddered. "Taylor, don't be so stubborn!"

Pickle leaned down closer and clicked his tongue. "Old Pickle sawed that leg off and that man twitched and yelled for a long time. But that old leg just laid there like a piece of junk. It might be I could saw your leg off for you."

"Get away from me!" James tried to inch away, but couldn't. "Taylor, help me! Please!"

"No amount of begging or anger will get you your own way this time, James." Taylor started to walk away. She said over her shoulder, "Court, get everyone back to whatever they were doing."

"You heard Mrs. Taylor," Court said with a wave of his hand. "Let's go watch Reid ride that bay."

James groaned.

Taylor turned to Treet. "Tie Andrew Simons up and leave him lying on the ground in the sun. Right on that anthill."

"Yes, ma'am." Treet hid a grin. He knew Miz Taylor was strong, but he'd never expected her to hold up under such pressure.

"Don't let that crazy man touch me again!" Andrew shouted, cowering away from Treet. "Rawlings, tell them what they want to hear!"

"It's too late." Taylor strode toward her cabin while the others hurried in other directions.

"Wait, Taylor!" James moaned.

She turned back and waited with her arms crossed.

"I confess! I killed Floyd Craven with a carriage. Now, fix my leg."

Her face set, Taylor commanded, "You will sign a paper releasing Floyd from all debts."

"I'll sign."

"And sign a paper making Cammie a free woman."

"I'll sign! Now, tend my leg!"

Taylor turned to Kendra. "Bring paper and ink." Taylor motioned to Pickle. "As soon as he signs, take care of him."

"You want me to saw off his leg?" Pickle chuckled and James cried out.

❦

After the transaction was completed Taylor turned to Andrew Simons. His nose had stopped bleeding, but blood spotted his face and fancy clothes. Taylor shook her finger at him. "You caused a great deal of trouble for me."

"I'm sorry. I don't know what came over me."

"You will return my money to me and you will sign a paper stating that you and Captain Crawley swindled me out of the money."

"Or what?" Simons asked coldly.

"Or I'll have Treet take you to the swamps and leave you to fend for yourself."

Simons's blood ran cold, but he didn't let it show. Taylor would never do anything to hurt him. "You're too kind-hearted for that."

"I know. But Treet isn't." Taylor waved her hand. "Take him away, Treet."

"Be real glad to, Miz Taylor." Treet bent down to lift Simons to his feet.

"No! Wait!" Simons opened his money belt and flung the money at Taylor. "Give me the paper to sign."

Taylor nodded and reached for the paper Kendra held out to her.

Just then Cammie walked slowly across the yard and stopped beside James Rawlings. Her stomach fluttering nervously, she held her baby down to James. "This be Daniel. I want you to know about him. I don't never plan to tell him his daddy be a mean-hearted man."

James stared at the miniature of himself and a strange feeling swept over him. His baby boy! This baby was his beyond a shadow of a doubt. "Daniel," he whispered.

Cammie held the baby to her and walked proudly back to the cabin.

❦

Later Maida sat with Taylor at the table and poured a cup of tea for her. "It's my turn to tend you."

Taylor smiled weakly. The papers James and Andrew had signed lay beside her on Maida's table. Pickle had already removed the ball from James's leg and had bandaged it the best he could. With Court and Bard guarding them, James and Andrew were sitting under a tree waiting for Yates and Ward to return. Slowly Taylor sipped the hot tea. "Ward is hurt because I didn't tell him about James Rawlings."

Maida shrugged. "He'll get over it."

"He is a proud man." Taylor took another sip of tea, her ear tuned for Ward's return. She figured he'd get to town, learn James wasn't there, and race back home for fear he was there. What would he say when he found James and Andrew shackled together under the tree?

After two cups of tea Taylor managed to pull herself together enough to look closely at Maida. "You're well again! I'm pleased and thankful."

Maida smiled and nodded. "It was like I was in the middle of a ball of cotton. I couldn't make sense of anything, then when I heard you scream, something inside me clicked, and I could think clearly again."

"Thank God!"

Maida nodded and dabbed tears from her eyes. "Now maybe I can find the strength to talk to Yates."

Taylor nodded. "I think the worst of our problems are behind us."

❦

Taylor thought of that statement later when she faced Ward after Court had driven James and Andrew to Darien. Baby Daniel was asleep in the bedroom and Treet had taken Cammie out for fresh air even though it was dark out. Brooke was asleep in the loft. Ward's jaw was set and his eyes hard.

"I wanted to tell you, but I couldn't," Taylor said again for the third time since Ward had returned.

Ward sighed heavily. "Will I be able to trust you again?"

"Of course! I don't lie!"

"Then tell me the truth about Sippy. Did you write her a paper that said she was free?"

Taylor swallowed hard and barely nodded.

Ward's stomach knotted. He'd known it, but to hear her say it made it even worse. "Would you do it again if a runaway stopped here and begged you?"

Taylor lifted her chin. "Yes!"

Ward helplessly shook his head. He thought of the other women he'd been acquainted with and he couldn't think of a one who'd put herself in such danger for slaves she didn't even know. Audrey Smythe never put herself out for anyone! The thought surprised him. He'd thought Audrey was practically perfect.

Suddenly Ward laughed. "Will we ever be an ordinary husband and wife?"

Taylor smiled. "I don't know as I'd like ordinary."

Just then the baby cried and Taylor jumped up. "You haven't seen Daniel yet."

Reluctantly Ward followed Taylor to the bedroom. She picked Daniel up wrapped in his soft blanket and held him out to Ward. He took the baby and looked down at him.

"James Rawlings is the father."

Daniel puckered up and cried harder.

"I don't blame the little guy for crying over that." Ward held the baby to his shoulder. "We'll give him a home here at Catawba."

"And an education," Taylor said softly.

Ward thought about that a while and finally nodded. "All right."

"I love you, Ward." The words just popped out, taking her by surprise. She'd wanted to wait and say them at just the right moment, but now seemed the best time.

His heart stood still for a moment before he realized what she said. She loved him! "Thank you," he whispered. He didn't know how to deal with her open admission of love. Did she expect him to declare his love to her? Well, he couldn't do it yet.

He held the baby out to her. "You take him. I can't get him to stop crying."

Taylor chuckled. "Only Cammie can. He's hungry." Taylor opened the door and called into the darkness for Cammie to come feed Daniel.

In the loft Brooke whimpered.

"I'll see about her." Ward climbed the ladder to Brooke. He lifted her in his arms, sat on the side of her bed, and rocked her back to sleep. "This is what life is all about," Ward whispered against Brooke's hair. How would it feel to hold a child of his flesh and blood in his arms? He wanted to build Catawba into a great plantation for Brooke and for his blood children. Would he have any?

Her eyes sparkling, Cammie rushed in and took Daniel from Taylor. "Oh, Miz Taylor, that Treet says he love me. He says he promised hisself he would never love nobody ever again, but he just couldn't help himself when he seen me way back when he was on that auction block in Charleston."

Taylor darted a look toward the loft. Cammie didn't know Ward was there. "This is not the time to talk about Treet. Sit down and feed Daniel."

Ward smiled and shook his head. He hadn't realized Cammie and Treet cared about each other. What would Yates say about that? He'd have to give Treet permission to marry in order for them to wed. Would Yates do it?

With a long sigh Cammie held Daniel to her breast. "I still praying Treet got enough love for me that it spills right on over to Daniel. But I know Jesus will answer that prayer just like He's answered the rest."

Sinking to a chair across from Cammie, Taylor said, "I'll take care of Brooke by myself for the next several days so you can tend to Daniel and get your rest." Taylor glanced toward the loft again. She had to get Cammie to talk about something else!

"You is one sweet lady, Miz Taylor." Cammie nodded and smiled. "I is still praying Master Ward will love you. He already loves Missy Brooke."

Taylor's cheeks burned with embarrassment.

Ward sat perfectly still with Brooke in his arms. He did love Brooke. Could he love Taylor the same as he had Audrey Smythe? He frowned. It made him feel strange to have Cammie praying for him to love Taylor. Was Taylor praying for him to love her, too? He wondered about that.

Taylor cleared her throat. She had to get Cammie on another subject. "Maida is in her right mind again."

"Praise Jesus!"

Ward carefully laid Brooke down. He couldn't sit in the loft all night long. He climbed down, but since he couldn't look at Taylor, he grabbed the water bucket. "I'll get fresh water."

Seeing Ward's embarrassment, Cammie laughed after he had walked out of the cabin. "Why didn't you tell me he up there? We done embarrassed Master Ward."

Taylor covered her face. "He'll think I set my cap for him from the beginning."

"He should be proud if you did."

Taylor laughed and helplessly shook her head. "What'll I do with you, Cammie?"

"Lets me stay here at Catawba till I go to be with Jesus. And help me raise Daniel to love the Lord and know reading and writing."

"I promise!"

❧

In their bedroom Yates sat on the side of the bed beside Maida and touched her cheek. "I'm happy to see you well again."

"I am, too." Maida laid her cheek against his hand. "There's something I'd like to say."

He tensed. Did she want to return to her aunt and uncle like she'd said before? "Can't it wait?"

"No." Maida took a deep breath. "I was happy to be married to you just to escape my aunt and uncle. I thought it would be enough. But it's not."

He forced back a groan. He didn't want her to leave, no matter what had happened with Bromley.

"Yates, I want love in our marriage. I want us to get to know each other and learn to love each other. Is that possible?"

Relief washed over him. "Could you love me?"

"Yes." She ran a finger across his lower lip. "Can you put Ellen in the back of your heart and love me?"

He nodded. "I already have."

"What about me being with . . . Bromley?"

A muscle jumped in Yates's cheek. If the man weren't dead, he'd rip him apart. "I don't know."

"Jesus said to forgive him." Maida cupped her hand along Yates's cheek. "I refused to forgive my aunt and uncle and then Alden Bromley, but then I realized the damage I was doing to myself and all of you. Today I forgave them with God's help." She stroked his face. "Yates, you must forgive Alden Bromley also."

"I can't," Yates said in agony.

"You can with God's help. You must or we'll never be rid of him. He'll rule our lives from the fiery pit!"

Yates thought about it and about what Taylor had said. He told Maida of his talk with Taylor. "I do forgive the man," he said hoarsely. "With God's help and strength, I do."

"Good. Now, we can get on with our lives."

Smiling, Yates brushed her black hair off her cheek, then kissed her cheek.

She closed her eyes and sighed.

He wrapped his arms around her and brushed her lips with his, then kissed her with rising passion.

Maida's nerves tightened, but why should she be alarmed? This was Yates Marston, her husband! She relaxed in his arms and returned his kisses with passion.

❦

With Musket beside him Ward paced the yard between the magnolia tree and the well. Why wasn't he glad Taylor loved him? What was wrong with him? She could easily be in love with Court Yardley, but she wasn't. Ward leaned against the magnolia tree with his head down. She loved him! She was different from Audrey Smythe and he'd loved Audrey for years. But had it been love? He respected Taylor. He'd had moments where he felt glad she was there. He enjoyed being with her. But would he ever love her totally, as he had Audrey?

In Ward's cabin Cammie held Daniel to her shoulder to burp him as she looked across the table at Taylor. "You go on out and talks to Master Ward. Sometimes it be easier to talk in the dark. Your tongue just comes loose and words pour out."

Taylor looked longingly toward the door. She did want to settle everything with Ward. But could she run after him like a lovesick calf?

"You do it, Miz Taylor," Cammie said softly. "Don't you waste no time."

Taylor rushed to the door, but couldn't bring herself to open it.

"You go, Miz Taylor!"

Her nerves tingling, she pulled open the door, stepped quickly outdoors, and closed the door. She stood there to adjust her eyes to the darkness. Light glowed from Yates's cabin and from one shack. Stars twinkled overhead and a half moon shone a feeble light.

"Taylor," Ward said softly from where he stood a few feet away. The empty water bucket sat beside him. He'd forgotten he'd brought it out to fill.

Taylor caught her breath and slowly walked toward him. "I came to find you."

"You did?" His palms were suddenly damp with sweat.

"Yes." She couldn't find the words she'd wanted to say.

He smelled the clean smell of her hair. Was it possible that he loved her and didn't recognize love for what it was? "I'm glad you did."

"You are?" Her heart beat so hard she was sure he could hear it, even over the noise of the night bugs. "Can we talk?"

"I think we should."

Trembling, Taylor stepped closer to him. Could she say what was on her heart or would her pride stop her? She shook her head and resolved to speak no matter what. "Ward, you are the finest man I've ever known."

"Finer than Floyd?" Why had he said that? He wanted to grab back the words, but it was too late.

Taylor bit her lip. "Yes, finer than Floyd. And he was a fine man." She took a deep breath. "I loved Floyd, but I love you in a different way."

He frowned. "Different? Like friends love each other?" he asked stiffly.

Taylor laughed softly. "I do love you as a friend, but much more. I love you with a passion I can't contain, a passion I didn't know I had until today."

He frowned. "Why didn't you know?"

"I'd hidden it from myself so I wouldn't feel guilty about not loving Floyd as much."

"What do you expect me to say?"

"Nothing. If you love me or not, it doesn't change my feelings toward you. I love the way you play with Brooke, the way you talk to your nieces and nephew, even the way you wrestle with Musket." Taylor laughed shakily. "I love the way you take care of me, the way you kiss me, the way you laugh, the way you walk." She slipped her arms around his neck. "I love you, Ward Marston, with a love that will grow stronger every day."

He hesitated, then circled her waist with his arms. Words failed him. Could she really love him as much as she said?

She pulled his head down and kissed him.

Suddenly something burst inside him and love flowed out like he'd never experienced before—not even with the girl in England who'd broken his heart. He tried to think of her name and he couldn't. The only woman he could think about was Taylor Marston. Love for her rose inside him until it consumed him.

She pulled her lips from his and whispered, "Now it's your turn to talk."

Ward laughed softly. "I'm a man of action," he said against her lips.

Her heart fluttered. "I like this better than talking," she whispered.

He touched his lips to hers in a light, quick kiss, then kissed her eyelids and the corners of her mouth.

She moaned as fire licked through her veins.

Finally he held her from him and looked deep into her eyes. "I love you, my sweet precious wife. Love was inside waiting to break free and you set it free."

Tears of happiness filled her eyes as she touched her lips to his again.

He returned her kiss as if he'd never let her go. And he wouldn't! She belonged at Catawba with him—always!

About the Author

Hilda Stahl was a writer, teacher, and speaker before her death in March, 1993. Born in the Nebraska Sandhills, Hilda grew up telling stories to her five sisters and three brothers, but then she didn't think of becoming a writer. Instead she wanted to be a rancher and raise horses and cattle.

It wasn't until after Hilda wed Norman Stahl and had their first three children that she began to write. She published ninety-two fiction titles and 450 short stories, and was a member of the Society of Children's Book Writers. Her name is listed in *Foremost Women of the Twentieth Century*, *International Authors and Writers' Who's Who*, and *The World's Who's Who*. In 1989 she won the Silver Angel Award for *Sadie Rose and the Daring Escape*.